Gwendoline
Goes Underground

Gwendoline
Goes Underground

by Gwendoline

Gwendoline is a fictional character.
That is:
She is as real as you or I.
She is a Story
Such as those we tell ourselves
And those stories are
What we are.

TWIN RIVERS
PRODUCTIONS

Issued in print and electronic formats
ISBN 978-1-990255-01-4: *Gwendoline Goes Underground:* Paperback
ISBN 978-1-990255-00-7: *Gwendoline Goes Underground:* EPUB
ISBN 978-1-7771580-2-6: *Gwendoline Goes Underground:* Kindle
ISBN 978-1-7773141-9-4: *Gwendoline Goes Underground:* Amazon paperback

Cover and text design by Counterpunch Inc./Linda Gustafson
Illustrations by Niki9door

Published by
Twin Rivers Productions
20 Bloor Street East
PO Box 75070
Toronto, Ontario, M4W 3T3

To receive a free book or novella, sign up at:
https://gilbertreid.com

CONTENTS

CAST OF CHARACTERS

Aisara – woman warrior, member of Kaleem Baluchi's militia

Alison – head of James Hewett Spencer's NY office

Annette Weiss – Hamburg tattooist, works with Werner Beck

Antoine Parillaud – Host of a popular French TV talk show

Anton – militia man, underground Russian agent

Boris Konstantinov – paramilitary officer working for Sergei Platonov

Claudia Clermont – Gwendoline's grandmother, novelist, sophisticate

Freya Hussain – owner of the Vamp tattoo parlor in London's Soho

Giuseppe – concierge of building in Rome, husband of Maria

Gus Foreman – rapist boyfriend of Misty Hoyt's mother

Gwendoline Clermont – mathematician, erotic performance artist

Harry Redford Cornwall – alias of an MI-6 operative

Igor – professional torturer working for Sergei Platanov

Irene von Plato – a German fashion photographer

James Hewett Spencer – British millionaire and venture capitalist

Jamila – female commander of Kaleem Baluchi's militia

Jo Delyle – black choreographer, dancer, model

Kaleem Baluchi – one of the world's greatest arms dealers
Kate – epidemiologist, Gwendoline's close friend
Khalid Nassir – one of the world's most wanted terrorists
Kirill – militia man works for Sergei Platonov
Lou-Lou Jade – French makeup artist
Lucinda Roberts – Gwen's landlady in Cambridge, England
Maria – concierge of building in Rome, wife of Giuseppe
Marlene Richter – German artist, partner of Jo Delyle
Martine Aubin – French actress and film star
Martin Stern – Czech journalist, murdered by Sergei Platonov
Maurice – French Secret Service operative
Max Ebersbach – German biker, friend of Heinrich Streiffer
Misty Hoyt – Gwendoline's alias as an Appalaichan waif
Nicole – French sex expert, owner of a high-end sex shop in Rome
Oriana Ricci – young Italian model, tattooed to be Misty Hoyt's double
Philip d'Este – famous French-Italian film director
Professor Ralph Higgins – Cambridge mathematician
Sandra – American pianist, multilated by Sergei Platonov
Sara Baluchi – adopted daughter of Kaleem Baluchi
Sergei Platonov – sadist, ruthless drug and arms dealer
Séverine – French Secret Service operative
Sonia – a member of Sergei Platonov's harem
Stephen Clermont – Gwendoline's grandfather
Tamika – woman warrior in Kaleem Baluchi's personal militia,
Tracy – a member of Sergei Platonov's harem
Werner Beck – tattooist active in Hamburg, Germany
Yo – Lou-Lou Jade's makeup artist assistant
Zoe Parillaud – teenage daughter of TV host Antoine Parillaud

PROLOGUE – VISITING CARD

Wham!

The oil rig guy slapped me.

"You bitch – you freak!" His scream echoed in the night, piercing the thick falling rain.

The man was a giant. He loomed over me like the Shadow of Death. "You bitch – you freak!"

I backed up, shielded my eyes.

The guy's big, handsome face glowed – it was as crimson as the flames of Satan's very own Hell. "You goddamn freakish fucking pervert!" he hollered, his mouth wide open. It was huge, like a cartoon. His fillings and tonsils glittered in the lamplight.

Gosh, I thought, maybe I've gone too far.

Wham! His fist slammed into my face. The impact rippled through my jaw, a stinging straight-razor slash. My ears rang.

"Ouch! Goddamn you!" I rubbed the smarting flesh, and gave him my fiercest look.

It was a dark and stormy night. Fat greasy raindrops had begun to fall in Typhilis, the capital of the New Democratic Republic of Old Transbeckistan, a so-called nation lost somewhere among the ragtag mishmash of quarrelsome countries and murderous fanatical outlandish weirdly religious tribes strung out for thousands of kilometers in the jagged mountains and windy steppes that mark the endless southern border of the Russian Federation. No wonder the Russians are paranoid. Of course, I exaggerate. Lots of those countries are adorable, picturesque places, fine tribesmen and women, courageous and outstanding warriors, splendidly progressive and democratic republics, as we will see. But right then, at that particular moment, I was in a foul mood.

Wham! The bastard hit me again.

"Ouch!"

Then – with me staring up at him and growling obscenities – he casually hooked a giant forefinger through the steel ring of my Punk-Goth steel-and-leather collar.

He tugged. With one smooth, nonchalant, almost indolent gesture, he lifted me straight off the cobblestones, leaving my stilettoes kicking frantically, dangling in the air. While I hung there, he slapped me again, a slashing glancing blow, from right to left, almost dislocating my jaw – or that's what it felt like.

I gasped. The man could have broken my neck. Well, maybe not. After all, he was an expert – or so they had assured me.

"You bitch! You fucking bitch!" He dropped me.

Wham!

I landed on my feet. How I managed it – landing on my feet, and staying on my feet – I have no idea. My head spun. Stars whirled. My stilettoes wobbled. The blond giant paused. He stroked his jaw. He grinned, a big grin, full of perfect big bright white teeth. Narrowing his eyes, he murmured, "You stupid, stupid bitch!"

He punched me again; it was slow-motion this time, teasing style, plunging forward, then dancing back, one, two, three, and finally smashing me – wham! The blow slammed me against the wall of a fancy perfumed candle shop, old Soviet-style concrete faced with false-antique stucco, a nice restoration job, really, if one had time to appreciate it.

I picked myself up.

"You filthy little freak – you pervert, you bitch!" he screamed – utter hysteria, utter hatred, strangely feminine coming from such a big guy. Then, his fist came out of nowhere. Wham!

"Ouch!" I felt my jaw. "Bastard," I muttered.

It was raining harder now – big scorching drops, coming down thick and fast – polluted and sticky, like bursting bubbles of hot molasses. There was no sheltering from it. I rubbed my eyes. The oil rig guy had almost finished working me over, beating me up pretty good.

He was a big bulky guy, about six-foot-four. He had giant fists, and bulging tattooed biceps. But, generally, he was gentle, well, as gentle as he could risk. He had to be careful, too, not to damage the invisible earpiece – microphone and tiny speaker – cutting-edge technology, they'd told me and a really, really bad idea, I had told them – that lodged inside my left ear.

He'd slugged me three times, then a fourth, then a fifth.

Each time, until the last, I got up, my fists out, miming a boxer's stance. Me, a slender, near-naked female, as cheap and trashy and grotesque as a Punk-Goth girl could possibly be, equipped with black stilettoes, skintight false black leather hot pants, and a skimpy, open, sleeveless, unbuttoned fake black leather vest. Dancing around, I was, boxer-style, knees out, elbows out, like an idiot imitating some TV show, shouting insults. I was tiny compared to him, but crazy – begging for more. I never landed a single punch. When I look back on it, it was a pure pratfall comedy.

We'd been drinking in a bar favored by foreigners, the Smoky Flea's Bottom, this Harry Redford Cornwall and I. Then, we got into a ferocious argument. It became a fight. We shouted insults. It was a true, top-of-the-lungs bellowing match. Then – after the owner told us to shut up or get out – we staggered outside, two drunken foreign sots, utter idiots, asking for trouble. Out we went, into the dark sultry rain. Our faces were instantly wet. The mist moved in like an army of ghosts under the old-fashioned wrought-iron gas lamps, all lit up in the gas-light glow, and creeping in, spooky tendrils, over the wet black cobblestones.

"You freak!" Harry slugged me. It was gentle, as gentle as he could make it and still be real. I figured it looked good. It sure hurt. After that last punch, I reeled against the false-antique wall. I fell down hard on my backside between two metal garbage cans that made a heck of a racket. The lid of one of them bounced off and spun, clattering, into an alleyway, sending a posse of rats scurrying frantically along the river of runoff that rushed and foamed and overflowed down the gutter. I stood up. I did it slowly, shaking my head, trying to get rid of all those damned stars that were swirling. I wondered for a moment where the hell I was and who the hell I was. Then I remembered who I was and saw where I was. Harry stood there, hands on his hips. "Fuck off – bitch!" he shouted, "You fucking freak!" He walked away – leaving me in the rain – and to my fate.

I shouted, "Fuck you!" I staggered out onto the street. The traffic and shop security cameras had been watching the whole thing. I was sure of it.

"Fuck you!" I shouted. I waved my fist in the air. I stood in the rain, staring down the street where Harry Redford Cornwall, the big blond oil rig guy, was heading off. "You cheap fucking bastard," I screamed. He didn't turn around. "Come back, you cheap fucking bastard!" My eyes were glossy with tears, flooding over. I was trembling, blinking, half-blinded, sniffing, choking up, tears streaming down my cheeks; they mingled with the rain. "Come back! Coward! You fucking coward!"

He was gone. An unmarked car would be waiting for him in the underground garage of a nondescript safe house five streets away. Without the beard, his hair trimmed and combed, with a fresh but realistic spray-on tan, and dressed in a merchant banker-type business suit and carrying a passport with a different name and nationality – Harry – whose real name I would never know – would be on the next flight out of Typhilis, which, if you didn't know already, is the capital of the New Independent Democratic Republic of Old Transbeckistan.

And that's where I, Gwendoline Clermont, BA, MA, Ph.D., Fellow of the Royal Society, lecturer at Cambridge University, England, and MIT in Cambridge Mass., and occasionally at the University of Paris, a math whiz, infamous hacker and cryptographer, icon of fashionable perversity and a submissive squeeze of scandalous film star Martine Aubin, now found myself – in Typhilis, the capital of Old Transbeckistan.

I wiped my nose. Yes, blood on my fingers and in the palm of my hand. Good. The large steel nose ring felt funny. It touched my upper lip. I hoped it wasn't damaged. I hoped the septum piercing hadn't been torn. Everything was so new I wasn't sure how anything worked. I began to walk down the street, away from the bar and away from my man, Harry, the oil rig guy, who had already hightailed it out of sight.

Inside my ear, a tiny voice said, "Good, Gwen, good, steady now, steady as she goes."

"Yeah, yeah, good," I muttered, and wiped at my nose with the back of my hand. I didn't like the idea of the tiny cutting-edge flesh-colored two-way earphone gizmo they'd planted in my ear, powered by my body heat and movement, and I'd told them so, in no uncertain terms. I was sure it would get me killed.

"Loud and clear," said the tiny voice. "We'll go silent now."

"That's right, that's right," I growled, as if mumbling to myself. That's what I felt I was doing – mumbling to myself. The voice in my ear was not close. It was coming from Paris, more than 3000 kilometers away.

The rain hammered on my shaved naked skull, dripped inside my flimsy open vest, catching on the nipple rings, and running down my skintight pseudo-leather hot pants. I was soaked to the bone. It didn't matter; the rain was warm, positively voluptuous.

In front of me, there were a few neon signs. One of them was my target: the SS Marquis Club. The letters were flashing, bright red. A few hookers stood, desperately waiting, or indolent and bored, just out of the rain, in narrow arched doorways; flashes of short skirts, long white legs, net stockings, stilettoes, platform shoes, enormous hungry eyes, Moldavians, Ukrainians, Russians, mostly. There wasn't much business. It was a hot wet night, rain pouring down, steamy mist leaking in tendrils out of side alleys; just a few clients were slouching along the sidewalk, some with umbrellas, some soaking wet, mostly foreigners, mostly Americans and Norwegians, oil guys, in sad, bright, multicoloured Hawaiian shirts and baggy shorts, totally soaked, with lots of useless bulging pockets, and in their wallets platinum credit cards, and with rolls of dirty, well-fingered, untraceable dollars and euros in those pockets and wrapped in elastic bands. Some of the oil men tourists – and even the hookers – glanced at me, and recoiled instantly, grimacing, glancing quickly away. Yeah, I thought, I'm a horror show, aren't I – and it's not only the blood.

You see, I was – I am – a monster.

Looking in a mirror was not something I wanted to do. I, Gwendoline, had been turned into a freak – scary even to myself.

I focused on what was ahead of me. There they were – lingering in front of the SS Marquis Club – four or five bouncers – or bodyguards. They were probably both, bouncers and bodyguards. Big muscular guys in black jeans and black T-shirts, with open jackets, and holsters. They'd seen the fight. Now they were watching me, a slight, slender, vulnerable-looking Punk-Goth female, probably really young – maybe even what used to be called jailbait – my stilettoes wobbling on the sidewalk, weaving like I was drunk, but not too drunk, not fall-down-vomit-all-over-everything filthy drunk. Yes, there I was, in the spotlight, looking down at the puddles and rain pocked-sidewalk, staring as if hypnotized at the dancing kaleidoscope reflections, red and blue neon, pure poetry, like in an old-fashioned film noir, except in color. Glancing up, I saw one of the men talking into a shoulder mike. I hoped he was getting permission to let me into the club. That was where I needed to go.

My girlfriend, the exquisitely kind and beautiful Martine Aubin, had said, "Darling Gwen, this is a suicide mission. I hope you realize that." "I know," I said. I kissed her, and the kiss turned into a full, raging, beautiful long consolatory embrace and kiss of farewell, perhaps our last kiss ever, until my controller, "Frederick" was the name he went by, said, "That's enough, girls, that's enough." We disengaged, and giggled, and, in unison, said, "Yes, sir!"

"So, what have we here?" One of the bouncers was standing in front of me, his forehead wet with rain, arms akimbo, staring at me as if I were a truant schoolgirl. I turned my face towards him, so it would be fully illuminated and catch the lamplight.

"Holy fuck," he shouted, "Mother of God!" His eyes went round. "Come and have a look at this! Hey, guys, we have a real live freak on our hands."

Suddenly, they were all standing around me, Russian guys mostly, a few Georgians, rain streaming over them, ignoring the rain, all staring – at me. One of them put out his finger and touched my nose ring, pure steel; I glowered and slapped his hand away.

"Jesus Christ!" He grinned.

"Mother of God!" One bent down to examine me carefully.

"You are a masterpiece."

"No, she's not a masterpiece; she's a fucking monster. It's grotesque! It's a violation of the sacredness of the body!"

"Sacredness of the body!?" One of the guys slapped the man on the shoulder. "Where did that come from? Where do you get stupid shit about the sacredness of the body? Are you religious or something? You're a pimp for fuck's sake."

"I studied to be a priest," the guy said, his face glistening. He looked sheepish. His eyes were shifty. He glanced at me, hungrily, and then away.

"Jesus Christ almighty! A priest! You – a priest!"

"Yeah, the theological seminary in Novgorod."

"Shit – the secrets this man has!"

"He's a fucking saint, he is."

They laughed.

Curious eyes, all of them now, narrowed, focused right on me. One of the biggest of the men – shoulders like the front of a Mack Truck – moved up close. He stared down. "Does this go all over, the tattoos? I mean, are you pierced and tattooed everywhere?" He seemed to be the leader. He laid his hand on my shoulder, a warm, heavy, strong hand. He nudged the flimsy leather vest open and nodded. "Nice tits, very nice, ripe and firm – classic." He grinned. "Nipples pierced too, and navel. You are a cute number." He tugged at a breast ring. And he asked the question again. "Does this go all over? You tattooed and pierced everywhere?"

I looked up at him – snuffled, and rubbed my nose, "Who the fuck wants to know?"

He laughed and took my chin between his big powerful fingers, forcing me to stare him in the eye. So I stared, held his gaze, didn't flinch. Steady, steady, steady. The rain was getting in my eyes, eyelashes dripping. Need to blink. Refuse to blink. He laughed again, mimicked, high-pitched, "Who the fuck wants to know? Listen to it?" he said, "Hey, listen to what it says!"

8

"Feisty little bitch."

"Good for a tumble."

"Let's have a closer look." A handsome, unshaven, heavy-set guy moved forward; he had a black leather shoulder holster high under his armpit, a white shirt with fine vertical blue stripes open down to his flat tanned midriff, and over his shoulder a snub-nosed chrome submachine gun. He hooked a single finger into the big steel ring on my leather and steel collar – pulled me with him, smiling all the time. He pushed me under the bright overhead light, and they all gathered around. A security camera was blinking down at us – little red light, blink, blink, blink. Good! The show was on. The rain poured down. It was like being in a shower, a hot shower. Not unpleasant, not unpleasant at all. I love running naked through warm rain, and I love lying in the rain on the terrace of our flat in Rome. If I get out of this alive, that is one thing I'm going to do – I'll run naked on the beach under the hot rain – with James or with Martine, or all alone, just me. Maybe with a dog. Maybe I could buy a dog. The dog would run with me, kicking up spurts of sand, just next to the surf, both of us naked, me and the dog.

The handsome man flicked one of my breast rings, then held it, then caressed my nipple. It was erect, as hard and high as an HB pencil eraser, but thicker – loyally doing its job. Terror and arousal all in one neat little tumescent package. "Ah, yes, you are the real thing, the real damned thing," he said, "Nipples hard – she's excited already." He listened for a second to his earphone. Then he let his gaze rest on me for a long time, and he said, almost gently, "Kid – I think we have somebody wants to meet you."

"Somebody wants to meet me?" I sniffled, wiped some blood from my nose, and looked at it; then I looked back up at him. My eyelashes were dripping water.

"Yeah, you'll like it. He'll give you everything you ever dreamed of."

"He will, huh?"

"Definitely – all for free too!"

"For free, huh?"

"Yeah, kid. For free."

I licked my lips and pretended to consider. "What the fuck! Okay!"

"Ivanov, take our little Punk-Goth tattooed friend inside, will you. Be a good lad now."

"With pleasure," Ivanov pushed me ahead of him. "What's your name, kid?"

"Misty."

"Misty! Fuck! Misty." He laughed, "The very idea – Misty!"

"Well, it's Misty, that's what it is." I shot him a surly glance. "And fuck you!"

Ivanov recoiled, pretended to be terrified. "You sure went overboard with the tattoos, kid. You really belong in a circus. You're a clown mask and pure freak, not a person." He grinned. "But don't you worry – some people actually go for this shit. You know, specialists, collectors, connoisseurs. You'll fetch a high price." He took me through the entrance, past two more doors, with a couple of guards standing at each one, and into a sort of vestibule. "And now, Misty, go meet your fate!"

I looked at him.

"Go ahead, Misty, don't hesitate. Let's you and I go right through that big, black, rubber-lined door there!"

CHAPTER 1 – SS MARQUIS CLUB

Okay, Gwendolino, I said to myself, so now you die. I straightened my shoulders, turned around, and pushed open the big leather and rubber padded door; it swung back, and we entered the room – it was huge. Music thundered, strobe lights flashed. It was a jumble of impressions: Guys in suits. Guys in leather. One guy was naked except for what looked like a leather or rubber jockstrap. Women – dressed and naked, too, or in G-strings and pasties, moved among the crowd. Ivanov had his hand in the small of my back, pushing me gently forward. "Go to the bar, Misty, and have a drink," he said, and he patted me on the shoulder. "It's on the house."

I walked ahead, and then I looked back. Ivanov was watching me. I plowed ahead. I looked over my shoulder. Ivanov nodded and then disappeared, through the door, back out into the rain.

The topless bargirl – well, she was wearing sparkly turquoise pasties – stared at me, and blinked. She curled her lip, "Jesus Christ!"

The strobe lights flashed, flickering images like in an old silent film.

"Sorry, I'm not Jesus Christ," I said. I smiled. She jerked back as if I'd punched her. My smile I suddenly remembered is so grotesque it will scare the bejesus out of anybody and everybody. It's interesting to watch people's reactions. Frankly, up to two days ago – and for the last three years – I'd gotten used to gazes of admiration, even lust, from everybody and anybody, from strangers and non-strangers – quick covert glances, smiles, nervous indirect stares from geezers, from young guys, and from women too, desire and envy and speculation in each glance.

It's a funny experience, being considered beautiful. You are on display all the time. You evoke reactions from people – hardly any of the reactions are neutral. And people – both men and women – feed you into their fantasies. Some are jealous. Some want to know you; some want to possess you; some are intimidated and turn away; some think you will be an ideal soul mate, or maybe a perfectly malleable perverse sex toy, complicit in every forbidden thought, eager to try any scenario. Some people think you will be the only human being on this whole bloody planet who could possibly understand them. It's as if beauty were a sort of apostolic consecration, a sort of embodiment of the soul, and your smile and approval a seal and sacrament of comprehension, forgiveness, and pardon. All of this is illusions and wishful thinking, mostly, though such impossible yearnings for "beauty" and "perfection" go deep. And of course, until a few days ago, I was an icon of chic perversity, the partner of a famous actress and the lover of a rich, powerful man.

How things can change in an instant! Now it's like I'd been maimed after a disastrous accident or had horrible plastic surgery. It's as if I am polluted, a pariah, as if my monstrosity was the plague – and infectious.

The bargirl pushed a drink towards me – some sort of cocktail. "This is the recommended medicine." She smiled, softening a bit. I could see what she was thinking: Maybe this freak isn't dangerous; maybe she's just pathetic. Yeah, she's some street waif who got herself turned into a tattooed hard-metal monster by some sadistic pimp or boyfriend.

I glanced around the room. Things were coming into focus. It was all black walls and chrome and silver and gold, black leather couches, black marble columns and tables, and chains and dark mirrors and people sitting clustered in groups.

Golden buff waitresses in stilettoes and sparkly rose-colored G-strings and pasties circulated among the groups bringing drinks, sometimes perching on guys' laps. It was darkly lit, except for the strobes, which hurt my eyes.

One group was clearly more important than any other group – and there he was, the man himself, my objective, my target, in the center of the most important group, slouched back on a black leather couch, Sergei Platonov, the leader, the trader in human flesh, drugs, arms, the merchant of atomic weapons and bio-logical death packages, the man who almost certainly had kid-napped my man, my love, my master, James Hewitt Spencer, and was holding him prisoner somewhere right now. Next to Sergei on the couch was a spectacular blonde in a white blouse and leather mini-skirt who had her arm around his shoulder.

The strobe lights started again. I tried to blink in rhythm with the flashing strobes. But I couldn't do it.

The bargirl offered me another drink, the same one, and told me I'd better drink it, or they'd kick me out of the club. "It an in-itiation ritual," she said, "and part of the entrance fee."

"That's nice," I said, "The fee is a free drink."

"Absolutely," she said, her smile a bit too tight, "It's real nice of them."

I sipped at it slowly – there was nowhere to hide the glass and no way to dump it without being seen. I didn't like this, and I figured that – at this rate – I'd be really drunk – and probably drugged – and maybe utterly helpless and hopeless by the time I met the great man.

Up behind the bar, a petite golden girl in a G-string began to twist herself around a brass pole. She had the cutest of ponytails. She swung down, stared at me for just an instant – Vietnamese, I thought, and beautiful. Lustful thoughts surged. She smiled a big smile, blinked, and then swung away.

Then a big hulking smooth guy who called himself Andrei was on the next barstool, leaning close beside me, radiating heat. Where did he come from? How and when he got there, I hadn't noticed. This was a bad sign; my radar was failing; time was breaking apart into disconnected bits and pieces, black holes were opening, memory was shattering into bright separate shards. "I'm Andrei," he had said, I was sure of it, but I couldn't remember exactly when he'd said it. Yes, the drink was spiked – but with what?

Andrei put his hand on my shoulder, a heavy, strong hand. His leather vest was skimpy and displayed his muscles. He smelt of tangy aftershave, and his breath smelt of mints. His hand was so heavy, and his massaging fingers so strong, I thought he might break my collarbone. "Now, you are truly a cute one, you are," he said. His mouth was full of teeth. They were overly bright. He must brush and floss five times a day, I thought. I wanted to ask him about his dentist. On the other hand, maybe they were false, maybe his teeth had all been kicked out in a fight, and these were dentures or implants. They looked gigantic, his teeth, his smile. Hallucinatory! Such big teeth! "The better to eat you with, my dear," said the Big Bad Wolf. I am Little Red Riding Hood. I am lost in the woods. Oh, oh, I thought. The drink was certainly taking effect. I wondered what was in it – certainly not just alcohol. His English was accented, Russian, maybe Ukrainian. Most of them, the men in the room, they were Russians, Ukrainians, Georgians, and Armenians, and –

The strobe lights started again and didn't stop. They blasted on and off, on and off. Everybody and everything looked like a zebra. They were all striped in flickering flashes and lines of light, the chrome, the leather, the rubber, all shiny, all glossy, ribbed with lines of blazing, flashing white, the naked women, the beefy muscular guys with their bare glossy waxed pectorals showing under their open leather jackets, the bar, and the bottles lined up in arrays behind the bar where on the runway the petite golden stripper curled herself around the pole.

Andrei laid out a line of coke on a small mirror.

"Sniff," he said.

"No, I think I'd better ..."

"Sniff!" His hand was even heavier on my shoulder, his fleshy thumb digging deep. Yes, he could crush my bones. He ran his fingers over my shaved skull, it was almost affectionate, but it was also like he was going to smash my head down on the glass, crush my face.

"Okay," I said. I leaned down, pressed a finger against one nostril, and sniffed.

I don't do drugs. So I didn't have much experience. But ... it was so pure I almost reeled back and fell off the barstool. I managed to stay upright. "Wow," I said. I looked at him. In the old days – like two days ago – my dark fiery glance – with the dark eyelashes and eyebrows – was a pretty effective weapon, or so people told me, but now it was only grotesque and weird; pathetic, maybe, yes, pathetic. I had been stripped of all my power as perverse-girl-enchantress, turned into a parody and negation of myself.

The strobe lights were making me dizzy. I might really begin to hallucinate. Things looked too damned bright, too damned intense; everything was too real, more real than real. And everything was really, really important too, infinitely important. The doors of perception had been smashed open, all the way, no barriers, no filters, nothing between me and everything. That round black metal button on Andrei's jacket suddenly seemed to be the most significant thing in the universe. It was the universe. I wanted to take hold of the button and discuss its metaphysical and cosmological significance with Andrei. Everything, I mean everything, was contained in that button. It was a liminal experience, on the frontier between being and non-being, between the mundane present and the transcendent infinite! The button was the gateway to the beyond, to the secrets of eternity. I sneezed and wiped my nose – the bloody ring getting in the way. I looked at the back of my hand: Silver snot, not so bad, mucus quicksilver from the nostrils, smeared across the back of my tattooed hand. I realized I was having a goddamn mystical epiphany: I was seeing the universe in a button on the lapel of the jacket of Andrei, the hitman, the eternity of the instant in a string of my very own dribble of snot. I was turning into William Blake, whose poems I adored, that London visionary, engraver, and poet, who saw the world in a grain of sand and eternity in the palm of his hand or something like that – it might have been the other way round. I probably have it upside down, or backward, or both. Next thing I'll start dancing like a Sufi dervish, whirl away my soul and lose myself in mystical abandonment. I don't know if I'll survive this.

It was four days since James disappeared. It seemed like a lifetime. So much had changed. So much had happened. And I'd gone crazy, literally crazy, with grief and fear. But, at the same time, I'd been as cool as a cucumber and as hard and lucid as a diamond, with my life reduced to the simplicity of one mission – get James back – and I had decided to act.

I was going to rescue him – me, Gwendoline Clermont, cloistered mathematician, winner of major prizes in international mathematics, the bright-eyed icon of perversity, lover of film star Martine Aubin, as well as "art performer" and model in my spare time! I was going to rescue James Hewitt Spencer, the multi-millionaire venture capitalist – and part-time intelligence source – who'd made some dangerous enemies – very dangerous. James had stumbled into something – well, we both had stumbled into something – much bigger than even he was, and much bigger and worse than we had imagined.

So here I was – a waif, a tattooed freak – on the trail of James' kidnappers. If they hadn't killed him already, but I couldn't believe that – I refused to believe that. They needed him; he knew things; he had things ... shares, bonds, partnerships, patents, information ...

So they would keep him alive – and they would torture him.

That was what I believed.

The nightclub was in the old quarter of Typhilis, the capital of the Independent Democratic Republic of Old Transbeckistan. Old Transbeckistan had been carved out of the Independent Democratic Republic of New Transbeckistan. This happened when a group of rogue Russian mercenaries allied themselves with some rebellious mountain tribes and greedy oil executives and overthrew the Islamist New Transbeckistan Government of dictator Mohammed Jihad Moses Nadir. They set up a puppet regime, despised by the West, and of extreme annoyance to Moscow. Moscow was trying to decide what to do – let the regime collapse from its inner contradictions, subvert it in multiple and ingenious ways, engineer another proxy coup, or invade the place and kill everybody. The oil rigs made dramatic action difficult. A lot of expensive equipment might get blown up. Pipelines might be ruptured. And, then, if you did take it over, you'd have to administer it, and the Russians knew it was a tricky territory to police. It had mountains all over the place and endless incomprehensible tribal feuds. Every man and many girls from age ten up knew how to wield an AK or strap on a bomb – and possibly a niqab – and blow up a school, a barracks, a theater, or a mosque or church. And then, too, there was a vicious slow-motion civil war – between the people of the mountain and the people of the plain – that had been going on for centuries. The New Independent Republic of Old Transbeckistan had oil – and lots of foreign oil workers. This also made things difficult for the Russians. They had shares in some of the companies that would be damaged. And they did not want to kill expensively dressed foreigners – Americans and Chinese and Norwegians and French – whose powerful governments might express a certain amount of displeasure at the massacre of their very own well-fed citizens. The oil business had been my entrée into the place, and my pretext, as a whorish hanger-on and true loser, for being here.

Andrei was talking – it was like he'd watched ancient American gangster movies; I thought I really was hallucinating.

"So, what's your name, babe?"

"Misty."

"Misty, what?"

"Misty Hoyt."

"Misty Hoyt?" He laughed. "That's a killer!"

"Stupid, I know," I said, "And not my idea."

"Well, Misty, you are a one-girl tattooed hillbilly freak show," he said.

"Yeah," I said, I blinked at him. My blink by now must be dull and shiny at the same time. The drops I'd applied before Harry and I slugged it out were supposed to make it look like I was drugged – or very drunk. But now I really was drugged – and really was drunk. The coke I could understand – that focused, diamond-cut, burnt-out gaze it'll give to your eyes, pupils shrunk to tiny startled paranoid points, the fidgety sharpness of attention, and the illusory sensation of transcendence and clarity. But I wondered what was in the drinks the nice bargirl had insisted I gulp down. That was something else again, whatever it was. I'd had three of them. Now I was apparently helpless, befuddled, and all prepared for sacrifice. It was clear Andrei was calculating: He was trying to figure out what I was worth to his master – if I was worth anything. Right now, I was jumping through a second or third hoop on my way to the man – to Sergei Platonov. Would I be a good victim, sufficiently perverse, sufficiently interesting?

Misty Hoyt was the cover name they'd given me. I'd objected. I thought it was too transparently idiotic, hyperbolic Appalachian hayseed, like something out of a cheap reality show peopled by scrawny, unwashed, bearded Bible-thumping crazies. But the experts said that ridiculous was good – ridiculous was credible, because Sergei Platonov, who was far from stupid, would not believe that anybody could be so stupid as to choose such a stupid transparent cover name, etc. Espionage, the experts explained, is like a hall of mirrors: it goes like this: She thinks that I think that she thinks that I think that she thinks and so on to infinity. It consists of multileveled deception and forms of self-consciousness which coil in on each other, like a spiral of smoke, or like an Escher drawing, that sort of thing – infinitely regressive. "Like some forms of math," I said. "Exactly," said my controller, Frederick, looking pleased with his pupil. Still, I was not convinced by "Misty Hoyt," but I didn't want to waste time arguing; I wanted to get into action. I wanted to slug somebody. I wanted to grab James, free him, and get him home, safe and sound, and make love to him for two weeks without stopping.

My Misty Hoyt background story – if anybody asked – was this: I was a girl from backwoods Appalachia hillbilly country – abused by my foulmouthed drunkard of a daddy and my addled drunkard addict of a mommy. I had indulged when sweet fourteen in consensual incest with my brother, who was three years older than I and who left home shortly after we did the dirty deed – a total of four times – on the old curling black-and-white checkboard linoleum floor in the kitchen. After daddy disappeared never to be seen again and after my mommy acquired a new lover, who decided I was as sexually interesting as mommy was, if not more so, I decided, somehow, that just maybe I'd had enough. So, after this series of catastrophes, I had somehow gotten myself to Europe, gotten myself addicted and tattooed – by my sadistic German biker Neo-Nazi drug-dealer boyfriend, Heinrich Streiffer, originally from Dresden but who hung out in Hamburg – and I'd been left here in Typhilis by an American oil rig guy who'd picked me up in Rotterdam on a stop-over, got me to the New Democratic Republic of Old Transbeckistan, had fun fucking me out of my mind in a small hotel and out on the riverside quay somewhere under the plane trees – the Beckistan River has nice leafy quays below the Typhilis embankment – and who promised to take me back the States or to Europe, but who instead left me dead drunk asleep in an unpaid hotel room without so much as a goodbye kiss, and that – the ungrateful bastard – after I had most obligingly, and enjoyably, satisfied all his most deviant desires, so it was that I'd found myself on the street, picked up by another big hunk of an oil guy, who called himself Harry Redford Cornwall – probably not his real name – who then had a fight with me because after drinking his liquor I declared that I didn't want to sleep with him unless he paid up front, one thousand dollars for the night. I was worth it, I told him, because I was one of a kind, unique in the grotesquerie department, and he'd never ever fuck anything as kinky and contorted as me anytime ever in the rest of his whole goddamned fucking useless life. Harry did not take kindly to this, and so I ended up bruised and bloody, weaving my way down Joseph Stalin Boulevard towards the SS Marquis Club. I was looking for fun and for booze and for food – and for trouble. That was the idea. And underneath, since I was trained in masochism and addicted to humiliation and mistreatment, I was looking for a man who would beat up on me, and beat up on me real good and real hard, like they did in the hills in the old country, which for me was the USA. This package – aka Misty Hoyt – was tailor-designed as bait for Sergei Platonov. While Andrei leaned over me, they were all watching, Sergei Platonov's bodyguards and hangers-on, men and women. It was a rite of passage, I guess, an initiation and a test.

The bargirl put another drink – double size this time – in front of me. Oh, goddamn, I thought. Andrei lifted the drink and put it to my lips. Fight or cooperate? I opened my mouth, tipped my head back. He poured the drink down. It overflowed; I choked; it dribbled over my chin, under my collar, and down my breasts and belly. I was all sticky wet. Even the nipple rings, I noticed, had liquor dripping from them – golden drops.

The petite golden Vietnamese stripper swung down, glanced at me, licked her lips, blinked, sketched a quick flirtatious pout, and swung away.

Andrei handed me another glass. I drank it down. I was feeling groggy and dizzy. I slid off the barstool, and declared, "I'm going to the ladies' room," assuming all the slow-motion drunkard's dignity I could muster. Andrei laughed. "You go right ahead to the ladies' room, Misty. It's over there!" He pointed and, groggily blinking, I swung around sluggishly, as if wading through glue, laboriously following his outstretched pointing arm.

"Over there?" I said, half a question, half a statement, "Over there." I hiccupped.

"Yes, over there," Andrei said. He pinched my shoulder. "We'll be waiting for you right here." His voice echoed from a distance.

The bargirl was grinning – she seemed to be miles away and yet very close. I could see the pores in her skin, and tiny glistening beads of sweat, though her skin was very fine and had that golden buff perfect tan that strippers and bargirls seem so often to have – or is it the flattering magic of the lighting?

Behind her, the petite golden Vietnamese girl was wrapping herself around the pole; she swung down again – jackknifed her body, and gave me a look, just a quick, focused glance, burning intelligence, then she swiveled back up, and twirled around. The lights reflected off her legs, and perfectly buff bum, two perfect golden cheeks, polished and glowing.

I bumped into a few barstools and chairs, and I leaned on a few tables on my way – it seemed a very long zigzag voyage – to the ladies' room.

Finally, I was there. I pushed open the door, entered a tunnel, all black, pink-speckled marble and subdued overhead lighting and flushed side lighting, sort of like entering an Egyptian tomb in the time of the Pharaohs, if they'd had electricity, which, so far as I could remember, they didn't, the Pharaohs I mean. Okay, I muttered to myself, now I'm almost sure to get myself killed. I'm too drunk and too drugged to control any of this.

I made it to the ladies' room, again all marble and luxury. I headed to one sink in the long row of sinks. The mirror glowed opaque black, like dark mica, but when you stood in front of it, it lightened up and suddenly became a real mirror – frighteningly clear – an intriguing lighting effect. And there I saw myself, the new me: Misty Hoyt.

"Fuck!"

Each time I see myself, even I am surprised. That's the new me: There I am: Shaved bald except for a single comic, round, puff-like, bright scarlet tuft in the middle, right on top. My face is entirely covered in massive, thick, closely-patterned matte black-and-scarlet tattoos, including my nose and lips, and my nose and ears are pierced with heavy metal rings. I've turned myself, pristine, chalk-white virginal Gwendoline Clermont, mathematician, and occasional Vogue model, into a Punk-Goth freak, a sideshow attraction, a midway monster, a biker's moll. Tattoos are pretty normal, obviously, but I, my dears, I have gone overboard: full-body, full-face, and full-skull. People recoil when they see me – I noticed it on the sidewalk, outside the club. And the bouncers did a double-take and then didn't stop joking. These tattoos, though, are my entrée into the inner sanctum.

The earpiece went alive, its tiny voice, only for me: "Gwen, can you hear us? Gwen?"

"Yes, yes, yes – look at me!" I said, staring at the mirror. "What a monster!"

"Gwen, Gwen, can you hear us? Gwen?"

"Yes, yes," I sighed. I stuck out my tongue – truly grotesque. "It is clear, clear, clear! I don't need another drink!"

"I don't think she can hear us," the voice said. "Gwen?"

The earpiece sputtered, turned to static.

Damn it! They told me it was cutting-edge technology, the newest thing, ultra-miniaturized, powered by the heat and movement of my body. I said I preferred old and dull and tried-and-true technology, particularly if I'm out on the front line alone with no easy way back. Cutting-edge is untested stuff, and untested stuff is, well ... Gwendoline Clermont is a firm believer in Murphy's Law: if anything can possibly go wrong, it will. And Misty Hoyt totally agrees.

"I'm here because I'm here," I said, and splashed water on my face; it dripped off the mask, down under my collar, under my skimpy open vest.

Just static in my ear. I grimaced: I'm going to have to tear the goddamned thing out and flush it down some goddamned toilet before it gets me goddamned killed.

Suddenly there was a girl next to me, leaning over the sink, a blonde, like pure spun gold. I figured she was Russian, one of

Sergei Platonov's gang; then I realized, yes, she was the one sitting next to Sergei out in the club, and she had her arm slung around his shoulder – she was obviously somebody. Maybe she was the key to the kingdom.

She leaned towards the sink, cut a line of white powder on a small purse mirror, and sniffed it. She stopped sniffing, wiped the little mirror clean, put it back in her purse – a small, sleek black leather purse hanging by a slender black chain from her shoulder. She stared at herself, then splashed her face with water, and again stared into the mirror, eyeing her hair.

"Fuck!" she said, "This is so kitsch!"

For the first time, I noticed how her blond hair was lacquered, combed up bouffant or honeycomb style, a glittering cone of spun gold, as if she had climbed straight out of the Soviet 1950s or 60s. Her face was oval, slightly triangular, with a high forehead and enormous blue eyes, a classic beauty tricked up with a touch of vulgarity. She puckered her scarlet lips, revealing perfect bright teeth; then, she tried out a mock Marilyn Monroe pout. Strangely, it was an exquisitely intelligent face; her glance was focused, attentive, missing nothing. And she was a beauty, no doubt about it, flawless skin; even the blond hair was probably natural.

"Nostalgia for Soviet times," she said, looking at me.

"What?" I pretended I didn't understand. Part of my cover as an amateur underground agent – alias Misty Hoyt – was supposed to be that I'm under-educated and not very bright. But as I'm an irrepressible pedant and bluestocking show-off with something approaching a photographic memory for the most arcane and useless and bizarre facts and theories, it's not easy to keep my mouth shut. Maybe I'll just give up – and show off. Sometimes paradox and contradiction are the spice of life; also, they are good diversionary tactics, smoke screens. Like my controller said: deception is best practiced as a multilayered game, and paradox is not to be neglected in the construction of one's underground persona. "Remember, Misty, exploit your emotional memory and inner conflicts," said Frederick. Stanislavski could not have put it better.

"I saw you looking at the hairdo," she said, "It's one of the many things Sergei likes." Her English was excellent, a touch British, hardly any Russian accent.

The earpiece made a burping sound. I was astounded that the woman next to me couldn't hear it. "Gwen, we've had confirmation. Gwen? Gwen, we've had confirmation – the packages are with Sergei. Repeat: the packages are with Sergei."

Then there was static. Shit! I tightened my grip on the edge of the sink. The "packages" were four thermonuclear devices, maybe six, maybe more. They were miniaturized to suitcase size, ideal for a containership, an aircraft, or even a guy with a bulky backpack. Shit! Sergei had been trying to buy the nukes. Now, if Paris was right, he had them. Shit!

The earpiece burped again. A voice said. "I don't think she's getting any of this."

"Ah, he's eclectic, then, your man, this Sergei," I said, slightly distracted, and turning to the blonde and realizing as soon as I opened my mouth that I was betraying the fact that I had a vocabulary. "Eclectic" was a bridge too far, much too far. Fuck – oh, well, I guess I'd better ride with it. As a spy, I'm utterly hopeless – and right now, I'm totally drunk and certainly drugged out of my mind, so my self-control is not perhaps what it should be in such a duplicitous life-and-death situation.

The blonde's eyes narrowed slightly, considering me more carefully. Her tongue passed over her lips. "Yes, he's a man of catholic tastes, of infinite variety, truly a renaissance prince, lavish with favors, capricious in his moods, capacious in his appetites, and, let me warn you, darling, he's very, very dangerous." She touched up her lipstick, bright scarlet, which didn't need any touching up. As she talked, she was looking at herself, studying the effect. "Sergei is a true artist. He likes to mix his genres – schoolgirl and whore, 1950's Soviet mother type and black leather biker girl, blond schoolmarm wearing oversized glasses and naked and gagged and in chains. Tattooed and marked for life, above all, he absolutely loves that – marked for life. You get the idea."

"It doesn't sound easy." I wanted to throw up. The room was spinning, not very fast, but it was spinning.

The earpiece muttered, "Gwen … static … Gwen …" I stared at the mirror; my image danced – a kaleidoscope of bright colors, tattoos – Who the heck is that clownish horror? Me, it's me! Of course, it's me.

The earpiece burst into static. "This is a catastrophe." And another voice said. "She's as good as dead." Then another voice, "She's probably dead already." They seemed to be all talking at once.

The blonde was staring at herself in the mirror, taking on a thoughtful, reflective tone. "Well, it isn't easy. And his mood changes in an instant. But he collects different girls for different flavors – so one girl doesn't have to be everybody and everything."

"Oh." I splashed water on my face and stared for a moment at the mask in the mirror. The lips had been tattooed so black they blended into the elaborate skin design; it created a sort of a skull-like effect. It seemed strange my teeth were still normal. I still had a smile, but …

"You're just his type, totally. With all the tattoos, you are utterly monstrous, if you don't mind my saying so. Punk-Goth gone mad." She swung around to take a close, direct look. "I never saw the point of tattoos, mind you, just fad and fashion. But," she focused on me, stared, grinned, and rolled her eyes. "My God, darling, you really are perfect! How could you do that to yourself?"

Her eyes were wide open and extra bright, as if startled, as if drugged, which she was, clearly. She licked her lips. "I think you will be a success. As I said, Sergei loves tattoos. He's totally into the weird and the monstrous. He adores freaks – and kid, you are about as freakish as they come."

"You think so." I turned my mask towards her and gave her an extra big smile – I was even more grotesque, Martine told me, when I smiled. "Oh, Gwen, how totally utterly horrible!" she'd declared. And then she kissed me as if to console me for having become a monster. As I grinned at Sergei's girl, the metal rings in my ears clanked against each other. I could feel the large ring nose, warm, smooth steel, against my curled upper lip.

"Yes, you look like a masterpiece of self-loathing."

"It's called body art," I said, "It's a statement."

"A statement?"

"Absolutely," I hiccupped. Everything was fuzzy; I forced myself to focus.

The earpiece emitted a hissing stream of static. If I survived this little adventure, I would kill somebody. Maybe I'd kill the guy or girl who invented the earpiece satellite hookup, but I'd torture them first. I was also, at the first opportunity, going to tear the little thing out of my ear and flush it down some toilet.

The earpiece hissed again, with the shadow of a voice. "Intended targets for the nukes are ... Paris ... Tel Aviv ... New York ... Tehran ... and maybe Moscow." And it sank into a cosmic hiss, background radiation left over from the big bang. If the voice was right, half the bloody world was going to be blown up.

"Whatever it is, you'll be a big success. Sergei collects waifs who suffer from extreme self-hatred. Self-destructive and self-hating girls are one of his hobbies. You can do so much with them."

"Oh. You figure I hate myself?" Again I turned to the mirror, splashed water on my face, and let the drops slide down my cheeks, my chin, and my neck, tiny rivulets, traveling all the way to my belly, and the ring that pierced my belly button. "It's really hot in there."

"Yeah, it's steamy. The air-conditioning's off. Everything in this god-forsaken country breaks down. They should never have had the goddamn revolution or invasion or coup or whatever it was." She leaned against the sink. Her minuscule mini-skirt was black leather, skintight, and, under the open black leather vest, I noticed that her white blouse was semi-transparent, and no bra, and then there were the black stockings, and black patent leather stilettos. She smiled. "Yes, I'm sure of it: you must have really self-destructive tendencies."

"Really?"

"I mean – yes, really! How could you do that to your face?"

I shrugged, and glanced at the freakish mask in the mirror, pure skull-like geometry – black-and-scarlet arabesques, shaved head, scarlet puffball or tuft at the crown, large nose ring anchored in the septum, big metal circles dangling from the ears, four on each side. Yes, truly, a work of art. I suddenly had an overpowering vision of me as a naked cannibal, utterly tattooed, a clanking monument of hard metal; I'm on some steamy prehistoric island, about to eat somebody – my neighbor in the mirror looked scrumptious. I was about to bite her arm, I was salivating for it, I could feel, under my teeth and lips the tenderness of her flesh, the smoothness of her perfumed skin, but she interrupted the flow of hallucination, and ...

Meanwhile, the earpiece was saying, "We'd better plan a strike, take the whole place out, for once and for all." Then it belched and hissed and went dead.

"Let me see. Your mummy didn't love you. Your father – or maybe it was a brother, or an uncle, or a priest – raped you."

Again the earpiece hissed. "Can't hear a damned thing ...

Could you order me a Reuben ...? Two pickles ... Thanks, thanks," then hiss, then static, then dead silence.

"Maybe, and maybe all of the above." I grinned, and stuck out my tongue.

She was watching me in the mirror. "Smartass! You'll go far."

"You figure?"

"You want me to introduce you to Sergei? I'm sure you do! That's why you're here." Her skimpy black leather vest hung open, and under the transparent blouse, her breasts were perfect, with large areolae and nipples, and both breasts were pierced with large rings, and her tummy looked as flat as a drum, as resilient as a trampoline. Her arms were buff too. Her legs shapely, perfect, but muscular. I blinked and bit my tongue: this girl must work out. She might even be dangerous – another obstacle. A silver ring shone in her belly button, above the low slung black leather skirt. She grinned. "Yes, I do figure. You are a bloody masterpiece." She shook her head and sighed, and said softly, as if talking to herself. "How could you do it to yourself?" She was staring at me in the mirror. Her English was more than good; it was literary, and of the cosmopolitan mid-Atlantic British variety. "Sergei will adopt you," she said.

"You think so."

"I know so, as I said: Sergei adores your type of look – utterly depraved."

"Who's this Sergei again?"

"Who's Sergei? Come on! You know. Now let's have a closer look at you." She moved closer, and we gazed at my image in the mirror. The contrast between the two of us could not have been greater. She was a classic beauty, and impeccable, even in that skimpy outfit – perfectly symmetrical features, fine and chiseled, dark eyelashes and eyebrows and blonde hair. She was a Vargas pinup from the old days, a young Catherine Deneuve.

As for me, it was true. I was Goth-Punk-Retro gone wild. Each detail had been carefully thought out. My head was shaved on both sides and at the back; the tuft of purple-scarlet hair stood up in the middle, dense and curly, like the silly puffball at the end of a poodle's tail; the thick steel nose ring pierced my septum and was so big it touched my upper lip; my eyebrows had been shaved – so carefully it looked like permanent depilation – and replaced by an elaborate black-and-scarlet tattoo design that covered my whole face and went down my neck. My whole body was brightly tattooed, down to my ankles, down to my wrists – dragons, serpents, mermaids, rising suns, flames. The whole of me was a work of art.

"What does it feel like, honey." She put her hand on my breast and tugged at the nipple ring. "Those tattoos are fab." She ran her finger along the edge of one of the tattoos. "This is top quality, deep ink, dazzling, bright. Must have cost you a fortune."

"Yeah. Cost me pure blood," I said.

"There's no accounting for taste." She tickled my breast with the point of one fingernail, tilted her head, considered the bright swirling design, a serpent about to bite a nipple. "Seriously, I used to teach English literature, mostly 18th and 19th-century novels, in Moscow, even in a university, but then I got hooked on some serious habits. Besides, it's better to live than to read about other people doing the living for you – right?"

"Right."

"And you?"

"I didn't finish high school. I tended bars – in Philadelphia, Baltimore, and then New York. I figured I'd see the world. I hitchhiked around Europe, Asia a bit."

"You hitchhiked? Alone?"

"Sometimes. Yeah. Anyway, I ended up in Hamburg; I got a German boyfriend."

"Let me guess. He liked tattoos. And heavy metal rock. And he had a big greasy bike with a high rev motor that made a lot of noise."

"Yes."

"And he thought Adolf Hitler was the greatest."

"Yes. Adolf was totally cool."

"He liked black leather, greasy engines, and setting fire to houses with immigrants and refugees in them."

"Yes. That was Heinrich."

"We have those types in Russia too."

"We were in Dresden and Hamburg, and then Leipzig, yeah, he liked tattoos. It started small. Then he wanted more and more." I glanced at my ruined face. "He paid for it all. He had money – so it was the best tattooing money could buy, and the brightest. We had a fight – that's when he had my face done, to prove I loved him and something to remember him by when we split which he did as soon as I was complete, my face was complete, I mean." I looked away from her and splashed some more water on my face. It was beautiful in a way, an abstract pattern of thick coal-black marks, and scarlet, stark, and brilliant. But it wasn't human. It was a mask. I was a mask. I was Misty Hoyt, the mask.

"And he said it was love, and so you let him turn you into a freak."

"I guess so. That was more or less how it happened. You don't like it?"

"I adore it, kid. What can be better? Marked for life! Ugly as hell itself!" She turned and took my face in her hands and kissed me on the lips, a real kiss that lingered. "You know if I introduce you to the man, it will be like I'm sending you into the meat grinder."

"Yeah. How so?"

"He likes cruelty, and he'll see that you like to suffer and that you adore humiliation. He's already noticed. So he'll oblige – beyond your wildest dreams."

"A match made in heaven," I grinned my grotesque grin.

She put her finger under my chin. "You are either the stupidest or the most perverse twisted and calculating girl I've ever met – and, believe me, I've met some loonies."

"So – have I passed the test?"

"You'll do – it gives me the shivers just looking at you."

"So ... this Sergei, guy, he's interesting?" I was hoping that the ear microphone was picking this up, but I doubted it was; it was not making a peep, not even a hiss, just dead air. And here I was, doing great! I was closing in on the guy.

She laughed. "You could say that."

"Well, then." I ran my tongue around my lips, leaving a heavy gleam of saliva. I was a very moist girl – that was the signal that I was apparently ready to do anything.

She grinned and shook her head. "You go wait at the bar, honey," she said. "I'll get Sergei to invite you over. He's been eyeing you since he first caught a glimpse of you – I'm sure you'll be a hit. But, you know ..."

"What do I know?" I gave her the innocent perverted waif wide-eyed double blink.

"It will be very tricky – and, as I said, very dangerous."

"I like tricky. I like dangerous." I fingered one of my nipple rings, and again licked my lips.

"My name's Sonia," she said.

"Misty," I said, "My name's Misty."

"Okay, sweetie. Okay, Misty, it's your funeral." She smiled a big smile, put her hand lightly on my tattooed shoulder – a bright, glossy, coiled serpent in scarlet, turquoise, and black – squeezed, turned on her heels, and was gone.

"Well, that was interesting," I said, as if to myself, hoping the mike was picking it up, hoping I'd get some response.

A burst of static, then nothing.

Four or five nukes, maybe more. Hmm ...

I waited for a minute. I splashed water on my face. I felt like I was sobering up. But there are moments like this when you think you are sober or the drug is out of your system, and then, a second later, you discover that you are still as drunk as a skunk and drugged to the gills and the world twirls around again and you think you may never regain control.

It was interesting what the voice had said – the packages were with Sergei. Four atomic bombs, maybe more ... interesting ...

The apocalypse.

I somehow made it back into the salon, sat at the bar, and ordered vodka. Vodka sounded like a good, sober, honest drink. I don't know what I was thinking. The barman – now it was a barman – I wondered where the bargirl had gone – told me it was on the house. Two girls were pole dancing just in front of me. I caught glimpses of their golden legs and torsos in the mirrors between the bottles. The slender golden Vietnamese girl was no longer there. Then Andrei was sitting beside me. Where had he come from?

"You ever do any stripping?" He leaned closer.

"Once, in Berlin, for a bet," I sniffed and blew my nose on a serviette.

"Ah, were you tattooed and pierced?"

"No, it was before – white as the driven snow I was."

"Ah," he said, "I'll try to picture that."

"You do that."

A hand was on my shoulder, another voice, female, "Come on, meet the great man." It was Sonia, suddenly there, beside me.

I got up. Andrei slapped me on the bottom. "Go get it, kid!"

Sonia and I wove our way through the tables. People looked up at us, distracted, glazed, and curious glances. One woman sitting on a guy's lap put her hand to her mouth when she saw me. I thought she was going to scream. But she managed to choke it off.

When Sergei stood up, I saw he was bigger than I thought, and he had muscles that bulged and showed lots of workouts and lots of steroids. It was clear he could afford anything he wanted.

"What is this?" He said, giving me the once-over. "Have you brought me another gift, Sonia? A tattooed waif?"

"Indeed, she is," said Sonia.

Sergei's eyes sparkled, but they were flat too, reptilian, as if nobody human was living inside, behind them. "What are you, waif? Come here."

I stepped forward.

Sergei put his big hand on my belly. It was warm. With one finger, he toyed with the ring in my belly button.

"Here, lift this off." He slipped me out of my vest. So now I was topless.

"Hey," I said, but it was pretty feeble.

"Let's have a look." He rubbed his chin. "Oh, I like this."

"Yeah?" I tried to strike a defiant pose; actually, I was scared, really scared, and exposed, totally exposed.

"I want to see all of you." He grinned, the grin of a pure predator.

I was sweating. I realized I was terrified, suddenly up close, suddenly staring into the abyss. I decided not to resist. I was, in fact, on one level, feeling pretty light-headed. "Hey, I don't know ..."

"Never say no, Misty. When opportunity knocks, never say no, and never say never," Sergei grinned and helped me out of my shorts and my panties – very gracious, a true gentleman. He left my stilettoes – otherwise, I was naked.

"Beautiful," he said. "Piercings and rings everywhere! Truly a work of art, don't you think, Sonia?"

"Truly."

Yes, there I was, revealed, my mind spinning with a cocktail of alcohol and drugs, Paris hissing and hiccupping in my ear, and me nude as a newborn babe, clothed only in sweat, tattoos, and dangling rings, in the middle of this club in the middle Old Typhilis in the middle of the New Republic of Old Transbeckistan. What the fuck is going to happen now? I glanced shyly around at my new – and edgy, deadly audience. Maybe they all knew who I was. Maybe they were just playing with me. Maybe I was just minutes or seconds away from ritual execution. I noticed an enormously fat man sitting on one of the divans in our group, only a few meters away. I let my glance slide over him, indifferent. His naked stomach, visible under his open jacket, bulged out, huge, and glowed with sweat. I recognized him from the briefings in Paris. He was a Pakistani arms dealer, perhaps the greatest merchant of death in the world. Kaleem Baluchi was his name. He was the man who, if the mutterings out of Paris were right, had just sold four or five or six – or maybe more – nuclear weapons to Sergei Platonov, and Sergei was going to sell them to … Who? These two men were the midwives of a sort of scenario for the end of the world. I licked my lips, took a deep breath. Sergei stared at me, his eyes moving up and down my body – calculation in his narrowed pupils. He flipped and tugged at one of my nipple rings. All eyes of his little group were on me – the naked tattooed freak, the waif, the offering, and the sacrifice. Sergei Platonov – known among other things as the killer of four continents – he'd personally murdered more than fifty people, so went the CIA estimate. He grinned. "Now, let's see what you can do, Misty Hoyt."

They all laughed; some of them clapped. Sonia smiled,

encouragingly. Kaleem Baluchi, patting his bulging, glowing tummy, chortled, and winked. I noticed he was trying to catch my eye, so I gave him a look and quickly returned the wink, while wondering what the fuck I was doing, oh, well, improvisation is essential to creativity, so they say, even for a mathematician.

Now I must perform – whatever it was they wanted me to perform. I swallowed. Sweat trickled down my back. I took a deep breath and I thought back, just for an instant, to how I had gotten myself into this fix and whether there was any way out of it – whether I would rescue James, help save the world from a nuclear holocaust, and live to tell about it – or not. And what the devil did Sergei mean by "perform"?

CHAPTER 2 – ASSASSINS

Four days earlier – it was a sultry beautiful Parisian day, sensual and electric, with a violent thunderstorm predicted for the evening. James had just left for Istanbul. The last glimpse I had of him, he was standing at the corner of our little street in Paris, just next to the patisserie where we got our croissants, hot and fresh, every morning. He stopped, turned, smiled and waved at me, where I stood, tiptoes, on the balcony. I waved and blew him a kiss. He returned the kiss, waved, turned away, and was gone. I stood there, staring at the empty corner, feeling, absurdly, a sense of loss. Then I shook myself. I shouldn't worry. I shouldn't mourn. He'd only be gone for three days, and he was going to phone as soon as he got to his hotel, which would be – I glanced at my watch – in about five-and-a-half-hours. Even with him away, we'd be together.

The humidity was rising. The sun was high and bright, but the light had already turned milky, as if anticipating dusk. I moved away from the open French doors and balcony and sat down at my computer; I stared at the screen; I was working on a mathematical network analysis of terrorist groups and the illegal arms trade. I made a few adjustments to the matrix and the parameters. Time races when I am working. The hours rushed away without my noticing.

I ran a few simulations – plugging in the behavior of specific gangs, of specific gang leaders. The model could predict, with a range of probable scenarios, what the arms dealers and terrorists might do next. It was part psychology, part history, part mathematics. And, graphically, a massive amount of information was quantified, and presented in an elegant, easily understandable format. You could zoom in on any part of the diagram for more details, and then zoom out again. I was proud of it. It made connections visible that otherwise could easily remain hidden. Law enforcement and intelligence organizations often operate in silos; they don't share information, and they don't know what they don't know, and they don't know what other people know – and what other people don't know. Criminals and terrorists slip through those gaps.

I sat back. I crossed my legs. I uncrossed my legs. I was antsy and horny. When James was not available, all the desires surged up. I wanted him. I felt his absence like an edgy emptiness in the pit of my stomach.

I stood up and stretched.

I sat down, and I uploaded the schematics and all of the day's work to the encrypted ultra-secure cloud storage.

I stood up, stretched again – wiggling my shoulders, making the voluptuous feeling last this time. I went to the balcony, and looked out on the narrow Parisian street with all its 19th Century buildings, the standard Parisian dwelling from the 1850s and 60s when Baron Georges-Eugène Haussmann redesigned Paris for Napoleon III, creating all those grandiose straight boulevards, all those uniformly designed, stately-looking blocks of apartments. The sky was by now milky rose, and the air was sultrier. The storm promised by the forecasters was closing in. I made myself a double espresso latte, slipped out of my sandals, lifted off my T-shirt, shorts, and panties, folded them on a chair, and walked around the flat barefoot and naked, offering my body to the caressing, ticklish, humid, warm air that drifted in from the windows. I took slow, comforting sips of the coffee. The air was super-soft, intimate as a body, melting into me, and me into it. It was one of those days when the world itself is your lover.

In the bedroom, the sheer white muslin curtain drifted in from the balcony. I stood by the bed, looking down at the sheets. It was neatly made! Perfect! It almost military in its precision, with no sign of this morning's marvelous wrestling match – I was on top of James, teasing him, bringing him to the very edge, then leading him back to sweet gentleness. Then James turned the tables. He had me pinned down, then tied down, spread-eagled and blindfolded, and he did wonderful slow-motion teasing things!

I turned around, and around, holding my arms out, balancing the coffee cup in one hand. Yes, the air was a sultry caress. It comforted me, aroused me, and made me even edgier.

I put the cup down and touched myself, scrutinizing myself in the full-length bedroom mirror. Chalk-white skin, jet-black hair, I seemed not to have changed at all in the last three years. My body was hairless except for the neat little gleaming coal-black "Bermuda Triangle," my "Heart of Darkness," as Kate used to call it. Outwardly I still looked like the 19-year-old girl who had been working on her Ph.D. in Boston, the girl who was tearful saying goodbye to her beautiful flatmate, Kate. Ah, Kate! Life had separated us. She had recovered from her illness in Africa. She was now in Hong Kong, monitoring an outbreak of a deadly new version of a coronavirus, once again risking her life to save humanity from present and future plagues and epidemics.

"Ah, Kate," I said out loud as I stared at myself – dark, dark eyes, and dark eyelashes and eyebrows. I lowered my head and gave myself my mutinous little boy look, and stuck out my tongue:

Oh, yes, aren't I charming! Then, out loud, I pronounced, "Gwendoline, you are an asshole!"

Tonight I was seeing Martine Aubin, my girlfriend, and lover. It was a date, definitely a date. I had proposed cooking for her here at home, a fresh plate of lemon spaghetti, perhaps some veal, and a bottle of excellent white wine. But Martine said she didn't want me sweating over a hot stove on such a warm summer evening. "Let's eat out," she said, "just downstairs from my flat, at Pierrot le Fou. Then we can come up to my lair and fool around. Okay?" "Yes, definitely okay," I said, thinking I would make myself very seductive – and then we would, if Martine still desired it, spend the night at her place. I could, in my mind, taste her soft liquid insistent hungry kisses. I could feel the skillful knowing intimacy of her touch. Each finger was a magician. In my imagination, her kisses and touch mingled with those of James. I felt the liquid rising. Saliva flooded my tongue; my legs trembled, my yearning soared, and ... "Okay, Gwendoline," I said to my image in the mirror, "time to sober up, my girl."

I went into the bathroom and turned on the shower. Yes, tonight I would be ultra-sexy – I wanted to drive Martine crazy! I closed my eyes and envisaged the whole thing: Let's see! I would slowly strip her of every piece of clothing. I wanted her alone, naked, offering herself to me, all mine, while I remained fully dressed, which, I thought, would be a nice touch.

The hot water poured down, steaming up the shower curtain. I stepped in under it. I began to soap myself, making of each movement of my hand an imaginary lover's touch. I would kiss her and touch her; I would run my fingers slowly down her thighs; I would caress the – oh, so familiar – moist inner side of her thighs, each side, in turn, I would have her sit, like a goddess, on the low divan, and I would kneel before her, I would be her acolyte and worshiper, I would kiss her nipples, and lick them, and suck them, and then with my tongue, I would force open her legs and twist her clitoris and milk it; I would liquefy her, and enter her; and I would still be wearing my tight sexy dress, and I would not allow her to touch me, except, when I ordered her to do so, and then only with her lips; I would drive her to the edge of orgasm, and then beyond; and then, slowly I'd peel out of my dress – or have her peel it from me – and I would bow down, naked, before her. I would worship her; I would –

I closed my eyes. I shuddered. I had almost brought myself to orgasm just with soapsuds and thinking about it. Perhaps I should go all the way. Yes, why not? And so I did. The shower went on and on.

I groaned, I screamed, I made an exhibition of myself – but there was nobody there to witness the show, just me and the steaming stream of bubbling water.

Finally, I stepped out of the shower, turned it off, and, walking around the flat, I toweled myself down, slowly, carefully, reveling in the voluptuousness of it. By now, despite the relief of orgasm, I was even more aroused. I opened the wardrobe and looked at the selection. Hmm! I faced an embarrassment of riches.

I considered several possibilities. Finally, I changed into the dress I would wear for Martine – It was a classic, a twin of the one she often wore: a skintight, one-piece, ultra-thin black latex dress, no underwear, no stockings, and to be completed by black patent leather lock-on stilettoes. It was extremely revealing, offering the body, in great detail, to even the most casual gaze. It was thus, in its exhibitionism – I am an object – subtlety submissive, and yet, in its metallic sleekness, promising a suave touch of the dominatrix. I would be her mistress and her master; I would be her goddess and her slave. I would be her worshipper, and she would love it, and succumb, and be on her knees and –

I checked myself in the mirror – yes, tummy still sufficiently flat, just a nice sensual little roundness, and my breasts, well, rather fine breasts, if truth be told, sculpted in black latex, nipples, and areola quite evident – perfect! Oh, you dreadful show-off, Gwendoline. Well, this was the way James liked me. This was the way Martine liked me. She loved displaying me like I was some sort of work of art – or her very personal pet – and when I could, I returned the favor. I often made her dress in revealing costumes of my very own devising, which gave great pleasure to her man, Philip, too. Sometimes he and I would join efforts in designing her outfit – and so this was the way I would be tonight. She would be my naked slave, and I would be her stylish, fully dressed mistress, just for her, visibly for her. I liked the feeling – I wanted to feel her hungry gaze upon me and that of passers-by. They made me feel alive.

It would be another half an hour before James would call from Istanbul. I worked. I read two articles I had intended to read, but had never found the time. Wearing the dress aroused me. I was ready for action, bubbling with mischief. I fidgeted and waited for WhatsApp to sound its little alarm. The appointed time came and went.

James didn't call.

James was late.

This was strange. James was always so punctual! And he had his cellphone. I rang the cell and got his voice mail. Hmm!

I checked his flight. It had left and arrived on time. I phoned his hotel in Istanbul. He had not checked in. They asked if they should cancel the reservation.

"No," I said, "No, don't cancel." On the Net, I checked the local Turkish and Istanbul news to see if anything had happened – an exceptional traffic jam, a big accident, or a terrorist attack. No, nothing.

My first thought was to go to Istanbul and try to find out what happened. But that was stupid. He was only an hour late – Perhaps I was overreacting.

I rang his cellphone again. It rang and rang and then went to voicemail. I left a message. "My love, it's me. Where are you? Let me know. I love you, and I want you. Call me right away!"

Hmm! I walked up and down. Had James run into trouble? Had he been hurt? Or kidnapped? I'd have to check and see if he'd actually got on the plane and then gotten off in Istanbul. He might have been stopped in or outside Paris on his way to Charles de Gaulle Airport. I had to get the passenger list.

The phone rang. Without looking at the name on the phone's screen, I picked it up. My heart was racing. "Hello," I said.

It was Martine, calling to set up the details for our evening date. Dinner for two at the bistro Pierrot le Fou under her flat, then monkey business in her flat, then maybe watch a video or two, then bed and more monkey business – then talk and caresses and sleep and caresses and talk and caresses and –

"James didn't get to his hotel," I said.

"What? Do you want me to come over?"

I heard a click on the line; the tonality was different; the line was bugged. Somebody was listening.

"No, actually, I think I'd better get out of here – and now."

"You think ..." Martine was savvy and quick, and I'd shared my fears for James' safety with her; she knew he had dangerous enemies; she realized what I was saying – that I was in danger and that the line was bugged.

"Yes, I definitely think ... Let's meet at the place in Paris where we first drank the chilled Chablis."

Martine hesitated for just a second. "Right!" she said. And she hung up.

I stood up and looked around. Yes, somebody was listening. If James was in trouble – if he'd been kidnapped – or murdered

– and if people wanted his secrets, then they could come after me. James was tough. He wouldn't give in. But I was his weak point. I would be the kidnappers' leverage. James would do anything to stop people from hurting me. I had to get out of the flat. If I had mentioned on the phone where Martine and I were going to meet – then when we got there, there'd be somebody waiting for us – and it wouldn't be the good guys.

I always kept a pre-prepared overnight bag, toiletries, and all. I grabbed it. I slipped my laptop – already in its unbreakable case – over my shoulder, and my purse. I wouldn't bother to change. The slinky tight black latex dress that I knew Martine would like, and the stilettoes, with their little locks, were not the best costume for a chase scene, but I didn't think I'd have time to change. And ... at that moment, the doorbell rang. I went to the monitor – it wasn't the concierge, and it wasn't the police. Two big hulking guys wearing leather jackets. True to form, I thought, Russian hitmen out of Central Casting. The camera was disguised. They hadn't noticed it. I had to get out of the flat – and quick. I turned on the shower, closed the bathroom door, and I triggered the fire alarm; a siren began to emit a high-pitched scream. The guys looked around, and then one of them drew a pistol. They were going to shoot the locks and smash in the door. It was armored, but lightly; it would resist for a minute or two maybe, but not for long. I went to my desktop computer – which was on, since I'd been reading the articles online – and I triggered the self-destruct program: in under a minute, it would destroy the hard drive and everything on it. In any case, everything of interest had been uploaded, encrypted, to an ultra-secure site only an hour ago and wiped from the hard drive.

I pulled open the French doors and went onto the narrow balcony and looked down – four floors below, the street looked normal. I slung the laptop, purse, and overnight bag over my shoulder, and I hitched up the dress – which was already damned short – and swung myself over the balustrade. I hung on, with just a foothold about two inches, a neat trick in stilettoes, and with one hand I reached for the next balcony; it belonged to our neighbor, a TV talk show host, Antoine Parillaud. At that moment, I noticed movement in the open window of an apartment on the opposite side of the street. The curtains stirred – as if in a sudden breeze. There was a gleam like that of a reflection off a gun barrel. I dropped down to a crouch, and a section of wall exploded above my head, just a bit in front of where I'd been standing. Fragments splashed into my face and my eyes. No explosive sound – the hunter was using a silencer.

"Bugger," I said. I was talking like Kate or Martine, "Bugger."

I grabbed the other balustrade and shimmed over onto my neighbor's balcony. I smashed the window of the French doors of the Parillaud flat with my laptop case and reached through the shattered glass, turned the handle, forced the French doors open, and slid into the apartment.

Just behind me, outside, a section of the wall exploded. The sniper wasn't trying to kill me. He – or she – was trying to stop me or slow me down. Or just scare me. Whoever they were – and I had a pretty clear idea who they were – they probably wanted me alive.

Now the killers knew I had changed flats. They might not know, though, that the Parillaud flat had a second-floor attic studio and spiral staircase up to the attic studio and another spiral staircase to the roof and a tiny little roof garden, and that there was a walkway over to the next building. Of course, they might know all of this; but I had to take a chance. I was in Parillaud's living room. Nobody seemed to be home.

Oh, no – the flat wasn't empty. Standing there was Antoine's daughter, a teenager, Zoe Parillaud; she was wearing a black

T-shirt and tight black elastic shorts and black plastic flip-flops. Dangling from her hand was a big book, a thick hardback, its pages fluttering like a fan. Her mouth was open, and her eyes wide. "What the hell, Gwendoline!"

"Sorry about breaking in! Get away from the windows, Zoe! People are trying to kill me or kidnap me. You'd better phone the police, and then hide under your bed; they'll probably break into your flat." A side of the studio wall exploded just beside Zoe. She ducked, turned around. Half her face was white with plaster.

The room suddenly smelt like a construction site. A wooden bookshelf – all sunny varnished pine – collapsed, peeling away from the wall, and hundreds of books cascaded, a regular avalanche.

"I'm not staying here," she said.

"Right," I nodded. Both of us moved out of the line of sight of the window. Zoe grabbed her purse from a divan. Books were still falling. The room was filling with dust.

"To the roof," she said. "Hey, this is like a film."

"Yes, Zoe, but it isn't a film." I pushed her in front of me up the spiral metal stairs, all chrome and black steel, very modernist.

We clattered to the top of the metal stairs and came into the little studio, her father's workplace. It looked like a perfect creative nest, bright and orderly. In one glance, I took it in: a neat little desk, a powerful desktop computer, a pinup board, and a calendar with production schedules outlined and little cards showing scene sequences. The bookshelves were piled up with dictionaries, an old-fashioned encyclopedia, and a shelf of fiction – classics, Balzac, Dickens, Tolstoy, in the Pléiade and Gallimard editions. I absorbed it, without even thinking, it gave me a whole sense of Zoe's father's life – before I'd only greeted him in the elevator or on the landing or seen him on TV. Now, suddenly, I understood what kind of man he was. A TV or movie script, with yellow highlight on certain lines, lay on his desk. Everything was in light wood, very Scandinavian really, very clean and neat. A large clear window looked out over Paris. "The glass is bulletproof, Dad told me," Zoe said. I could see Montmartre, and the round white dome of the church of Sacré Coeur, a strangely gloomy and lugubrious building; it was conservative Catholicism's revenge for the sins of the Paris Commune of the spring of 1871, when revolutionaries took over the city after Napoleon III was defeated by the Prussians. The vengeful conservatives decided that Parisians, whenever they looked up, were to be reminded that they had revolted against the Word of God and were destined for punishment. Huge clouds were building up to the west. I saw a flash of lighting. Yes, the storm was almost here.

"Dad has a pistol." Zoe was kneeling next to a safe. "It's locked in here." She opened the safe and handed me the gun – a Glock 43 9mm Luger caliber pistol. I weighed it and checked the magazine – it was loaded. When I'd gone out on the anti-smuggling operations, Interpol and the DEA or US Drug Enforcement Administration, and the Italian police, in particular, had insisted I learn about firearms, and how to use them. I don't particularly like guns, but you never know what is going to come in handy.

All this had happened in an instant. We were already climbing up the spiral staircase to the roof.

"Hold on," I said, motioning Zoe to stay back. I went out onto the rooftop platform. I crouched down, sheltering under the trellis of vines, and looked around. A vast sky and the city looked like a tapestry laid out just for us. It was beautifully lit, a violent-looking, stormy Parisian evening, high purple clouds reaching up to the west, yellow bars of sunlight radiating out like a saint's crown, slanting lines of rain heading towards the city. I felt big hot raindrops against my skin. Already, the rain had come! There was nobody in sight on the platform, nor the rooftops. I scanned them again. Tiles and corrugated-looking roofs with little chimneys rose everywhere, a classic Parisian rooftop landscape. Here and there, there were a few rooftop gardens, luxurious little islands of green. There was nobody dangerous, not that I could see. The walkway to the next building looked clear.

"I'm coming up," Zoe said.

"Okay," I said, "but crouch down. These guys shoot first and ask questions later. They want me alive, I think, but I don't think they care about you."

"Cool," she blinked at me and grinned. "So, I might be collateral damage."

"Yes, Zoe, you well might."

We skittered along the walkway. We came to the backside of the next building. A metal service staircase went down one level to a work platform. We clambered down and paused to catch our breath. The air was getting heavy. More raindrops splashed on my arm. I looked down at myself – skintight figure-molding black latex, black stilettoes, and nothing else – except a Glock, a laptop case, a purse, and an overnight bag.

Just below us, people were having an early dinner party on a terrace surrounded by a trellis heavy with vines. We jumped the last five feet, landing right next to their buffet table – where a strawberry and spinach salad was set out, among other delicacies.

"Sorry, sorry," I said.

"Hi Pierre, Hi Amelie," said Zoe, "We're escaping from some killers, and they have guns. They're going to shoot us."

"I'll phone the police," said the man Zoe had addressed as Pierre. He stood up. Bullets exploded next to him. He flattened himself against the wall.

"Get to cover," I shouted as Zoe and I leaped into the flat, everybody tumbling in behind us. I stopped just long enough to see that they were all safe. Amelie was shutting the terrace door – she pulled a metal grill across the entry and locked it, and then she slid the plate glass door shut and locked it. "That should keep them out," she said, and turned to me.

"Right," I said, "But get away from the door. They might try to shoot their way in."

Pierre was on the phone, giving the address.

"We have to go now," said Zoe.

"Yes," I said, "Sorry for all the fuss. Goodbye! And thanks!"

We left their flat, and galloped down the stairs, Zoe following, me first, with the Glock drawn. We came out on rue de Buci. I looked left and right and up towards the rooftops, didn't see anything threatening. We raced around a corner, past the Chinese restaurant, where Mrs. Chang, who was out front watering the flowers on their terrace, gave us the once-over – staring at my latex dress and high heels and Zoe half-covered in stucco dust – and then she smiled, and shouted, "Hello Gwendoline! Hello, Zoe!" She was probably thinking that I was doing one of my public sex pranks or performances, but puzzling perhaps as to how I had inveigled Zoe Parillaud to partake in my misbehavior.

"Hi, Mrs. Chang!" I waved the Glock.

Mrs. Chang's eyes widened.

Zoe and I were already halfway down the street – heading straight for the Metro Station. Zipping under the floral Art Deco Metro sign, we clattered down the stairs into the subway. "Have you got a ticket?" I was glancing behind us and wielding the Glock and thinking – this would be funny if it weren't so dangerous.

"I've got a pass," she said.

"Me too."

We slid our passes into the slots and slipped through the turnstiles. We galloped down to the platform, breathless, almost laughing. Zoe put her hand on my arm. "We're going to make it, aren't we?"

"I hope so." I scanned the platform and the stairs behind us, the Glock ready.

"We'll take the same train," Zoe said, "Then I'll get off four stations along and change trains. Dad's at his girlfriend's in the Marais. She and I are pals, and I often eat over there with them. They can put me up for the night. It'll be cool. I like her though mom can't stand her. It means I have to be a diplomat, you know, shuttling between Dad's and Mom's points of view, and Julie's of course – she's the mistress, I mean, the girlfriend, she's hardly older than me, so she's sort of more like a sister than an extra mother if you see what I mean."

Zoe was talking; I was watching. I also slipped the SIM and battery out of my cellphone and slipped them down behind a bench, into an invisible niche. I looked around. There were a few curious glances directed our way. Maybe it was a bit strange, this sight, one woman, luggage hoisted over her shoulder and with a black latex dress and a Glock, and a teenager with flip-flops, tight-pants, and T-shirt, and covered in white stucco dust.

The train came into the station. A guy – surely one of the Russians – came running down the stairs. A guard intercepted him just as the gates were closing. The man turned and shot the guard in the face. The doors of the train opened, then we were in the train, the guy sprinted for the train, the doors closed, and the train began to pull out of the station. I shouted to everybody, "Get down!" They stared, and then they understood. Zoe and I knelt close to the floor.

A ripple of bullets smashed through the windows, and then we were accelerating, and we were out of the station. Nobody had been hit. Maybe the guys didn't care if I was alive or dead. Maybe I had overestimated their subtlety; maybe James was dead, and they wanted me dead because I almost certainly knew what he knew. I was afraid the train would stop. It didn't. It did slow down at the next station, and it looked like it was going to stop, and then it went on, not stopping, to the following station, and it stopped there. The platform was full of police. How they had gotten there so fast, I had no idea.

"Do I look okay?" I asked, slipping the pistol into my purse.

"Just a bit of dust," she said, and she wiped it off my cheek and my shoulder.

"You too," I said, "But maybe a bit more dust." I wiped the plaster dust from her cheeks and lips. Half of the rest of her looked like she'd come out of a bomb blast – but there was no time for a total dust-down and shower.

"Maybe we should look innocent," she said, her eyes round, and mischievous; this was a game for her.

"We are innocent, I said.

"With that dress and those shoes, you hardly look innocent," she said.

I looked down at myself. Yes, I kept forgetting that I was wearing a black latex skintight single-piece dress, no underwear, and stilettoes. All of this meant for Martine and our evening tryst and my plan for wild and sentimental sex and sympathy – eons ago, in another world, when happy dinosaurs were grazing on prehistoric mushrooms on the Champs Élysées. No, I didn't look like a virgin.

Zoe suddenly wrapped her arms around me and kissed me – a long passionate kiss, a lover's kiss. I had my hands full. I submitted. The doors opened, and we went out into the crowd, our arms around each other, laughing.

"What an adventure," she was saying, and, as we sashayed ahead, arm in arm, the police let us through, and they said, "If you could wait over there, ladies and gentlemen, we would like witnesses to what happened two stops back."

We went where indicated, but just behind us was an exit to the street and to another subway line; in the crowded confusion, nobody paid attention to us, we were two giggling young women in a crowd. We slipped through the exit and went up the stairs and along a corridor to the other line. A train pulled in just as we got there, it was serendipitous, like things were sliding together just as they should. The doors slid open, and we got on. The passengers looked at us. We were an odd couple. The butt of the Glock was sticking out of my purse. Then the passengers plunged back into their smartphones, iPads, and newspapers.

"I liked that kiss, Gwendoline."

"So did I," I said. Zoe was as fresh as a rose, a real teenager, a kid. I would probably be arrested for diddling a minor.

"I've wanted to do that for a long time," she said.

"Hmm," I said.

"I've watched you, and you and James and you and Martine Aubin."

"Hmm," I said.

She grinned. "My boyfriend will be jealous if I tell him. Can I tell him?"

I shrugged and smiled. "As long as he doesn't come after me with a gun," I said, "Or denounce me to the Vice Squad."

She kissed me again. "I'm getting off here," she said. "Will you be okay?"

"I'll be okay," I said, "be careful, don't go back to the flat, and warn your father, maybe you'd all better stay at the girlfriend's for a day or two, or maybe in a hotel, and warn your mother, too, if she ever goes by your flat. And thanks, Zoe – you saved my life."

"Can we kiss again sometime?" She was going out the door.

I nodded, smiled, blew her a kiss, and mouthed, "Yes, I'd like that!"

And the doors closed the train was on its way, and for the first time, I had time to think. What had happened to James? And how could I save him? I was sure he had not left me. And now I was sure he was being held prisoner somewhere – or he had been murdered. They could kill him, but they would almost certainly want things first. They would need to know where his investments were, and what information he had on their companies and their networks. They might even want him to sign over shares. The fact that they came after me – and wanted into the flat – probably meant that they needed information, stocks, and documents. And they almost certainly wanted me as leverage, or to get rid of me as a possible obstacle to their plans. James might not crack, but if they threatened me, he would crack. He'd give them what they wanted. We were coming into Châtelet station. I watched for any dangerous characters. No, there didn't seem to be anybody who looked like a killer.

I got off and changed trains. One fragile-looking old lady looked me up and down and said, "That is a very nice dress, dear." "Thank you," I said. "Once I liked to wear things like that, but those days are long gone." "You are beautiful, madam," I said. "You are a dear," she said, "I wish you all the best. And I hope he or she is worth it." And she went to sit down and got out an iPad.

James didn't keep anything of his except clothes and sex toys in the apartment. It was my apartment, not his, he said. And I didn't keep vital information in there either. I encrypted everything and uploaded it to a secure server. Well, I hoped it was secure. I regularly eliminated all traces from the desktop of any vital information or work I had done. I did it every time I left the desk for more than a couple of minutes. And, before leaving, I'd activated self-destruct, so probably even the most ingenious hacker wouldn't be able to get any information from my desktop. Besides, it was new, and there wasn't much of interest, to them at least, on it. I'd taken all the precautions possible. Or I hoped I had. I'd pushed the hard drive destroy button just before climbing out the window. And I'd eliminated network links to my cellphone. Should I contact the police, Interpol, my intelligence contacts? Yes, I should. And, I thought I had a pretty good idea of who had done this – Sergei Platonov, arms dealer and killer extraordinaire.

I changed trains several times, and I got out at La Motte-Picquet-Grenelle station. I climbed up to the street. It was now raining hard, and I didn't have an umbrella. In a few seconds, I was soaked. The latex was even more clinging that before – well, that was impossible, but it was certainly more sculptural. I looked like I was painted in black varnish, glistening with beads of rain.

I was next to an overhead railway – part of the metro system – and close to the place where Martine and I had our first chilled Chablis in Paris. It was a small side-street restaurant, just under the overhead section of the metro. It had a tiny intimate trellised and enclosed terrace which they heated in the winter, and where they served oysters in the winter too, and where, in the summer, the trellis was entwined with vines and flowers were everywhere. You could listen to the muted rumble of the trains going by over-head and to the cries of vendors in the little outdoor market. It was a cherished, quiet, romantic spot, utterly unpretentious with delicious family-made food and a super – simple and not pricey – wine list.

Martine and I had gone there one hot summer afternoon, and we had swallowed oysters and drunk chilled Chablis, and for some reason, everything we said or did seemed utterly hilari-ous. We had been very amorous too, smooching shamelessly, but the owners did not seem at all offended; in fact, they offered us another bottle of wine – free, on the house. Then we had gone out onto the street, feeling horny and happy and giggly and full of energy; we had ended up in Martine's flat for a session that seemed to last for hours and hours and ended up with us going out to see a midnight movie on a screen set up in a park. I seemed to remember every detail of that day. I turned a corner and looked around. Martine was there already, waiting in a taxi. I climbed in. I asked, "Did you phone for the cab?"

"No. I grabbed it on the street, more than a block away from home and around two corners. And I took the battery and SIM card out of my mobile, crushed and burned the SIM card, and dropped what was left in a sewer grate, and left the mobile hidden at home – in the freezer."

"Good," I said.

Martine smiled – a good pupil.

"Could you please take us to Boulevard de Port-Royal at the corner of rue Pascal," I said.

The driver said, "Yes, Madam."

We began to head through the streets. The rain was heavier now. The windows fogged up.

"I also picked this up," Martine said; she was wearing a black T-shirt, black jeans, and cork-soled pumps, and she had what looked like an overnight bag. She handed me a disposable cellphone. "I got eight of them, you never know." She displayed a plastic bag full of brightly colored phones.

"You are a genius."

"All those spy films Philip and I have watched."

I phoned a number I had memorized, and that had been given to me at one of the security conferences I attended at the École de Guerre, the National Military School. It was a Paris number. In one of the top-secret sessions, I had learned – the quick course – how to be a spy, and I had even been taught a code. A man with a British accent answered: "Exotic Edwardian Antiques."

"Tabletop for two," I said. "Ah, tabletop! Greetings," he said,

"Do you mind phoning back in one minute, exactly?" "In one minute," I said, and hung up.

"Code?" Martine blinked at me.

"Hmm, yes."

"So, what do we do?"

"You stay close to me," I said. "You may be in danger."

"Me?" she raised an eyebrow. I saw the light dawn in her eyes. "Ah, yes, I understand – they've got James, they want something from him, you are leverage against James, and I'm leverage against you."

"Precisely. I'm sorry I got you into this."

"I'm not. It's exciting. Actually, I already thought we might be in a bit of trouble – Philip and me. So, I used a throw-away phone to text Philip to watch out and not phone me or email me on our usual accounts. He's in India scouting locations. He should be okay. But in any case, he's got four bodyguards with him. And the locals are very keen on his doing the film in their village, so he should be okay. He's famous. Sometimes fame is like a shield."

"You're famous too," I said.

"Yes, but then so are you."

"Yeah, sort of," I said, "Thanks to you."

"You exaggerate. You are famous all on your own." Martine kissed me on the cheek; l squeezed her hand.

The minute had passed. I rang the number again. The same voice answered. "Okay, we meet – now," he said.

"Yes," I said.

"Humpty Dumpty's Second Omelette."

"Right," I said. "I have an overnight bag."

"Trusty old bag, I trust," the voice said.

"Yes," I said.

"Bring the bag with you." He hung up.

I gave the taxi driver an address. It was three blocks from the target address.

"I'm an overnight bag?" Martine whispered. She put her hand on my thigh, pulled my latex dress up slightly. Both my thigh and the dress were beaded with hundreds of water drops. My hair, I realized, was soaked; trickles of water dripped down my back. I smiled, nodded, and put my hand on her hand.

"So, I'm an overnight bag. Charming," she whispered again; she leaned closer and gave me a warm kiss. "I like being your overnight bag," she breathed into my ear. The rain began to splash harder against the windows.

"Terrible weather," said the driver.

"Yes, it is," we said in perfectly synchronized chorus, and then laughed,

"You sound coordinated, like you are part of a chorus or a TV vaudeville sketch," the driver glanced into the mirror.

"I think maybe we are," said Martine.

He laughed. "Well, invite me to your show, whenever you put it on."

We got out at the corner of rue Pascal and Boulevard de Port-Royale, about three blocks away from our objective. I paid the driver in cash. "You're going to get soaked," he said. "We'll be okay." We smiled and waved, and he did the same and drove off.

Martine and I, neither of us had thought about umbrellas, so we were standing there, in the rain, under the plane trees, getting soaked.

"I really love the dress," said Martine, as we set off down a side street.

"Well, I make an effort," I said, and glanced at her, "It's an exact knock-off of one of your favorites – as you can see."

"That's right!" she said, half closing her eyes. Blond, and tanned, and blue-eyed, she looked trim and buff and perfect in the jeans, T-shirt, and cork-soled pumps. She took my arm. Standing there under the rain, we offered, I'm sure, a very romantic image, if anyone was looking.

We walked down another side street, went through a covered alleyway, and went around a corner; we stopped at a newspaper kiosk, and I bought Le Monde and Le Figaro. This was something I was supposed to do. I remembered the whole routine — or at least I hoped I did. We lingered for a moment under the awning of a café, rain pounding on the canvas, as if we were considering what to do. Then we walked about ten meters down the street and went into a variety shop and bought some chewing gum. We came out again, and I glanced up and saw that a third-floor window was open. "Okay, let's go."

We crossed the street and entered a dimly lit, nondescript hallway, where dirty cream paint was peeling off the walls, and got into an elevator whose doors slid open as we approached. Inside, it was made of burnished steel, and had no buttons or lights indicating floors; but it did have several cameras and other sensors, that were evidently peering at us. It looked like it could be isolated – and perhaps filled with gas to paralyze or kill intruders. "High tech creepy," whispered Martine. She rolled her eyes, made a goofy expression, and put her arm under my arm and leaned against me.

We went up to what felt like the third floor. The elevator stopped – and for at least 45 seconds, nothing happened. We were locked in a steel box.

"Double creepy." Martine licked her lips and tightened her grip.

The elevator door slid open, and we were in a modern corridor, with on the left, two offices, lawyers, to judge by the nameplates, and, on the right, an insurance office.

We entered the insurance office. It was a very plain elegant room, with what looked like steel walls. Two bodyguard-looking gentlemen, unsmiling, blond, tanned, and wearing expensive suits, were standing there; and behind a desk, sat an elegant and very fit-looking black woman. Her badge said, "Claire." She smiled, stood up, and said, in French, "Could you give me your bags, please? Thank you. And I shall just scan you both, if you don't mind."

She scanned us, several times, and she felt me down, which was easy for her – and for me rather pleasant – as the latex dress was micro-thin and she quite clearly realized I wasn't wearing anything underneath it. She gave me a cute smile. The two guards watched impassively. Claire let me keep my computer, but the other bags – purse, overnight bag – went into a sort of steel cupboard. She felt Martine down, stopped, gazed at her, and the two smiled at each other while Claire felt around Martine's breasts.

"Mr. Wilson will see you now." Claire gave us a big smile and pushed a series of invisible buttons – a code – and opened a door – visibly an armored door – and we went through into a short corridor – a sort of decontamination security corridor, it seemed to me – and we waited another twenty seconds while we were scanned. And then the next door slid open, and we were in an empty corridor with cameras watching us – I was sure they were there, though I couldn't see them – and a series of unmarked doors which also were probably armored. I imagined that the corridor could be flooded with tear gas or something like it if Martine and I happened to be assassins or jihadist terrorists with bombs strapped to our bellies and AK-47s in our fists.

One of the doors opened, and a handsome tanned man in a very expensive-looking suit – Hugo Boss, I guessed – came out. I recognized him immediately from one of my mathematical seminars at the security conference, and he said, "Very nice to see you again, Doctor Clermont. And I see you have brought us a special guest."

"Yes," I said, "Martine Aubin, please meet Frederick. Frederick, this is my friend, Martine Aubin."

"I am delighted." Frederick bowed and kissed Martine's hand. Martine glanced at me, crossed her eyes slightly, and flapped her eyelashes – the girl didn't take anything seriously, not even old-fashioned male gallantry.

Frederick ushered us into the inner sanctum, and we sat down in what looked like a windowless, sound-proofed boardroom, except the table was smaller than a boardroom table. There were mirrors at one end, which meant, I suppose, that the room could double as an interrogation chamber. There was a large screen on the other wall. Coffee and tea were available on a side table.

Two people appeared: a woman and a man; they were both French: Frederick introduced the man as Maurice and the woman as Sévérine.

Maurice was dressed in blue jeans and a blue shirt open at the collar. He looked trim and athletic. His tan was even; his teeth were bright, and his blue eyes seemed to take in everything at a glance. He had the sharply defined features of an old-fashioned French or Italian movie idol, and he moved in a very deliberate way, as if ready to spring into action at any moment. He's a killer, I thought. Martine blinked at me and grinned.

Sévérine looked like an executive or lawyer – she had a thin face, sharp very regular features, a deep tan, jet-black hair going straight down to her shoulders, and a trim black business jacket, and black tapered trousers, and a white silk T-shirt under her jacket, and no bra that I could see. Her eyes were hazel and very bright – she looked straight at me as if she were going to drill right through my skull.

This was, I began to figure out, a sort of joint French-British-US intelligence coordinating center.

"May I set up my computer?" I pulled it out if its case.

"Of course," said Maurice.

I put the computer on the table, opened it, and turned it on.

"That is a very fetching dress," said Séverine.

I looked down at myself. I once again felt naked. "Yes, well, it was – it is – for Martine. We were going to go out – we had a date – that was our plan, at least."

Martine looked down at the table and then up at me, and it was strange, the wide defenseless look in her eyes – it was love, almost adoration. I suddenly realized, yet again, how much we meant to each other, how much we were in love. We played games, we joked, we pretended to be cynical libertines, we loved to make love to each other, we put on exhibitionist displays for ourselves and for James and Philip, whom we loved fiercely. But in fact, we were also in love with each other, too, desperately head over heels in love.

Frederick swiveled back in his chair. "So, let's get to the point. Doctor Clermont ..."

"Gwendoline, please call me Gwendoline."

"So, Gwendoline, what exactly happened?"

I explained what had happened: James was going to call me when he got to his hotel in Istanbul; he is always very precise; but he didn't call; when I tried his cellphone, it didn't answer; he hadn't gotten to his hotel; there seemed to be no reason for a delay. I tried his cellphone again. Then Martine phoned, and I realized the line was bugged. And then several killers came visiting, and I escaped from my flat. "They took a couple of shots at me and at my neighbors, they followed me into the subway. I was with Zoe Parillaud, the daughter of Antoine Parillaud, the TV personality. The killers followed for a time – but I am sure, as sure as I can be of anything, that we lost them."

"Did they want to kill you?"

"No. I think they wanted to capture me."

"So, we already know what the central problem is. James Hewitt Spencer is missing."

"Yes."

"You do realize, Gwendoline, that this is not an entirely private matter."

"Yes. I assumed you would want to know. I haven't gone to the French police, though I am sure after the shooting the police must be at my flat and Antoine Parillaud's flat. After escaping, with the help of Zoe Parillaud, I met with Martine, and following your instructions, we came here." I did know what he meant when he said this was "not entirely a private matter." James – and I – were "assets": James because he used his contacts, and his economic power, to acquire information and to acquire properties that were of interest to various intelligence services, those of the USA, UK, France, Germany, and so on. He worked to defend the interests of the "West" – and to prevent those properties from falling into hostile or terrorist hands. And me, well, that was because of the math and my hacking and decrypting skills and my ability to decipher networks – criminal networks, terrorist networks, etc. Since I'd already been on several "missions" against people smuggling and organized crime, I was, in a way, already an "asset" and "part of the community."

Hearing "this is not entirely a private matter," Martine had raised an eyebrow, but she didn't ask any questions; I knew she had guessed, though I had never discussed it with her, that I was more than just an academic math geek; that I worked on "practical" things too. She did know a bit – from allusions James and I made – about my role in analyzing smuggling and terrorist networks.

"Well," Frederick looked at his two colleagues, as if for confirmation, "We do know that James got off the plane in Istanbul as planned. And that he took a taxi. Presumably, he was headed to his hotel. And we know he never checked in at the hotel. So, we will for the moment presume that, somewhere between the airport and the hotel, James was kidnapped."

I said, "I put a GPS locator in James' shoes."

"You did?"

"Yes, I did."

"Does he know?"

"Of course, he knows. He thought it was a joke. But I insisted. I've been worried about his safety. He tells me I am a worrywart. But he let me install them." I pushed my computer towards Frederick. "It will take a moment for the link-through to work," I said.

"Good, let's see what you've got."

"Okay, I'll put this on the large screen – if that's okay."

"Absolutely." Frederick handed me a connection cord; I plugged it in.

The screen lit up with the image from my computer, then a map of Istanbul and surroundings. But the GPS trace was not yet there. It was often slow.

Frederick said, "Well, while we are waiting for Gwendoline's GPS, we have these other indications. A taxi – almost certainly the one used by James – was found here." He used a light beam to point to the map. "The taxi was burnt out, just a smoking carcass. The taxi driver has disappeared, and he is presumed dead. The normal routes between the airport and the hotel are several. Usually, which one is preferable depends on the time of day, level of traffic, and so on. For the day in question, that is, today, and the time of day, the taxi probably took this route." He traced it with the light beam.

Séverine leaned forward. "We also are trying to get the GPS indications from James' cell phone and the cell phone of the missing taxi driver. That way, we can try to pinpoint where the taxi deviated from normal."

"And of course, we will have Gwendoline's GPS indicator," said Maurice; his eyes moved between Martine and me; it looked like he was trying to decide which one of us he'd like to gobble up first. Yum! Yum!

"Yes, that too," said Frederick, and he glanced at me as if I were a particularly precocious schoolgirl about to win a prize.

The image on the screen changed. And Séverine used the luminous pointer. "Camera footage from the taxi lineup at the airport, as you can see, shows James ceding his place at the last minute to a woman with two children. She apparently didn't ask him. He seems to have taken the initiative – that indicates his choice of taxi was random, it would have been difficult for the kidnappers to arrange a setup or ambush at the airport. The taxi driver's record is clean."

They sat back. "Miss Aubin, do you wish to stay for all of this?"

"Yes, if you allow me to stay, I will stay."

"Good. So, you are now part of the team, Miss Aubin." Frederick seemed pleased.

Maurice gazed at her. "Once you leave, Miss Aubin, and for the next little while, we will provide you with protection, if you agree. You are known to be close to Gwendoline and James – so you could be leverage. You will also have to sign a confidentiality statement."

"Yes, I agree to protection. I don't want to be a pawn in anybody's game, and I don't want whoever it is to get at Gwendoline and James through me. Yes, I'll sign the statement. And please call me Martine."

"Yes, Martine, of course," Maurice favored her with a long, lazy, eyes-half-closed gaze.

"We will alert New York for your grandmother, too, Gwendoline, if you agree."

"I agree, certainly. I'd like to talk to her myself."

"So, Gwendoline, what do you think happened?"

"I think it is Sergei Platonov," I said. "He is behind the Gremlin North Star network, which has been trying to get the Czech company Bio Futures, and here is the ownership structure of Gremlin North Star." I downloaded the diagrams I had made, plus the footnotes, which provided the proof for each link in the diagrams.

"You've been hacking, again, Gwendoline!" Frederick pretended to be shocked.

"Yes." I looked down at the desk. Martine pushed her leg against mine, like I was a school kid being scolded.

"Well, we approve; generally, we approve, Gwendoline."

"And Sergei has his headquarters, here, just outside Typhilis, the capital of the breakaway New Independent Democratic Republic of Old Transbeckistan. So, if he were to take James anywhere, it would be there."

"Yes, how would they get there?"

"I don't think he would be transported by land," I said, "Platonov uses a small airport outside Istanbul for many of his operations, drug transport, and up-market people smuggling – high-end prostitutes and shady entrepreneurs, and cash. So, if he wanted to take James to a secure location, for lengthy interrogation, that might be the route he'd take. I don't think he'd want to operate in Turkey. The security forces there are not particularly friendly to him."

"Nor are the Russian security forces," Séverine said.

"That's true. For the Russians, Platonov is a dangerous turncoat, selling arms to terrorists, particularly Islamist terrorists."

Finally, my GPS schematics came up on the screen: A series of little dots appeared on the map. They coalesced into a line.

"Damn it, Gwendoline, yes, you were right." Frederick took up the pointer. "Look."

The GPS took James from Istanbul airport to a certain point on a small side street, still on the way to the hotel; then it went sideways, off to a private airport, twenty kilometers from Istanbul. And then the line went straight up, and across the Turkish border, eastwards, to the Republic of Transbeckistan.

Then, at an airport in the Republic of Transbeckistan, just outside Typhilis, the signal stopped, well, it didn't stop, but it remained in the same place. The GPS transmitter was alive. So, either James was in that place, alive or dead. Or he had taken off his shoes or been stripped of his shoes, and was somewhere else.

"Let's zoom in on that place. Have we got satellite images?" Frederick leaned forward.

"Yes, here we go," said Maurice, glancing at Séverine.

A satellite image zoomed up, and then zoomed in on the small airport outside Typhilis. The GPS signal map was then superimposed on the satellite image. The signal was not far from the airport runway, about three kilometers away, on what looked like a side road.

"I'll they probably made him change clothes there, and they possibly scanned him for any signals," said Maurice.

"Just made him strip and change clothes I would bet," I said, "Otherwise, they would have either destroyed the GPS, or they would have used it as a decoy.

"Yes," Séverine glanced at me. "Put it on a delivery truck or had someone drive it off in the opposite or an oblique direction."

"Or maybe they've figured out we would figure out those things – and react accordingly, by just leaving it there, as a teaser." Maurice raised an eyebrow. He was a very handsome man and quite conscious of the fact, and he was ultra-conscious of sitting across the table from film star, sex symbol, Martine Aubin, and of Little Miss Perversity Me in my black latex semi-see-through. He was a very sexually self-conscious man, our dear Maurice, narcissistic, highly intelligent – an interesting type.

"I'm not sure Platonov thinks we are watching him," said Frederick.

"Really?" I raised my eyebrows. I was surprised. I'd been watching him; I presumed everybody else was.

"We've been very laid back on this one." Frederick glanced at me.

"We've allowed him a lot of latitude. We've given him lots of space," said Séverine.

"To hang himself," Maurice smiled. It was a rather self-satisfied Oh-I-am-so-clever smile. Oh, Oh, I thought, maybe he's not as intelligent as he thinks he is.

Frederick leaned forward. "Platonov has been negotiating for nuclear technology, and to be more precise, for miniaturized nuclear weapons with some elements of the Pakistani and North Korean armed forces. The go-between, if any of these deals go forward, is one of the world's biggest arms dealers, one who has managed to avoid the spotlight; but he is one of the most dangerous men alive. We have been waiting to catch him with Platonov. He would be a huge prize. As for Platonov, he wants to get an atomic weapon and sell it to some terrorist organizations in the Middle East. The idea is an attack on Israel, or perhaps on Iran, even in the US or Europe. Moscow is also one of his targets – a personal vendetta against the Russian President."

"Oh." That was something I didn't know.

"So far, Platonov has not been successful. Or at least we think he has not been successful."

"Oh. You *think* ..." This, I thought, was not very encouraging. Martine's leg pressed against mine: Atomic weapons, and uncertainty about whether the guy had acquired them! We were beginning to appreciate the stakes.

"He has also been attempting to acquire biological weapons and chemical weapons."

"That's why he wants Czech Bio Futures," I said.

"Precisely, that's why he entered into conflict with James. James was determined to block the acquisition and to bring the company into the Western orbit. It was an indirect conflict, of course, with Platonov hidden behind layers of proxies and holding companies."

"We noticed you were following this business, Gwendoline," Séverine favored me with her intense razor-like glance, and with the slightest suggestion of a smile.

"And so, we followed you following Platonov. Though you covered your tracks so well, it was almost impossible to follow you – but then we decided we would piggyback on your efforts. You are quite shifty, Gwendoline, and very sly, and we had to change our decoding methods every few days to keep on your trail." Maurice seemed pleased to give me this little lecture.

Frederick smiled. "I was going to call you in, Gwendoline, and give you a rap on the knuckles."

"But you found out lots of things we didn't know, so we followed you, and, yes, we were planning to bring you in for a little conversation." Séverine glanced at me through half-closed eyes.

"Great, thanks!" I was annoyed that somebody had been able to follow me without my knowing it. I frowned.

Séverine read my frown quite accurately. "We needed our best hackers and cryptographers to do it – to follow you, I mean – a whole team, and to do it so you wouldn't know we were doing it."

"Okay, now I feel better."

"So, we can try to extract James – if we know where he is. This will, of course, mean revealing our hand with Platonov, and perhaps terminating him."

"Right ..." Hmm, I thought. It was obvious: if Platonov had

James, and if we rescued James, then it would probably follow – no, almost certainly follow, that Platonov would have to be captured or terminated – killed. We would have to fold up his operations; and that might have all sorts of implications, since Platonov had contacts in terrorist organizations, in governments, with scientists, with –

"In any case, we have allowed Platonov a very long leash; it is a dangerous game we've been playing. If he acquires what he wants, the nukes, and if they are used before we ..." Frederick let his thought trail off.

"Yes, but we are still waiting for him to contact the major target, the arm's dealer. I'm not sure we can get approval for any move at this stage. We'd compromise everything. We want Platonov's source as well as Platonov, and we are hoping to rope in some of Platonov's Islamist customers too." Séverine looked unhappy.

I was beginning to get angry; they were stalling, and they were setting forth the arguments for stalling; I realized that if we didn't move against Sergei, and now, James would die. Their delaying strategies and priorities meant he would die. I'd have to break loose and go after Platonov on my own. That would be damned difficult. Meantime ...

"Gwendoline," Frederick turned and displayed a sad, fatalistic little smile, feigning sympathy, probably another stalling tactic, "show us everything you have on Platonov. Let's see if we missed anything."

"Okay," I said, deadpan, trying not to sound furious. I brought up my little database on Sergei Platonov. I summarized what I knew: Sergei owned shares in the Czech company through a holding company in Moscow, which held shares in a company in Switzerland. There were about five layers of "holding companies" in various permissive and opaque jurisdictions: places where you can do virtually anything and where it's difficult to find out about anything. Platonov also held a controlling interest, probably, in the Moscow-Swiss International Trading bank. The titular holder was a comrade of Sergei's, they'd fought in a couple of wars in the Caucasus, but the guy himself was dead, and apparently, his mother was the titular owner of the shares. The mother was an ex-school teacher, a widow, and a pensioner who lived in Georgia in a tiny house with a tiny garden and none of the appurtenances of wealth or luxury. So, she was just a front, one of many.

"Let's have a look at that."

"Right, here it is." I showed them the screen. "Here is the ownership network." I'd laid it out in a series of diagrams. There were holding companies that held holding companies that owned holding companies. Sergei was in control of a vast number of companies. He knew people in North Korea and Pakistan and Iran, and, as was now clear, he was trying to get his hands on nuclear technology and on a cluster of lightweight, portable, easily hidden atomic devices.

"And here is the logistics network." I brought up another diagram. It showed the infrastructure behind his cash flow. It showed where drugs were refined, along which routes they moved and how they were transported, by train, airplane, human mule, truck, or boat. It traced where the money came from and went. It pinpointed some of Sergei's informants and contacts in important places. It marked his arms deals: Where the arms came from, what they were, where they went, and how they were transported and paid for. "There are a few gaps, here, here, and here, where I don't have information. If you click here, you get a list of unanswered questions – and some suggested lines of research."

"Very, very impressive, Gwendoline," said Frederick.

"Yes, damned good," said Maurice, "Do we have all of that, Sévérine?"

Séverine gave me her stare and then a big smile. "No, we don't, actually – not all of it."

So, I was ahead of the game. I was pleased, like I had aced an exam. I guess I'm still a schoolgirl. But I was now calculating how I could leverage what I knew to help set in motion a rescue operation for James. Under the table, Martine had put her hand on my thigh. She had followed the logic; she knew what I was thinking. I flipped to a new screen on my computer. "I also obtained some – well, hacked – some footage and photographs of Sergei at a meeting in Typhilis. This image is from five days ago. It's a warehouse, just beside the small private airfield outside Typhilis. There was security footage linked to the security company's mainframe, which uploads every half-hour to a server and cloud storage unit in Tbilisi in Georgia. So I was able to get it and grab some material without their noticing. I'm incurably snoopy, I'm afraid. Here they are." The images came up, and then the footage. It showed Sergei, with several other men, on a loading dock. They were loading several boxes – four boxes to be precise – onto a truck.

"Mon Dieu," said Maurice; all the blood drained from his face, revealing creases and lines, as if someone had suddenly sculpted him in dried and cracked clay; it was what he would look like as an old man.

Séverine let out a whistle between her teeth. Her hazel eyes blinked, flashed to me, and then to the screen, and she sat up straight.

I felt Martine's body stiffen. She sensed something extraordinary had happened.

Frederick had raised an eyebrow, and now he took a deep breath and bit his lower lip. "Could you roll that one back, please, Gwendoline?"

"Of course." I did so.

"Freeze it there."

"Okay."

For a rather long minute, nobody said anything. The room was silent, not even traffic noises from outside. Martine's leg moved against mine. Then Maurice said, very slowly, "Yes, that's him. That's Kaleen Baluchi"

"The fat one?" I asked.

"Yes, the fat one," said Séverine in a whisper.

"I wondered who he was," I looked at them. Martine's hand had tightened on my thigh; she stroked me, like calming a nervous feline. I glanced at her and decided I'd better ask. "So, who is Kaleen Baluchi – or what is he?"

Frederick cleared his throat and looked at the other two. They nodded. Martine and I were going to be allowed to know. "Kaleen Baluchi is our main target, the invisible man, what used to be called a merchant of death. He is one of the greatest, if not the world's greatest, dealer in illegal arms. As I said, he is the invisible man. He has always escaped detection. He deals in biological and chemical weapons. In this case, he has come into possession of a number of atomic weapons."

"... four ... we think," said Séverine, "at most five or six."

"... four ... probably four miniaturized nuclear weapons, or, at most, five or six. Maybe seven, possibly more ..."

"Oh," I said. *Nuclear weapons?* Seven or possibly more?

"He was the one negotiating with Sergei." Frederick looked at me and then at Martine. "It looks as if the sale has been completed."

"We had no idea ..." Séverine shifted in her seat.

"... that it had gone this far." Maurice was still pale as a ghost, his face rigid. It was the shock of the moment, I guess, when you realize you are in a very high stakes game, and that you have made a terrible mistake – a mistake that may cost lives – in this case, millions of lives. They had been letting Platonov run around – and right now, he might have the nukes, and the nukes might be on their way to their targets. Those boxes might contain the nukes.

Frederick blinked at Martine and me, but it was as if he was far away, as if his mind was thinking of other things, seeing other things. "These devices have a 6 to 10 kiloton range. That means they could obliterate a quarter to a half of Manhattan, most of central Paris, Tehran, or Washington, or Tel Aviv, or London – or a large hunk of Moscow."

"The Russians have told us they think that these bombs have been enriched with extra radioactive material, making them extra dirty."

"Yes, they could make the site uninhabitable for many, many years, centuries perhaps, and of course, depending on winds and dispersal patterns, cause huge numbers of additional casualties."

"Oh!" Martine and I said in one voice.

Frederick almost smiled. "Sergei is not a Russian patriot. He hates the Russian President, for one thing, an old feud that goes back a bit. And we know he has been negotiating with some anti-Russian terrorist groups, and with anti-Israeli groups, and anti-western groups, particularly with some Jihadist End-of-the-World fanatics. So, everybody, virtually everybody, is at risk – including the Iranians. We now need to stop Sergei and get our hands on those weapons."

"I'd guess that – if he hasn't already sold them – they are in his castle-fortress outside Typhilis," I said, "If you look at the next two diagrams, you can see where the truck went – it headed towards the castle. But I did lose contact with it after it went under the mountain tunnel – right there." I used the pointer to indicate. "I'd hacked or hitchhiked on a satellite, but then it moved beyond the effective horizon."

"The castle is heavily fortified."

"Yes." I took a deep breath. My mind was racing. I'd been particularly interested, given my extra-curricular interests, in Sergei's sex life and his sexual quirks, his obsession with tattoos for one thing. He liked tattooed girls, very heavily tattooed girls. "I have an idea. Sergei owns a night club, the SS Marquis, in Typhilis. It's not far from his castle."

"We know about that. Difficult to get into."

"And his headquarters is impenetrable."

"We'd need somebody inside."

"Sergei is tough, and he knows about security."

So there it was. We now knew the background. But we went over it again. Martine listened intently. Sergei had served in Russian Special Forces; he was a karate black belt; he had been accused of the murder of a prostitute in Paris; he had sadomasochistic tastes; he was usually the sadist, though sometimes he liked to be dominated. His sadism was not symbolic, not sublimated. It wasn't a game. It was real. He had beaten a number of women terribly, and he had killed several of them. And, though not tattooed himself, he had a strong fetish for tattoos and tattooed women. He collected lost, vulnerable waifs. He liked to get lonely women drunk, or drugged, and then to tie them up and have sex with them. Often he would hurt them, beat them enough so that they died.

I took a deep breath and then said what I had in mind: "Point number one, I'm almost certain the bombs – and James too – are in Sergei's headquarters. His chateau – he considers it invulnerable."

"Well, it virtually is, damn it." Séverine brought up an aerial photograph of Sergei's chateau.

Frederick had formed his hands into a tepee and was staring at the image on the screen. "Yes, Sergei's HQ – we need it disarmed before we can get in. It's got anti-aircraft, surface-to-air missiles, and it's got drones policing the perimeter."

"And it is a country where Sergei owns most of the politicians. So, he's protected."

Frederick looked at his hands, finely-manicured deeply tanned, virile looking hands, the hands of a surfer or hunter, and that contrasted with the suit, the starched shirt cuff. "I'm not sure what at this stage we can ..."

"Okay, I'm going in. I'm very good at infiltrating."

"What?"

"I am going to go and open the way for your attack – or whatever you want to do – and I'm going to find James and bring him out," I crossed my arms on my chest and gave them the gift of my dark fiery glance, jet-black eyebrows, and eyes as dark I have been told as hell itself.

"You can't."

"There's no such word as can't. I'm going to do it."

"That's absurd. You're not a professional."

"Not a professional, what?"

"Spy, undercover agent."

"I can be pretty undercover."

"And you well-known, your face on all those magazines."

"We'll disguise me."

"How?"

"Hmm ... Tattoos. And a bit of quick surgery."

"This is absurd."

"This raises severe security problems."

"Well, we'll see about security problems."

"You can't get near to Sergei."

"I'm sure I can get near to Sergei. I know him. I understand what he wants."

"Gwendoline is extraordinarily intuitive," said Martine,

glancing at Frederick. "She perfectly understands every nuance of the perverse mind. And, if I understand you correctly, Sergei is quite perverse – even obsessively perverse."

I shot Martine a glance – then smiled.

She turned serious. "But, Gwen, darling, it's a horrible risk – you are going to get yourself killed, or worse, tortured and maimed."

"It's a risk I'm willing to take – nothing ventured, nothing gained. I am going to stop Sergei, and I am going to get James or die trying."

"Darling, you are crazy."

"I also know where Sergei goes – rain or shine."

Frederick raised an eyebrow and slowly swung his chair towards me. I think he suddenly had an inkling of how my plan might be useful. He nodded. "Yes, we have seen how effectively you had traced his movements. You are very thorough, Gwendoline. Show us, Gwendoline. I don't know if your friend Martine is aware of the extent of your gifts."

"Okay," I said. I swung my computer around and projected everything on the big screen. On the computer, I had graphed my analysis of Sergei Platonov's movements, the patterns day after day, and I had correlated where he went with other elements of his schedule or events that he might be involved in. I'd set up a program that did this automatically. I had hacked into the system his portable telephones used, and those used by some of us bodyguards, and the one used by his driver. I had done all this – with help from James – because I was worried about James and about Platonov's schemes and I was also going to use my analysis an example of tracking and tracing and hacking at an upcoming security conference, though I would have heavily disguised the actual target of my investigation. "Sergei moves between his HQ in the chateau here, and the nightclub he owns in Typhilis.

Almost every night, if he's in the Republic of Transbeckistan, he goes to this club."

"And what is this club?"

"As I mentioned before, it's the SS Marquis Club, a sort of sado-masochistic playpen for Sergei and his men. There are other clients, but they are carefully screened and almost always people who do business with Sergei. The Burmese Triangle gang, the Georgian Black Ops faction of the local government, and two or three Thai drug dealers."

"Yes, we've tried to place an agent inside, or bug the place; but we haven't managed it. So, what is your plan, Gwendoline?"

Maurice leaned back. "If you presented yourself as you are dressed now, you would probably be welcomed with open arms."

Séverine was watching me with half-closed eyes. "Yes, but then they would certainly recognize you, and you would be raped and tortured – not only for the pleasure of it, but to put pressure on James."

"Yes, they would recognize me, and I imagine you are right: they would not be very nice." I glanced down at myself: the single-piece skintight ultra-thin black latex dress seemed to have gotten thinner; it looked like a coating of semi-sheer lacquer.

Maurice shrugged; he half closed his eyes and smiled.

Séverine stuck her elbow into his ribs; he turned to her and winked. Their relationship, I surmised, was more than professional; I wondered if this was against the rules, or not.

Martine licked her lips and rubbed her leg against mine. I thought, here we are, with James in danger, and trying to save him, and atomic bombs about to kill millions, and still, we are flirting – trading simple animal comfort and jokes, showing we understand each other and desire and love each other, and it is totally natural and James, I am sure, would approve.

I put my hand on Martine's thigh, and I sat up straight. "Okay, my plan is to get to Typhilis, to turn up at the club – as a tattooed wastrel, a really desperate case."

"Yes, but still ...?"

"My face will be tattooed, my head shaved, my ears and nose pierced ..."

"Oh, Gwen," Martine opened her eyes wide; her expression was so appalled it was comic.

"And they can touch up my features – a bit of filler here and there so that the shape of my face will not be the same. I'll be tattooed everywhere. I'll be the perfect waif, precisely adapted to Sergei Platonov's tastes."

"Yes, that all sounds very splendid and romantic, Gwendoline." Frederick leaned back. "You mutilate yourself to save your lover. But how can we effect such a transformation, and so quickly."

We all looked at each other. Yes, that was a problem. There was a long silence in the room. Martine caressed my thigh. I turned and looked at her. She blinked at me and nodded. Oh, I thought – of course, she has the solution.

"Okay, tell them," I said.

"I think I know the person," said Martine, "the person who can transform Gwen into ... a Goth-Punk freak. And do it quickly."

"Yes," I glanced at her, thinking even in this desperate situation, she is so utterly cool and utterly beautiful. "I think we are thinking of the same person."

"Yes. Lou-Lou," Martine said. "Lou-Lou, I'm sure, can do everything temporarily, but very realistic. Even a tattooist will be fooled."

"Lou-Lou?"

"Is this person in Paris?"

"Actually," Maurice said, "if you are talking of Lou-Lou Jade, we have used her on occasion – she has very high clearance, strange as it may seem. She is one of the world's greatest tattoo artists

– and she has an encyclopedic knowledge of tattoos and tattoo styles and meanings – very useful in the war with biker gangs, neo-Nazis, the Triads, and the Japanese Yakuza. She can mimic virtually any tattoo style or technique."

"Well, then," I looked around the table.

"Are you sure, Gwen?"

"Yes, I'm sure."

"This is most unorthodox. But ..." Frederick looked unhappy and perplexed; he ran over the alternatives: send in commandos, but that would be almost certainly suicidal, the castle was a fortress with anti-aircraft missiles, and radar, and several dozen heavily armed guards; there was no intelligence on the internal layout of the castle, or at least not since the changes Platonov had made in the last five years, and James was undoubtedly being held in one of the bomb- and missile-proof underground chambers; James would be dead before anyone could reach him. And the bombs could be set off before anybody could get to them, or, possibly, even be smuggled out of the castle. Without somebody inside, any attack would go in blind.

"This might, actually, be the answer to all our problems," said Frederick, and he let his gaze rest on me; and in that moment I saw a certain logic, from their point of view, in my crazy plan: and Frederick knew I understood; by letting Sergei out on a "long leash," they had given him time and space to acquire nuclear weapons; if disaster occurred, and millions died, then it would look like they had dropped the ball – to put it mildly – and the consequences, on all levels, would not be very pleasant; but if I were parachuted in, even if I didn't succeed, it would show they had taken the initiative and ... If I did by miracle somehow succeed, and guided in the troops, and stopped the bombs, it would be, for them, a tremendous coup ...

"Are we ready to do it?" Sévérine was toying with a pencil and staring at it, perhaps to avoid looking at me. "I mean, aren't we risking a fiasco? I mean, Gwendoline is brilliant, I give her that, but …" She turned and looked directly at me. "We may be sending you out there to die, Gwendoline. And if you fail, well, the consequences could be … catastrophic, and not just for you and James."

I stiffened slightly. I didn't care if I died. I would not let them sacrifice James on the altar of realpolitik – I'd rescue him myself if I had to, even if it meant putting the whole world in danger. Besides, by acting now, I might help, in a small way, stave off the apocalypse. Martine put her hand on my hand – she clearly saw where this was headed.

There was silence in the room. I could hear something that sounded like a ventilator; I could hear our breathing; I wondered whether it was still raining outside; I wondered – and I didn't really dare to even think this – I wondered if James was still alive or if he was dead, and if he was dead, how he had died; and if he was alive, what condition was he in and what were they doing to him. I closed my eyes, and tried to control my breathing; Martine tightened her hold on my hand; as always, she was hypersensitive to what I was feeling; we had been so intimate and played so many intimate games and confessed so much to each other that we were like one soul. She picked up the slightest tremor of emotion, the subtlest nuance of thought. I opened my eyes.

Frederick was looking at me. He glanced at Maurice and then at Séverine. They both nodded. Without exchanging a word, they had decided something. But I didn't know what it was.

Maurice nodded toward Frederick.

Frederick cleared his throat. "I think we have to act now. We were hoping to head off the transaction before it took place, but we clearly failed. This is our failure, and it is massive. And for the moment, we have no plan in place, no appropriate assets in place, and so …" He spread his arms.

"The bombs could be sold at any moment," Sévérine said in a whisper. "Maybe they already have been."

"Yes." Maurice nodded.

"So perhaps, then, the moment is now." Sévérine looked straight at me, favoring me with her deep, focused gaze, "right now – acting with what we have on hand."

Frederick leaned back in his chair. "We'd need agreement from the highest level, of course."

"Of course," said Maurice.

"Yes," said Sévérine. "I'll speak to the Minister. And he'll speak to the French President."

"I'll see about the British Prime Minister," said Frederick, "And the Americans – I'll be on the line with them in the next few minutes. The White House will be informed, in general terms probably."

"The Americans have been impatient for us to act."

"So now, we can tell them that we are going to act."

"The Russians will not, I think, be hostile to our doing this," Maurice seemed to be getting enthusiastic about the whole thing. "Perhaps they could even help out. It's their backyard, after all. Perhaps some Russian Special Forces could be added to the mix, that joint US-Russian outfit for example. We give them the information, prepare the ground, and when Gwen has compromised Sergei's fortress, identified the bombs, and secured James, they strike."

"Hmm. That raises the danger of leaks. Platonov has friends in Russia, friends in high places."

"Yes, but so do we."

"Yes, yes, that's true."

"Well, let us say we envisage doing this. The first thing is to prepare Doctor Clermont – sorry, Gwendoline – here for her adventure, and to construct a back story, and to arrange for her entry into Typhilis and into the night club, at the right time, when, hopefully, Sergei will be there – and hopefully he will take the bait. And, hopefully, he will take Gwen back to his castle."

"Do you think he will be in the club when he's interrogating James? I mean, you would think he'd want to be on hand."

I cleared my throat; this was becoming real. A sinking feeling opened in the pit of my stomach. "I think Platonov has professional interrogators, and before, yes, he's gone to the club even when he has a guest – I mean a prisoner. When he was holding Frank Castro and Joseph Cantor, he continued to go to the club. It's a ritual, almost obsessive, I think."

"Well ..."

"And I presume you have satellite surveillance of Transbeckistan and even of the castle – so you will be able to see if a column of cars – and 90 percent I'll bet that's him – sets off for Typhilis at 8:00 pm. Sergei may be a wild man, but when he's in Transbeckistan, he's predictable; he's a man of habit." I thought I was almost there; I almost had them convinced.

Frederick nodded and looked at me with thoughtful eyes. "You may well die, you know, Gwendoline – and worse, much worse."

Maurice sighed and smiled. "You are a mathematician – and your work has been widely applied. If you die, it will be a great loss."

"Thank you," I returned the smile, "That's very kind."

"Hmm, I say we give her the chance." Séverine stared at me through calculating, half-closed eyes.

"Yes." Frederick leaned forward. "So, we bring in this Lou-Lou Jade of yours."

"Now, Mademoiselle Aubin ... Sorry, I meant to say, Martine. Martine, you will have to sign all sorts of confidential documents. Promise not to say a word, all that sort of thing."

"Of course," Martine nodded.

"And we might provide you with a Gwendoline lookalike so it can be reported that you are comforting Gwendoline, or something. We could use a decoy, to establish that Gwendoline is in Paris, to confuse Platonov and his killers."

"Ah, a Gwendoline lookalike – that's interesting." Martine favored me with a fluttery smile.

"The tabloids can be encouraged to speculate, to say you and Gwendoline are on the verge of a breakup or something. Platonov's people will assume that this is a cover story and that, in reality, you, Martine, are comforting Gwendoline because of the disappearance of James and because she was shot at. Some of the media will speculate about the shoot-out on the Left Bank, certainly: Was Antoine Parillaud the target, for instance? That will add to the confusion. And we will make a show of security around your double and make it seem for the media you, Gwendoline, were the target of the violent events – the shoot-out – near rue de Buci, in the Left Bank, some sort of crazy fan, or puritan movement that disapproves of you. So, between the Parillaud hypothesis and the Gwendoline Sex Icon hypothesis, there will be lots of smoke, but with no connection to James. Platonov will know differently, and we and you know differently, but Platonov's people will, hopefully, assume the cover story, or stories are for your security and that you are here in Paris, under our protection. They may even try to get at you again here in Paris – we might provide them with hints as to where you might be. Martine will come in very useful in this. Plotting to capture you in Paris will perhaps keep Platonov's various teams busy and distracted. A very discreet appearance of your double and Martine together – perhaps more than once – I think would be in order. We'll set up a little set of scenarios. Then your double and Martine will go into protection, perhaps with us offering a bit of false bait here and there."

"Show business," Martine said, under her breath.

"Yes, precisely, Mademoiselle Aubin – sorry, Martine – it's show business."

"Yes, I do insist. Please call me Martine."

"Certainly, Martine. Well, as you suggested, much of espionage and counter-espionage is show business. So, we will set up a situation room. And we will prepare our little bit of show business involving Martine and the Gwendoline double as a distraction – hints, bait, and decoys. And we shall prepare Gwendoline for her mission."

CHAPTER 3 – MISTY HOYT

I was naïve; I thought it would be simple – I'd just get myself covered in tattoos; and this would disguise who I was; I would be dropped into Typhilis in the New Democratic Republic of Old Transbeckistan, turn up at the nightclub, and since Sergei had a tattoo fetish I would wiggle my way into his company and his confidence, and find out where James was, and try to free him, or call in the troops who would free him – and possibly me – and we would capture or neutralize the bombs. I had obviously not thought this through. Sergei knew a great deal about tattoos. So, we needed an elaborate backstory – regarding me and the tattoos – and the tattoos had to be very authentic, and each tattoo had to have its own backstory. Lou-Lou Jade would be essential for all of this.

We also had to decide on my biography – who I was, how I came to be tattooed, who did the tattoos, and this meant the type and style of the tattoos had to be analyzed and chosen, and also my appearance and psychology had to be tailored to be bait for Sergei which required, apparently, an elaborate psycho-social-sexual analysis of the guy, though I thought I had a pretty good instinctive handle, as a fellow practitioner of kinky sex, on what made him tick.

Lou-Lou Jade, my nemesis during The Story of O caper, when

she turned me into Owl who could only talk owl, Too-wit-Too-Whoo, was, it turned out and as Maurice had said, truly expert in the culture of tattoos. And it turned out too, that there was a tattoo parlor in Hamburg – a very prestigious tattoo parlor – where they did classical Japanese type tattoos and were masters of design and radical techniques, just the kind of thing that would draw Sergei's attention. So it was decided that I had had my tattoos done mostly there, in Germany; this meant a German backstory, and this meant they had to use some "assets" in Germany to provide the confirmation of the backstory if Sergei's men checked it – so I was provided with a "boyfriend" who had encouraged me – forced me was a better word – to have tattoos. One tattooist in Hamburg was an "asset" of the German intelligence services; he would confirm, in detail, that he had tattooed me. Another tattooist, in London, was also an "asset," and she would attest to the fact that she had tattooed me, if the question were put to her. Lou-Lou knew their styles intimately – very elaborate classical styles and brilliantly colored, using special new glossy inks that, it was claimed, would never fade. So, also, I had to appear as an ex-drug addict; so, some of the signs had to be on my body, not much, just a few marks here and there.

Soon we were in a room with the screens showing the tattooed women who had appealed to Sergei, tattoos done by the studio in Hamburg, and tattoos done by the Japanese master who worked in Hamburg and by the German guys – and our girl in London – who had trained with him. And, also, facial tattoos, radical total facial tattoos, done by an extra mad hatter tattooist in London, who was also, it turned out, an "asset." Lots of the tattooists had "problems" – drugs, alcohol, lack of money, kinks, and minor or major criminal convictions. The problems made them easy to recruit, and they had contacts in criminal and other milieus, which made them valuable as recruits. This was yummy. I was learning new stuff all the time.

So, it was decided: I would have a full-body set of tattoos, my lips and cheeks would be redesigned, I would have extensive piercings, my face would be totally tattooed, my head shaved, and tattooed.

"Oh, my god, Gwendoline, how horrible!" Martine took my face between her hands and kissed me. There were tears in her eyes. "You will no longer be you!"

≈

Within two hours, a room was prepared for my transformation. It had no windows, gleaming fresh white walls, bright overhead lights, and a sort of operating table where I could lie on my tummy or on my back and in the center was a chair which looked something like a dentist's chair, where I could be strapped in – and tortured – if necessary.

"Please hand me your clothes, Gwendoline," said Lou-Lou.

"Okay." I'm a bear for punishment.

She stood and watched, observing me closely, as I undressed.

"The shower is that way." She pointed down a corridor. Then she disappeared through another door, carrying my shoes and my latex dress over her arm.

So I showered, and shampooed, thoroughly – I was saying goodbye to the old me, goodbye to Gwendoline Clermont.

When I came out of the shower, dripping wet and shaking myself like a dog, Martine was waiting in the corridor with a huge white towel. I kissed her, and I toweled myself as we walked back to the operating room.

Lou-Lou was nowhere to be seen, but there was a pretty girl I had not seen before. She looked Vietnamese. "I'm Yo," she said. "I will do the waxing and the piercing. And I will help Lou-Lou with the tattooing. It will be simpler if you stay naked. I want to study your body."

"Of course, Yo," I handed the towel to Martine. Now, I was, as Yo ordered, naked.

"I'm going to stay during the procedure," Martine put her hand on my shoulder. "And Séverine asked me to brief you on Sergei Platonov." She waved a small red folder – TOP SECRET. "It contains the stuff they think you might not know – and that you need to know."

"Good," I said.

Lou-Lou came into the room carrying a sheath of drawings and photographs – the designs for my tattoos. She had been busy putting together the finishing touches for my "look." She began to pin them to a corkboard.

"Lie down on your back, please." Yo smiled and pulled on white latex gloves. They made a snapping sound.

"Okay." I lay down on the operating table, and, as she instructed, I opened my legs.

Yo leaned over and began to prepare for the waxing.

"This has to be total," Lou-Lou was staring down at me. She grinned.

"Sadist," I growled.

Yo went to work.

"Okay. Here goes." Martine sat down on a stool next to me and opened the file.

I closed my eyes and just let myself float with the sensations. As the whole process went on, Martine was reading.

"Sergei Platonov, 32 years old, his mother is Russian, his father was from Chechnya; his father was killed by Russian paratroops when Sergei was eight. The boy witnessed the killing and was wounded. He was brought up in Moscow by his mother and his Russian grandmother. He joined Russian Special Forces, but was let go and imprisoned after several incidents of rape and torture of women and young girls. He escaped prison and ..."

I was almost lulled to sleep as I listened to her, what with the waxing, the warmth, the burning sensations, and a bit of tugging here and there, and then the application of creams, and disinfectant, and a washing of parts, and Yo and Lou-Lou working in such a concentrated way as Martine talked on, and on.

"I'll use a local anesthetic so I can do the piercing quickly," said Yo.

"Okay," I said.

Yo had a row of instruments lined up, I noticed; most of them looked like long needles of varying diameters.

Martine's voice was like a melody. "He escaped prison and ..."

"This is stuff I will know, but I won't know," I said, realizing I'd have to compartmentalize my mind as I developed my separate identity. I would know many things that my new "self" could not possibly know. I opened my eyes and looked at Martine.

"Yes," Martine nodded. "You will know this stuff and a lot of other stuff, but the new you, the tattooed you, the Freak Goth-Punk you, won't know any of this. You will be ignorant of all of this. So you have to keep your different roles clear – and what you know, and what you don't know."

"Right. Go on," I reached out and stroked her thigh. "I'm all ears."

Yo was working on my pubis and labia, and the clitoris hood. I felt an injection, some tugging. "I'm piercing now, cauterizing, and inserting the rings," she said.

"Okay," I breathed it out and bit my lip.

Martine glanced at me and narrowed her eyes. Her lashes were wet. "Okay, I'll continue. Platonov escaped prison, and he went abroad, to Africa, and then to the Caucasus as a sort of free-lance mercenary. There are several accounts of rape, in Kinshasa, in Lagos, and two in South Sudan. He set up his own company, began to trade in arms, and Russian, and US and French troops tried to intercept one of the shipments. Sergei killed two of the Americans, and one Russian officer – who happened to be a young cousin and close childhood friend of the Russian President ..."

"Right, so Sergei's not popular in Moscow. I'd heard hints of that, but I wasn't sure it was true."

As Martine's voice continued, Yo worked on my labia, and she moved up to my belly button – apparently, it was going to have its very own ring.

Lou-Lou was working on my nipples. They felt funny, rubbery, with the local anesthetic.

"Ouch," I said. I felt the piercing go through my right nipple.

"Wimp," said Lou-Lou.

"Cruel monster," I glared at her.

"We'll be shaving your head in a few minutes," Lou-Lou said as she concentrated on the piercing, "except for the puff-like topnotch; tattoos will cover both sides of your head, right up to the little puff-like topnotch, a spiky bit of fluff. It will look cool, like the parody of a poodle."

"Parody of a poodle?" Martine rolled her eyes.

"Exactly, she will be the parody of a poodle." Lou-Lou ran her fingers through my hair – I still had hair.

"I'll do the nose piercing – a steel ring – and the ears – three rings on each side – last, after we've finished the tattoo work," said Yo.

Martine sighed, rolled her eyes, and turned a page. "Sergei worked in human trafficking – lots of women and children, boys and girls – for the sex trade; he recruited his slaves from Eastern Europe, Thailand, and so on. He also exploited and used many of his victims personally. In Africa, he captured a French woman – an aid worker. Here's a picture."

I glanced at it. The woman was pretty, a smiling blonde, blue eyes, sporty, buff look, her arm around the shoulder of an African co-worker.

"He kept her for two years. When they found her body, it had been completely tattooed. Here's a morgue photograph."

"Oh, boy! How did she die?"

Martine frowned, blinked at the page. "Torture, electric shocks, sexual misuse – repeated rape – dehydration. For months she'd been kept in a cage, never cleaned, never let out. Then she was strangled. You can see the marks there."

"Yes. I see them." The body was totally tattooed; the face was so battered it was hardly recognizable as a face, except for the eyes, which were open.

Martine held up a glossy color photograph. "Here's another victim. She was already tattooed when he met her. Are you sure you want to look at these pictures?"

"I'm sure," I said, "I have to."

Martine lifted more photographs up – a cute black girl with elaborate arm and back tattoos. Then the same girl with her throat cut and her nose cut off. Her eyes were open.

And then another one, covered in bruises, and with broken and bloodied teeth; and another one with strangulation marks around her neck; and then another one with an elaborate and beautiful full-color body tattoo and a bullet hole in the middle of her forehead; and then another one ...

Martine's mouth was set. "I would like to send Sergei Platonov to the deepest hell and let him burn in sulfur and lava for all eternity. Death is too good for this guy." She shivered. Goosebumps rose on her arm. Her perfumed breath was warm against my cheek. "Okay, here's the last one," she said. She held out another photograph: the body was so battered, and the face such a mishmash of twisted bloodied slashed features, like a sketch by

Picasso at his angriest, that it was difficult to see who or what she might have been.

Yo tapped me on the arm. "Would you please get up and sit in the dentist's chair, Gwendoline? I'm going to shave your head now, and Lou-Lou will be giving you a few small facial injections."

"Hmm," I muttered.

Without looking at myself, in fact, closing my eyes, I got up and sat in the chair. Moving, I felt a dull numbness and vague pain between my legs and at my nipples, and I also felt the metal – the rings, labia rings, a clitoris hood ring, a belly button ring, and nipple rings. Oh, boy! I kept my eyes closed tight as Yo went to work – clipping, and soaping and shaving my head, eliminating my eyebrows. She'd put a sheet over my body, to keep the hair off.

I opened my eyes.

Martine glanced at me, and then she put down the stack of photographs and went back to reading – out loud – the report on Sergei, on the way he killed and tortured his victims, and on his people smuggling and arms trading networks. The list of his murders, mutilations, and assassinations was long. And he also helped a variety of different totally evil terrorist organizations with their logistics and arms supplies.

When Yo finished shaving my head and eyebrows, Lou-Lou crouched close and gave me a few injections to change the shape of my lips and cheeks.

"Poor Gwen," Martine put her hand on my arm.

Yo applied thick gooey dye to my poodle-like topnotch and, wearing a new set of latex gloves, she massaged it thoroughly. "We'll let this set. It will take about half an hour."

"Okay," you can stand up now and have a look," said Lou-Lou.

"Right. Okay!" I stood up, took a deep breath, shut my eyes, and turned towards the full-length mirror. I opened my eyes and looked at myself.

"Holy Mackerel!"

"Holy Mackerel? I never heard you use that before," Martine was standing right beside me.

I cleared my throat. Gwendoline, the pedant, came up from her depths and took over. "It's a bit old-fashioned. It's probably an 18th – 19th-century euphemism cover-up for 'Holy Mary'," I said.

"I adore it when you give lessons," said Martine.

I studied the image in the mirror: standing beside Martine – whose blond, tanned, fully dressed beauty sparkled – I looked like a large featureless slug, no pubic hair, no eyebrows, totally hairless, except for a dyed, flaming, purple-and-scarlet puffball perched the middle of my skull. Two rather large steel rings decorated my nipples, and one shone in my belly button, and, when I spread my legs, I saw the gleam of the clitoris hood ring, and of six labial rings, three on each side. "Holy Mackerel!"

"Now, Gwendoline, we begin the tattooing," said Lou-Lou. "You will become a total work of art, a symphony of color and design, ein Gesamtkunstwerk. Yo will assist me."

"Whew!" I muttered.

"Gwendoline, if you don't mind, please lie down on your delicious little tummy." Lou-Lou put her hand on my shoulder and grinned; she was eager to begin. I was to be putty in her hands.

"Yes, ma'am." I climbed onto the operating table and lay on my stomach on a layer of soft white towels. I felt the nipple rings, the bellybutton ring, all the other rings, clearly imprinting themselves on my consciousness; and more rings were to come – nose and ears!

"Comfortable?"

"Yes, ma'am."

"Good." Lou-Lou picked up brushes and needles and specialized pens and ink pots and set to working tattooing my back while Yo began to work on my left buttock. I was being attacked from all sides.

The door hissed open, and Sévérine looked in. Lying on my belly naked and hairless, I blinked at her; Sévérine had not yet seen the new me, but she didn't seem to notice or care. She merely blinked at the bright lights. "Martine, may I borrow you for a few moments?"

"Of course," Martine squeezed my hand, mouthed a kiss, and followed Sévérine out the door. The door hissed shut; it sounded as if we were in an air-tight chamber.

I lay there, thinking. Lou-Lou and Yo worked their magic. I felt a stinging tickling sensation, a pitter-patter of fine-webbed marks, intricate design and ink work, spreading over my skin, like an army of little ants marching over my back and backside.

After what seemed a very long time, Martine came back, holding a sheath of notes. She had been assigned the task of making sure I had my back story right. Since the whole project had to be quick, everything was being improvised, and everybody was being put to work. "Sévérine will be bringing the full briefing book in a few minutes," she said.

"Lou-Lou, should I make this brighter?" Yo had her finger on a point just above my bum.

"Yes, make it the brightest scarlet, the brightest possible," said Lou-Lou, "with a deeper stippled outline mark, there, to the left, shading off a bit as you go upwards."

The door hissed open. Sévérine came in, carrying a very thick binder, with a red cover, and a title, "OPERATION WAIF: TOP SE-CRET: Briefing Notes."

She crouched down next to the operating table and showed it to me. "This is the complete back story. We've had to whip this together. I have to prepare some of the other aspects of the operation, so I can't stay with you now." She stood up. "Martine, will you rehearse the rest of the back story with Gwendoline? Make sure she knows every aspect, every detail. If any questions come up, if anything comes to mind, anything at all – Lou-Lou, Yo, Martine, and Gwendoline – ask. We don't want to overlook anything."

"Of course," said Martine as she took the binder. Lou-Lou meanwhile was working on my shoulder. And Yo had moved on to my right buttock. I felt the dance of little pricks moving along my skin and a warm feeling as if I were having a particularly elaborate intimate massage. I wondered if the designs would ever wear off.

Séverine stood at the door, one hand on the door handle, "By the way, Gwen, this is new you. You are a kid from backwoods mountainous Kentucky, a white trash runaway, abused, promiscuous, angry, desperate, and headstrong. Your new name is Misty – Misty Hoyt."

"Misty? Misty Hoyt? That's ridiculous." I muttered.

"Well, the Committee has decided."

"Humph. The Committee has decided!" Here I was – lying on a table, like a slab of meat, or like an artist's canvas, under the bright lights, my body being redesigned and my life being re-created, all without any input from me. I snorted. "Misty Hoyt is a dead giveaway."

"As I said, Misty," Séverine gave me a thin smile, "the Committee has decided."

"Humph." I made a face.

"Goodbye, Misty," said Séverine. The door hissed shut behind her.

Lou-Lou was working down my arm, a buzzing sound and little prick points dancing merrily along.

"Misty Hoyt," I muttered, "Misty Hoyt! Ridiculous!"

"I think it's cute," said Martine, "a whole new you."

"You are cruel, my impeccably beautiful darling blonde." I closed my eyes.

"Hold still." Lou-Lou was now preparing to ink the back of my neck.

"Okay." I was drowsy; maybe it was something to do with the bright lights. I blinked and opened my eyes. I'd better stay awake.

Martine sat down on a little stool next to the operating table. Her face was only about a foot from mine. Somehow, even after all our adventures, she smelt like lemons and sunshine.

Martine cleared her throat. "Okay, Misty, let's begin." She put her hand on my arm. "This part is about the tattoos in Hamburg, and how and where you got them. Werner, the Hamburg tattooist, looks like this. Here's a photograph." She stuck the photo in front of my nose.

"So that's Werner," I said.

"Yes," Martine smiled. "That's Werner – Werner Beck. Werner did your body, almost everything on your body. Werner lived in Japan and in Thailand in the late 90s. He studied with the masters, Horiyoshi III, and others. He spent some time doing drugs in Goa in India. He talks about making love to a girl on a beach. He told you the story a dozen times. She was French Polynesian. She went by the name of Alice. He never knew her last name. 'Like a girl out of Gauguin,' is what Werner used to say. They lived together for three months. Then one day she up and disappeared. After she left, Werner began, and he told you this many times, to notice the smooth-skinned Indian boys, particularly when they dove from a dock, into the sea, into the rolling surf towards sunset, just wearing shorts, their bodies gleaming in the setting sun. They looked so beautiful, so sensual. Werner wondered if he was turning into a pedophile. While in India, he worried about this; and, while he worked on your tattoos, he confided in you. Werner likes to smoke cigarettes – old-fashioned French Gauloises – but he goes outside to do it, stands on the sidewalk, in front of the tattoo studio, and cups his hands, bends over, walks up and down. His studio is in a little side street in Hamburg, Benner Strasse, just off the Reeperbahn, in the St Pauli quarter. Here are some photographs." Martine held the photographs under my nose. I looked at them. She turned a page. "After Alice disappeared, Werner began to watch the boys, the young men, and he realized that he wasn't a pedophile; he was gay. This was a huge liberation."

"That tickles," I said, clearing my throat.

"Sorry," said Lou-Lou. "I'm putting in some tiny little bumps along the design edges. We have to give the tattoos a little edge here. It's like the needle leaving very small bumps along the outlines, where the needle goes deepest, to get the deepest clearest delineation. We have to make this totally realistic."

"Okay, I see – little bumps."

"And we'll put in nuances of fading where the skin bends, at the elbows, on the inner side of the arms, say, here, and here and here." Lou-Lou touched my elbows and my underarms, to illustrate. "But these are quite new tattoos, the best of the new inks, so they will be very bright."

Martine showed me more photographs. "This is Werner's tattoo parlor in Hamburg. This is the entrance. Try to memorize the details." She read me an exhaustive description of the tattoo parlor and its instruments and of what you saw when you looked out the window.

"It's like acting, Gwen, plunge yourself into the role."

"Right," I said.

"Imagine yourself – you *are* Misty Hoyt – going into the tattoo parlor – with your guy."

"Right. I'm Misty Hoyt." I closed my eyes, and I forced myself to live the situation, really live it. I am Misty Hoyt. I am Misty Hoyt! Going down a Hamburg street, sleazy tattoo parlors, strip joints, cheap eateries, the sounds of Hamburg ... "Like method acting," I said, keeping my eyes squeezed shut, concentrating on being that drifting, damaged, headstrong Appalachian wastrel, Misty Hoyt, plunging into her body, her thoughts, her hot pants or short skirt, her naïve stupid illusions and hopes, her fears, her innocence, her love for her guy, her willingness, maybe even her eagerness, to be inked, to be deformed, to be destroyed, and all for love, for the desperate, hopeless need for love.

"Exactly, darling," Martine's voice came out of the darkness, "Exactly like method acting."

"Shift your neck, a little to the right, will you, Gwendoline? Thanks," said Lou-Lou.

"Call her Misty," said Martine.

"Right, Misty," Lou-Lou said; there was a smile in her voice.

"And keep your arm still, Misty," said Yo. She was working just below my shoulder.

I blinked, leaving Hamburg behind. The overhead lights burned down hot and steady; it was like being half asleep and sprawled tummy down under a tropical sun on a sumptuous beach. I wanted to yawn, but I didn't. Both Yo and Lou-Lou were hard at work. It seemed like there was not an inch of skin that was going to be left clear, not underarms, not hands, not feet, not nothing. I closed my eyes. Fuck! I really am going to be a freak.

"Ready for more?" Martine turned a page. "Misty?"

"Yes, Misty is ready." I opened my eyes, closed them again. Just let Martine's voice carry you along, I told myself.

"Your boyfriend was Heinrich Streiffer. He's now in Dresden. He joined a biker gang in Leipzig. Here's a photograph. Hmm, he looks a bit like a German James Dean."

I opened my eyes. "Hmm, yes, he does, handsome guy! How did I get so lucky?" I stared at the photograph while Martine held it in front of me. Lou-Lou was again working on my bum with Yo.

They were filling in some details, I guess – was my whole backside going to be tattooed? Hmm ...

"Heinrich's father was a Lutheran pastor, and his mother worked in an insurance firm. Their names are Angelika and Rupert Streiffer."

Lou-Lou cut in, "Misty, you can sit up now – and turn over and lie on your back."

"Okay."

"Do you want to have a look?"

I thought for a moment. "No, I don't. I don't want to see a thing until you've finished the whole job."

"Everything?"

"Yes, the whole job," I said, "I don't want to see a thing until you've done my face and everything." I kept my eyes shut, sat up, and then lay down on my back. I opened my eyes, stared upwards at the bright lights, and then turned my head and looked at Martine. I reached out and touched her lips. She smiled. Her eyes were wet.

While Lou-Lou and Yo worked, with Yo doing my legs, and Lou-Lou concentrating on my pubis and belly, Martine continued to tell me of my life as Misty Hoyt. In Hamburg Heinrich got me to do some stripping and pole dancing; which I did, and it brought in some money; but Heinrich was trading drugs and really didn't need money, so he decided I should be tattooed, and that was when Heinrich introduced me to Werner Beck, and I got my body tattoos and piercings. The piercings were done in the same studio and by Werner's colleague, Annette Weiss.

"Is that all clear?"

"Yes, it's clear," I said.

Martine began again. "You went to London with Heinrich. Your body was already tattooed and pierced. But your face and head had not been touched. Heinrich was arranging for some big drug shipments through Hamburg and Rotterdam to London. He didn't tell you much, but you guessed. You both stayed with a buddy of his in Islington, a narrow little house on a small lane. Here's the photograph. Here's the interior. And here's the address. You had a fight. Heinrich said you were flirting with his buddy and whose house it was; his name is Max Ebersbach, he's another biker, who plays, strangely, the ukulele. He's a sentimental guy with curly red hair and buck teeth. You denied the flirtation. You'd smiled at him, and you'd smiled because you thought he was funny, and funny looking; that was all. Heinrich didn't accept your excuses or ex-planations or your smiles. Heinrich beat you up, slapping you hard, back and forth, back and forth; then he pushed you down on the bed, you leaped up, fought, and ran; he chased you around the house, had sex with you on the tatty old Persian rug in the little front room of the house, then you went back up to the bedroom, and he made love – very rough love – to you again, the sun stream-ing in, yellow paint on the walls, a picture of Karl Marx above a chipped, cream-colored, stand-alone wooden dresser – here's a pic-ture of the room – and it was so violent and insistent that it hurt, but you liked it too. Then Heinrich was sitting naked on the edge of the bed, you lying there, naked, aching. He said he loved you, and he adored you. And you said you loved him and adored him and that you would do anything for him."

"Oh, oh," I said, "Do anything sounds like trouble."

"Yes, oh, oh," Martine paused, and cleared her throat. "So he said he wanted you to prove it – that you loved him so much, you would do anything for him. You said you would. So he took you to a tattoo parlor in Soho, one of the famous ones, the Vamp Stu-dio, and he told you that you were going to have a new look, and it would be a surprise. You didn't want to do it, but you didn't want to disappoint him either. And you didn't want to go back on your word. You are a stubborn girl, right? And so ..."

Time went by. Yo completed my legs, thighs, and hips, and now both she and Lou-Lou were working on my breasts and collar-bone and arms.

As Martine told the story, I could see it. I applied the "method acting" approach. I lived it as if it were real. It was like a waking dream, but maybe even more intense than a dream. Heinrich took me to the Vamp tattoo parlor in London's Soho.

Yes!

He took me to the tattoo parlor.

"Please stretch your arm out, Misty," said Yo, "Yes, that's right – just like that!"

Heinrich took me to the tattoo parlor.

And he said, "Every time you look in the mirror, you will think of your love for me."

"Oh."

"Yes. Your face, your beautiful face, will be mine." He took my face in his hands. His hands were strong and rough and weath-ered – hard hands with a delicate touch. When he wanted to be delicate, Heinrich could be delicate, oh, so delicate. He held my face in a vice, almost crushing my jaw. "I love your face. Your face will be forever mine. You will have your face tattooed for me." He was speaking English, but his German accent had become stronger. His voice was throaty. He was excited, excited erotic-ally, excited by the cruelty of it, the perversity. I realized I was in a trap; it was too late to back out. I was sweating fear. I saw a strange hard sparkle in his eyes. He ran his fingers over my face, every detail, the tip of my nose – which he kissed – and my lips, and my cheeks, and forehead, and earlobes.

"Yes. Yes," I said, "I love you." I said, knowing that by those words I had doomed myself. I didn't know exactly how, but I knew that I had doomed myself. He let my face go, and he kissed me, and it was a wild, violent deep kiss, and his hand slipped down my shorts, and he fingered my clitoris, and forced my labia open, with the labia rings pressing against them and against his fingers, and I was already wet and breathless, and he turned to the tattoo-ist, a young woman, Freya Hussain, and he said, "Yes. Now, do it." And I sat in the chair, and Freya worked on my face and skull for hours and hours, including shaving my skull and leaving only a topnotch, which she dyed bright purple-scarlet. People came and went, customers stopped to admire, and some said things like, "Shit" and "Fuck" and "Awesome," and so on. The session lasted late into the night and well past midnight.

Heinrich was there all the time, commenting on the work, "Yes, yes, that is right – heavier there. Yes, and fill in that bit, please. Yes, scarlet there, the brightest strongest possible. Yes, the ring should be the largest, Yes, that's right!" I didn't look at myself at all. I just sat there rigid, avoiding mirrors. At one point I had to close my eyes when my eyelids were being tattooed. Then my nose was pierced, and my ears, and my skull was tattooed, and then, finally, it was already deep into the night, I was allowed to look. My face was gone – an intricate monstrous mask had taken its place. And I knew I was a freak. I would be a freak until the day I died. Heinrich said it was a masterpiece and I was his and we went back to the house in Islington, and we made love on the floor and on the divan and in the bed, and he took me every way he could, and he kissed me and he caressed every part of me, and made me kneel before him and worship and service him, and, then, finally, he said, now I would never forget him, and we left the next morning for Rotterdam and we again made love in a small hotel. And in each instant outside, in each instant in the streets, I saw how, now, in the streets and in the hotels and in bars – everybody saw me as a freak. I had been changed, utterly changed. There was no going back. Four days later, Hein-rich fucked me in the morning, very early, and he was very rough about it, and then he tossed me a roll of banknotes and, standing in the doorway, he laughed – now I was eternally his; he had no more need of me. "Goodbye, sucker, goodbye freak," he said. And he left.

I screamed at him. I ran out into the corridor naked, and I chased him downstairs, and I screamed in the lobby. The hotel manager came and calmed me down. "I will have to call the police if you make more of a fuss," he said, "but the room is paid to the end of the week, so you can stay here if you want." And he added, giving me a look, "I know people who would pay a lot for somebody like you, a freak like you." "Fuck that!" I said. "Well, think about it," he said. "What can you do now? I mean, look at yourself. Nobody's going to hire you, not even to clean toilets!" "Fuck you!" I shouted. I stayed in the hotel for the rest of the week, and I met an oilman who specialized in sexual oddities, and told me about his adventures with bearded ladies and such like. I didn't believe him, but at least he wanted me – or seemed to. We made love and got drunk for a few days. He was heading to the New Independent Democratic Republic of Old Transbeckistan and said, "Come on, babe, you are uniquely horrible. You need to see a uniquely horrible place!" So that's how I ended up in Transbeckistan.

Martine and I went through many of the aspects of my life. She cross-examined me. I kept my eyes closed mostly, applying "method acting," approach, visualizing, imagining, worming my way into the skin and life of tattooed pierced Goth-Punk freak Misty Hoyt, drifter, and masochist, and more and more, as the needles and brushes beat their tattoo on my belly, legs, and breasts, I truly became Misty Hoyt.

"Okay, we're ready to do your head and face now," said Lou-Lou. "First, we do a few extra injections. They will take effect immediately."

"I don't want to look at anything until you're finished," I said, still lying there, staring at the bright ceiling lights. Tears flooded my eyes. Misty had had such a fucking rotten life! It was tragic, really. Martine laid her hand on my shoulder, "There, there, Misty," she said, "Don't worry, Misty." I blinked at her, all blurry, a golden blonde, a goddess from my distant, fading past.

Yo disappeared and came back with a black dressing gown so I wouldn't see the tattoos on my body. I put the dressing gown on and pulled up the collar and knotted the belt. It went down beyond my ankles. I couldn't even see my feet. I refused to look in a mirror.

We had a snack of sandwiches and coffee – I touched my head and forehead and found it strange to have no hair, just utterly smooth skin, except for the impertinent puffball on top of my head.

"Well," said Lou-Lou, "Let us now finish this masterpiece."

"Yes," said Yo.

"I really think it is our best work yet."

"We should do a video – and keep a photographic record, of course."

"Of course, we shall document this work of art," said Lou-Lou, "Okay, let us begin."

I closed my eyes, slipped out of the dressing gown, and sat back in the dentist-like chair, and I kept my eyes closed. Martine squeezed my hand. Through my eyelids, I felt the warmth of the bright lights, and I could see a blotchy pattern of red and black drifting over my retina. There was pressure on my eyelids as Lou-Lou applied the ink, deeper and deeper, and harder and harder. "Sorry," she said, "this may be uncomfortable."

"Hmm," I mumbled. I was not allowed to move my jaw.

"So, now we complete the facial design; this will be very heavy and charcoal black, with some strong scarlet and turquoise serrated arrows and sweeping lines, it will be a masterpiece if I do say so myself."

And so they worked and worked, and I felt my whole face being tattooed, every single millimeter of it, including my skull and ears and eyelids and lips.

Then Yo pierced my nose and my ears and inserted the rings. She stood back, and said, "Well, I think that is perfect."

Lou-Lou reached out and ran her fingers over my tattooed collarbone. "We will add the leather and steel collar with its nice ring, too, just to complete Misty's new look."

And she added the collar and clicked it into place. I swallowed.

"Voila," said Lou-Lou, "You, Misty Hoyt, are now a total work of art, a bright symphony of color."

I stood up. I let the sheet fall away and handed it to Martine. Her eyes were glossy. She smiled, but I could see it took all her strength to smile.

"Okay," I said. "Let's look at the bare naked truth."

≈

I turned towards the full-length, three-sided mirror.

Then and there, in that instant, full length and naked, and from three sides, I saw what I had become. I was Misty Hoyt, sideshow freak.

"Holy Moly!" I swallowed. Saliva rose, a sickening wave. I wanted to vomit. I wanted to pee.

"Holy Moly?" echoed Martine, "Don't tell me. I'm not going to ask."

"Yes, don't." I stared at Martine, standing beside me in the mirror, my golden beauty, utterly perfect – flawless, lightly tanned skin, blond hair, blue eyes, a voluptuous trim body, a body to die for. Tears ran down her cheeks.

I held my breath. My heart stopped. My throat was dry. I licked my lips. I put my hand – my glove-like, matte black, bright scarlet, patterned tattooed hand, at the end of my bright multicolored arm – to my throat, to my thick leather collar, touching the large steel ring. The creature in the mirror put its hand to its throat, and touched the collar's steel ring, but it couldn't be me – not really me.

Misty Hoyt was tattooed, fully tattooed, everywhere tattooed, arms, torso, legs, face, and skull, with dense bold swirling utterly luminous designs – flames, serpents, dragons, flowers. The breasts were circled with tattoos, and scarlet flames around the edges, licking fiercely towards and touching the nipples. The nipples and areolae, already in normal times prominent, had been tattooed glowing scarlet. A large metal nipple ring hung from each nipple. I blinked. The unrecognizable eyes in the mirror blinked. Yes, it was me, really me – Misty Hoyt.

My ears stood out from my naked tattooed skull. Both ears glowed, red and black, brightly tattooed, with large black metal earrings – three on each side – dangling, sparkling. They clanked every time I moved, even the slightest bit.

I licked my coal-black lips; my tongue, pink and normal, seemed like an alien being, a serpent, a weird unground sloth, peeking out. My face and skull were boldly restructured, my lips much fuller, tattooed black and upturned at the corners like in a fixed and grotesque smile; my boyish smile had been turned into a lippy carnivorous pout, a heavy, sensuous scowl, a sort of parody of an angry smile. My cheekbones were more prominent, narrowing my eyes, making them crafty, angry; my face and skull were entirely tattooed, in brilliant blood-scarlet and the deepest matt jet-black; my nose and lips were black, with ribbed scarlet lines, and scarlet flames on the wings of my nostrils, and my eyes – eyelids and all – were entirely surrounded by flames of black and scarlet. A heavy ring hung from my nose, touching my tattooed lips. Caught and imprisoned in the cage of a black-and-scarlet mask, my eyes seemed like wild shifty things, darting desperately this way and that.

I reached up and touched my skull – utterly smooth. My head was shaved on both sides and at the back, and tattooed in a bold black-and-red pattern, and with only the bright dyed tuft or puff, standing straight up, boldly, in the middle. Yes, like a poodle, I thought, like a fucking poodle.

My lower belly and sex were covered in a diabolic flame-like tattoo that flared up, yellow and scarlet and black and green, to my belly button which, of course, had its own design, like a target, and its own glittering steel ring, as did the hood of my clitoris. Yo had really gone to town. I hadn't fully realized. I glanced at her. She grinned and shrugged.

My labia had six rings, three on each side. I felt a burning sensation, just looking at them. Heavy thick black lines separated the different designs, and other than my breasts, not an inch of skin had been left uncovered.

"Here," Martine said, gently. She swung out one of the full-length side mirrors so I could see my back.

I turned sideways. My back was a riot of color and design, with hardly an empty spot, and the tattoos spiraled up the back of my neck to my head and the bright scarlet and turquoise puffball topknot. A brilliant dragon design in scarlet and turquoise went down from the nape of my neck to my left buttock, which it covered. My buttocks shone liked they'd been waxed or covered in a sheen of oil. On the other side of my back, an emerald green tropical jungle with parrots and peacocks and cobras flared upwards, from my thigh to my neck. My right leg was entwined by a snake.

"Well, this is the new me, I guess." I saw the grotesque mask in the mirror smile, the web of black-and-scarlet, skull-like with the black nose and lips, bared its teeth what looked like a smile. I felt my smiling upper lip press against the nose ring. I touched my belly. It was aflame with tattoos. The labia rings sparkled between my legs.

Lou-Lou had a camera out. She was shooting me in extreme close-up, details, details everywhere, and then a series of full body shots, me alone, naked, against the white background of the walls.

"May I touch her?" Martine reached out her hand.

"Yes, go ahead." Lou-Lou stood back, looking very proud, with her arms crossed, contemplating her creation.

Martine turned me around and put her hands on my shoulders, which seemed suddenly slender, not able to bear all this weight. "Oh, Misty," she whispered. There were tears in her eyes. She wiped them. She kissed me. I felt her mouth and lips brush and press the steel nose ring against my flesh.

Martine bit her lip, looked down, then looked up, put her hand to my breast, touched the erect nipple, and flicked the nipple with her finger. "You are a work of art, darling Misty. When you're back, I'll never let you go! I will lead you everywhere on a leash." She tugged at the thick ring in my collar. "I shall lead you everywhere on a chain, and we will kiss and kiss and never stop. I must confess, part of me," she whispered, "wants to keep you like this forever."

"Grrhh," I growled, "Grrhh."

"Oh, Misty Hoyt, oh, beautiful Misty Hoyt!" Martine kissed me.

The door opened. Sévérine entered. "It is time, Misty. We have a final briefing, some equipment you will need, and then you are on your way. Your flight will be taking off in two hours."

CHAPTER 4 – SERGEI PLATONOV

"Misty Hoyt," Sergei Platonov grinned up at me, and repeated, "Misty Hoyt!"

There I was, in middle of the SS Marquis Club, naked except for the black stilettoes, perched on the edge of the marble table, facing Sergei Platonov, killer and sadist and arms dealer. Sergei was slouched down low on the leather couch, eyeing me, up and down. I tried to steady myself. I saw double. I was stoned and drunk and naked in the midst of the crowd of gangsters, hangers-on, call-girls, slaves, and hitmen, and me naked except for the purple-scarlet pompom that festooned the crown of my head, and the stilettoes, and a full array of brilliant tattoos, and a collection of rings, dangling, piercing my flesh, and me gleaming with sweat. Right now, an oily trickle of sweat was snaking lazily down my back, and a silver drop of sweat, which seemed icy and gigantic, was gathering at the tip of my left nipple.

A few feet away, patting his bulging, sweat-covered belly and grinning at me through fluttery half-closed eyes was Kaleem Baluchi, the man who had apparently sold the atomic bombs to Platonov; Baluchi, so Frederick had told me, was Mr. Death himself, the world's foremost purveyor of nuclear and chemical and biological weaponry. Catching my eye, Baluchi grinned, and gave me a thumbs-up. When I blinked and licked my lips, he patted his belly again, and then he clasped his crotch and began slowly to massage it, with a huge fist and huge fingers.

"Misty Hoyt!" Sergei said again, narrowing his eyes, staring straight at me. I sniffed and stared back at him.

"What's in a name, eh, what's in a name?" Sergei declaimed, looking around. "Misty Hoyt. It's a nice name, Sonia, very apt, don't you think?"

"It's a delicious name," Sonia said. Her arm was around Sergei's shoulders. She was watching me closely.

"Sonia is a very wise girl, aren't you, Sonia?"

"I am if you say I am, Sergei." She smiled and snuggled closer to him.

"You see, Misty, I can be rather demanding, can't I, Sonia?"

"Yes, Sergei. You do make your admirers pass little tests now and again."

Sergei seemed pleased. He grinned. "I asked Sonia ... well, do you remember that time? The Italian girl ... Why don't you tell Misty the story, Sonia?"

Sonia frowned and then stared straight at me. "Well, you see, Misty, Sergei doubted my loyalty, and –"

"Oh, Sonia, I wouldn't be that harsh. I just wanted to make sure you were as perfect as you seemed to be, and as you have proved, again and again, to be." He kissed Sonia on the lips. Then, he pulled away, turned to me, and said, "Go on."

Sonia looked straight at me, eyes narrowed, serious. "There was a young woman whose loyalty Sergei doubted. She was Italian, from Venice. She had a very nice accent. We picked her up in a bar in Berlin. I liked her very much." Sonia hesitated.

"You and she made love," Sergei said, "I seem to remember."

"Yes, we did, and you watched, several times you watched, and you made love to her too."

"Oh, yes, that part I had forgotten. It must be old age." Sergei grinned at Sonia, and then he turned his grin – like a searchlight – on me. His teeth and his ice-blue eyes shone, like floodlights.

"She was so sweet, a wonderful lover," Sonia's eyes took on a faraway look. "I liked her very much. She knew a great deal about Venice and sailing in the Adriatic and about Cesare Pavese, the Italian writer from Piedmont, whom I adore. I can still remember the taste of her lips. But she was, it turned out, a spy."

"Yes, very unfortunate." Sergei picked up his glass, toyed with it, and stared straight at me.

"So?" I said, perched on the marble table, which seemed to be spinning, or maybe the room was spinning, "How does the story end?" I wanted to hiccup, but I swallowed it down.

Sonia's fingers were in Sergei's hair, caressing, playfully, but as she spoke, she stared straight at me. "It was a beautiful day. I took the girl out into the garden of the chateau, where we were living at the time; we sat down and had a drink. I suggested she would like a massage. I got her to take off her shirt and her bra, and then her skirt and her panties. She lay down naked on her stomach on a towel on a bench. I stood up, went around behind her, and massaged her shoulders. I took my time; it was very pleasurable; she purred, pretending to be a cat. I said I was getting some extra spicy cream from my purse. 'It will be even more sensual that way,' I said. I pulled out my pistol and shot her in the back of the neck. I don't think she had any idea what was happening. It was instantaneous. Her last moments were of pure sensuous pleasure."

Sergei leaned forward, lifted his glass, took a gulp, and looked up at me. "Yes, it was very neatly done, Misty Hoyt. I watched. Sonia didn't hesitate."

"No, I didn't."

"That is a very interesting story," I said, trying to keep myself on an even keel. I swallowed a hiccup. I was going to vomit. The room swayed. I was terrified that the deck of this wallowing, staggering ship, the table on which I was sitting, would lurch up and spill me off, and I'd fall on my knees at Sergei's feet. I took a deep breath and glanced around. Kaleem Baluchi had a naked girl – a blonde with very long legs – on his lap. He was holding a vodka bottle up high, forcing her to drink. The vodka spilled from her lips, gurgling everywhere, running over her shoulders, down her breasts and belly. She was sputtering. I wondered if she'd survive. Inside my head, the coke was whirling around, diamond-sharp; I was utterly high, totally stoned, and floating free from my body. Sergei grinned at me like the Big Bad Wolf that was about to eat Little Red Riding Hood. "Stand up, Misty," he commanded.

"Yes, sir." I hiccupped and stood up, tummy out, offering myself. Sergei leaned forward and began stroking my belly, and he reached down and touched the labia rings and the labia itself and pressed inward, and I was wet, goddamn it, and he sampled the liquid and then brought his fingers to his nose and sniffed and then licked his fingers.

I was more and more conscious of my nakedness, and how exposed and vulnerable I was, standing in the middle of Sergei's group, squeezed between the low table and the divan, with Sonia, sitting beside Sergei on the divan and smiling up at me like a protective but unpredictable and deadly goddess.

Baluchi's blonde choked on the vodka. He made her stand up and then had her lie tummy down over his lap while he spanked her. She was still choking and coughing. It looked playful – until Baluchi took off his belt. I heard the whap, whap, whap, as if it was coming from another world. His huge belly gleamed, the buckle on the belt, which was gold, flashed through the air. Bright red strokes appeared across the girl's glistening white buttocks.

"Well, Misty Hoyt," Sergei grinned. "Why don't you go up there on the stage and strut your stuff? I'd like to see you pole dance."

"What?"

"Pole dance."

"Oh, pole dance," I mumbled, slurping back saliva. I figured I would hardly be able to stand up, let alone pole dance. I had never pole danced in my whole life though Misty Hoyt had pole danced, and had admitted as much at the bar to Andrei, but I hadn't had time to catch up with all of Misty's skills. This was definitely a hole in the planning of my backstory – giving me experience, as a pole dancer, I would not be able to fake. I would look utterly grotesque too, tattooed as I was; the vanity of self-consciousness never dies   I shuddered at the thought of me tattooed and pierced among those buff, golden, perfectly beautiful girls.

Whatever! I had to do it.

"Okay," I said, "You are the boss, Mister Sergei." I managed somehow to stand up, wobble, and then make my way, through tables and guests, and get over to the runway, and climb up onto it. It seemed very high. I weaved, tottered this way and that, and then somehow I pulled myself together.

I pole danced with one of the pole dancers – me weaving around one pole, and she around the other. She was the petite, fine-featured golden Vietnamese girl I had noticed before. I'd seen movies of pole dancing, so I managed to fake it; and then I was the tattooed pierced clown, a freakish waif, I didn't really have to be very good.

Then – I'm foggy about actually when – the golden Vietnamese girl and I were ordered to make love on the runway in the bright lights. The strobe lights had stopped. The other pole dancers had disappeared into the crowd. And now, except for the spotlights on the two of us, the whole place was subdued in dull amber light, a sort of nightclub twilight. The music went down, and it was quiet. I thought maybe I was hallucinating the silence. But no, it was real.

Sonia appeared beside the platform and started to give directions. "Down on your knees, Misty. Down on all fours, Misty. Lick her, Misty, suck her, put your lips to her breasts and suckle her milk, Misty. Go down between her legs, Misty." So I tongued the Vietnamese girl, and sucked on her neat cupcake breasts, with her nipples erect and tense and elastic under my tongue, and I licked her tummy and her clitoris, and I did my best and since I'd learned from Kate and from Martine, and I had practiced on Martine, extensively, and she had practiced on me, every sort of variant of girl-on-girl lovemaking and sex, so I guess I sort of had a Ph.D. in licking and sucking and twirling and nibbling and kissing and caressing and teasing and fingering and slapping. I think I was pretty good and the girl pretended to have an orgasm, well, maybe she really did. In fact, I'm pretty sure she really did. She cried out, an ululating sort of scream, and her neat, perfect body arched up and lurched, and her thighs closed on me, taking me prisoner.

Then ...

Then I lost track.

The music was wild, and people were dancing, and strobe lights came on, intermittently, adding to the spotlights that lit up the golden girl and the tattooed grotesque, which, of course, was me.

Thundering in my ears, like the surge of ocean surf and breakers, was the sound of the crowd, the music, and, coming through it all, there was Sonia, giving instructions.

By now I was excited too since being naked and performing like that with a girl I didn't know and with another woman giving instructions and with a crowd of criminals and gangsters and strippers looking on, was something new, and I was, of course, drunk and drugged and without any clothes and without my purse or any object at all, so I could feel the erotic and almost mystical excitement of total dénuement – total nakedness and destitution – abasement and abjection – despoiled of everything and reduced down to my anonymous bodily essence – this dénuement being something French philosophers used to talk about, as Kate had informed me one hot, rainy morning when I was slouched down, buck naked, under the awning, in a cream canvas pine deckchair out on our deck, sipping from a big mug of strong black coffee and reading The New York Review of Books.

Now, truly totally despoiled of myself, I had become just a piece of anonymous brightly tattooed naked flesh gyrating under brilliant warm lights, showing off, which was inebriating, all those eyes on my naked, tattooed, pierced, shaved, and waxed body. I could feel the sweat beading on my skin, and I could taste the salty sweet sweat on the Vietnamese girl's skin. As I licked and sucked, as my tongue twirled and swirled, my golden girl was splayed back, staring at me through narrowed golden eyes; and then, to my surprise, she cried out again, she screamed, she screamed, again, and then again, and then she whimpered, and her half-open lips, her gleaming teeth, and her chin, were wet with saliva, so she really did come, again, and then again, at least I think so, but time and space were getting pretty jumbled up, and then somehow – how did this happen? She was on her knees, and I was lying back, and she licked me and licked me, making sure I was already wet, but I was already soaked, of that I was sure, though I certainly relished her talented affectionately precise tongue – she was a genius in lovemaking, I decided – and her lips and teeth and tongue were sublime. I groaned.

She paused, looked up at me, her golden eyes blinking. 'What?' I wanted to say, but I just groaned again.

She stood up, looking majestic and imperious, her golden hair sparkling in her ponytail, her fragile shoulders gleaming and pure and golden, and she strutted proudly, stared down at me – I was crouching at her feet – a conquered bit of booty.

"Girl!" she said, "Look at me, girl!"

I looked up out of my tattooed mask, blinking.

She smiled, a stern smile, my Golden Mistress. "Get on your hands and knees, girl, and watch!"

I shifted to hands and knees and looked up, an obedient puppy. I wagged my tail, my rump flashing back and forth. She smiled down, displaying a wonderful smile, sweet, and all-forgiving.

The strobe lights sprang into life. Zoom, zoom, zoom! We were all zebras, striped, and rippling with light. The music hammered in my ears. Light flashes filled my eyes. As I, an eager little doggy, watched, my golden girl, my Golden Mistress, carefully inserted and strapped on a black double dildo – made to penetrate both of us at the same time – and which looked frighteningly enormous. She buckled it tight, and commanded, "Stand up, slave!" I got to my feet and then she was kissing me, and I was kissing her back – it was so fluid our bodies and mouths seemed to be one body, one mouth – and part of my mind was thinking what a ridiculous sight this must be – me, the bald tattooed pierced freak, festooned with rings, and she, the perfect golden girl, everyman's dream, and so, dancing me backwards, kissing me all the time, forcing me to submit to her every move, she marched me back and pinned me against the hot metal dance pole, and she opened me, delicately, with her fingers, and then she penetrated me with the dildo, which was tricky and strange with all that metal I had attached to me, the labial rings and the clitoral hood ring, but I was already totally liquid – seething hot like molten melted butter – and it made it even more exciting as the rings pressed into my flesh, and a little hook on the dildo pressed tight against my clitoris, clicking the hood ring, and then she turned the dildo's vibrator on, and the pleasure – no, it was too intense to be called pleasure – the crazy pure painful quivering ecstasy exploded, and I saw that she too was approaching orgasm, since the vibrator was designed for two, and, with my heart pounding and my saliva dripping and my hands grasping at her ass, holding and pressing her cheeks, forcing her deeper into me, I wondered what James would think, and I knew what he would think, he would kiss me and comfort me and reassure me that it was perfectly fine and he would most certainly enjoy it too, watching it, and afterwards giving me his analysis of the pleasure I felt and he felt – for James, in one mode, was a very self-conscious, detached and analytic person, but also capable of romance and total romantic and sexual abandonment which combination was for me one of the things that made him so unique and uniquely wonderful – and I wondered if he was still alive and my heart froze in horror at the same time as it surged with desire, and I kissed the girl now tenderly, suddenly realizing how petite she was, how fine her features were, and thinking that perhaps, yes, she must be Vietnamese. She had golden perfect skin and with her beautiful almond eyes and golden hair she was a perfect contrast, absolutely, to me the tattooed circus freak, and I wondered what this particular show looked like if you were standing watching it, and I saw people, vaguely, in the golden flashing shadows, lifting up their phones, taking photographs and maybe making videos and I thought, oh, boy, if I survive this, I'm going to be even more infamous than I am now. I did then, to my surprise, find myself swept up in another, yet another, wave of excitement, and I pulled away just for an instant, and gazed into her eyes, and then I kissed her with a deep, serious concentrated kiss, feeling I could eat her up and absorb her into me, and meanwhile the dildo, which was an excellent vibrator, penetrating deep into both of us, began a new particularly intense pulsation and again to my surprise I was swept away – still farther – and I came, I came, again, and again. Oh, my God, oh, my God ...

She turned the machine off. The excitement gradually ebbed, with echoes and returning waves like a giant tide slowly receding from a beach, but rushing back with sudden thunderous surges of energy; she slipped the dildo out of me; we separated. She unstrapped the dildo, and carefully removed it and set it down. I was dazed, leaning, starry-eyed, against the dance pole. Suddenly sounds came back. The place was noisy again. I saw Kaleem Baluchi standing there, hitching up his sagging pants. His shirt bulged out over his enormous belly, and, as he waddled forward, he began to put on his belt. He was staring right at me. He grinned, and blew me a kiss, and then he turned away and walked back into the amber shadows.

Now nobody seemed to be watching us, that was my impression, but it wasn't true, from the shadows they were watching us, and the girl said, "Come on, Misty, kiss me again," and so I did and we stood there, in our own isolated little space, in an entirely different world from all the others, kissing and caressing and stroking each other, and my Golden Mistress whispered into my ear, "You are beautiful, Misty Hoyt, I love you just the way you are."

Time roared along like a freight train, passing us by, and at the same time it was slowing down. I was swimming in glue. The golden girl was still naked, and playing with my nipple rings, and caressing my belly and breasts, and she licked my right breast and, while I stroked her hair and pulled her to me, part of my mind was saying, we are wasting time here, we have to get Sergei to take me to his compound, to his mountain fortification and hideout. Maybe I've shot my bolt, maybe he's seen enough – or too much – and so maybe he'll just leave me here. Then I'll have to kill him; I'll have to find a way to kill him.

Sonia was suddenly standing at the edge of the bar. "Come on, Misty," she said, "the boss wants to talk to you. Don't bother to dress. You too, Tracy, don't dress, stay naked: you're going to be part of the party."

Tracy – so that was her name!

Tracy slipped off the runway. I took a deep breath. Well, Misty, you asked for it. Tracy took my arm and leaned close. I could feel in the midst of my twirling fog of feelings and sensations that she was afraid.

"Sergei is curious, Misty," Sonia said, "He wants us all, I think, to perform some more tricks."

We wove our way through tables and past dancers. I hadn't even noticed people were dancing. One black woman was in a shimmering gold dress that looked like it was made of gold coins; she was dancing with a man who was shirtless and wearing black leather trousers. They glanced at Tracy and me, and grinned. Another woman, a blonde with her hair cut ultra-short, was in a black latex catsuit, and she was dancing with another woman, also blonde, with her hair cut ultra-short, in exactly the same outfit. They looked like twins. Their eyes, crystal-clear blue and wide with cat-like curiosity, turned towards Tracy and me – and Sonia, who was leading the way.

We got to Sergei's group. They were still sitting on the three long divans that circled, in a wide U-formation, the massive low black marble table. Sergei got up slowly, with the smooth, stealthy, lethal movement of a beast of prey, and looked me up and down and then he put his fingers to my lips and my nose ring; he jangled the metal rings hanging in my ears; he flicked at the puff of hair on my skull, tugged at one of the nipple rings, and he said, "You are a collector's item, Misty Hoyt."

"You figure?" I said.

"Yes, Misty, I do figure." He laughed, sat down on the divan, slouched back, sucked on his cigar, puckered his lips, and looked up at me. "Sit on the table, kid."

"Yes, sir." I cleared away a couple of glasses, and I perched on the edge of the table, my black stiletto heels on the floor, facing Sergei, and feeling, well, extra exposed. He leaned back and surveyed the rings in my labia, the colorful swirling designs on my belly, the rings dangling from my breasts, and he puffed a big smoke ring towards me. It broke apart against my face. I closed my eyes and opened them again. It was an Arturo Fuente cigar, I think, rich tobacco, and very expensive. The smoke curled around my face and breasts and tendrils drifted against my shoulders and belly. I blinked. Soon I would be perfumed in sweat and cum and cigar smoke; Sergei was putting his mark on me.

I turned my face away, to avoid the floating caress of the smoke. On the table in front of Kaleem Baluchi, the naked blonde lay sprawled face-up among the bottles and glasses and ashtrays and candles while people smoked and talked all around her. I couldn't see whether she was breathing or not. Baluchi caught my eye, patted his tummy, winked and raised his glass in a toast and mouthed, "Prosit!" I nodded back.

"Now," Sergei was saying, "Let's see if these girls know how to work for their living." He puffed out another smoke ring, paused, contemplated the glowing end of his cigar, and then he ordered Tracy to kneel on the floor in front of me, in the tiny space between Sergei's knees and mine; he spread his legs wide to accommodate her, and he pulled on her ponytail, so her head was jerked back, violently. I thought he was going to break her neck, but he just smiled, let go of her hair, chewed the cigar, and said, "Okay, you do a bit of work, Tracy, you lick and nibble and twirl and bite little Misty here, giving her as much pleasure and pain as you can, while Misty and I have a talk." He closed his legs, squeezing Tracy between them.

Oh, I thought, so I'm going to be displayed and pleasured and interrogated at the same time, pretty damned confusing, another exam to pass! Reminds me of high school. I hiccupped. Tracy glanced up at me and mouthed a kiss. Then her head went down, and her mouth was on me, delicately, softly, and her tongue exploring and her teeth touching my lips and tugging gently from time to time on the labial rings – ouch, the piercings were still tender. She had a definite technique: She would start, and stop, and then flick the tip of her tongue against my clitoris, which was extra sensitive with the ring on its hood. I tried to hold my breath and control my breathing. I was hyperconscious of people watching me, as I sat there, perched on the table, under a spotlight, gleaming sweat and tattoos, with Tracy, all golden, her neat ponytail, working hard, down between my legs.

"So, Misty, tell me your story." Sergei drew in a deep lungful of cigar smoke cigar and exhaled, slowly, in a thick stream, straight towards me; he narrowed his eyes against the smoke, and smiled. He had very bright even teeth and a perfectly even tan, as if it has been sprayed on; his black leather jacket was open on his body builder's chest, with prominent smooth pectorals and flat ribbed abs, and no hair, so it looked like either he was naturally hairless as many Slavs are in my limited experience of Slavs, or he had been waxed, or had all his hair removed with a laser. His pants were black leather, and skintight, and he was wearing black, thick-soled military boots, and while smoking the cigar, and holding it out to contemplate the glowing end, he was clutching his crotch and massaging it through the fine black leather. I could see, or thought I could see, that he had an erection – I wondered if this was just natural, or if it was my fault – or perhaps Tracy's or Sonia's.

"Here, Misty, take a puff." He handed me the cigar. Oh, God, I thought, I am going to be sick. I don't like cigars, I can't stand cigars, and I've never smoked one – though as an encyclopedia of useful and useless knowledge I knew a lot about them – a product of grandmother and grandfather's society – and now I've drunk those drugged drinks and I've sniffed coke, and now he's giving me a cigar. I took it, held my gaze steady, looking straight at him. The cigar was wet and sticky with his saliva. I licked it before I put it in my mouth. I took my time licking it, looking at him, but not in a challenging way, in a sort of worshipful neutral mildly submissive anti-feminist way. Finally, I put the thing in my mouth, chewed a bit, and I took a puff, managed not to gag, rounded my mouth and managed to puff out a big circle of smoke which headed straight towards him; but before reaching his face, it drifted up sideways and slowly dissipated. I handed the cigar back. And he took it, and he grinned. "I like you, Misty, you are spunky for a freakish kid. Tell me, tell me your story."

"What part?" I said, swallowing; the cigar was making me dizzy. It wouldn't do to throw up. Tracy was busy between my legs, her golden ponytail catching the light, bobbing up and down, slurp-slurp, it was getting pretty sticky and tickly and tingly down there, and in spite of myself, I could feel my excitement rising. I trembled, struggling desperately to keep control of my mind – and my body. I was not sure an orgasm would be very politic, or polite, given the circumstances.

One of the things that sometimes happens to me in difficult situations is that I have a sort of out-of-body experience – It's as if I am in two places at once, inside my body, inside my skin, somewhere behind my eyes, peeking out, but, at the same time, I'm also in another place, floating away, maybe sideways, or maybe up into the air, towards the ceiling or the clouds. Right now, I was outside myself, and I could see myself, perched on the edge of the black marble table, head shaved except for that one ridiculous pompom scarlet tuft, and covered in brilliant black and scarlet and green and blue tattoos, and with three big rings hanging from each ear, and an oversized ring nose that touched my upper lip, and nipple rings and Tracy, naked, golden and perfect, kneeling, working hard, between my legs. I was evaporating, I was drifting up towards the ceiling. It was terrifying: I thought that I was drifting so quickly outside my body I might never be able to get back inside my body, and at the same time, while I was drifting away from myself, I could hear myself talking to Sergei, giving him my life story – the made-up cover story – and taking the cigar and taking another puff and handing the cigar back, and holding his gaze, which I felt I absolutely had to do, glassy-eyed and all, while I told him how Dad left when I was born, but came back and beat up my mother and me, and then he went away again, and we were left alone in a wooden and tarpaper shack in the middle of nowhere like something out of the Great Depression of the 20th Century and how my mother was a sucker for bad guys and one of them she picked up – she worked as a waitress on the highway, in eastern Kentucky it was, and the guy came home, and he liked me, he liked me a lot ... and ...

"How old were you?"

"I was about eleven, I think, it's sort of fuzzy, I was in the 6th grade and –"

"What was the name of the diner where your mother worked?" Sergei's smile was bright, his eyes narrowed. He drew in the smoke, and he let out a big puff, a giant ring, headed straight towards me. His smile got brighter. "I like local color, Misty, I like details."

"Johnny Duff's Diner," I said, "it had an old neon sign – a red sign – which was broke half the time, so it spelled "John ... Du," which was sort of stupid, I remember thinking, even as a kid, I noticed things. It was like, 'duh!' We lived down a rutted mud and gravel side road, next to an open junk pit – old car carcasses piled up – I used to play in there sometimes though ma said it was too dangerous – with a rusted fence around it and sumac growing everywhere."

"Sounds very ... picturesque, poetic."

"You're fucking kidding me! Poetic! Fuck poetic! We had a fucking outhouse! I shat and pissed through a wooden board. It smelt like it too. Poetic! Fuck!" I blew a circle of smoke.

"Go on, Misty, this is most interesting." He took the cigar, narrowed his eyes, and puffed more smoke. My skin was coated in it. Soon every inch of me would stink like the butt end of a Havana stogie. Tracy was tickling my clitoris. I wished she would stop, and I wished she wouldn't. I wished she and I were alone, and I wished we were somewhere where we were not going to get killed in the next few minutes. Sweat dribbled from under my metal-and-leather collar, down my back, wriggling like a goofy icy little serpent tickling its way right down my spine and into the crack of my ass.

"We weren't totally lost. I mean, Ma had a car, but it broke down, and she lost her license from driving under the influence and couldn't get it back, so it was on foot or accepting rides all the time."

"What did he do to you, the boyfriend?" Sergei stared at me, smiling, half-smiling. He handed me the cigar. I took it, inserted it in my mouth, and breathed it in. I took my time to exhale, blowing another smoke ring; I was beginning to feel like I was God and could do anything, and get away with anything, and I was also feeling like I might throw up at any minute and vomit in Sergei's face and all over Tracy's perfect ponytail and her perfect golden back, with her beautiful spine, and her neat, perfect shoulder blades and the perfectly beautiful waist and ass. She would probably never forgive me.

"You are very observant, Misty." Sergei grinned at me, and I smiled, and I said, "Oh," and I thought maybe this is not so good,

Misty Hoyt being so observant and all, was probably not such a good thing.

"And you have an exceptionally good memory." His grin became tighter, and he took a puff of the cigar and blew the smoke straight into my eyes. I didn't know whether he was trying for a metaphor – blowing smoke in my eyes – or not; but I had no choice, it seemed to me, but to plunge onwards, into my story, so I told him about the little room, and my bed which was an old bed with lumpy broken springs and a thin stinky and piss-stained mattress, jammed up against the wall, the shitty fly-splattered wallpaper, and the coils of yellow flypaper hanging down, rattling and swinging in the wind, with the one dirty broken window, and how Gus – Gus Foreman the boyfriend's name was – came in when mom was working the night shift and how he took his time, he allowed me to lick and grease his thing before he stuck it in me, he was not rough with me – but I was frightened and he was sort of gentle and like I said he took his time and he used lots of spittle to ease his way into me and how it hurt – even though my older brother since decamped had done it with me several times before Gus – which detail I spared Sergei – and how Gus told me it was our little secret because mom would get really mad and be jealous and he was always really nice to me, like a father or a nice uncle, when Mom was home, and she said once – it was raining and really hot in the house and you could smell all the smells – the rotting wood, the mildew, the grass, the piss, mouse turds, fresh piss and old piss, the creosote, and the raw earth – and her voice was sort of slurry because she'd been drinking and it didn't take much – just a glass or two of cheap wine or beer – for her to slide off sideways into slurred words – her mouth taking on weird slow deliberate shapes like her saliva had turned to syrup, and her tongue had gotten lots bigger – and not making any sense, and, turning to Gus, she said, 'You really like Misty, don't you,

Gus.' And he said, looking at me and winking, 'Yeah, it's like she's my own kid, my very own kid.'"

Sergei smiled his big broad, perfectly even smile, and said, "You knew it was not right." And he handed me the cigar. I was all tense at this point because Tracy was kissing my labia and licking my clitoris in a particularly savvy way – quick little up and down and sideways flicks with the very tip of her tongue – and the way she was doing it was so sweet and loving and delicate that I wanted to cry – and to scream. I drew in a cloud of the smoke and handed him back the cigar, and then I exhaled – a long thin stream with some twirls and curlicues in it.

"Yeah, of course, I knew it was bad. I'm not fucking stupid!" I said, "We had a television, and I had a computer. I wasn't born in the fucking Stone Age for Christ's sake!"

"Did your mother ever find out?" Sergei licked his lips, blinked, and picked at a bit of tobacco that had stuck to his lips. And, yes, he did have an erection; the bloody leather was stretched, stretched and glossy, a neat little phallic tepee.

"Yeah, she found out. And she screamed at him and pounded her fists on his chest and took up a kitchen knife and wanted to carve out his heart she said, and he beat her black and blue, and she beat me, slapping me mostly on the face. I thought she was going to break my jaw or snap my neck, she hit me so hard. And then she said, 'I want to see it.' And he said, 'What do you want to see?' 'I want to see you and her do it, the filthy traitorous fucking little bitch.' And so he said, 'Okay.' And he looked at me and grinned, like isn't this going to be fun; so, we put on a little show for her, for Ma, he and me humping, fucking, right there, right in front of my old lady. Then he made love to both of us. And then he made love to me again, all our liquids intermingled – and she watched, always she watched."

"I like this." Sergei handed me the cigar.

I took it and puffed and blew a smoke ring and then another smoke ring. "She sat on a wooden chair next to the creaking fucking bed, and she watched. The springs weren't worth shit. She was smoking a cigarette, it hanging from the corner of her mouth, real lazy like, totally lost like, and her hands dangling limp-wristed between her legs, and she took a puff and she just watched and so it became a regular thing – sometimes he took me first and she watched and sometimes he took her first and I watched. He didn't treat me nice anymore. We didn't have our little secret anymore. He just called us both sluts – slut number one and slut number two. I was slut number one, the top number. She was slut number two, the bottom. That was our rank – me first, her second. He liked to keep us naked, mum and me. No clothes for the females in the house, that was the house rule." I sucked on the cigar and puffed out a big smoke ring that turned slow summersaults and drifted off to the side. "Ma had a good body for an old fucking broad, at least I thought so. She was a looker, smashed-up, but a looker." I handed the cigar back to Sergei. "More traffic started to go down that side road where we had our shack because they opened an old gravel pit and the garbage dump became more active, and the place got really dusty, sand drifting in all over the place, and the trucks made lots of noise, so you couldn't sleep. Even the sex was gritty. Sweaty and coated in fine dust – I didn't bother to wash – that's the way I tried to sleep, gritty, sweaty, filthy, listening to the trucks. I couldn't sleep. I stopped doing okay in school. I was furious at my mom. I wanted Gus for myself. When I told him that, he slapped me, and didn't stop slapping me and said I should show my mom some fucking respect. And so when I could – I was sixteen – I left."

"Where did you go?"

So I told him. I was listening to my own voice. I heard, too, in my head, Martine's voice, as she rehearsed with me all the aspects

of the story, sitting next to me, on that little metal stool, back in
Paris, while Lou-Lou and Yo tattooed their way over my back and
buttocks and skull, the overall tickling intimate sensation of it,
every inch of skin being possessed, not by me – but Lou-Lou and
Yo, who were putting their mark everywhere, Lou-Lou delighting
in the opportunity to transform me into a Punk-Goth freak, a
perfect Lou-Lou work of art, a sort of fun-house mirror image
of some aspect of her own self, where she wanted to go, maybe,
but hadn't quite dared, and Yo, piercing me, inserting the rings,
massaging the ointment, testing everything. I was conscious, too,
of Tracy, crouched between my legs, of her lips and tongue and
teeth and beautiful perfect little face and breath close and warm
to my belly, and I was conscious of Sonia, her short tight leather
skirt, her long white legs crossed, lounging back on the divan,
one arm around Sergei's shoulder, watching me closely, studying each word I said, and I was conscious of Baluchi and of the
sprawled drunk, unconscious blonde, who might be dead by now
for all I knew, and of all the women and guys who were sitting
in our circle, the guys, in particular, leaning forward, watching
me and Sergei intently, waiting for him to move in for the kill,
or slouching back, talking to each other – bodyguards, mostly, I
think, muscle, they had muscle, they certainly looked like muscle,
some with lots of hair, some with shaved heads, and me in the
middle, naked and sweaty, talking on and on …

Everything was beginning to look too bright, too detailed. I
could see every bead of sweat on Sergei's upper lip. I could see
every strand of his blond hair. I was so aware of everything I
thought I would explode; my skin couldn't contain me, I was going to …

Then …

Oh, oh, oh!

I saw a, a, a – It couldn't be!

I saw a snake – a huge creamy white and mottled snake – it looked like an albino python – which was sliding over the top of the couch just behind Sergei, and I was going to say something, but then I thought, No, this is a hallucination, I've got to control myself, I can't admit I'm going crazy; if they think I'm going crazy, they might just drop me and leave me behind or worse, kill me and throw me in a trash can. No, I'm not going to recognize it. Everything was increasingly intense, and time seemed to be slowing down. The snake curled towards Sergei and raised its head. Sergei reached out and put his hand around the snake's neck. He seemed to be caressing the snake. It slithered forward, across Sergei's lap, and reached out towards Tracy, busy between my legs, and now Tracy looked up at me, and she seemed to see the snake out of the corner of her eye, but she didn't scream or leap up or do anything in particular, but she began to kiss my belly and to play with the bellybutton ring with her tongue while the snake, slithered over her shoulder, and then recoiled slightly, raising its head towards me, and it started back a bit, recoiling still more, its head and snake eyes and snout drawing away, as if to get a better look at me, at my decorated metal-laden face, as if it were puzzled, wondering what I was, or what it was supposed to do with me – attack and eat me – or curl around my neck like a feather boa and be decorative – it's skin was like a pale latte with mottles of darker brown and its eyes were like flattened calculating sparkling yellow lozenges and its narrow thin tongue flickered out, flashing quickly – and I thought for a moment that it was going to leap and attack, but it didn't. It turned and slithered back over to Sergei's lap and up over his shoulder, and across to Sonia, and began to curl and drape itself around her shoulders.

"This is Betty," Sergei said, laying his big hairless hand – he had long sensitive fingers like those of a classical pianist – on the mottled snake. The snake's body bulged here and there and it was big and fluid and maybe eight or more feet long.

"Betty," I said, rather stupidly, but I wanted confirmation that it was not a hallucination.

"Betty," Sergei repeated, looking me right in the eye; his eyes were the bluest blue; how was it I had not noticed before how blue his eyes were. They were truly a beautiful blue, like the bluest of blue skies or like a swimming pool, into which you could dive, and drown, and ...

Once again, I was inside myself, and at the same time, I was outside myself. I could see me, sitting on the table, with Tracy on hands and knees between my legs, and I could see the colorful tattoos, and the metal, and the shiny sweat-covered tattooed body that was me and the bright comic scarlet tuft, and I could see the mirrors and the metal columns and the leather walls and the marble floors and the specks of mica in the table I was sitting on, and then I could hear everybody talking – some in English, some in Russian, some in Georgian, and two guys in Italian, it was as if five or six different soundtracks were running simultaneously in my head. One of the Italian guys was saying, in Italian, "The little tattooed bitch is perfect. Yeah, Sergei will have a real circus tonight. He'll fuck her until she's dead. Yeah. Literally dead. She's already dead, only she doesn't know it. Well, no accounting for tastes." I felt I was going to be sick again. Too many sensations were pouring into my brain. Every inch of my skin felt like it would explode. "Get a grip on yourself, Misty Hoyt," I said to myself, "Yes, Misty! Get a grip."

My ear implant came alive in a burst of static, and it was saying, in a mixture and babble of voices, in French and English, woven with chaotic static.

"There's a lot of interference."

"Be careful. Traffic is heavy."

"We have interference."

"I think we've lost her."

"No, we haven't lost her."

"Yes, we've lost her."

"She's in the club. She's met the target."

"Yeah, she's met the target."

"She doing some sex routine. It's hard to tell what."

"Too bad. She can't hear us. She's out of the loop."

"Damn! She's cute. I wouldn't mind shacking up with her, tattooed or not."

"Shut up, Maurice." Séverine's voice.

"Yes, the tricks she plays. Makes a man wild, just thinking with brains and a body like that and a mind to keep you awake at night."

"I said, shut up!" Séverine's voice, very annoyed.

Different voices were mingling together; a lot of channels had somehow leaked into the one channel. Damn! "Keep calm, Misty." I was now Misty inside my own head. Gwendoline was fading away. Who the hell was Gwendoline anyway? Did I once know a Gwendoline? Gwendoline was gone. Another burst of static, somebody saying, "Could you order extra surveillance?" Another voice saying, in French, "Have the Russians answered yet?" Then a burst of static and – nothing. I was almost certainly getting much more of the office soundtracks than I was supposed to be getting. And, really, they didn't seem to know if I was alive or dead.

Sergei was saying, "So, Misty, what was it like, being out on the road, all alone?"

Somehow I was answering him. I heard my own voice as if it were somebody else in another room talking, "So that's how I got myself to ..."

"That's very interesting," Sergei was smiling, the smile of an excited predator, of a sadist. "Those tattoos hurt a lot, I'll bet. Must have been a shock when you first saw yourself."

Somehow my voice was gabbling on; it even seemed pretty coherent, though I didn't have enough focus to really listen to what I was saying, but Sergei seemed happy.

The earphone came alive again, and it was saying, in French, "Thanks, Pierre, I'd like a double espresso."

Fuck! I was hearing office chatter from control, a whole lot of mikes must be open. Then somebody, a guy, on another channel, was babbling, with an American accent: "The drones are going to be delivered to the Shetland base at 08:45. Repeat. The drones are going to be delivered to the Shetland base at 08:45. I'm not sure that will be in time ..."

Then a female voice, again American, mid-west and a bit nasal: "Who the fuck is this Betty they're talking about? Is Betty an agent? Have we got a Betty on our lists?" Then a guy with a French accent saying, "Maybe it's just a casual whore they've picked up. Or maybe it's a new alias for somebody we've already cataloged?" "And this Tracy, and this Sonia – do we know anything about them?" "Yeah, who the fuck are all these dames? Anybody got any ideas?"

"Yes, that's really interesting," Sergei was saying, and then he turned to whisper something to Sonia.

Another new voice, speaking in English, had a French accent; it was saying. "I can't find any Betty in our database. But of course, we haven't been able to get inside his inner milieu. Could have changed the code name. Maybe this Betty is ..."

"Shut up," I said.

"What did you say?" Tracy looked up at me – an amorous quizzical glance. I put on a silly grin, and shook my head, my earrings jangled: "Nothing," I said, "nothing." She smiled and kissed my belly and then kissed my breasts, and began to massage them, her fingers spread, looking up, almost worshipfully, or seemingly so. They were quite firm, and overly proud, my breasts, I thought, again looking at myself from an astronomical distance.

Tracy's hands were skilled, sculpting all of my self-conscious desires. I am clay, dear Tracy, please birth me out of the dust! Bring me to life! Sculpt me, carve me, create me! Oh, oh, goddamn, but that felt good. Oh, oh, oh. Tracy smiled up at me again. She knew her touch was magic. It gave her pleasure to give pleasure. Well, somebody seemed happy, at least for a moment. Tracy blinked at me and then kissed my belly and the inner side of my thighs, very tenderly – it was like a declaration of love.

Sergei stood up. "I think it's time we left." He pulled Tracy's head back, by her ponytail, and he said, "Kiss Misty on the lips."

Tracy got up on her knees, and then stood up, and she looked at me, her eyes wide, and she kissed me on my lips, and I tasted my own fluids and hers all mixed together, and I returned the kiss, and then Sergei put his hand on Tracy's shoulder and said, "Now, let's go. You're coming too, Tracy. We are going to have some fun with our new friend, Misty Hoyt."

We got up. I went to get my clothes. And Sergei said, "Don't bother about that – you and Tracy don't need clothes. Sonia will bring your clothes, won't you Sonia dear, and you'll bring Misty's little purse, too, won't you Sonia, dear."

"Certainly, Sergei, darling," said Sonia, bowing her head slightly, looking vexed, as if jealous, and she went to the bar and picked up my clothes, which were on a heap on one of the stools and my purse which – I suddenly realized – I'd forgotten that it existed – was sitting on the bar all lonely and all by itself.

Sonia returned, smiling. "I think you are going to be a big success, Misty. You are just the ticket, Misty!"

I noted that Kaleem Baluchi got up at the same time as we did and that he and Sergei exchanged a glance, and I figured that Baluchi was probably going where we were going – and that could be good or bad, I imagined, depending on how it turned out. Both merchants of death in the same place might turn out to be very useful. Baluchi's blonde was now lying sprawled, like she was crucified, spread-eagled, naked, face-up on the marble table. Baluchi signaled to one of his men who pulled the blonde to her feet. Her head lolled down and her hair flopped over her face, but she looked like she was not dead, and when she belched and threw up all over the table, I knew she was alive. My own stomach echoed with a lurch of its own.

Baluchi laughed, and put his fingers in her sweaty, disheveled hair, and she looked up at him like a beaten and resentful dog, an exquisite face, a total mess, and in a wild-eyed panic, wiping vomit from her chin, and Baluchi laughed again and nodded, and the guy who was holding her by the arm dragged her along with them as they headed for the exit. Baluchi again caught my eye, and he blinked and nodded. For some reason, I nodded back. We had made a connection – our destinies were linked.

Tracy took my arm, squeezed it, and held on as we went towards the exit, our stilettoes clicking, giving us that swaying-ass-look that guys seem to like so much, and not only guys. I still felt I was conscious of too much, of every sparkle and glimmer and sound, and I really did think I was hallucinating. Some of the drugs must be kicking in with a delayed reaction. Maybe it was the cigar. Everything was too intense. The inset amber wall lights with the false art deco design – smoky turquoise and smoky yellow glass in abstract triangular shapes and curved, flattened floral shapes, held by sculpted flaring brass fittings. And the contrast with the black leather and rubber walls, and the strobe light installations, and the gold spotlight shining down on the stage and pole where Tracy had been dancing. I could see every single tiny detail. My mind was racing. I could see beads of sweat forming on Tracy's golden skin like raindrops on a windowpane.

In my ear, the thing had woken up again and was saying. "We've lost her. I think this thing is dead. What do we do now? We've lost Misty. Anybody got any trace on Misty? No, no, no ..." "I think we're fucked. Are we going to go in? Are we going to just write her off?" "Can't go in – no assets near enough. Not even the Russians can get there in time and –" Then it again went dead.

Tracy held on tighter and leaned in close, like she was my date, or I was hers. We came out a big metal side door. I noted that it had giant bars on the inside, and more hidden cameras outside. Guards dressed in black jeans and black T-shirts with bulletproof vests and with submachine guns at the ready, stood on either side of the door. One of them gave me a look and raised his eyebrows: Naked tattooed girl and naked golden girl hugging each other in an alleyway. You don't see that every day, or maybe you do.

There was thunder, it rippled between the buildings. The storm had come back – or had never gone away. The air was sultry, sweaty. Big wet drops. It began to rain. Tracy leaned closer and brushed her lips against my ear and against my heavy steel earrings that clicked like little castanets. Her breath was warm. I suddenly realized she was afraid, afraid again.

I put my arm around her waist, and she put her arm around my waist, and it was suddenly like, and I felt really like I was hallucinating, like we were two high school girlfriends, true sweethearts.

Our high heels – we'd probably borrowed them from our mothers – made us sway in unison and made a nice click-click chorus on the cobblestones.

I felt her body, close, warm skin on warm skin, leaning against me. The walls, tilting inwards, glowed with sweat. More guys with submachine guns came out of the club. The steel door closed behind us. With guards in front and guards behind, we went down the narrow side street. There were guards too, I saw, at the far ends of the street, blocking it off. The rain was warm, and coming harder now. I kissed Tracy on the cheek. Her skin was wet, glossy with raindrops, and it shone gold in the lamplight. The rain gushed off my skull, getting under my thick metal-and-leather collar, trickling everywhere. The drugs raced through my blood. I wanted to grab Tracy and make love to her right there, right in front of everybody, on the cobblestones. The streetlamps loomed up, and stared down at us, charming grotesque glass and metal cages perched on ornate wrought-iron poles, imitation or real wrought-iron, and, it seemed to me, like they were 19th-century gas lamps, out of some expressionist German black-and-white silent film of the 1920s. I was tottering on the edge of hallucinating again, thinking we were all on a movie set, playing in a vampire film, set in some archaic expressionist Germanic corner of Transylvania. Sonia was walking in front of us, wearing Betty wrapped around her shoulders, and Betty's long undulating mottled pale brown and gold, contrasted with Sonia's long chalk-white legs and swaying walk, accentuated by the stilettos and the tight short skirt. Sonia handed Betty off to one of the muscle-bound guys. I don't think he was amused. "What the fuck do I do with this?" Betty stretched herself out in a long vertical line, hanging out from the guy's arm, her head turning around to check on his face: Was he a worthy place to linger, or should she move on? Sonia laughed, and turned to look back at us. Her face was pale and her smile bright in the lamplight.

The ear thing sputtered into life, just for a second, "She's dead, I'm sure she's dead." And that's all I heard – nothing more. I figured they'd given up on me. They couldn't do anything for me anyway – "no nearby assets," as the voice had said. I'd better get rid of the thing; it might sputter again or squeak and give me away. Next time I go to the toilet, if there is a next time, I'll pluck it out and dump it.

At the end of the street, on the bigger street, which was a medieval fantasy of a street, with overhanging second stories, and wooden beams, and what looked like white stucco, and leaded, peaked windows, and picturesque peaked roofs, there was a black stretch Mercedes limousine with shaded windows, and there were three black SUVs, one behind the Mercedes, and two in front of it.

Tracy and I stood in our stilettos, clinging to each other, waiting, there, on the sidewalk, like two lost hookers. Like I said, it was a narrow medieval-looking street, and I didn't see anybody, just Sonia, Sergei, and the muscle-guys, including the guy who was carrying Betty. Betty had wrapped herself around his shoulders like a scarf. She hovered out in front of him, and then swung around, looking over his shoulder, I guess sniffing, and exploring, probably wondering if there was anything to eat. She was too small and docile to eat a human, I think, though I guess, if she were hungry or pissed off enough, she could try.

The doors of the Mercedes opened, and Tracy and I climbed inside, with Sonia. Sergei slid in beside us. The muscle man handed Betty to Sergei, who handed Betty to Sonia, who said, "Hello, Betty, how are you?" Betty's narrow flat head recoiled and she hissed and stuck out her slit tongue which flickered catching the lights of the interior of the car and then she coiled herself up, around Sonia's shoulders with part of her body – yes, she must have been about eight or nine feet long – curled beside Sonia on the seat. I didn't need to hallucinate; this was hallucination enough.

The doors clunked shut, the motors revved, all in unison, and we went roaring through a series of tiny twisting back streets. I lay back, and Tracy and I sort of continued our night club sex act;

she leaned against me and kissed me and I allowed myself to be kissed and then I kissed her back. And Sergei, sitting opposite us, said, "That's right. Why don't you join them, Sonia?"

"You are a real bastard, Sergei, there's no limit to your creepiness," she said, but it was said lightly, with a smile, and she blew him a kiss. "Besides, I have Betty to keep happy."

"Just shut up and take off your clothes, Sonia," he said. "Betty likes you even better when you're naked – and so do I."

"Yes, Master, anything to please my Master." And, being careful to avoid disturbing Betty, Sonia carefully removed her clothes, a slow striptease, as I could appreciate from the corner of my eye. She lifted off her little vest, she opened her transparent blouse and slipped it from her shoulders, easing it out from under Betty, and she opened her belt and took it off, and she opened her skirt and slid it down her legs and held it up – as if it were proof.

"That's right, that's right," Sergei was saying, lazily, his eyes half-closed. "Panties, too, Sonia. Panties too – I want you naked. I like to see you naked. And I will love seeing you grovel, in the mud, in the slime, in the clay. Later you will grovel for Misty. You will be her slave."

Sonia tossed the bits to Sergei. I followed this in a distracted way as I was busy kissing and being kissed by Tracy, and Tracy had also slipped her hand between my legs. I sighed, thinking this is going to be one long acrobatic night! I wonder if I can last the whole marathon. The leather seat was cool and sticky like adhesive under my bare bum. The air-conditioning was on. The voices in my ear had definitely stopped. I was on my own. I hoped that at least we were going to Sergei's headquarters. Then, hopefully, I would find James and find him alive. And I'd see too if the four or five nukes or more were there, or if they had already been sold onward – to the final users – whether the doomsday machine had yet to kick off, or whether it was already ticking down to zero.

"Hey," I made a feeble protest, as Tracy brought me close to orgasm, and she whispered, "I like doing this, I like touching you, I like you, let's keep doing this."

I took her chin between my hands, and I kissed her. "Yes," I whispered, "Let's not stop – ever."

Sonia had tossed her panties away and was naked and wearing Betty like a boa around her neck, and draped around her shoulders, and down between her breasts and legs. Betty was curious. Her head was hovering out beyond Sonia, and it came up quite close to me, and considered me I thought with quizzical serpent eyes, and recoiled slowly, and brushed along Tracy's shoulder and then returned to Sonia who was sitting quite still, just watching us.

Sergei, who seemed half asleep, said, "Open your legs, Sonia," and she did so and stuck her tongue out.

"Touch yourself, Sonia."

"Yes, Master."

"Your pleasure is my pleasure. You know that, Sonia."

"Yes, Master."

We were rumbling along what sounded like a corduroy road, made of logs, since the bounce-bounce-bounce was rhythmic, almost like racing over corrugated iron, and maybe it was something like a bridge or a road constructed over a swamp.

Sergei was watching us, but now he shifted his seat, swung it around, and began to kiss Sonia – and Betty slid away into a corner and coiled up on a seat and raised her head as if she were watching us all through narrow carnivorous eyes, and occasionally she hissed, and her tongue flickered in the amber light. I wondered what her reptilian mind made of all this.

Sonia was on her knees, kissing Sergei on the mouth. "No blow jobs in a moving car," he said, "it's too dangerous."

"Biting off your penis or castrating you by biting off your balls would give me great pleasure," Sonia said, and kissed him. He kissed her back, and laughed, and slid his arm between her legs, and kissed her again. Her body glowed chalk-white in the dim interior of the car. We rumbled across a narrow bridge, it made a hollow, echoing sound, the rattle of the beams – so we were going over the Beckistan River, and into rebel and gang-held territory, Sergei's territory, his own little kingdom within the kingdom. We sped between tall trees, pine and cedar, down a narrow valley, or so it seemed, cliffs looming up on both sides, and then through a fairly long tunnel, the tunnel lights racing by in a blur outside the car windows, and then we were on a winding road that went up a hillside, and then we were on a sort of plateau and racing between plane trees and fields, and then we entered a forest and then again a winding mountain road, a precipice plunging down on one side of the road, and a sheer mountain wall soaring up on the other, and we came to what seemed to be a narrow plateau, and a short while after, we came to a giant set of gates, which had already been swung open; we drove through the gates, past massive walls; and we came to a stop in a large courtyard in front of a building that seemed to be something between a chateau and a fortress. Clouds raced by, up above, silver and black. The moon was out. I looked up. This was the sort of place where Count Dracula would hang out. I could see him now, pale skin, long fangs, black cloak, and loathsome ghoulish eyes, with filthy claws for hands, and infinite dark desires and blood-lust yearnings that needed, desperately needed, to be slaked. I kissed Tracy and bit her lightly on the lip, and she drew back, smiled, kissed me, and bit me, ever so gently.

CHAPTER 5 – THE CASTLE

The car doors opened. We got out. Sergei stretched, twisting his shoulders, lifting his arms up over his head in a strangely delicate ballet-like, almost effeminate gesture. "Sonia, look after our guests, will you."

"Of course, Master." Sonia still naked, and once again wearing Betty dangling glamorously around her neck, turned to us, "Come along, Misty, come along Tracy, we girls must go and clean up a bit, and Betty too. Right, Betty?" Betty's head swayed out in front of Sonia and her snout brushed my shoulder and her tongue flickered and touched my skin, and I again wondered what thoughts were churning over in the python's mind. I just hoped I didn't smell or move like food. But I guess I was too big a mouthful. Betty veered away and her head seemed to float in front of Sonia, about two feet away, swaying, curious, surveying the kingdom, her tongue darting. Our high heels crunched on the gravel.

I pretended to wobble – as if my ankle had twisted slightly – just to seize a moment to take my bearings and I looked up and around – the walls surrounding the "castle" were maybe 50 feet high or 15 meters; the castle itself was huge; in front of us, a baronial-style, arched entry loomed up, and above it, there were windows, three or four stories up; to the left was a suspended third-story closed-in walkway going over – perhaps 200 meters, a little over 200 yards – to a huge square building that looked like a bunker, built into the cliffside; on top of the bunker-like building were antennae and disks an lots of wiring was visible, and at the bottom of the bunker were garage entrances – they looked like they were armored – and there was a pedestrian entrance, a single door, that looked like it led down to a basement or underground fortifications. There were guards stationed in front of the bunker, walking back and forth, carrying submachine guns. So – if you were going to torture somebody, or store nuclear weapons, that might be the place. And it was probably also the communications and control and command center. I could see a few guards walking on top of the big bunker, and what looked like the silhouette of a ground-to-air missile launcher. All this I took in with a single, quick glance – it's amazing what the mind can see when adrenaline is racing. I straightened up and said, "Ouch!" I tested my high heels, took Tracy's arm, and we tried to catch up to Sonia.

"The festivities, I imagine, are about to begin," said Sonia, turning to me with what looked like a sly smile. We went in under the baronial arch, we walked up a few steps, a massive door opened, and we entered a surprisingly narrow hallway – a tactical choke-point – and then we came into a big, high-ceilinged room with arches crisscrossing on the ceiling and with oak and stone buttresses and where a fire was burning in a giant baronial-size fireplace; Persian rugs covered the vast tiled floor and paintings hung from the walls, and branding irons – or so it seemed to me – were heating in the fire and there, in one corner, next to several sofas and a low marble-topped table, was a large Plexiglas cage – for Betty, I guessed it was.

Sonia took the snake to the cage, and opened the door, and aimed the snake towards the door and without any resistance,

Betty slid into the cage and coiled up. "Home sweet home," said Sonia, "Betty smells rabbit. And soon, she will be fed a nice plump little rabbit or three or four."

"Ugh," Tracy shuddered and tightened her grip on me, her arm around my waist.

"Nature is cruel, you know that, Tracy. You should know that, better than anyone." Sonia knelt down and adjusted a dial. "Betty's flat has its very own heating; she likes it to be about 80 degrees Fahrenheit – or, for we Europeans, 27 Celsius. Right now, it's hotter than that anyway, but just in case ..."

I looked around. All this was grand and weird and scary. I had to focus. Now, the important thing was to find out if James was here, and to get to him and free him – and, somehow, get him out of here. But, in the meantime ...

"Come, ladies," said Sonia.

She led us up a staircase. We came to a landing, and a corridor, and we entered a modern-looking bedroom with a king-size bed, wall lamps, a modernist dresser, and a Jacuzzi and two very large bathrooms. I excused myself and shut myself in one of the bathrooms and relieved myself. I wasn't sure my digestive system was working normally.

After checking for hidden cameras – and trying to do it without seeming to do it – I began to pry the earphone out of my ear. I intended to smash it under my heel, and flush it down the toilet. But the moment I touched it, it went live again – "Misty, Misty – can you hear me?"

"I've got all these fucking voices in my head," I muttered, as if talking to myself, "must be the drinks – or the fucking drugs!"

A voice said, "Yes, she's alive – confirmed, she's alive."

"Good, Misty, we hear you – loud and clear. We go silent now."

"Okay, okay, okay!" I flushed the toilet, "I'm a fucking idiot – how do I get myself into these fucking fixes."

When I came out of the cubicle, I tried to take note of everything. The bathroom was splendid and had ventilation and even a very large window, which afforded a splendid moonlit view over the mountains, in the distance spectacular storm clouds were piling up in the moonlight; the window was barred with thick steel bars. Getting out this way would be impossible, without using dynamite, that is. Down below, in the courtyard, a new convoy of black SUVs had arrived – and two stretch limousines. It looked like Sergei had guests.

I came back out of the bathroom and found Sonia and Tracy waiting for me.

Sonia said we three would all shower together – it would be much more intimate, and it would be good training. While in the castle, we would not wear any clothes, unless we were explicitly given permission to do so. And we were each to be given a collar to wear which would indicate, via a local little GPS-type system, to fortress security exactly where we were at any given moment.

Since I already had a collar, Sonia attached and locked a metal tracer tag to the metal ring on my collar. It was titillating, her naked body brushing mine, as she marked me with the metal tag, making her my mistress and me her slave. She looked straight into my eyes and smiled, and I wondered at the meaning of the smile. It seemed so intimate, as if it were more than just a smile.

I watched – and Tracy licked her lips nervously and watched me watch – as Sonia fitted a collar to her. "I really don't like wearing this," Tracy said.

"Nothing to be done about it, darling slave; our master insists," Sonia said, clicking it shut around Tracy's neck and locking it, and then Sonia clicked her own collar into place and locked it.

"We are all slaves then," I said.

"Yes, we are," said Sonia, "All slaves. Repeat after me: I am your slave."

"I am your slave," I said.

"I am your slave," said Tracy.

"Good, now you will just excuse me for a moment." Sonia smiled, caressed the side of my face, tugged at my collar for just a moment, flipping the little tracer tag back and forth, and gazed straight into my eyes, licking her lips and giving me that special little smile. Then she was gone.

Inwardly, I was itching to spring into action; I had to find James and I had to find out if the nukes were here; but I didn't dare make any move at all, since if I was found out and they killed me, I wouldn't find out anything and I certainly wouldn't rescue James.

Tracy and I stood awkwardly for a moment, then Tracy moved towards me, and kissed me and whispered, "This is a very dangerous place, Misty, I hope you understand that."

"I'm sort of getting the idea," I said, thinking, not even you, Tracy, know how dangerous this place is, possibly stacked up with miniaturized nukes. We kissed again. Her naked body was sweet, pressed against mine. "I adore your topknot," she said, smiling, and she kissed my forehead and then my breasts. "And I love all the rings."

Sonia returned, smiled graciously. "Well, slaves, let us begin."

This would be fun, I thought, but how long would it take?

First, we brushed our teeth. I brushed and brushed and brushed with the toothpaste, and I gargled and gargled the mint-flavored mouthwash – all provided free gratis and for nothing – and I watched myself in the mirror as I brushed. My teeth, at least, were the same; but otherwise, I was Misty Hoyt, the pouting tattooed monster. Even the shape of my eyes had changed. Gwendoline was a ghost, a faint memory.

We showered, Tracy and Sonia and I together in the big shower, which was like a small room, all in dark ceramic tile, decorated with complex arabesques, as if it were part of a sultan's harem, and the effect was made even more glamorous by the amber-colored romantic lighting, and misted glass doors; the shower had six nozzles all pouring forth hot water, plus flexible little hoses with slim rubber nozzles for extra-specific spurts of intimate cleansing; steam rose all around us. "You will wash Misty, and Misty will wash you, Tracy," said Sonia, "And take your time, be thorough. Leave no millimeter of skin and no orifice untouched."

"Yes, Mistress," Tracy bowed her head, and looked up and smiled – directly at me.

"And, Misty, you are to address me as 'Mistress' even if you don't like it, and Sergei as 'Master.' Understood?"

"Yes, Mistress." I bowed my head. This was one game I should be good at – I'd had lots of practice.

There were large urns of body soap, very foamy stuff, perfumed and suave, and bubbling over with promises of sensual sensuous pleasure.

While Sonia watched and occasionally gave directions, I soaped Tracy, carefully, taking my time, covering her in a thick layer of suds and then slowly washing her down, letting my fingers go everywhere, every nook, every smooth cranny, every orifice, and every lusciously slippery curved surface. In the hot cascade of water and the steamy atmosphere, Tracy was more golden than ever.

"Kiss her now, Misty, show her you love her." Sonia stood under one showerhead, water cascading over her shoulders, her hair still pinned up in the old Soviet schoolmarm beehive.

I obeyed and kissed Tracy's lips. The water poured over us. The soap cascaded down Tracy's body, drips of soapy water ran from her nipples. I pressed myself against her, and looked into her eyes. Tracy grinned – the first time I'd seen such an expression on her face – it seemed to say that we two were very naughty children and getting away with something. She kissed me, slowly, hesitantly, while staring at me, while her tongue danced a little dance along my lips, then she pried my mouth open, entered my mouth, and it became a full kiss, mouth on mouth, and tongue on tongue. My nipples and nipple-rings pressed against her breasts.

We separated for just an instant, to get our breath, and we stared at each other. She hooked her finger in my collar ring and pulled me to her. Again we kissed. I rinsed her and then stood back and contemplated my work.

Tracy looked like a statue in some wonderful baroque garden caught in a summer thunderstorm. Then it was Tracy's turn to wash me.

Martine and I had played such games, but this little game, between Tracy and me, who were strangers to each other, was somehow more daring and more intimately exciting. Tracy took her time. And with the tattoos and the piercing and rings, there was a lot for her to explore. She and Sonia commented on various parts and aspects of my anatomy. I was not me, not a person. I was a bizarre work of art being examined by aesthetes and connoisseurs, or I was a whole gallery of art, with serpents, dragons, peacocks, flowers and a myriad of designs; they were observing, touching, evaluating; or maybe I was a wild and exotic animal, captured, brought in to be examined, categorized, and given a name.

"Now, slaves, you can wash me. Misty, you do my back. And take your time and use your imagination. I want to be stimulated. And Tracy, you do my front. At halftime, you will change places."

"Yes, Mistress," Tracy said

"Yes, Mistress," I said.

"And, you, Misty, disentangle my hair. And give me a nice vigorous shampoo. I want to get rid of the stiff, lacquered Soviet look."

"Yes, Mistress," I whispered, bowing my head; I got a bottle of shampoo from the ceramic shelf where all the unguents, soaps, creams, ointment, and shampoos were lined up in splendidly various jars, bottles, and vases.

And so it was that Misty Hoyt shampooed Sonia, her mistress, and gave her a very vigorous, almost sadistic, scalp massage. While I shampooed Sonia, Tracy was washing Sonia's belly and breasts and covering her everywhere in creamy suds, and then Tracy began caressing Sonia's breasts and caressing her between the legs. Sonia's hair, freed from its beehive prison, was luxurious and long.

"Do it again, Misty. Another shampoo and massage, please." She looked over her shoulder and blinked at me.

I obliged, and shampooed her again, and massaged her scalp again.

She bent her head back towards me, in a sort of ecstasy, eyes closed like in Bernini's Ecstasy of Saint Teresa, as I washed and rinsed her hair. I was not sure whether the ecstasy and pleasure came from my massaging her scalp or from Tracy kissing and licking her nipples and exploring between her legs or from both.

Sonia's hair was now long and wild. I began to wash her back; I was careful to wash everything and everywhere, penetrating into the most intimate corners of her anatomy, giving her anus a very thorough and very soapy cleaning; I stretched her wide.

"Oh, Misty," she signed and reached back and played with the purple-and scarlet tuft that stood up – even when soaked – so proudly on my skull, and she laughed. "Oh, Misty Hoyt, you are a naughty girl. You will be punished."

And then halftime came, and I was assigned to face Sonia. She was already sparkling clean, of course. Her blond hair, darkened by the water, was plastered down to her skull and snaking down her neck and spilling over her shoulders and collarbone. She looked like a seductive beautiful version of the Medusa, about to devour me or turn me to stone. "Kneel before me, Misty," she ordered.

"Yes, Mistress," I knelt in front of her on the shower floor – amidst the Niagara of hot steamy water.

"Now, Misty! Do be a good girl and use your lips and explore, and, again, show some initiative, darling, be inventive. Go wherever you feel you should go."

"Yes, Mistress," I looked up worshipfully from my tattooed mask, and she smiled down at me, winked, and said, "Oh, Misty Hoyt, whatever shall we do with a monster such as you?" And she caressed my shaved tattooed skull and played with the bright, perky tuft, and I looked down, thinking that time was passing but that this ritual was a part of the price of entry, and thus necessary, and was very enjoyable in itself, and thinking, too, that there seemed to be – or was it an illusion? – some extra meaning in her smiles, her winks, her glances, and in the sinuous, insinuating way she pronounced the phrase, "Oh, Misty Hoyt, whatever shall we do with you."

I wondered. Was she onto me? Did she know who I was? Maybe she and Sergei were preparing me for torture and execution? Just teasing me, just playing me along?

Keeping my head down, utterly submissive, I kissed her belly button, the tip of my tongue toyed with the little ring, and I kissed her labia, her nether lips, she was waxed as smooth and naked as I was, except for a thin slender closely trimmed vertical blonde triangle, barely a pencil stroke; I explored with my tongue her labia and her clitoris, doing my best to display to the utmost all my virtuoso talents – trained by Martine – with my lips and tongue and teeth.

As I did so, she was playing with my comic topknot. I tingled with the excitement of my heavy round steel nose ring pressing against the smooth skin of her belly and her clitoris as I licked and nibbled and sucked, and the water poured over me, bathing me like a benediction. As I felt Sonia's excitement rise, as I felt her whole body go tense, my own excitement soared. I teetered on the edge of orgasm, seeing myself, in this drama of abjection, kneeling, a tattooed naked, shaved, and pierced slave, in front of my blond goddess mistress, and I was vaguely aware, too, of Tracy, working her way down Sonia's backside. "Oh, Misty," Sonia sighed. She reached down and pulled me up by my collar, so I was facing her. "Kiss me, Misty Hoyt, kiss me!"

I stood up, kissed her on the mouth, and whispered to her, "I am your slave, Mistress. I am your slave, and I will do anything you command." And out of her wild beauty, her blue eyes shining brightly, with her blond hair like a storm of serpents around her face and plastered on her forehead and cheeks, like a wild, primitive goddess rising from the waters, she kissed me and whispered, "I too am your slave, Misty Hoyt, and we are united unto death itself." She kissed me again. I closed my eyes, almost swooning. Our kiss was dark and deep and passionate as life and love and death itself.

My heart was beating. I fought to keep it from jumping out of my throat.

Finally, we stepped away from each other, and we stood still, just letting the water cascade over us. Sonia turned a handle; the water stopped, and we were left standing, soaked and dripping, in sudden steamy silence.

Just outside the shower, there were big fluffy pre-warmed towels and a giant blow dryer you could step under. We had fun, the three of us, drying each other. Since I was bald and had no real hair of my own – except the impertinent puffball topknot – I was tasked with toweling Tracy's hair and Sonia's hair. But even while we laughed and horsed around, Sonia insisted on calling us 'slaves,' and we bowed our heads humbly, and bent our knees, and called her 'Mistress.'

I noticed that there we several cameras in the shower room, but what they could have seen – or recorded – in the steamy atmosphere, I couldn't imagine. Had Sergei been watching us all the time?

"This is like the chateau in The Story of O," I was about to say, but then I held my tongue because I knew that such an allusion would be absolutely out of character, almost certainly, for Misty Hoyt, and that it would evoke dangerous ideas, and – for anybody who followed these things – above all, it would evoke images of libertine Martine Aubin and her lover, owlish submissive Gwendoline; and that, if such ideas and images came to mind, I could easily be uncovered at any moment. In fact, it did seem to me extraordinary nobody had recognized me – but the facial modifications and the tattoos and the baldness and the hard metal accessories seemed to have been enough to obliterate the person I had been up until four days ago. In fact, when I thought about Gwendoline, I realized she was a memory, a stranger, a dust-covered fragment from an ancient mosaic or fresco in a ruined villa of Ancient Rome. I was Misty Hoyt – and I might never return to being Gwendoline. Perhaps Gwendoline had already died, somewhere back there, perhaps Gwendoline was only a dream, a memory, a hallucination. Maybe I really was Misty Hoyt.

Sonia spoke into an intercom. "We are ready," she said.

A voice said, "Come, we have guests. A feast has been prepared."

"We are going to a feast, Mistress?" I opened my wild tattoo-framed eyes wide: more delay, more complication!

"Yes, a feast, my slaves."

Sonia led us, naked and collared as we were, to the feast. It was in a huge room with a massive wooden table and a fireplace as tall as a man, and, in spite of the hot weather, there was a fire flaming up, worthy of a Renaissance prince or barbarian from the dark ages. Sergei was standing by the fireplace, a glass of wine in his hand, and a broad smile on his face. He came over to us and kissed Sonia on the lips; he slapped Tracy on the bottom; he stared at me for an instant, grinned, and hooked his finger in my collar ring. "Come, Misty Hoyt, there is an admirer whom you must meet."

Kaleem Baluchi was sitting at one corner of the banquet table, his jacket open, and his vast dark belly gleaming. He smiled as he saw me approach. He got up and kissed my hand. Sergei released me and handed Baluchi a chain leash, fine steel links.

Baluchi bowed, and said, "I hope you will not mind, my dear, if I make you mine, and put you on a leash. I have watched you from afar, and I have dreamed of the things we might do together."

I bowed my head and said, in as sullen and submissive a voice as I could, "Okay, if you really want to."

"Oh, yes, indeed, I really want to!" Baluchi grinned and hooked the leash to my collar, and locked it. He seemed delighted that I might prove petulant and difficult. Resistance, after all, is the spice of courtship – and of torture. All the romantic comedies say so. A totally submissive slave would be a bore. I felt perky and ready for a fight. The shower had refreshed me, and though it was warm in the room, the air here in the mountains was much drier than down in the city.

"Here, sit here," Baluchi patted a cushioned seat that was beside him, to his left. I sat down, trying to muster some dignity, sitting as erect as I could.

The table was laden with piles of fruit, and large bowls of hot food were steaming under elaborately decorated lids. Sitting on the other side of Baluchi, to his right, was the blonde who had been forced to drink the vodka. She was naked, except for a thick collar, like all of the women. She had a glazed look, though for a moment her eyes focused and she did nod at me, a petulant, pouty, intense stare, which left me wondering – was she jealous? Did she despise and hate me? Was she dangerous?

Across from us was a handsome sharp-featured, dark-skinned man with a trim beard and whom I took for an Arab. His eyes were like black coals – the burning eyes of an angry prophet – and he stared at me with what I immediately realized was utter contempt and hatred.

Baluchi leaned toward me and puckered up and was offering me his lips. "May I?" I let him kiss me, and I kissed him back, timidly at first, but then with a bit of an aggressive surge, biting his lip, very gently.

"Ah, excellent, excellent!" He put his hand on my thigh. The man across the table had been watching us. He was eating with his fingers. I was hungry. I glanced at Baluchi. He said, "Go ahead, my dear! Eat, eat and drink and make merry, for soon we shall die. What do the pagan philosophers say? Carpe diem? Seize the day?"

I nodded but immediately concentrated on scooping up food. I decided I would remain with a knife and fork – and so I began to eat, shoveling food into my mouth. I suddenly realized I was starving.

The handsome man watched me and bared his perfect teeth in a bright wicked smile. "An abomination," he said.

I blinked at him.

"She is an abomination. She is a painted and defiled whore, a piece of human filth. All that is evil in the world in incarnate in this creature," he said, staring at me, his handsome eyes not even blinking. "You are a pervert, Baluchi."

I blinked at the sharp-featured prophet and gave him a silly grin. In that instant, I recognized him. He was Khalid Nassir, one of the world's most wanted terrorists, a fundamentalist end-of-the-world sort of fellow, addicted to beheading infidels, apostates, archeologists, doctors and nurses, and of raping any women – or child – his men had captured and declaring that in so doing he was carrying out the work of Allah. I let my eyes rest on him for just a second: I would dearly love to murder the man. I looked down at my plate. The chicken vindaloo was excellent. I licked my lips and forked up a mouthful.

Khalid Nassir smiled; it was a very handsome smile. "It is a portent, the presence of such painted whores, it is a portent of the end," he said, picking up a piece of meat, "All of this will perish," he smiled again and nodded at the table, the guests, and his nod encompassed the whole chateau and the whole world. "You have provided the key, dear Baluchi, the key to the kingdom and to the end of the world."

"Ah, you do me too much honor, dear Khalid, I am merely a businessman and, in my spare time, a scientist too, I am curious about all things, and I like to solve problems. And, if I can give you pleasure, and give you what you want, then I am indeed happy."

Khalid Nassir said, "Well, Kaleem, I am delighted you are happy, for such worldly happiness will not last. Only the will of God is eternal. And through your good offices, the will of God will be done."

Kaleem had left his thick pudgy hands on my thigh, and he was massaging me, lightly, softly, it was not unpleasant. I glanced at him and blinked. He smiled. He had a very nice smile. And he was the man who would be the willing instrument in the death of millions. I was sitting within a few feet of some of the most dangerous men in the world, and one of them was massaging my thigh. On the other side of Baluchi, the blonde was picking at her food. She clearly wasn't hungry. She picked up her wine glass and emptied it.

Sonia was seated beside Sergei and had her arm over his shoulder, and I once again thought that she was quite forward for a slave; it was clear she fully possessed, and had for a long time, Sergei's trust; when the moment came, I would have to kill her too; though how I was going to free James and kill anybody I had no idea. I shoveled more rice onto my plate.

Khalid Nassir was staring at me. "You are like a pagan idol," he said.

I blinked at him. "You figure?"

"Yes, the ancients worshipped painted and gaudy images, sinful abominations. Queen Jezebel, of which the Bible speaks brought such worship into the kingdom of the Jews."

"Now, now," said Kaleem, "Misty is just a girl."

"How old are you?"

"I'm nineteen," I said, which was the age my backstory had determined, it was very nice losing three years lickety split, just like that, so easily. One of the reasons, too, my face had been filled out, just a bit, by the injections.

"You see," said Kaleem, waving a drumstick that dripped sauce, "She is nineteen. She is a child. Behind all of this, she is innocent. She is the image of the goddess, but she is innocent."

"There is no such thing as innocence," said Khalid Nassir.

Tracy was kissing, or being kissed by, the man next to her. He was a blond, Germanic-looking man, in a dark jacket and with no shirt. Her eyes, over his shoulder, glanced at me. I almost waved. Her ponytail reflected the light. I felt a surge of tenderness. Tracy was the destined victim, I supposed, innocent, and loving, and petite, and whenever the moment for action came, she, I supposed, would be sacrificed. "There will be collateral damage," Frederick had told me, "Whatever happens, however it goes down, there will be collateral damage."

Sergei stood up, banged a spoon against his glass. "I want to welcome my friends. They have never met before. What we have done together will make history, my friends. We shall change the course of history. We shall bring down the imperialists, and we shall destroy the Zionist regime, and we shall further the cause of righteousness and deliverance. Just think of it, five simultaneous attacks that will ignite the holy war!"

Those who drank, drank to the toast; Khalid Nassir was abstemious; he twirled his glass of water and looked at me with eyes that burned, dark like fiery coals. I think if he could have set me alight and turned me to a column of ash there and then he would have done it. And if he could have raped me on the banquet table, he would have done it. And if he could have cut my throat, he would have done it. And it would all have been done in the name of God. Such true believers have no pity, no sense of measure. I curled my fists. I licked my lips; I would tear his eyes out.

There were many toasts, and much drinking and plates and servings came and went, and I ate my fill. Finally, the feast wound down, and the guests began to wander away.

"My dear, come with me," said Baluchi. He took me with him, leading me by my leash, through several doors, up some stairs; Baluchi's vodka blonde followed us, but at a certain distance, barefoot, and silent. Baluchi led us along a corridor and then to a very secluded suite at the top of a wide spiral staircase that went down to the ground floor. He unlocked and opened a door, and led us into a large alcove-like room, which turned out to be his bedroom. It was dimly lit, had a huge bed, a divan, several tables, and hanging tapestries and a desk with a laptop computer sitting on it. He waited until the blonde had come in, and then he closed and locked the door. The blonde glanced at me, and bared her teeth in what looked like a smile. Her eyes, a mixture of gold and blue, were like those of an animal, not human. She was very pretty, more than pretty, with a stunning wildness about her, her blond hair long, straight, and uncombed.

Baluch glanced at me and licked his lips.

Oh, oh, I thought.

156

"Sit down, my divine Misty Hoyt," he said, motioning towards a divan and handing me my leash.

I sat down, pressed my legs together, and coiled the leash in my lap.

Baluchi turned to the blonde. "On all fours," he said, making a gesture with his hand. She crouched down, on all fours. "Bark," he said, making another gesture. Sign language, I thought, some sort of sign language.

Crouched on all fours, looking at us with her wild eyes, at me, then at Baluchi, the blonde barked; she let out a series of yaps, like a nervous dog, and then she snarled, baring her teeth.

"Good Enough!" Baluchi said, and raised his hand. "Down, crouch, animal, crouch! Sleep!"

She lowered herself onto her side and lay down, curled up.

"She's totally deaf, and she can't speak," Baluchi turned to me, "Sergei had her vocal cords removed, and her hearing destroyed. She was a violinist, an American, very talented. She is like an animal. He turned her into an animal."

"Oh," I said. I stared at the girl. Crouched on her side in the fetal position, she opened her eyes, blinked, and stared back.

Baluchi walked up to me, and stood for a long moment before me, looking down at me. He licked his lips. Then he undressed, shedding his clothes casually. He stood before me, naked except for a tiny loincloth, a vastly overweight dark-skinned, completely hairless bald man, he gleamed with sweat. So did I, gleam with sweat. So, there we were, both naked – well, in his case, almost naked – two alien human animals, facing each other, while the blonde lay curled on the floor, her eyes open now, watching us. I blinked up at Baluchi: he was enormously heavy; if we had sex, he would crush me under his weight. I stood up. He waved his hand, "Do not worry, I will not hurt you. I will not rape you. Sit down, sit down on the divan."

I sat down, pressed my legs together, hands curled in my lap. He gazed at me, an unblinking gaze, impenetrable, but not, on the surface at least, unfriendly. He wiped at the sweat on his forehead. Sweat gleamed in the folds of his enormous belly.

I pushed my legs tighter together. I did not want to have sex with this man. If worst came to worst, I could try to kill him. One of my earrings could be opened and pulled out; it would automatically straighten out, into a weapon – a miniature razor-sharp blade: enough, perhaps, to cut his throat. I began to wonder, should I kill him, and then set off to explore the castle, to find James? But they would certainly immediately know what I had done, and they would be able to trace my movements through the electronic tag on my collar. It obviously transmitted my coordinates to the security control room in real-time, all the time. And there were guards everywhere, and I had no idea where James was. I had to find another way.

Kaleem was looking at me with what looked almost like fondness. "Misty," he said, "That is your name, is it not, Misty." He walked away from me, and looked down at the blonde. She looked up and uttered something between a growl and a purr. She kissed his foot.

"Yeah, I'm Misty, Misty Hoyt."

He crouched down and stroked the blonde's hair. I was amazed that he could crouch. He was so fat. He turned towards me. "I bought her from Sergei. I paid good money, a great deal of money. She is mine now." He stood up and lumbered towards me. I wondered if I was about to be bought or sold. And I wondered at the woman lying there like a pet. A violinist? An American? I wanted to know her story. She was gazing at me; she licked her lips. I took a deep breath and I perched on the edge of the divan, legs squeezed together, the leash coiled like a snake in my lap, waiting – wondering if I should pretend to fool with one of my dangling bits of metal, and then, pull it out and skewer his jugular. Baluchi was not visibly aroused, not at all aroused. Or so it seemed.

He lowered himself to his knees and gazed at me with a strange look. "You are a work of art, Misty," he said.

"Ah," I said, licking my lips, "Yeah, well, that's very kind of you."

"And you are, Misty, as that fanatic Khalid Nassir said, an idol, and a goddess – a return perhaps of the primitive mother goddess who preceded all the gods."

"Well, well," I said, "that's very nice; I'm mean, my being a goddess and all." I hoped I was not up against an iconoclast like Khalid Nassir himself, who, having called me a goddess, would decide it was his duty to destroy me, to cast me out of life and into the wilderness or into the darkness of death. Like Queen Jezebel, murdered by the thugs sent by that jerk Elijah, and whose body, if I remember correctly, was thrown out a window or cut up by said thugs and fed to dogs or something like that. I don't like prophets. But, you know, murderers, if successful, get to write history.

Kaleem laid his hands on my thighs, but lightly, his two big pudgy strong hands, just touching, just caressing my skin, as if he wanted to make sure I was real – as if all the brightly tattooed skin was tangible, as if it were something that could be probed and possessed. There was a strange soft light in his eyes. "You are a painted idol. That is true, absolutely true."

"Hmm," I muttered. I put a hand, gently, on his hand. He nudged my legs open. I let him. He had tears in his eyes.

The blonde sat up, arms around her knees, and watched us.

"Are you okay?" I touched Baluchi's face. His bald shaven head gleamed.

"Yes, yes, Misty. I am entirely fine. But I must confess, Misty ..." He hesitated and licked his lips and gazed straight into my eyes.

"Yeah?" I smiled. "You can tell me anything."

"I am not a man," he cleared his throat. "I am not a man."

"Oh?" I took a deep breath. "What do you mean, Kaleem, you are not a man?"

He lowered his big head to my thighs and began to kiss my legs, my tattooed legs. The blonde blinked at us; it was like we were being watched by a cat, lofty, indifferent, and alien. I felt the wetness of Baluchi's fleshy lips and his hot tears against my skin. I said nothing. I caressed his head, the smooth naturally bald part, and the raspy stubble where he had to shave it. His kisses were soft and somehow respectful. I felt almost tenderness for this merchant of death.

"I am not a man," he said, his voice muffled.

I leaned forward and kissed the crown of his head. He looked up at me. "I am not a man," he repeated.

I looked down at him and caressed his head, and I said, "Hey, there. Shush, now, shush now, little baby."

The blonde blinked, wide-eyed, she put her hand to her mouth, as if in surprise or awe.

Baluchi's eyes stared up at me; they were liquid and dark, as if he were about to cry. A sliver line of tears had formed at the rim of his eyes, his eyelashes, long and thick like those of a woman, had little silver beads of tears. His eyes looked as if they were circled in kohl.

He looked down. "There was a feud in our village, Misty. And my family had dishonored another family, or so people said. So people died. The feud was deadly. It was going to consume all of us on both sides. And in the end, it was said that there must be a sacrifice to end the feud and to end the bloodshed. And the sacrifice was chosen. It was to be me. And my father said, 'He is my only son. I do not want him to die.' And the chief of the other clan said, 'Then he will not die. But he will no longer be a man.' And so it was agreed. And so they took me outside, and they took a knife, and they plunged the knife into the fire until it glowed red, and then they held me down and held my legs apart and then they did it. You understand what it means, do you not?" His eyes again stared at me, as if he were tempting me to laugh, to mock him, to judge him.

I nodded. "Yeah, Kaleem, I understand," I whispered. The blonde was still sitting, cross-legged, watching us, soft, sparkling animal intelligence in her eyes. I wondered if she had been driven mad by what had been done to her. I wondered if Baluchi had been driven mad by what had been done to him.

"You and I, Misty," he wiped at his forehead, "you and I are outsiders, monsters. When I saw you, I knew you would understand. Your eyes are so intelligent. You are not what you seem, Misty Hoyt, you are much greater than what you seem."

"Yeah. That's very nice, but I wouldn't say that." I didn't catch any second meaning in his compliment, for that is what it seemed to be, a compliment; but, still, any suggestion that I was "not what I seemed" made me nervous, a little trickle of fear and sweat rippled and dripped down my spine.

"May I add to your splendor," Kaleem asked.

"Well ..."

He pulled out from under the divan several lengths of sparkling chain with clips on their ends.

"I don't know about this," I said.

"It won't hurt."

I sighed and rolled my eyes. "Okay."

He attached the small chains – snapping the clips shut – so that they linked the ring in my collar to the nipple rings and then to the labia rings. His fingers were large, but surprisingly deft and quick.

"Done," he said.

"Hmm." I looked down at myself.

"You are now truly a goddess." He sat back slightly, and beamed at me. The lamps reflected off his baldness, off his belly.

"Well, thank you, Kaleem, I guess." I wasn't sure these new chains were safe, but really they didn't make much difference, just added, I guess, to the stigmata and symbolism of being a fallen goddess.

"I can offer you the whole world," Kaleem said, "I can offer you anything you desire."

"The world, Kaleem," I leaned forward kissed him on the forehead, "That is real nice, Kaleem, the whole world, but –"

CHAPTER 6 – EXECUTION

Someone unlocked the door from the outside and slid it open. Sergei Platonov appeared. "I am sorry to interrupt your confession, Kaleem, but I do need a word with Misty." He smiled at me.

Kaleem wanted to keep me. I could see that. He looked at me, sheepishly and then he turned to Sergei, "But Misty and I were only beginning our little talk ..."

The blonde stood up. She glanced at me – fear in her eyes. It almost seemed from her expression that she wanted to protect me, that she was fearful for me, not for herself.

I could see Sergei was not going to take no for an answer and I had already begun to wonder if Kaleem confession was a prelude to murder; if, having told me of his castration, he would perhaps take his revenge for the wrong done to him by strangling me or slitting my throat or worse. Goddesses are often sacrificed, are they not? Or maybe he really did see me as an understanding fellow soul, a fellow freak, a fellow outcast, someone to whom he could talk, to whom he could lay it all bare. After all, I did look like somebody who would do and accept anything. My tattoos and piercings and my nakedness were my badges. I was a totem, a painted idol, and, perhaps, I could be his goddess. Yes, I think that was it; he wanted to travel the world with a fellow exile, a trophy of abjection, a fellow outcast and scapegoat. He would keep me as a pet, a shield. And then, too, maybe Kaleem's wound was the reason he wanted to midwife the end of the world, the death of millions. Maybe he hated himself so much he wanted to destroy the world and all the creatures in it.

Sergei, his smile now of steel, and his eyes shining with a strange glassy brightness, raised his hand. "No buts, no hesitation. I shall talk to you later, Kaleem."

Kaleem bowed, ceding to the inevitable.

As I walked past the blonde, she touched my arm with her hand. I saw tears in her eyes, her lips parted, as if she wished to say something, but only a mute breath and a sigh came out.

We exited Baluchi's apartment, and Sergei closed the door behind him. Outside the room, several of Sergei's bodyguards were waiting. They all looked very serious.

"I think we shall go for a little walk." Sergei took my leash, clenched it in his fist, and held onto it. He did not look at me. We walked down the stairs, and out through the great baronial hall, the fireplace was still burning, and I saw Betty in her Plexiglas cage all curled up, and I imagined she had eaten her rabbits and was happily digesting and dreaming whatever dreams pythons dream.

We came out of the entrance. SUVs and armored cars were lined up, guards and drivers and militiamen and militiawomen standing around, smoking, gossiping.

We were joined by Sonia and Tracy and six of Sergei's guards. It became a whole procession, and, for some reason, I seemed to be at the center of it. This was not good. We left the castle and the SUVs and militia behind, and we walked down the gravel drive towards the large bunker-like building that was built into the cliff. It was about 200 meters away. I thought this was probably not good news on the one hand, since I seemed to be in some sort of deep trouble; but, on the other hand, it was quite possibly good news – if there were any secrets here, they were probably in the bunker; and if James was still alive and a prisoner, he was probably in the bunker.

But we walked beyond the bunker and down a path beside a mud-filled ditch. Up above was a platform with an anti-aircraft missile launcher, and beyond the muddy path, there was another, further bunker, even larger than the first. The rain had given way to a soft mist, and the ditch was brim-full of thick clayey mud that reflected the security lights and the lights from the castle. We stopped beside the muddy ditch.

"I think we should do this with a certain formality," said Sergei.

"Whatever you think appropriate, Master," said Sonia.

Sergei pulled a pair of handcuffs from his belt. "Turn around, Misty, put your hands together, behind you back."

"Is this some sort of new game?" I blinked at him.

"Naughty, naughty girl," he smiled; it was not a friendly smile; he slurred his words; he was drunk, or so it seemed.

"Do as he says, Misty." Sonia seemed excessively serious, her bright blue eyes focussing on me, her mouth set in a straight, unfriendly line; all the hints of playfulness and flirtation had disappeared. Tracy stood back, with the guards. She seemed wary – and frightened.

"Yes, Mistress. Yes, Master." I couldn't fight everybody. So I turned around, and offered my wrists, behind my back, thrust together.

I felt the handcuffs slip around my wrists, tighten, and then I felt them click shut, locked into place. I was effectively shackled. Well, I knew from the beginning this was a suicide mission, so ...

"Turn around and face me," Sergei again slurred his words. From all I'd read, he was supposed to be very good at holding his liquor. Why was he drunk? How had that happened?

I turned around and faced him. He towered over me. "Well,

little waif, dear little Misty Hoyt, you try to fool me, do you?" Sergei reached out. His hand was on my face; he played with the nose-ring; he caressed my cheek. He put his hand on my scarlet topknot. He could easily twist my head, snap my neck, and that would be that. "You are a very naughty girl."

"What did I do, Master?"

"Ha, ha, the waif calls me 'Master.' I believe that is called irony, or is it chutzpah, or is it both?" He let go of my topnotch and coiled my leash around his fist.

"I would say both," said Sonia, staring at me steadily.

Sergei pulled me to him; the leash was curled even tighter around his fist. "This little tag on your collar, Misty, you know what it is?"

"Yes," I said, and a horrible idea began to dawn.

"What is it, Misty? Explain."

"It transmits my position. It tells you where I am. But I haven't done anything wrong," I said.

"Of course you haven't, of course, you haven't." He patted me on the shoulder, and he caressed my breast and touched the nipple-ring, tugging at it. He could rip it off in a second, and half my nipple with it.

"Good. I haven't done anything wrong," I said. I could hardly speak; sweat dribbled down my back; the air was heavy; the smell of the plants and the earth and the fecund liquid clay was overwhelming. Every sensation was as if I were feeling and sensing it for the first time – and this might be the last time. Life was telling me that it was too sweet to be tossed away.

"But the thing is, Misty." He touched the little tag with his fingers, and then he touched my lips, running his finger along my lips, touching the nose ring, playing with it. "The thing is, Misty, that the little tag transmits your position. Like a little radio station."

I nodded.

166

"And Sonia noticed something about the little transmissions, didn't you, Sonia?"

"Yes, yes, I did."

"Sonia has been very useful to me. You remember that Italian girl, Laura?"

"Yes." Sonia smiled as if the memory gave her pleasure.

"And you remember how you uncovered that Israeli agent?"

"Yes."

"And you shot him, which was very nice of you."

"Yes, I shot him." Sonia said it deadpan, "in the back of the neck. I made him kneel, and I shot him."

"And, when we had to torture that Russian agent, you were very effective, Sonia. I liked the razor and the electric tongs in particular."

Sonia just nodded. Behind her, the guards shuffled. Some of them looked eager; some of them looked uneasy. Their eyes were bright; they had been drinking. They seemed dazed and drunk. Tracy stared at me deadpan, but when she blinked, I saw her eyes were wet. The lights from the castle and reflected from its walls, lit up the scene, sharp shadows, and bright splotches, like a movie set.

"When Sonia checked the signal from the little tag, and she is very thorough, my Sonia, she noticed something, and she asked me to tell the people in the control room up there to check on the signal from your tag. Sonia suspected that there might be some interference, didn't you, Sonia?"

"Yes, yes, I did."

"And the people who listen to that signal, well, who monitor it, who watch it on a map, they did, in fact, notice something."

"They noticed something?" I felt myself go numb all over. My skin was prickly with fear, beaded in sweat; I tried to control my breathing.

"Yes, indeed. They noticed interference."

167

"Ah, interference," I said, "Interference from what?"

"Tut, tut!" Sergei raised his finger. "You are an intelligent girl, Misty; actually, from what I understand, you are a genius."

I just stared at him.

"The interference was intriguing. So the lads who work for me, just upstairs, they investigated, and you can't guess, I'm sure you can't guess what they discovered." His gaze wavered, as if he were about to forget the question he had just asked and the answer.

I blinked at him. "No," I said, in barely a whisper, though I tried to make it sound bold and brazen; my throat was dry. "I can't guess."

"They discovered another little radio station that was interfering with their little radio station." He blinked. He had slurred the last words.

"Oh."

He steadied himself. "And so they listened in a little bit. Not much chatter, but we were able to trace a signal, and we did get a few bits and pieces, and we deciphered those bits and pieces, and we learned about a very interesting person – Doctor Gwendoline Clermont."

I said nothing, then "Who's Doctor Gwendoline Clermont?" And I was thinking: Damnation! I knew that gizmo would give me away. Cutting-edge technology – my eye!

"Don't treat me like a fool, Gwendoline. Where is it?"

I decided there was nothing to be gained by playing a silly game. "In my left ear, it's a small bump, flesh-colored."

"Sonia, it's your discovery, will you do the honors?"

"Yes, master." Sonia reached up, and with the point of her fingernail, she soon found it and detached it, being very gentle, I noticed, and she removed it and handed it to Sergei.

He looked at it, staring for a long time. He was swaying a bit, I noticed, but he caught himself, and said, "Interesting." He curled his fingers around it. For a moment, I thought he was going to drop it and crush it underfoot. But he slipped it into his pocket. "Perhaps we can entertain your friends in Paris, Gwendoline. I'm sure they will enjoy what is coming next."

"Yes, this is always the good part," said Sonia. Her eyes seemed very bright. I thought: She's on drugs; she's on drugs so she can do this; so she can kill me.

I shifted on my feet. The handcuffs pinioning my arms behind my back were uncomfortably tight. They were sure to leave a mark on my wrists, which was annoying, but not of any importance, really, not now. Maybe the time for vanity – even Misty Hoyt's vanity was over.

"Turn around and kneel," Sergei said.

I glanced at them both, Sergei and Sonia: so this was it; the end of the road, the end of the line. Look them in the eye, take a deep breath, and then die, die with dignity, I guess, if you can manage it. When you are dead, you are dead; it'll probably be quick. Well, I hoped it would be quick.

"Please turn around and face the ditch, Misty." Sonia nodded

"Okay." I turned and faced the ditch.

"Kneel."

"Okay." Kneeling on the slippery muddy ground while in stilettos and with my arms pinioned behind my back was tricky. I started to kneel but wobbled and almost slipped. Sonia took me by the shoulder and gently pushed me to my knees. My knees sank deep into thick warm muddy clay. "Thank you, Sonia," I said.

"You are welcome, Misty," she said.

"She's Gwendoline," said Sergei, "Gwendoline Claremont."

"I prefer the name I knew her by," said Sonia.

"Fair enough," said Sergei. "We shall all remember Misty – and how charming she was. Misty, our dear highly decorated Misty Hoyt!"

I tried to keep myself upright. The squishy mud was slippery; I could easily fall flat on my face. That would not be very dignified. I tried to steady myself, and I thought of James. Now I would never be able to save him. I wondered where he was, if he was still alive, if they had hurt him, how badly they had hurt him. I wondered what he would think – how he would suffer – when he knew I was dead. Would he ever know I tried to save him? I blinked. My eyes filled with tears. Damnation! I do not want to be weak! Damnation! I wanted to blow my nose. But, of course, I couldn't. Snot dripped from the nose ring – not very dignified. The handcuffs were tight, cutting off circulation. I wiggled my fingers.

Nobody said anything. Kneeling, I waited. So, this is the way it ends: A bullet in the back of the neck and the body falls into a muddy ditch. What a waste of an expensive education! And – what about Kate and Claudia and Martine and Philip and all the seminars I was supposed to give and the things I could still discover? Now, there would be nothing, just darkness. I blinked and looked around. The night air was heavy, redolent, and rich, with smells and sensations. Being alive is an infinitely pleasant experience. In a few seconds, for me, it would be over. My universe would disappear. Basically, for myself, I had no complaints – I had had a fantastic life.

"Do you want to execute her, Sonia, or shall I?"

"I shall do the deed if you wish, Master," Sonia said.

Anger surged up, and, inexplicably, since she had never offered to be my ally, I felt betrayed. I wanted to look Sonia in the eye. I tried to glance over my shoulder, but all I glimpsed was Sergei, handing her his pistol. "There you are, then." It was a Luger P08 I noticed, an antique, a collector's item. Very stylish!

I heard her check the magazine, quite effectively, skilfully, like in the movies. It made the deadly clicking sound, hard metal on hard metal.

"My pleasure," said Sonia.

I looked away, and I waited. I looked down at the glossy mud, reflecting the moonlight. I felt the cool metal muzzle of the Luger press gently against the nape of my neck. Suddenly, I was calm. In that instant, the moon appeared from behind a ragtag reef of dark clouds; the moonlight shone on the mud; the smells of the earth and of the stone walls and the plants were rich after the rain – a drunken pleasure. I breathed it all in. It was sweet, suddenly overwhelmingly sweet, with an infinite suggestion of perfumes and nuance. Oh, but life was good, and I had had a wonderful and privileged life. If I die now, the only thing I will regret is not saving James, not seeing him, not knowing ... And I will regret not having more time with my friends, Martine, Kate, Claudia, Philip, my grandfather ... my students ...

Sonia moved the muzzle up and down the nape of my neck. It tickled. "I do love all these tattoos," she said.

"Yes, your friend Misty is a work of art. Perhaps you can keep the skin, as a memento," said Sergei.

"Yes, of course, a true challenge for a taxidermist," Sonia moved the muzzle up and down the back of my naked tattooed skull, "A work of art, our little Misty."

"But she is also a spy, and ..."

"On the other hand," Sonia said, "Alive, our darling Misty Hoyt might be more useful than dead."

The muzzle stopped moving. It was pressed tight against my skin, right at the top of the nape of my neck, where the spine joins the skull, at the occipital bone.

"What are you thinking, my dear Sonia?" Sergei was slurring his speech more than ever. I glanced over my shoulder: how much had he drunk? He glanced at me; his eyes were blurry, watery circles in the moonlight.

Sonia laid a hand on my shoulder and began caressing the

nape of my neck with the Luger's muzzle. "Your guest, you tell me, has not responded to treatment, Sergei. But Misty may provide the leverage you need."

"Of course, of course," Sergei slurred, "That is a possibility."

"Misty – or Gwendoline – is his lover."

"Yes."

"She is his absolute passion."

"So they say, yes, that's what they say." Sergei hiccupped.

"So, her arrival is serendipitous, a gift from the heavens." Sonia still had her hand on my shoulder, and she was now holding the Luger steady, its muzzle in precisely the right place – instant death.

"Perhaps you are right." Sergio crouched next to me. His boots squished heavily in the mud. If he wasn't careful, he'd get his trousers dirty. I realized that, yes, my first perception had been right: he was drunk, very drunk. His eyes were too bright; his breath stank of liquor. "Still, I think she should die – or at least suffer. He put his hand on my shoulder, and he kneaded my muscles. "Feeling a little tense, are we, Misty?"

I nodded.

"Well, then," he laughed and pushed me forward. I slid and toppled face down into the mud of the ditch; with my arms behind my back, I couldn't break the fall. Sergei leaned forward and pushed my face deep into the mud and held it there, his big hand pressing on the back of my skull. My nose was crushed. My mouth was under the soup-like mud. I couldn't see, and I couldn't breathe. I held my breath. I struggled, twisting this way and that, thrashing desperately. My heart hammered in my ears. I could hear – as if through an ocean of glue – Sergei's laughter. He was going to suffocate me, drown me. When I did breathe, I would breathe in pure mud; then, he could let me suffocate, choke to death. Panic rose. I would have to struggle, to try to free myself. But how could I, with my arms pinioned behind my back? I kicked, trying to push him back.

Finally, he let go, and pulled me up, turning me over, so I was lying on my back, in the deep mud, my arms pinned under me. My eyes were full of mud. I blinked, tried to stare at him, tried to see. Everything was a muddy, tangled blur. Sergei crouched close to me, his boots and trousers and chest smeared in mud. "Roll in it, little tattooed sow, roll in it, you bitch, you waif-bitch, you self-mutilating waif-bitch."

I gasped for air. I had to blow out and sneeze to clear my nostrils. The nose-ring made it harder. I could hardly see. I was covered in thick sticky dripping clay.

Sergei kicked me, lifted me up with his boot, and turned me over. I rolled deeper into the deep muck. I flopped back and forth like a fish out of water, trying to lever myself out of the ditch. Pinioned as I was, it was impossible. I stared up at him.

"Roll, grovel." He grinned.

Behind him, the guards were laughing, clapping. Black and silver silhouettes, their teeth were bright in the moonlight.

He turned to Sonia. "You too, my dear slave, help her, cover her in mud, and you too, and cover yourself in filth. And you, Tracy, crawl, crawl in the mud."

"Really, Sergei," Sonia said. I could see she was annoyed.

"Do it! Do it." He hiccupped.

The guards took up the chant. "Do it! Do it!"

Sonia handed Sergei the Luger and crouched next to the ditch. She tried to pull me up. I was too slippery and too far away. She leaned forward.

"No, go in, join your friend, Misty." Sergei was now enjoying himself. "And you too, Tracy – grovel in the mud."

"Sergei, you are a real bastard." Sonia stuck out her tongue. Cautiously she lowered herself into the ditch, joining me in the abject display. She crouched on her knees, and she smeared mud all over me, though I didn't need it, I was already totally covered in the stuff. Her touch was surprisingly gentle. Then, looking straight at me, and glancing up at Sergei, she smeared mud over herself and lay down and wiggled so that she could cover her back.

Tracy slipped gracefully sideways into the ditch and covered herself in mud. She plunged her head under, swished around, and then, slowly, on her belly, she crawled out, dripping with the stuff. Even her ponytail was covered in it, a clotted bouncy little gray appendage. On hands and knees, she blinked up at Sergei, her beautiful face a muddy mask. "Are you satisfied, Master?"

"Yes, yes."

The men cheered. Most of them seemed even drunker than Sergei. This could be dangerous, I thought. They despise us because we are women, and we are extra vulnerable because we are naked; if they became too excited, I figured they wouldn't distinguish between me and Sonia and Tracy. We'd all be fair game.

"Let us applaud our lady friends – and Little Misty, too, who is not a friend, but who has put on a very good show." Sergei grinned down at us and clapped.

Sonia and Tracy helped me stagger out of the mud. Tracy cleared the mud from my nostrils, from the nose-ring, and from my eyes. At last, I could breathe, and I could see. The chains Kaleem had added to my costume were heavy and dripping with mud, and made me even more self-conscious, but they were not particularly uncomfortable.

CHAPTER 7 – DOUBLE-CROSS

"Good, my obedient children, now I wish to show you something."

The mud was drying already and getting crusty. Some of it was in my eyes. My lips were coated. It was squishy between my legs. Looking at Sonia and Tracy, I would have smiled, if the situation had been less dangerous. Sonia's face was a mask of drying mud, which made her large blue eyes even larger and more extravagantly blue. Tracy was a perfect statue of mud, petite and voluptuous, emerging from some sophomore mud wrestling match in Texas, the ones they used to have in the grand old macho chauvinist patriarchal fetishistic days where anything goes – or used to.

It began to rain. I turned my face up to catch the drops. It was a downpour, warm, overwhelming, a true flood. It would wash some of the mud away. I blinked, and just let it wash over me. I noticed that Tracy and Sonia had done the same.

"Keep walking, sluts," Sergei prodded Sonia with the Luger. He was still holding my leash, leading me like a tame, or maybe not so tame, animal. I wondered if there was some way to get rid of the handcuffs and free myself. But how the devil would I be able to do that?

We walked back up to the main pathway and then down into a shallow valley, and then we came to the farther bunker; I saw now that it was truly buried in the hillside, with only the front part of the giant building sticking out. Four guards stood outside; they seemed sober. One of them saluted; he was looking at Sonia, not Sergei.

The rain stopped as quickly as it had begun. The moon appeared. Now we were just streaked with mud, not coated in it; we were a bedraggled sight, Tracy, Sonia, and me, naked, wet, muddy, and silvered over with the light of the moon.

The guards opened a large iron door, and we were led into the bunker; the door shut behind us with a hollow clang; Sergei prodded us, and we went down a spiral metal staircase.

Sergei tugged on my leash and then turned to face me. "Here, we have something you will be very eager to see, since you can still see, my freakish little Misty, or shall I call you Gwendoline?"

Sonia, who was right behind me, put her hand to my waist for some reason, and ran it down to my buttocks, and slapped my muddy buttock three sharp times – slap, slap, slap. Was she on my side or was she just taunting me?

We came to the bottom of the spiral staircase, and there was another door in a wall of armed concrete. Three guards stood outside the door. Sergei gestured, and they opened it. And it closed behind us.

Inside was another metal staircase. It led down, deeper into the heart of the bunker, or into the cliff. It took us down five more floors; now we were far below ground. It was awkward, walking down all these steel stairs on stilettos, my arms pinioned behind my back, and being tugged at by the leash.

I looked around. The walls were of reinforced concrete; they looked very thick. There were armored doors that could be closed automatically. This was an extremely deep bunker, armed against aerial attack, or bombs, or even ground assaults.

We had come to what seemed to be the lowest level. There was one large door and a corridor leading off to one side, perhaps to a storage area. "You go back upstairs, all of you wait outside," Sergei said to the two guards who had accompanied us. "I want our muddy ladies and our friend Misty to help me with something." Sergei pushed a button. The door opened. And we entered, leaving the guards behind, all except one whom Sergei signaled with a wave of his hand should follow us.

As the big armored door swung shut behind us, I looked around: we were in a large, high-ceilinged room, with concrete walls and metal beams across the roof and metal and concrete columns holding the roof up. It was like the interior of a giant-sized bunker or underground warehouse. The neon tubes bathed the whole place in a ghostly cold light. It had reinforced walls, with arched alcoves like in an ancient dungeon, or an infernal parody of a cathedral; there were no windows or openings to anywhere that I could see – just the one giant armored door through which we'd come.

We walked past a steel column, and I saw him – James.

I took in my breath, and almost fell down, tottering, pinioned on the stilettoes, but, somehow, I steadied myself. Sonia pressed her hand in the small of my back, helping steady me.

James was hanging from a wall, naked and bloodied, blindfolded, chained spread-eagled, crucified, against a wall of steel and naked cement; his arms were manacled to a steel crossbar, and his legs were spread and manacled to another steel crossbar. His chest was crisscrossed with whip and slash marks and dark red burns. Blood dripped from the side of his mouth. His nakedness revealed burn marks on his thighs and belly, striped like a zebra, and around his testicles. The blindfold was soaked in blood, with dried dark, crusty trickles down his cheeks. Had they gouged or burned out his eyes? I held my breath. I choked back my rage. Oh, I will kill Sergei. I will eviscerate him; I will tear out his intestines; I will make him die in bloody agony. I will kill them all, slowly, totally, each and every one of them.

Sitting at a small steel table in front of James was a man who had a computer and with an array of instruments – whips, electrical tongs, knives and scalpels, and what looked like a Taser. He must be the torturer and the interrogator. He was wearing a black suit, with black shoes, and a white shirt, open at the collar; he looked rather like an Iranian political leader; when he turned around to stare at us, I saw that he was pale, pasty-faced, had circles under his desperate-looking eyes, and had unshaven stubble of perhaps three or four days – I understood: He'd been working on James, probably almost twenty-four hours a day since James was captured. He had exhausted himself trying to break James. Next to his table was a small brazier, a fire burning, with tongs resting on it, their points glowing a fiery red.

I looked back. The one guard who had followed us stood impassive near the closed and locked door, his arms crossed, with his submachine gun hanging by his side.

Sonia stood very still, pressed close beside me.

"James," said Sergei, in a loud, theatrical voice, as if talking to a deaf person. "I have a guest for you."

James lifted his head slightly. He licked his lips, but he said nothing.

"You may not recognize her, if you saw her, James."

James coughed, but said nothing. A drool of bloody saliva dripped from the side of his mouth.

"James has not been very talkative, Gwendoline," Sergei said, in the same loud voice.

James twitched; he moved his head as if trying to see – trying to see if I was really here, if the name "Gwendoline" corresponded to reality.

"Yes, I'm okay, James, I'm here," I said, "I'm really here."

"Go to him, Misty, go to James. Let us remove his blindfold. Let us let him see what you have become."

I stared at Sergei – was this another part of his cruel game. They would take off his blindfold, and I would see empty bloodies sockets, nothing, where once there were eyes.

"Come, I'll do it," Sonia said, she moved close to James.

I walked up close to James. "I love you, James," I said, "I will always love you." I wanted to prepare him for the new me, but if he were blind, then he wouldn't see the new me, he wouldn't know. If he were blind, I would dedicate my life to him; I would love him as nobody had ever been loved. I would love him to the end of time. I didn't say anything.

Gently, delicately, Sonia removed the blindfold. James' eyes were rimmed with blood, but he had eyes; one eye was closed, and the other eye seemed bright and feverish. That one eye fixed on me. It was preternaturally bright. I saw doubt at first, then a flash of recognition. He bared his teeth. Blood dripped from the side of his mouth.

I glanced at Sonia; she nodded, as if telling me to go ahead, go to James. I didn't know what to think of her, so friendly, so warm, and yet just a half an hour ago she had discovered the bloody earpiece transmitter, and revealed who I was, and condemned me to death, and, at the muddy ditch, she had been eager to kill me – or so it seemed.

James, with his single eye, again focused on me, and I saw the eye go wide in shock and then focus again, in recognition. "Gwen?" he whispered.

"Yes, it's me." I came close. And I leaned up, and I kissed him.

"Gwen – what have they done to you?"

"I did it to myself, my love. It is – it was – my disguise."

"Oh, Gwen!" He smiled. Then he laughed. "Oh, Gwen – you are crazy, and you are a genius!"

"You like, Master?" I blinked at him, smiled, and bowed as much as my pinioned arms and stilettos would allow; I wanted to seize him in my arms and cover him in kisses, but pinioned as I was, I could only bow, and then touch my lips to his chest.

"I love you, Gwen. You have surpassed yourself." He coughed and spat up some blood. I yearned to wipe it from his mouth.

Sonia stepped forward with a cloth and wiped his lips and dampened his forehead. "Thank you." He glanced at her and blinked; it was clear he had never seen her before.

"You are welcome, James," she said.

Sergei was rubbing his hands together. "James, since she has been here, Gwendoline ..."

"Misty," said Sonia.

Sergei turned and glared at Sonia. "Well, yes, Misty. You see, James, Gwendoline re-baptized herself as Misty, Misty Hoyt, which is a dreadfully corny name, as part of her disguise. Well, Misty – or Gwendoline – has been demonstrating her sexual prowess. And I think we should let her give a little demonstration."

James said nothing, then he closed his eye – in a quick wink and nodded: I knew what it meant: Okay, Gwen, anything you have to do, anything you do, is okay with me. Besides, we have to gain time.

I licked my lips and smiled at him and nodded.

Sergei was rubbing his hands and more and more slurring his words, and this was stranger and stranger because he definitely had a reputation – as I had read in the intelligence briefings – of being able to hold his drink. "Let us have a little fun. Let us see the two of these ladies here make love. This will amuse James, I am sure. Tracy – you will supervise."

Sergei sat me down on a stool, my arms pinioned behind my back.

"Kneel, Sonia, kneel. Down on your knees!"

"Yes, Master." She knelt and bowed her head. Like me, like Tracy, Sonia was still streaked in mud, disheveled, and even in this horrible moment, even after she had almost executed me, I couldn't resist thinking how beautiful she was. But there was something about her which I didn't understand – the strange mixture of cruelty and ruthlessness combined with tenderness and sensitivity.

Sergei grinned. "Give Misty some pleasure – the last pleasure she will ever feel. Make her squeal in ecstasy!"

So, he was going to kill me, or, more likely, torture and maim me to put pressure on James.

Sonia glanced at James – he gazed at her steadily and nodded – and then she looked up at me.

"Tracy!" Sergei commanded, "Take the whip. Prod them if you need to. You are the instructor, Tracy. Tell Sonia what to do."

Tracy went to the interrogator's desk. He had continued to sit there, impassive, watching the proceedings, glancing at the three naked mud-streaked women, but looking exhausted and bored. His tools were lined up on his desk beside the computer. He glanced at Tracy sleepily, and, with half-closed eyes, he handed her a whip.

Tracy took it, curled it tight, stepped forward, coughed, and cleared her throat. "Sonia! Caress Misty's breasts, please and kiss her breasts, and lick your way down to her belly." She coughed again.

Sonia touched my breasts, with their rings and Kaleem's chains, and she licked her way and kissed her way around the muddy rings and the chains, and she kissed my belly and then, bending lower, she kissed my naked, tattooed pubis.

"Yes, yes," said Sergei, "Go on, go on!" He glanced at Tracy.

"Now, Sonia, give Misty pleasure, true pleasure," said Tracy. She was curling and uncurling the whip.

Sonia glanced up at me, her eyebrow arched, and she lowered her head and kissed and opened my labia, already liquid, and still muddy, and her tongue entered me, and she began to caress my clitoris with the tip and the surface of her tongue, licking kisses, and kissing licks, and sucking too, gently. Sensing her cheeks pressing against the rings in my labia, and the chains – which tugged at my nipples – was very strange. Pinioned as I was, I felt utterly enslaved and helpless.

Sergei walked back and forth, rubbing his hands. "Igor, why don't you add a little spice to the show. Giving James a few electric shocks and perhaps a bit of acid to add to the flavor."

I started. I was going to scream, "No!"

Sonia bit me, pressing with her teeth, just slightly. Ouch! I looked down. She shook her head and mouthed at me, "No, not yet!"

I thought: Yes, okay, we are entirely in Sergei's power; let's play for time, as James suggested – even if he's going to suffer. I gritted my teeth – and I wondered about the 'No, not yet.' What sort of game was Sonia playing?

"Tracy!" Sergei glared at Tracy.

"Back to work, Sonia," said Tracy. She prodded Sonia with the handle of the whip. As she did so, Tracy stared at me and nodded. What she meant, I don't know. She and I had been lovers, just a few hours ago, and there was a connection, definitely, but what sort of connection was it, and what help would it be?

Sonia began to kiss me, licking and sucking and licking and caressing with her tongue and her lips. This was both a game and not a game. It was exciting and horrifying. And James, crucified and helpless, was watching, as I, his pierced, shaved, and tattooed whore, was being pleasured by a beautiful naked blonde. I shuddered. I came in a whimpering, sobbing delicate little orgasm that rippled through my whole body. Sonia eased up slowly, she caressed my thighs, played with the rings and chains, and she stared up at me in an almost amorous way. There was a sizzling sound – we turned to look.

The man at the desk had taken an instrument that looked like tongs. It was attached to a long electric cord. He applied the thing to James' testicles. Sparks leaped. There was a smell of burning flesh. James lurched, but he didn't cry out. His mouth was fixed in a grimace. He closed his eyes.

"Oh God," I breathed out. "Sergei Platonov, I will kill you!" I said it between my teeth. Sonia shot me a warning glance and tapped on my thigh.

"You see what a whore your woman is, James." Sergei said, his words coming out slurred and vague, "She cavorts and has orgasms, while you are being tortured. What a little whore she is." Sergei came over to me and closed his fist on my topknot. I grimaced, waiting for the pain. But he just played with it a bit, and then he let go. "Now a little acid," he said.

Igor took a small vessel and squirted a liquid onto James' chest. A hissing sound. Smoke rose. James didn't cry out. He grimaced. He was gritting his teeth.

I trembled. I was about to spring up.

Sonia grasped my thigh in a tight grip, tightening and loosening – it seemed like some sort of signal, again something like, "Don't do anything, wait! Just wait!" She stared up at me and bit her lip. Her eyes narrowed and seemed to flare – in anger and hatred.

James opened his eyes, stared straight at me, and half closed one eye in a wink, the corner of his mouth turning up in a smile.

The torturer picked up a whip, a thick black thing, metal-and-leather twined together.

He smashed it across James' chest, twice, three times. Blood welled up in thick welts. I boiled. Tears filled my eyes.

"Now, let us stop playing games." Sergei was standing over us. I twisted my head back, so I could look up at him. He stared down at me. I blinked.

"Move away, Sonia," he said. She looked up at him, an expression of terror in her face, the first time I had seen her look frightened. I swiveled around on the stool, my body twisted back, with my hands locked behind my back. Sergei continued to stare down at me.

"We called you Misty, Misty Hoyt." Sergei slurred and grinned and touched my lips. He crouched in front of me. He played with my nose ring and with my nipple rings. "We took you in, off the street, out of the rain and storm. We clasped you to our bosom. And what did you do? You betrayed us. You are not sweet innocent lost Misty Hoyt, not a sweet vagabond tattooed waif. No, you are Gwendoline Clermont, the famous beautiful libertine – Gwendoline! You are known everywhere." He clasped my face between his hands. His breath was heavy with alcohol, and his gaze was blurred.

I thought he was going to twist my head and break my neck. But he continued his speech. "And look at her now! Behold this great beauty! She is a freak – the once beautiful Gwendoline – a monster. She destroyed her beauty for love. It is a sweet story. Each time she looks in a mirror, she must feel horror at what she has done." He let my face go. "So, there it sits, on this little stool, this monster, this fearful monster – afraid of her image in the mirror. You see what she has done for you, James – she has destroyed her beauty. For you, James, she has turned monster – and is horrified each time she looks in a mirror." He hiccupped.

I didn't say anything. I just stared at him. Sonia had backed away, and Tracy, I noticed, had backed away still further, close to the guard who was standing near the door, with his machine-gun slung down by his side. He glanced at her and smiled. She wiggled her shoulders as if suppressing a chill and she touched her pony-tail, stroking it, and she smiled back at him.

Sergei crouched in front of me. "But we shall fix that, Gwendoline. Soon you will no longer be forced to gaze upon yourself. In fact, you will no longer gaze at all. No eyes, no teeth, what a beauty will she be, unless, of course, our friend here decides to talk." Sergei glanced at James. James was staring at him and staring at us both.

So, I was going to die – be maimed and die – and I was not going to save James – I was going to make it all worse. I *had* made it worse; now, Sergei had leverage – and the leverage was me.

Sergei picked up a red-hot iron from the fire. He stared at it, and he grinned. "Oh, monster, shall we now make you yet more monstrous!"

He walked over, and he brought the red-hot point of the iron close to my face, close to my eyes. I could feel the heat, burning my skin. I stared. I didn't want to flinch. My eye watered. I was vaguely aware of Sonia backing away. I was vaguely aware too of her fascinated gaze, as if the point of the iron had hypnotized her.

"Don't hurt her. I'll tell you what you want to know." James' voice was strong. I felt the love and the burning hatred in it.

Sergei crouched in front of me. "Now, James, you are a stubborn man. And you are a much-loved man. You see what Gwendoline has done for you. She has horribly disfigured herself. She has turned herself into a tattooed and pierced freak, thinking this would appeal to my perverse side, and that this would hide her true beauty and disguise who she is, and she has been rolling in the mud and begging like the lowest of the low, all because of you, and she has had an orgasm, she has made love, she has been penetrated and defiled, all to appease me, and all because of you, and she has allowed herself to be delivered into my hands because of you, and now, she will pay, because of you."

"Sergei, I beg you, do not harm her." James was staring at the little scene out of his blood-rimmed eye.

"It's too late, James. In any case, you don't believe me; you really don't believe me." As he said this, Sergei nodded at Igor.

Igor smashed the big whip against James' chest.

I winced as if the whip had hit me.

Sergei put down the red-hot iron. "I think we will be more delicate. We will do this in stages. One little pound of flesh at a time. Hand me that scalpel, Sonia-swine. I think I shall remove one of dear Misty's eyes."

I took a deep breath; one way or another, this was going to end badly. James nodded. "I love you, Gwen."

"I love you, James, my darling. Oh, how I love you!"

Sonia went to the table, looked at the choice of surgical instruments, and picked one up. "This is the one you mean, Master?"

Tracy stood back, staring. She had not uttered a word. She had edged her way farther towards the exit, poor girl, and now she was standing right behind the guard, as if cowering behind him for protection. He looked around and smiled a reassuring smile at her.

Sergei glanced at Sonia, "Yes, you fool, bring it here. What an idiot. You see, James, not all women are as intelligent – or brave – as your foolish genius little Gwendoline here."

Sergei lifted me up from the stool, and he was holding me, with his fist clenched around my chin, squeezing it tight. With my arms pinioned behind my back, and balancing on the stilettos, I almost toppled over. Sergei grinned. His liquor-poisoned breath was hot against my face.

"I shall take the right eye first, I believe," he said.

"Stop, don't do it," said James, "I told you – I will tell you anything. Anything you want to know! Just don't hurt her."

"I knew she was your weak spot, James. Ah, true love! It is a wonderful thing." Sergei was still staring at me, his face very close to mine. "But, James, it is too late. I will take one eye. And then, if you are very, very good, I shall leave Gwendoline's other eye, plus perhaps a few scars to remember this moment by. I was thinking of removing her ears – and perhaps most of her nose."

"No," James strained against the manacles, "If you hurt her, you will never learn anything. And I swear I will kill you."

"That is very unwise of you, James, now I am tempted to take both eyes, right now, merely for the pleasure of it. Here, hand me the scalpel, Sonia-bitch."

Sonia suddenly stepped next to him, and in one quick move, slashed his neck with the scalpel. Sergei was staring at James and holding my chin with one hand, and he didn't see it coming. She hit the jugular, a glancing blow, as he instinctively had elbowed her back, throwing her aim off. Blood began to spurt. He stumbled back, arms flailing, and knocked her backward.

When Sergei let go of my chin, I kicked away from him and almost fell on my backside, but managed to stay upright, and I saw Igor turn towards his work table and reach for a pistol, and I charged at him head down and sent him spinning. The table turned over. The scalpels, knives, saws, and needles went spinning and flying. Igor was on the ground and trying to get up. I kicked him in the teeth. I heard a mighty crack. He went down and curled up in the fetus position. I kicked him in the face. He rolled over again and lay flat out. I kicked him in the crotch. Then I brought the full weight of my heel down on his windpipe. It's not for nothing that stilettoes are called stilettoes. He let out a wheezing sound and a coughing sound, and then he went into convulsions. All this happened so fast I really didn't know what I was doing. I looked up at James. He was staring at me. "Gwen," he said

"I love you," I blinked at him.

Igor was up again, grasping at his windpipe. He smashed into me. I fell down. He turned away from me as I struggled to get up. It wasn't easy, in stilettoes, with my arms pinioned behind my back. But I managed to push myself to my feet.

There was a clatter from near the entrance. I saw, as if in slow-motion, the guard drop his submachine gun. Tracy had something around his neck. She was strangling him. He kicked, he clawed at the air. She was clinging onto his back. He spun around and around, clawing desperately. Red blossomed like a flower at his neck and a crimson bib on his white shirt.

I heard a crash, and I turned. Igor was choking Sonia. He had her down on the ground, the oily bloody muddy concrete floor, and he was strangling her, her arms were pinned under his knees.

I ran into him, kicking in the side. He toppled off her, and, tottering on the stilettoes, I fell down and rolled. Igor grabbed for me. I pushed away, kicking with the stiletto heels, making a rasping grating sound on the cement, scraping my bum on the concrete. Sonia grabbed Igor by the belt and pulled him back. She flipped him over, and he flailed wildly, trying to get out from under her, she thwacked him on the temple, he went limp, then he tried to rise, tried to strangle her, she fought back, gouging her thumbs deep into his eyes.

I struggled to get up and go and help her. I staggered and fell down, back on my backside.

Igor went into a spasm. He jerked once, twice, then a third time – and he lay still; he was dead. Sonia's thumbs were deep in his eye sockets; she had ripped his eyes out.

"Gwen, look out!" It was James.

Behind me, I heard a spluttering growl. Still on the ground, kicking with the stilettoes, I swiveled around. Sergei! Surging up from hell, somehow, Sergei had gotten back on his feet. A massive bib of blood dripped from his chest. His neck showered drops of blood and blood drooled from the sides of his mouth. Even his blond hair was soaked in ribbons of the stuff. Pushing with the stilettoes, I shimmied myself farther away, scraping my bottom and my pinioned hands on the rough concrete. If only I could stand up!

He staggered, his face a face of pure hatred and horror.

"Can't talk, eh, Sergei!" I stuck my tongue out, "can't talk, eh? We cut your tongue out, eh?"

He gurgled. I pushed myself farther away and tried to get up. It was impossible, with the high heels and my hands pinioned behind my back. Then I came up against a smooth surface, the steel portion of the wall near the section where James was hanging crucified and helpless. Using the wall as leverage, I pushed myself to my feet, and tottered, swaying, pinioned, and almost but not quite helpless.

Sergei loomed up, bloodied, monstrous, a drunk madman, his face a mask of hate, his eyes wild, his hair flattened, streaked with blood, and his shirt soaked in blood, hanging out, his belt unbuckled and open. His mouth bubbled out dark clots of drooling blood. He looked around, madly, an insane animal, desperate, doomed. He reached out. He was going to try to gouge my eyes out. His bloodied fingers, his thumbs ready, in position ... closing in ...

Levering myself against the wall, I kicked out with every ounce of strength. The point of the stiletto caught him in the shin. He howled, like a banshee, and a huge gob of blood flew out of his mouth and splashed in my face. He staggered back. He gurgled. He turned in a dizzy circle, head down, like a massive, wounded bull. He looked up. His icy blue eyes, bright as diamonds, stared out of a mask of blood. He pitched forward and fell against me, drooling blood over my shoulder. I tried to kick away.

He put his hands on my shoulders. His eyes were close to mine, blue, blood-shot, wild, shining blue like two empty crystals. He gurgled, a shower of spittle and something that sounded like "Misty."

I kicked and tried to knee him in the crotch. But he had the strength of someone who is beyond life and death, all his energy gathered in one idea – revenge. "Misty!" His fists clenched around my throat, two thumbs, crushing my windpipe. I sputtered, twisting this way and that.

Suddenly, Sonia was behind him. In her hand, I saw a knife. She knocked him sideways, and as he fell, she curved in under him and plunged the knife into his belly and ripped it upward. "You evil pig," she whispered, "You evil pig. Die!"

Blood spurted everywhere. But somehow Sergei regained his balance; he lunged at her; she slashed at him, a broad sideways sweep, across his face, slashing a slab of flesh away; he careened away, knocking her down. He tottered and fell to the ground. Slowly, Sonia got to her feet, and she looked down on him.

Sergei lay there, face-up, gurgling, half his cheek and nose cut away. Sonia straddled him, using her legs to pin down his flailing arms; she forced the knife up higher into his gut, under his rib cage, deep into his chest cavity. He convulsed, shook, went into spasms; and then he was still, his blue eyes staring at the ceiling. Blood coated Sonia's thighs, and belly, and her arms were bright red to the elbows.

Tracy came up, her hands and arms coated in blood.

Sonia looked up at me. "You okay, Misty?"

"Yes. Now, we have to help James."

"Yes. Let us free Mr. Hewett Spencer," Sonia said. James was hanging, truly crucified, with the manacles holding his feet just off the ground. "Gwen," he breathed, "Princess!"

"Master, I am here," I managed to bow, even with my arms pinioned – and numb – behind me.

"These manacles work by screws." Sonia was unscrewing them. Tracy helped her while keeping an eye on the door.

"What about the other guards?" I glanced around – had they heard anything? Were there cameras? Had they seen anything?

"Maybe," Sonia said, "Our problems are just beginning."

James was soon free. He rubbed his wrists and rubbed his ankles. I wanted to comfort him. But I was still pinioned. Tracy searched Sergei's pockets for the keys for my handcuffs. She looked up at me. "I think one of the guards has them, one of the guys at the gate, outside."

"We have to get out of here." Tracy stood up.

"Darling, Princess," James said. He kissed me, and he held me, naked as he was, naked as I was. Oh, it was delicious. He winced. "Oh, I'm sorry," I pulled back, just a bit. "It's just the burns," he said, he hooked his finger in my collar and pulled me to him and kissed me. Our kiss tasted of blood and sweat, and mud mingled. I shuddered with delight. The kiss was deep; his body was hard and masterly against mine.

"Thank you, Master," I whispered. I pressed my body closer into his; I wanted to take him in my arms, but of course, I couldn't. James looked at me, and smiled, his teeth still all rimmed with blood, he caressed my topknot and my nose and my nose-ring. "You are a work of true beauty, Gwen!" He kissed me on the lips and played with the metal that dangled from my ears.

"In here we call her Misty," Sonia said, almost absently; hands on her hips, she was looking around; she glanced at us. "Okay, children, that's enough with the romance! We have to survive. And we have to find and neutralize the bombs somehow."

"Bombs?" James raised an eyebrow.

I cleared my throat. "Miniaturized or partly miniaturized nukes, up to twelve kilotons. They are supposed to be a development of the old Soviet model, made more powerful by North

Korea, then by Pakistan," I said. "Paris thinks Kaleem Baluchi has sold them to Sergei, who has probably sold them to Khalid Nassir. They may be here, or ..."

"Or they may already have been shipped onward," said James, and frowned. "I did overhear some chatter about 'bombs' and 'packages.' I'm not sure they are still here."

"So, we have to find the bombs, whether they are here not," said Tracy, who was kneeling next to Igor's body, searching his pockets. "And we have to neutralize the air defenses of this place, so that the airborne group can land."

"Airborne group?" James, I could see, was weak. He held onto my shoulder. "What airborne group?"

"Airborne group?" Sonia turned to Tracy. "What airborne group? Who are you, Tracy?"

Tracy, one hand in Igor's pocket, looked up. "At the moment, I'm with Russian intelligence, on loan to Russia from the United States CIA and DEA."

"Ah." Sonia half closed her eyes and licked her lips.

"And you?"

"Well, since we are in a confessional mode – and since we seem to need each other ..."

"Yes, at this moment, my dear Sonia, whoever you are, we definitely need each other." Tracy smiled – it was a knowing, calculating smile, not the innocent, trusting smile I had seen before; but, as if she were aware of the thought that had just passed through my mind, her smile broadened into its old amorous innocence, and she winked at me, and her mouth mimed a kiss.

"Mossad," Sonia looked down and then crouched by Sergei's body; she picked up the Luger and checked the magazine. "I'm Mossad."

"Damnation! Everybody's an agent, triple or double! And I thought I was the devious one." I breathed it into James' shoulder, and I kissed him; I was annoyed: all the time, in my masterful charade, I thought that I, Misty Hoyt, was the sneaky one. James, winked, kissed my forehead, and stroked my buttocks. "You *are* the sneaky one," he whispered; somehow, he read my thoughts, right down to my choice of words.

"We have a Russian and US Joint Special Ops Group, in southern Russia," Tracy said, "They are ready to come in and take this place over, but we need to neutralize the aerial defenses here first, or it will be a bloodbath. Also, they are at least two hours away, maybe three." Tracy was still petite and golden as before, and then I realized, now her hair was free; the knot that kept her ponytail in place was a razor wire, the weapon she had used to kill the guard. She looked worried. "Also, I lost my communications early on. I've been 'dark' for almost two weeks; Moscow and Washington probably think I'm dead, so we need a way of linking up."

"Let's see if we can free you." Sonia examined my handcuffs. "These are very advanced and very strong. We need the keys or a tool kit. Shooting the lock would be too dangerous."

"And we need communications," said Tracy, looking around, "Communications with the outside world."

"Sergei's pocket," I said, "He's got my earphone. It's a link to Paris. They can hear us. The person wearing the thing can hear them. If it's still working, we can link through there to anywhere else Paris can connect to – which certainly includes Washington and Moscow – and Jerusalem."

"Of course! Why didn't I think of that?" Tracy went to Sergei and crouched over his body and rummaged in his pockets. Even now, covered in blood and streaked with grease and mud, she was the beautiful golden girl; her hair, now, tumbled over her shoulders – ah, how sweet!

James looked at me and, as always caught my thought, deciphered my wandering libido in a glance. He winked and kissed me on the lips. "And there's my friend Igor's computer," he said, holding me by the shoulders, pinioned as I was, helpless as I was. I could see he rather liked it, holding me helpless like this, and so did I. Staring into my eyes, he said, "Igor's computer is linked into the Net – I'm certain of it – He was receiving and sending emails. He was also cruising pornography sites, the contents of which he was occasionally kind enough to share with me in between whippings and electric shocks. We even discussed the merits of different types of rope knots in bondage scenarios. Alas, poor Igor. He was a rather nice fellow. In another world and time, we would perhaps have enjoyed a drink in Moscow or London." James looked down at the bloodied eyeless cadaver, glutinous ruined eyeballs, torn out by Sonia's thumbs, hanging from its cheeks. "In any case, we have the computer, and we have a secret weapon – Gwendoline – Misty, Misty Hoyt."

"Ah, yes, Miss Hacker Extraordinaire, I believe, and computer genius, yes, I've heard of her," said Sonia. "Well, Misty, get to work!"

"Of course." I went to the computer and stared down at it. I needed my fingers. I had no fingers! I nudged the computer with my thigh. The screen lit up. It showed two women making love, kissing, rubbing their pelvises together, one woman putting her hand on the other's pubis; it was a loop, the same gestures, over and over again.

I sat down on Igor's chair. With my arms were pinned behind my back, I had to lean forward. Igor's body, its eyes gouged out, lay next to the table. James stood behind me, his hand warm and comforting on my shoulder, gently massaging.

"Can you be my fingers, James?"

"Darling Misty, I'd adore being your fingers!" He kissed the top of my bald head and ruffled the tuft, "Just a second." He went over and got the stool I'd been sitting on when Sonia had been ordered to pleasure me, and he pulled it over. "Maybe the stool will be easier for you; it has no back, so it won't get in the way of your arms."

"Yes," I stood up and sat down on the stool – much easier, and James sat down in the chair, next to me.

I noticed again how crisscrossing burns marked his thighs. I yearned to touch him and comfort him – but my hands were useless, helpless yearning itchy fingers, locked behind my back.

"Let's see, my love," I said, and I gave him a quick string of instructions. James was extraordinarily good at computers himself – he was a genius at it really – and so he was quick to catch onto what I was doing. His fingers danced over the keyboard as I told him what I needed. "I think we should check security, outside this chamber. And then I'll see if we can hack into their defense system. There may be a way to neutralize their anti-aircraft system from here."

"By the way," James said, one hand on my shoulder, the other typing instructions into the computer. "I don't believe there are any cameras in this room. Sergei didn't want to share what went on here, and he didn't want to share any of the information he might obtain here."

"Right, that's logical enough," I said, staring at the screen.

"Well, that is good news," Tracy said, kneeling beside Sergei's body. "That probably means nobody knows Sergei is dead."

"No, and they don't know that we, for the moment, are in charge," said Sonia, who was searching some shelves for weapons or useful material. "How are you guys doing?" She glanced over at James and me.

"I'm checking the security cameras in the whole castle-fortress complex," I said, "Just to see how safe we are, whether the alarm has gone out, and how much time we might have to do whatever we are going to do."

Checking the security cameras didn't require hacking, as the computer was linked directly into the castle's security net, but it was linked in one way: to watch and listen; it wasn't feeding out information itself from where we were. This was lucky. So, yes, nobody knew that Sergei was dead, and that we were free, well free, but inside a cage, inside a bunker, inside a castle, inside a tribal area, inside a mountain valley, inside the New Revolutionary Democratic Republic of Old Transbeckistan. "It all looks clear," I said, "The guards are just loitering around. Some of them look like they are still drunk. There don't seem to be any guards inside the staircase. It looks like they have all gone outside."

"I managed to spike the drinks with a slow-acting narcotic after the feast. The men were sitting around with vodka glasses. That's why Sergei was groggy and erratic." Sonia came and stood behind James and me and stared at the screen. "So, they still don't know what has happened. That is good. For them, Sergei is still alive, still the boss." She put her hand on my shoulder.

"Yes, I presume that's so," said James.

"Great. We can use this."

"I think the command and control center is upstairs, in this building." James turned to me, took my face between his hands and kissed me. I tasted his blood, delicious blood now that he was safe. "You are beautiful, Misty, oh, so beautiful."

"Yes, she is," said Sonia, "And so are you, James. I'm jealous."

"Here," Tracy held the Paris earphone gizmo up. She used Sergei's pants to wipe some blood from it. "See if this works. You'd better be the contact for Paris, Misty. They know you."

"Yes."

"Okay, now, let's see if it works." Tracy crouched next to me and inserted it into my ear.

"Hello, guys, can you hear me?"

There was a burst of static, and then, Frederick. "Yes, Hello Gwen, we thought we'd lost you for a moment there, Gwen. You appear to have established a special kind of totem-like relationship with Kaleem Baluchi. That could be useful. Then it sounded rather like you were going to be executed, tossed into a muddy ditch. Spell-binding tension, I must say, everybody sitting on the edge of their seats, forgetting to eat their popcorn. Of course, it would have been better if we had had the visuals; but we had to make do with sound. And, then, if we understand correctly, you and Sonia put on a sort of sex show, with Tracy orchestrating, while Sergei's handmaiden – Igor I believe his name was – was doing nasty things to James. Very titillating in a sick sort of way, though, as I said, we missed the visuals. And then it sounded like Sergei was going to poke your eyes out. But if we understand correctly, you and Sonia and Tracy put an end to that. Glad it didn't happen, and jolly good show that you made it through all that, Gwen, and I believe James is free too, and that the four of you are together. Give us an update."

"You can hear all of us, right?" I spoke normally. If it was working correctly, Paris could hear us, but I was the only one who could hear Paris.

"Yes, indeed, we can hear James, Mossad's Sonia, and the admirable Russian-American agent, Tracy. We had no idea so many people were on the trail of Sergei. Good show for the whole team, international cooperation is just what we want, I say. Maurice and Séverine join us in that – and Martine has been sitting in, helping us with the psychology side, you know. She has been biting her nails, metaphorically speaking, of course."

"Hello, Gwen, hello James!" It was Martine's voice, "I love you both – we'll get you all out of there!"

We confirmed the situation for Paris. Sergei Platonov was dead; James was free, but the four of us were locked in a dungeon about seven stories down in a mountainside; four, perhaps five or six, or more, atomic weapons were presumably here, possibly in the storage at the castle, though we hadn't seen them; assuming that Sergei had purchased them, he may have already shipped them elsewhere – James thought this was a distinct possibility – without even taking physical possession of them, and so the bombs could be anywhere, but they would, probably, have been planted or transported onwards by Khalid Nassir's network; so they would have to be tracked down – and right away! Otherwise, we were facing a nuclear holocaust.

The air defenses of the castle-fortress were intact, so attacking it from the air would be very dangerous. Nobody outside our dungeon yet knew that Sergei was dead; Khalid Nassir, leader of what he called "the Universal Caliphate Jihad," was in the castle, or had been a few hours ago, and Kaleem Baluchi, the cleverest and most wanted arms dealer in the world, was here too, with his guards and a young American woman prisoner he kept as a pet. The important thing now, was to find out where the atomic bombs were. Also, we four would like to get out of here alive, which would be nice.

"I'm Sonia, Mossad. One of the first targets, we think, is Tel Aviv," said Sonia.

"Hi, I'm Tracy, Moscow intelligence, seconded, as you seem to know, from Washington. We have an airborne joint Russian-US force two hours, maybe three, away, ready to come here. But first, we need to neutralize Serge's air defenses."

"To neutralize the defenses, we need to get to the control room," said James, "There's a slight possibility that Gwen – sorry, Misty – may be able to turn them off or block them from here, but –"

"Yes," I said, "But I agree with James, I think it's probably a very slight possibility that I can turn it off from here. I think they probably have independent systems. So, we may have to get to the control room. Or we may even have to attack the launchers themselves and their crews."

James picked up my thought. "But if we can get to the control center, we might be able to block the radar systems and partially disable the air defenses from there." He glanced at me – his very own tattooed pinioned genius hacker and willing slave.

I could hear Frederick giving orders, and then he spoke to me. "Splendid work, all of you. We shall try to get as much satellite information as we can, and we shall alert the Russians and Americans so that they can set the helicopter assault team in motion. They will need you to clear the landing for them, because they will be violating the – hostile – air space of Transbeckistan, and in that zone, there is no other friendly place for them to land. Meanwhile, priority number one is to find the nukes."

I repeated this to the others.

"Good," Sonia said, glancing at Tracy, "We'll be in touch. We will try to find out about the nukes, and we will try to take their air defenses out of action."

"Tracy here," Tracy said, "Please tell Moscow Central that Curly Sparkles the Third is okay, that she is fully operational, and that this message – about the operation – comes from her as well as from Sonia and Misty and James."

"Curly Sparkles the Third," said Frederick in my ear.

"That's right, Frederick. You heard her, Curly Sparkles the Third."

"It shall be done. Curly Sparkles the Third!" I heard him explain, and his voice faded, but I was sure that Paris was still listening. Unless the link failed, they would hear what we were saying and doing.

Tracy knelt and examined my handcuffs. "This is a new RM-78 Russian model, based on the old Soviet RM-70 model. I think I can open it." She got the thin wire she had used to cut the guard's throat, and she began to probe the lock. I swiveled around in the chair to make it easier, and so she could get a better look.

I wiggled.

"Stay still, Misty, don't wiggle," she said.

"You're tickling me." I licked my lips. James put his hands on my pinioned shoulders to steady me. I was antsy; I wanted to get into action; being trussed up could be fun, but right now, it was annoying and frustrating – and even dangerous!

Tracy and Sonia crouched next to the handcuffs, and Tracy probed and probed with the wire. I heard a click, then another click; then, one hand was free. I rubbed my wrist. And then there was another double click, and both my hands were free.

"That is a very elegant handcuff," James said.

"Yes, in another time and another place, we should ..."

"Don't worry; we will." He placed his hand in the small of my back and pressed, stiffening my resolve, and making me yearn too, for a time when we could just be ourselves. But, before we could get back to playing our little Master-Slave Dialectic, we had to survive this exotic adventure.

"The handcuff still works," said Tracy.

"Keep it. We'll certainly find a use for it," said Sonia.

Now that my hands were free, I could work quickly. I tried first to hack into the security system and into the anti-aircraft system that protected the castle.

At the same time, I was getting updates from Paris through the earphone, and, from time to time, I spoke so that Paris could know what we were doing, while Paris was linking with Washington and Moscow and London and Jerusalem.

Sweat dribbled down my back, gathered in my collarbone, and put a sheen on my whole body. James found a bottle of water and fed me from it, and splashed some water down my tummy and back.

"Thanks," I breathed.

It was stifling and muggy. It occurred to me that none of us had bothered to dress — not even James. Well, there weren't any clothes except for the blood-spattered clothes of the guard, Sergei, and Igor.

I was still wearing the chains Kaleem Baluchi had attached to my rings and my neck collar. Well, they were, in truth, rather decorative, and, with all his faults, Baluchi was a worshipper. So, I figured I'd keep them – they were part of the new me, of Misty Hoyt, Pagan Goddess of the Appalachians.

Sonia and Tracy were rummaging about looking for weapons in the storeroom at the side of the torture chamber, and I could hear them talking. James was sitting beside me. He looked down at himself. "I'm going to improvise a loincloth," he said, "Do you want one?"

"No, being naked is my disguise. I like it."

"True." He kissed my bald pate and ruffled my topknot. "You are decorated and covered enough as it is – stunning. Naked women are beautiful – but a naked man is but a silly, ridiculous unmanned thing."

"You are beautiful naked or dressed," I said.

"Thank you, Misty."

"Thank you, Master," I said. I typed furiously, "I thought my new head-to-toe tattoo decorative scheme might be right up your alley."

"Anything you do is right up my alley. And this, well, Misty, this is positively awesome!" He gave my colorful puffball tuft a flippant encouraging little fillip, a cute flick with his finger. Very exciting!

"Look, here," I squinted at the screen, and, talking both for James and for the people in Paris, I explained: "This is on Sergei's computer system: it is a timetable of departures and arrivals of shipments of material. The bombs are possibly here, in the bunker, on the second-floor underground, but probably deep in the mountain. I think, there's a tunnel that goes to the storeroom. We are I reckon about 100 meters away from the place the bombs might be. I'm uploading this to you now, Paris. Okay?"

"Loud and clear, Misty,"

"Misty," said James, "I do like Misty." He crouched down next to Igor's body and tore the man's shirt up; he turned it into a knotted loincloth. "I don't want to wear the man's clothes," he looked up and smiled a blood-rimmed smile at me, "besides, with you and your friends naked, I don't want to be overdressed."

"Master, I like you precisely the way you are." I glanced at him. He was crouching, tanned, naked, lean and muscular, haggard, streaked with blood and oil and sweat, his eyes red, his flesh marked and scarred with by the whip and electric branding and splashes of acid, his hair long and greasy and disheveled, raw manacle marks around his wrists and ankles, his penis and testicles bloodied and looking oh so vulnerable: He was utterly, sublimely, beautiful. He took my breath away.

He stood up and knotted the skimpy and bloodied bit of Igor's torn shirt around his waist. "Now I am modesty itself," he said, looking down, checking the flimsy bit of stained white cotton, "A true man."

"You look like a mystic from ancient times, in the desert or in India," I blinked at him, "a man casting off all the baggage of civilization, setting off all alone with a begging bowl to discover the bare truth of the universe, renouncing all the pleasures of the flesh."

"Yes, that's exactly how I feel. I am renouncing all the pleasures of the flesh." He pressed himself against me, and knelt and kissed me, and held my face to his.

Sonia and Tracy came out of the storeroom, they were carrying submachine guns, some grenades, and a couple of pistols. They were heavily armed for two naked women.

I turned back to the computer screen. My fingers danced over the keyboard. "I haven't been able to get to the defense systems. It is on a separate circuit, and not linked to the Net or to this subnetwork."

"So if we are going to bring down Sergei's defense systems, we have to get out of this room," said Sonia

"Yes," I felt a nice little rivulet of sweat meandering its way down between my breasts, to my bellybutton, and beyond. "Let's have a look at the layout – who is where and what they are doing and how heavily armed they are."

While they gathered around and watched, I again hooked into all the security camera system – Sergei had linked the torture room computer to the security system so that he could check on what was happening elsewhere in the castle complex.

And, yes, James was right; there were no cameras where we were, since Sergei didn't want to be seen torturing his prisoners – and, as James pointed out, Sergei didn't want anyone to know what information, if any, he pried out of his prisoners.

"Okay, look here," I said.

The camera showed the guards outside the bunker; they were getting antsy. Their boss, Boris, I could see, was making a call from his cell phone. Sergei's cell phone rang, and rang, and rang.

Sonia picked it up. "Sergei doesn't want to come to the phone. He's having fun right now." Sonia glanced at James.

James screamed.

Sonia said, "Yes, that's right. He's working with the prisoner, and we are making progress. Misty is a great help!"

James screamed again.

On the screen, Boris looked doubtful. After Boris hung up, he walked back and forth. He phoned another number. Glancing at the computerized security switchboard panel, I was able to identify it. "He's phoning main security," I said.

"We'll have to do something."

"Meantime, let's see what we are facing." I flipped through the whole range of security cameras: several cameras showed the entrance, and the main gate, and the exterior of the main gate, beyond the walls of the fortress; another pair of cameras showed the interior and exterior of the SS Marquis Club, eighty kilometers away in Typhilis. Four cameras showed the main entrance to the castle itself, the grandiose arched baronial entrance, and the groups of SUVs, Hummers, and limousines parked in front of it, with various drivers, bodyguards, and so on, hanging around, smoking cigarettes.

"Those are different groups," Sonia said.

"Yes, Sergei's men, then Baluchi's men, and Khalid's men," said Tracy.

"The three groups don't love each other, I presume," James said.

"No, they don't," said Sonia. "They hate each other. And they are all heavily armed because the three gentlemen don't trust each other."

"I see an opportunity," said James.

"Yes, that might be useful, get them to kill each other." I licked my lips and flipped through another series of cameras: There were several cameras in the main entrance hall and facing the baronial entrance from the inside; images were showing the giant fireplace, and there was even a close-up image of Betty curled up in her Plexiglas cage; it looked like she was snoozing. Then several cameras showed bathrooms. Then there were two images of the shower room where Sonia and Tracy and I had been playing just an hour or two ago. It was empty now, with no steam and no water flowing and it looked hygienic and abstract, almost a painting by Mondrian, or maybe an Art Deco poster.

Sonia was saying, "I think we should storm out of here and grab those nukes. We've got grenades, we've got guns."

"There are too many of them," Tracy said, "they are well-trained. And they are in different positions. We might surprise some of them, but the others would know we are coming."

"Why are you working for the Russians? Aren't you, Vietnamese?"

"I'm Vietnamese American."

"So why the hell are you working for the Russians? And how is it you speak Russian like a Russian?"

"I worked for the DEA; then liaised with the CIA; then I started working on Sergei, here, his drug connections with the Italians, Columbians, and Mexicans; and then the Russians got interested ..."

"Because of the arms trade angle ..."

"Yes, that and the drugs, and so I was asked to liaise."

"And ..."

"And the Russians asked if they could borrow me – I speak Russian, as you said, and also Spanish and French, and I studied Russian at Georgetown and in Moscow, and so I was part of a joint US-Russian operation, and Sergei had taken a –"

"He'd taken a liking to you, darling. I saw that. I was almost jealous. You were his golden girl."

"Oh, well, yes, I guess, for a day or two, I was. I think he was becoming bored; he was going to eliminate me. A day of torture, and then ... In any case, you, Sonia, were always first in his heart. He loved you."

"Sergei was first in his own heart – and maybe his mother had a place there too, but, no, he hated her. No, I think for a moment, you held his attention."

"But you held it longest."

"I'm a survivor." Sonia sighed. "I've become what he wanted me to be. This has been a long project, three and a half years."

While I listened, I was flipping through screen images. Now I was in what looked like a boudoir designed by the Marquis de Sade. What looked like Kaleem's blonde pet, the deaf-mute American girl violinist, was lying spread-eagled on a bed; her wrists were manacled to the head of the bedstead and her ankles to the bedposts at the foot of the bed; she was blindfolded and gagged with what looked like a ball-gag; she seemed to be alone. Was she alive? Yes, I saw her tugging at the manacles and trying to flex her legs. I flipped away: there were images of a loading bay, of several trucks lined up, of men working loading cases onto trucks, and then images of warehouse-type rooms – all full of crates; they were enormous.

"Weapons," said Tracy.

"Yes. It looks like it. See the markings on that crate."

"Yes, Beretta: Italian – handguns, probably, rifles, light weaponry."

"And a whole underground parking lot full of armored cars."

"You could equip an army with this stuff," Sonia leaned close over me. Her breast brushed my shoulder. "You know, it's the first time I've been allowed in this room."

While he followed me flipping through images of the fortress and the castle, James had been drawing a sketch of the fortress and the castle, identifying where the guards and drivers were standing, where the different groups of armed men were stationed, and where the strategic points were located. He kept glancing up, checking the camera images I brought up on the screen.

With Sonia's hand on my shoulder giving me a tiny, itsy-bitsy massage, I ran through more images; they were in subcategories: exterior security; internal security; castle; warehouses and defense: there were cameras in bedrooms. There were lots of separate suites and quarters for guests in the castle. Sergei ran something like a luxury hotel for his clients and contacts.

"What's that?" Sonia's grip tightened.

"Is that who I think it is?" James was staring at the screen. "Why is he sitting like that?"

"Yeah, what's going on here?" I stopped on the image. Kaleem Baluchi was as I had left him, dressed only in a loincloth, but it looked like he was tied in a chair. He was sitting very erect; his arms seemed to be pinned behind his back; his belly bulged over his waist. "Look at this. Is Kaleem Baluchi a prisoner?"

"Maybe it's some sort of sexual game?" I said, but I didn't think so.

We all leaned towards the screen. Then Khalid Nassir came into the frame. He slapped Baluchi across the face, once, twice, then a third time. Baluchi's head jerked sideways each time. They looked like powerful slaps, more than slaps.

"It looks like Nassir is torturing him, or at least hurting him," said Sonia; it was barely above a whisper; it was as if she were saying it and thinking it with a certain foreboding. "I'm not sure that this is good."

"Can we get sound on that?" James leaned forward, his hand on my arm.

"Let's see." I moved the mouse around. "I think so. Yes."

"I'll only ask this once more: what are the codes?" It was Nassir's voice, and he was speaking in English, his rather cultivated version of British English; even knowing what I knew, I still found it disconcerting when terrorists, speaking in a Western language, used such an educated upper-crust version of the language, tones and accents one associated – certainly mistakenly – with civility.

"You have not paid. You have not paid in full. That was our agreement. And you promised you would let Sasha go."

"You will never see Sasha again – unless you give me the numbers and the codes. Besides, she will soon be married to one of my warriors. She will give him children – many children. You are not even a man, Kaleem, why do you care for this woman?"

"You know why."

"Ah, yes, because when her mother and father were killed, you adopted her, and you raised her as your own. Now, she will find her rightful place as the slave of a warrior who is fighting against the infidels and apostates and will with God's help bring about the Caliphate and create the world of believers from which the infidels and all the impure non-believers will be cast out or reduced to slavery and harlotry which is what they are in their hearts – harlots and slaves."

"Sergei promised me ..."

"Sergei – ah, Sergei is nobody and nothing. Sergei does not count! He cannot promise anything. He is a corrupt infidel, a pig! He wallows in debauchery. Just as you do, Baluchi." Khalid walked up to Baluchi and slapped him again. "I saw you look at that naked painted whore – that tattooed pierced idol; you were eating her with your eyes; you were slobbering over her, Kaleem. I shall have her stoned to death. Buried up to her neck, and then stoned, then the carcass will be dragged through the streets."

"She is human, Nassir. She is a child."

"She is not a child, she is an adult, and she is an abomination, this Misty of yours. She is filth and pollution like all Westerners, all infidels, and all apostates, like that fool Sergei. He promised you protection. Where is your precious Sergei now? Cavorting and fornicating with those naked women, with the tattooed whore. So, do you give me the codes, or do I cut off your nose and your hands? Better, I shall have Sasha executed – stoned to death like the whore she is." Nassir slapped Kaleem again, and then again. Blood drooled from the side of Kaleem's mouth.

"What are these codes he's talking about?" Sonia was leaning close to me, her hand on my shoulder. "What are these numbers?"

"I think he's talking about the bombs," said James.

"Yes, the bombs," Tracy crouched on the floor next to us. She pushed a muddy strand of hair away from her eyes. "That was the big deal between Kaleem and Sergei, and between Sergei and Nassir. That is what Moscow is terrified of. If Nassir has the bombs ..." She shrugged.

"He'll use them against anybody and anything," I said. "Let me see if I can find out a few things. Do you mind if we leave the Nassir-Baluchi show for a moment? I can shrink it down to a corner of the screen."

"Do it." Sonia was pacing up and down, chewing on her clenched fist. "Tel Aviv is one of Nassir's targets," she said, quietly, looking down at the floor, as if talking to herself.

"Yes, do it." Tracy nodded and glanced at Sonia.

"Okay, let's go. Let's see about the bombs." I opened a new screen. "Where are you, little bombs?" I plunged into a general search in the Net of the castle-fortress. I came across a file entitled "Shipment Schedule for Bananas." They thought they were secure, but it was pretty permeable and leaky as an internal system, because it was self-enclosed and local, or so they thought; but there were lots of back doors in and out. Inside the Banana File, I found a file that said Fat Thin Little – Hmm, I thought, the first atomic bombs were called Fat man, Thin Man, and Little Boy. This was like "Misty Hoyt." It was a red flag, but was it a joke, or arrogance, or carelessness, or a decoy? I opened the file. It had a series of timelines. I squinted at the timelines, delivery dates, and details of the logistics networks. I flipped through a sheath of files. "Holy, Moly!"

Sonia had come over and put her hand on my shoulder.

"Holy Moly?" I heard, echoing in the earpiece. The mike and speaker on the other side must be open. It was Martine's voice. "Did she just say 'Holy Moly?'"

I had to grin. "Yes, Martine, I did just say, 'Holy Moly'," I said, feeling Sonia's grip on my shoulder tighten. She had seen what I had seen.

"I think, Misty, that ..." James was beginning to say, "That the bombs are already ..."

"Yes, definitely," I said. "Hey, everybody, if these delivery dates are accurate, and they were only entered four days ago, then the bombs have already been shipped, and some of them at least are in place on their targets – or at best approaching the targets – and there are maybe as many of five of them, maybe six, maybe more."

"What?" It was Séverine in Paris.

"At least one of the bombs has already been sent on. In fact, it might already be at the destination."

"What is the destination?"

"I'll send you this as soon as I can – the connection is flickering here – and there are lots of 'walls' I have to go through – but the destination, according to this, is New York."

"You mean one of the nukes might already be in New York?"

"Yes. I think that's what this means. Here, let me send it to you. I think the other bombs are in place too or near their destination – probably."

"What?"

"Paris, I'm sending you the file now. Those boxes I saw a week ago, where Baluchi was at the airport with Platonov. I think the boxes were being sent away; they weren't being unloaded as we thought, they were ..."

"... about to go onto an aircraft, or several aircraft," said Frederick's voice in my ear.

"Yes, the trucks that headed to Sergei's fortress were empty, I'm almost certain of it, or at least partly empty. The bombs were about to go on several aircraft, private executive and transport jets, and so, given the lapse of time, they are quite probably in position by now."

"And Nassir wants codes from Baluchi," said Sonia.

"Probably the codes to trigger the devices," said Tracy.

"God Almighty," James breathed. He put his hand on my thigh.

I glanced at James "That's probably – well, almost certainly, what Nassir and Baluchi are fighting about."

"Explain, please, we didn't follow that part," said Séverine, "What about Nassir and Baluchi?"

"Nassir is slapping and punching Baluchi and threatening somebody Baluchi loves, somebody named Sasha."

"Sasha, Sasha ...?" James frowned. "I did some research on Baluchi. I seem to remember ..."

I asked Paris. "Could you try to find out who Sasha is? She is important to Baluchi. Whoever she is, she seems to be leverage."

"Okay – yes."

"Nassir wants codes – and telephone numbers, I think."

"Okay – yes."

"And Baluchi doesn't want to give them to him."

In the earphone, I could hear somebody in Paris shouting in English, with an American accent, "Get us all the satellite footage for the last two weeks over the Republic of Transbeckistan; get all the assets we have on this. Get Washington. I want to talk to the National Security Advisor. Yes, right now. Somebody notify the President! We'd better put all our assets on alert in all targets and anything remotely related to the targets."

Frederick's voice, "So the codes and the telephone numbers, their purpose may be to trigger the bombs."

"Yes," I said; I swallowed. It was muggy in the room; I was utterly coated in sweat. My nose was running too. I wanted to wipe at my nose-ring, but I didn't have time. James lifted a bit of cloth, and wiped it clean. "Thank you," I whispered.

Then, Séverine came on the line, "Misty, is there any indi- cation of the targets, other than New York. So far, we just have rumors."

"Yes, I think so. Let's see, other than New York ..." I was flip- ping through a list. "This might be a decoy list, but I don't think so. New York, Paris, Tel Aviv, Moscow, Tehran, and there's London too, with an 'X' beside London. I don't know what the 'X' means."

I explained to Paris that Khalid Nassir was in a room in the castle – more than 250 meters from us – with Baluchi and that he was trying to get "codes" from Baluchi. "We're not 100% sure what the codes mean, but we have a pretty good idea!"

"You have to stop Nassir somehow."

"Get both Baluchi and Nassir alive, if you can."

"We could knock the whole castle out with a missile," said a voice in Paris, a voice I didn't recognize; the accent was American.

"No," said Frederick. "We have people inside."

"People? I understand. But just consider, it's the lives of a few agents against the lives of millions. They will understand, your agents surely will understand, to weigh the lives of a few agents against millions of lives. They would die as heroes, and ..."

James and Tracy and Sonia hadn't heard this. I held my breath. If they obliterated the castle, then they would obliterate us with it, but worse than that. I cleared my throat. "I'm sure we'd all understand your priorities, and it would be very nice to die heroes – flattering indeed. But there's no guarantee that blowing up the fortress and killing everybody here will stop the bombs going off," I said, "We don't know what the trigger mechanisms are, and we don't know what these codes and numbers Nassir wants are. The bombs might be on timers that have been pre-set. There may be terrorists who can set them off on-site, individually, instantaneously or with timers, or just by making a telephone call or sending a text message. We don't know enough."

Sonia, unconsciously I think, was giving me quite a nice shoulder massage. Tracy was looking at me, wide-eyed. James put his hand on my thigh. I didn't need to explain what I'd heard. They had all understood: If the United States and Russia decided on a missile strike, we would die.

"Right," said Frederick, speaking into my ear. "And if we don't get to Nassir and Baluchi, we will never find out – and that may mean we won't be able to stop the bombs."

"I think we need to get the Joint Russia-US Special Ops force here ASAP," said Tracy.

"Yes, we heard Tracy, Misty," said Frederick, "Tell Tracy, we'll give the green light. Washington and Moscow have already approved in principle. If there's no hitch, they'll be off the ground in a couple of minutes. They'll give you firepower on the ground for whatever you may have to do."

I repeated what Frederick had said.

Tracy nodded, "Good – but that means we have to take out the fortress's anti-aircraft defenses."

"Yes."

James stroked my thigh. "And that code ... If we are going to stop the bombs, we have to get to Nassir and Baluchi, and ..."

"Yes," I said, turning to him, but speaking so everybody could hear me. "There is another problem. According to this document – Paris, I've already sent you a copy – these bombs can be detonated remotely, probably by a phone call or a text message, probably containing a code that has to be entered, or that the bomb's timer can enter itself once it receives the message. There might be two or three levels of code – and choices at various levels. And of course, Nassir or his people would need the right telephone number."

Séverine in Paris was saying, "Just to be clear, Misty: you mean that, from anywhere in the world, somebody who has the right telephone number and who has the right code can detonate a nuclear device which is quite probably right now somewhere – but we don't know where – in New York City – and in Paris, in Moscow, Tel Aviv, and Tehran, and possibly in London?"

"Yes, I think that is the situation," I said, and I repeated Séverine's summary for James and Sonia and Tracy since I was the only one who could hear what Paris was saying. I could probably have hooked up a workaround to put Paris on speaker, but that would take time, and I wasn't even sure it would work with the little earpiece gizmo – and I didn't have time.

Frederick said, "Nassir must not be allowed to get the numbers and the codes, whatever they are and whatever they do."

"Right." I glanced at James and Sonia and Tracy. "We must stop Nassir from getting the codes," I repeated. They nodded. I blinked at them. Our team was glamorous, but pretty bedraggled. Three naked mud-streaked women, one of them a silver chain decorated totally tattooed mostly bald Punk-Goth freak, and one rather battered but beautiful almost naked man in an improvised and bloody loincloth and covered in scars from whips, acid, and electric shocks and with a beautiful but blood-rimmed grin and tired – but infinitely charming – eyes.

"Misty, this is Jim Stanton, CIA, have you got any hints as to where the bomb might be in Manhattan and when it came to Manhattan? Or where it might be in any of the other cities?"

"Hi, Jim. No, not yet. There are reams of documents – they might contain something, but they might not. As you know, these terrorist groups give lots of their commands verbally, in person, to be untraceable. In any case, I'm uploading all the remaining documents to Paris right now. But our priority here ..."

"Yes, Misty, your priority there is to stop Nassir from getting the codes and the telephone numbers. Absolutely."

"Right."

Then Séverine was on the line. Her voice was, as always, cool and ironic. "Misty darling, so you do think that Nassir could trigger the bombs? He could blow us all up from where he is?"

"Yes, Séverine, I would guess he – or one of his proxies – can trigger them from anywhere, from a landline, or a cellphone, or a computer. Or get someone else to do it for them, if he has the telephone number and the unlock code. He could make a phone call, or he could send a text message. The bombs also might be on a timer. That is the code might trigger the bomb instantly, or it might set off the timer, so there might still be a delay – but we don't know if there is delay mechanism, and if there is, or are delay mechanisms, we don't know how long the delays have been set for. If there is remote triggering, then there's no need for a timer delay, except maybe as a backup – if, say, the order to detonate fails to come through by a certain time."

"Hmm," said Séverine, "That's rather discouraging, Misty. Do you think we could try to block down all communications out of Sergei Platonov's fortress, turn off the electricity, and cut the satellite connections?"

"The fortress has power generators. I believe they kick into action automatically. And if you cut off communications, then we wouldn't know what was happening, and we don't know, in any case: some of the bombs might already be on timers. The countdown might have begun. Maybe the only way to stop the bombs is to communicate with them and put the countdown on hold. We just don't know."

"Right, Misty. You and your team must get to Nassir and Baluchi."

"Will do," I said, "I'm not sure if it's possible – but we'll do it." As I said this, Sonia was stroking my shoulder, and James was kissing me on the cheek.

"Misty, this is Frederick. Jim is here with us in Paris; we are liaising with Washington and New York and London. They are hearing everything we are hearing. Moscow and Jerusalem are joining us shortly and Tehran as well. We will put a team on getting what we can out of the documents and correspondence. But you have to stop Nassir."

"Right!" I turned to James, who was seated beside me and to Tracy and Sonia, and explained the situation. I hate to admit it, but this was exciting. My blood was racing; my mind was in overdrive; we were faced with a horrible challenge – hundreds of thousands, millions of lives hung in the balance. Somehow, I thought we were going to win, whatever the odds. Maybe I'd watched too many movies with happy endings. Maybe I was convinced I could do something in my life that would really count.

"Is there any way to stop Nassir from here?" James said. "If there isn't, we have to get out of here and get to the castle."

Sonia and Tracy were leaning over us, staring at the screen. Sonia put her hand on my shoulder, "I don't see how we can stop him from here. He's alone in a room with Baluchi."

"No, I don't think there is," said Tracy.

James looked up at them. "Well, you two know the place better than we do." He held up the sketched map he had made.

"Yes, we know it pretty well." Sonia took the sketch and frowned. "Yes, this is pretty good – you've pinpointed all the dangerous bottlenecks."

James smiled. "I can do a pretty good imitation of Sergei's voice; I've been listening to it long enough. It's not good enough to give detailed orders, and my Russian isn't good enough – he gives orders to the lads almost exclusively in Russian. But I could shout a few things, probably."

I looked at him. He was right beside me, our skin touching, our sweat mingling. I thought about how to get us to the castle, "Right. I could probably work up a program to translate your voice into his, or arrange a link-up to do the same, and you could give orders to the men to seize or kill Nassir, but ..."

"But it would take too long and be too risky," James said.

"Yes," said Sonia

"Yes," said Tracy, "Hey, Paris, what about the joint force, the American-Russian group."

Frederick answered: "They're already in the air. Washington and Moscow have given clearance. They are at least two hours away, and a big storm system is moving towards you. It will make helicopter landings very dangerous – maybe impossible. In any case, before they can even try to land, you must neutralize the drones and the anti-aircraft system of the fortress."

"Right," I said, and passed Frederick's answer along.

"Consensus here, Misty, is that you have to get to Baluchi, liberate him take him prisoner, and capture Nassir. We need both of them alive. We need to know what they know. Otherwise ..."

"Okay," I said, and I explained to the others.

"Aside from the bombs, alive is much better," Sonia said. "Nassir has killed many of our friends. Israel wants him alive. He knows a great deal. If he dies, his group will continue without him; if he lives and tells us what he knows, we can cripple them for a long time. And if he dies, his group may still be able to explode the bombs."

"Yes, Russia wants both of them alive and the US too, we particularly want Baluchi," Tracy said, "Baluchi knows more than almost anybody about the arms and drug trades. We've wanted him for a long time." She was sitting cross-legged on the floor, like a kid, looking up at me. She pushed a strand of hair away from her eyes.

Martine was on the line from Paris. "Okay, Misty darling, they've given me the line for a minute: Paris is going to fall silent, while they let you work out your plan to get Baluchi and Nassir and to neutralize the air defenses. If anything new comes up, we will be on the line, okay. We are listening, though, so anything you need, we are here. I love you – I love James. Be safe, darlings!"

"We love you too," I said, and there was a lump in my throat, and I felt how little words could express, and how little they counted.

I swallowed, and I realized my eyes were wet. "Okay, now, we have to get to Baluchi and Nassir."

"And, between here and there," said James, "Let's have a look at what we are facing."

I brought up the schematics of the buildings – I matched them with the cameras and with James' sketch of where the guards were placed and where the probable bottlenecks were, and we came up with the obstacle course of what confronted us. "There are about sixty heavily armed guys here," I said. "So, how do we get to Kaleem?"

Sonia crouched next to Tracy. "I have free run of the compound, and Tracy, you do too."

"Yes."

"So we could take Misty up to the castle, and we could seize Nassir, and we could capture – and free Baluchi, and then we can get Baluchi to tell us what he knows, perhaps how to neutralize the bombs."

Tracy smiled. "Misty has a huge influence over Baluchi. She's his totem, his goddess."

"Hmm," I looked down, the chains and piercing rings twinkled, my breasts dripped sweat, I was steaked with mud; the tattoos glowed brightly, as if lit by inner neon, as if coated in oil. I cleared my throat and glanced at James. "Yes, I'm Baluchi's fetish, his totem."

"He has extremely good taste, our man Baluchi," said James.

"But he might just have been playing with me before pouncing.

People have very ambivalent attitudes to their totems and fetishes – and this explains a great deal; for example, in 1912–1913, in a series of articles, Sigmund Freud argued that –"

"Stop, Misty, stop." James put his hand on my shoulder and leaned down and shut me up with a kiss, and he tickled my ear, which made the three heavy earrings jangle. He realized I was almost certainly about to forget myself totally – and the impending end of the world – and give a two-hour lecture on Sigmund Freud and the theories of totems and fetishes. I really must learn how to shut up. "What I mean to say is, a fetish is often hated as well as adored: so maybe Baluchi just wants to cut my throat."

"Yes, worshippers often sacrifice the fetish object," said James.

"Yes, but this little fetish is our ticket to Baluchi." Sonia caressed my breast and flicked the nipple-ring, making the chain sway, and twinkle. It made a very jingly sound. I think she thought I was still her slave, still an object to be trifled with. People can get carried away with their roles. Spies sometimes forget they are spies. James put his hand on my shoulder and winked.

"Yes," said Tracy, "During the feast, Baluchi couldn't keep his eyes off Misty."

"As I said, a man of good taste," said James.

"We won't be able to carry guns," said I, and, as always, I was enjoying the attention, the caresses, the trifling, and playing around. Even in the shadow of the apocalypse! I am truly irresponsible! Well, seize the instant, that's what I say!

"No, we'll go just as we are," Sonia gazed at me fixedly, "naked mussed up slaves, part of Sergei's circus. But James, the prisoner, cannot come with us; he will stay here and act as our controller."

"Right," I said. I returned the gaze: we all knew this was almost certainly a death sentence for all of us.

"It's a mortal risk," said James.

"Let's analyze the obstacles. Where you have to go – who's there, and how they are likely to react," Tracy stood up, all business, but her grin was looking delightfully childlike.

I considered this little adventure: "We have to keep the mud, but get rid of the blood. You've got a few streaks specks of blood on you, Tracy, and you, Sonia, are soaked in blood, your arms particularly from cutting Sergei's throat and from gouging out Igor's eyes."

"We can say it is blood from James," said Tracy.

I nodded. My earrings jingled. "Okay, sounds good – you both helped in the torture."

"Right. It's the sort of thing Sergei enjoys – enjoyed – getting his female slaves to participate in the dirty work." Sonia grinned. "So, girls, we have to make this look real."

"You were handcuffed, Misty. They all saw that." Tracy blinked at me – the golden girl with dark eyes, and a sly grin.

"Yes, that's right." I looked down at my hands – free to roam the keyboard, free to caress, free to roam the whole world.

"I can put the handcuffs back, Misty," said Tracy, "but I can do it, so they are not locked – in fact, I can jam them so they won't lock – and you can just open them anytime by just pulling, and twisting, like this." She showed me.

"Great."

The voice in my ear spoke: "Misty, we can patch James through Paris, via your computer hookup, that way James and Paris can brief you in real-time while you head for Baluchi and Nassir. James will have all the monitors in front of him. So that gives us and James eyes on events in the fortress. We can warn you of dangers. And we can keep in touch with you as you are going after Nassir and Baluchi. Do you agree?"

"Absolutely," I said, and I explained to James and Sonia and Tracy; James would be able to talk to us, he would be watching all the monitors, and, via Paris, he would also hear in real-time, through my earpiece, what was happening to us, and what Paris was saying.

"Great, that's good, that's good." Tracy and Sonia looked at each other and nodded.

"Right," I muttered, and I brought up the images of the guards; the guards inside the bunker had left and had gathered outside and were loitering just at the main door to the bunker. "Well, the one nice thing is that nobody yet seems to realize that Sergei is dead. See, here, outside the door, everything is normal."

I surveyed the route. Sonia and Tracy analyzed the guards along the route, the best way to go, who was most dangerous.

James kissed me. "Good luck, Misty. We are going to get through this!"

"Yes, Master, yes, my love, we will." We embraced; he held me; he looked into my eyes. We kissed, and then, reluctantly, we parted. I let my hands slid off his chest, and I stepped back. I kept my eyes on him, and he watched as my arms were pinioned behind my back, and Tracy attached the leash to my collar.

"Ah, Misty," James sighed, "My beautiful Misty." He put his hands on my pinioned shoulders, warm and strong and comforting hands, and gazed into my eyes, and kissed me, a long delicate, exploring kiss which seemed like it might never end. We both knew it might easily be our last kiss.

I was led on a leash to the door and out the door of the torture chamber. James closed the door behind us, and we climbed up the stairs, our stilettoes doing their sexy click-click on the steel steps. Without meeting any guards, we came to the top of the stairs and to the giant door that led out of the bunker.

"Ready?" Sonia favored both of us with a steady and stern look. She tugged on my leash. "Are you ready, Misty?"

"I am ready, mistress," I said. I bowed my head, truly once again a slave, my arms now pinioned tight behind my back, pulling my shoulders back, tightening my breasts. I felt even more exposed than usual.

"Okay, here goes," said Tracy; she mimed a prayer.

"Hi, guys, Sonia here." She leaned towards the intercom to the outside. "I'm coming out, with Misty and Tracy. Sergei wants us to go up to the chateau and perform for Nassir and Baluchi."

"Right, Sonia," Boris's voice came over the intercom, "Just wait, I have to check with Sergei."

"Go ahead, Boris," Sonia said, crossing her eyes and sticking out her tongue, which was, I guess, was her way of expressing a prayer. It would now depend on whether James fooled Boris.

There followed a long second. Sonia kept the intercom open so we could listen. We heard Boris. "Yes, yes, yes, sir. Yes, Sergei."

Sonia rounded her lips and blew out a soundless sigh of relief.

"You can come out, Sonia." Boris sounded pleased. "The boys will be delighted to see you."

CHAPTER 8 – MERCHANT OF DEATH

"Okay, coming out," Sonia shouted, in Russian. The door slid open. We stepped out into the damp night air, the guards – six of them – gathered around to stare.

"A sight for sore eyes," said Boris, saluting Sonia, and ogling all of us with a lingering and caressingly appreciative gaze.

A new layer of sweat bubbled on my skin. It was still sweltering hot, even with the sun long gone; everything was damp, with white mist drifting up from the hollows, and curling up in tendrils over the soaring stone walls of the fortress.

Sonia favored the men with her brightest smile. "Well, you boys do deserve a bit of comic relief from time to time, look at Misty here. She has been amusing us, a true little performing sex pet, doing special tricks, all the while."

"If Misty needs extra interrogation, I'm always available," said Boris.

"We'll keep that in mind, won't we, Misty." Sonia tugged on my chain, and I pretended to stagger, and then I bowed and then lifted my chin and glared at Bois and growled. He and his men laughed.

"I'm in love with Misty," said one of the bigger men, a guy they all called Kirill.

They all laughed.

"Well, when we've finished with her, perhaps you can marry her," said Sonia, giving him an even more radiant smile.

"It's a deal! Let's shake on it!" He shook Sonia's hand. I stood by and watched this. I was a manacled pinioned clown – and the predestined sacrificial victim – an enemy spy, caught, and to be punished, probably with death; before dying, I would be their toy. Tracy was watching the men carefully, petite and golden and stunning, even streaked with mud and sweat and oil. Her fragility was an illusion. I figured she could probably take on, single-handed, and finish off, at least two of those big men, maybe more.

As we headed up the path towards the chateau, the men tagged along, making remarks and jokes. I could see that Boris was particularly fond of Sonia, very fond of her in fact. The men – except for Boris – seemed still drunk after the big feast – and I had noticed some bottles of vodka near the bunker exit. But they were in good humor, joking, not molesting us – after all, Sonia was Sergei's, and she and Tracy had been part of the gang for quite a while. The men knew these two women were tough; they were killers. Both girls, even naked, were one of the boys.

"Remember that time in Azerbaijan, Sonia, when we took out those Armenians," Boris was saying, "those were good times, good times – it makes life worthwhile living, having had times like that to remember. You were cool, really cool, the quickest shot around."

"But not like you, Boris," said Sonia, laughing. "You were Mr. Cool himself; those three killers didn't know what hit them."

"Yes, yes," Boris had that far away down-memory-lane look in his eyes, "They were nasty folk. We make a good team, all of us."

Krill was following close by. "And Tracy, what do you think of Misty? You're always so silent."

"Misty is beautiful, and very special," Tracy said, putting her hand on my shoulder. "If you don't marry her, Kirill, I'll marry her myself."

Kirill and the others laughed.

Boris woke up from his nostalgic reverie. "Sorry, Sonia, but I'd better take the men back, if Sergei sees we've left our post there will be hell to pay. You will be okay from here on?"

"We'll be okay, Boris, thank you!" Sonia blew him a kiss.

"Well, good luck, ladies."

"Don't forget, Misty! I'm going to marry you!" Kirill blew me a kiss.

I turned, glared at him, grinned, and stuck out my tongue; Sonia tugged at my leash. "Come on, Misty, stop flirting with your fiancé."

The men laughed, and their laughter echoed and then faded in the mist as they walked down the path, under the lamplight, under the sloping hillside. Their voices became even more indistinct as they started back up towards the bunker and its towering cliff.

We walked past the mud pit. Our stilettoes made a muted click-click on the stone pathway.

"Bring back fond memories, Misty?" Sonia nodded at the bubbly mud surface, "Our mud bath?"

"Were you really going to shoot me?"

"Well, someday, maybe I'll tell you. But the mud wrestling was fun."

"Absolutely," I licked my lips. "Let's do it again – soon."

Tracy grinned. "Come on, guys, get serious."

Other guards were watching us. One of the anti-aircraft missile launchers was parked on a platform-like outcropping of rock to the right of us, up above our mud wrestling pit. Another had moved out onto a platform to the left above us, on an outcropping of the cliff. A couple of the gunners turned and watched us go by. Several whistled. One shouted, "Come and visit us, ladies, we're lonely up here."

One guard, who was walking down from the chateau, came up to us and said in Russian, "I'll accompany you, ladies, if you have no objection."

Sonia glanced at him. He had a pistol at his belt, a knife attached to the side of his khaki trousers, and an automatic rifle slung over his shoulder. His militia uniform was pressed and neat. He was an open-faced young man, and not at all drunk. His smile was pleasant, beautiful even. I figured he was about eighteen or nineteen years old, maybe younger. Strangely, there was nothing lascivious or gloating in his glance. He looked at me, but he looked me in the eyes, a direct, friendly gaze. I smiled at him. I couldn't help it. And he returned the smile, with a sort of twinkle in his eyes, just the suggestion of a wink.

"No objection, we are honored," said Sonia. I glanced at her. She was being very accommodating. Was it wise to have a guard with us, even if he was a handsome young man with a big smile? Sonia was a gorgeous woman, and in my opinion, even more beautiful now, so disheveled and muddy and mussed up, and her hair plastered down to her head and neck, and her naked body and face streaked in clay and covered with grease and oil. The high heels, on the uneven terrain, made her sway, in the most sensually promising way; her super buttocks, moving in syncopated rhythm, glowing with sweat, offered an image of perfection, a superb, proud ass. I wanted to slap it; I wanted to touch it, but of course, as a pinioned prisoner, I couldn't. She glanced back, smiled, and tugged on my leash. It was as if she had sensed my glance and captured my inner libidinous musings, as I sculpted the pleasures of her body in my mind. I swallowed and licked my lips. Her inner beauty, too, shone through, brilliant in her smile, in the tangle of muddy blond strands of hair on her cheeks, in her immense eyes and penetrating glance. We had traveled a long way in one night, from the heights of Eros, through the valley of death, and onward to the Crusade to Save the World. She put one hand to her tangled hair, and straightened a few muddy Medusa strands. The vulnerable delicacy of the gesture gave me a little shiver. A sweet disorder in the dress, kindles in clothes a wantonness, I thought, remembering the subtly perverse eroticism of a suave poem by one of the 17th Century English puritan poets, though of course, Sonia wasn't wearing any clothes at all. I did imagine her, though, in a torn and shredded shift and ... Oh, well! Misty, stop that!

As if to wake Misty up from her mental meanderings, Sonia tugged at my leash, a trifle impatiently, and Tracy gave me a hard loud slap on the bottom. When I turned, Tracy had the effrontery to grin at me. I stuck out my tongue and growled a mutinous Misty Hoyt growl deep in my throat.

Tracy, truly, was as cute as a button. She growled back. "Remember, Misty, if Kirill doesn't marry you, I will."

The young man laughed. "You seem to have fun, the three of you, even the prisoner."

"Yes, Misty is a prize," said Sonia, "She's a high-stepping, high-spirited little filly, and, even if she is a traitor and a spy, we value her very much."

We came to the castle-like residence. In front of the entrance, SUVs were lined up. Sergei's stretch limousine was parked off to one side. Guards and drivers were lounging around. Most were Sergei's men; others were wearing the uniform of Nassir's terrorist group, and still others belonged to Baluchi. Presumably, Baluchi's men – and some of Baluchi's troops, I noticed, were women – didn't know what was happening to their master. All the men – and the women – straightened up, and stared at us. Some seemed to like what they saw; Nassir's men, though, glared, and then turned their backs. We were clearly, all three of us, an abomination. These divisions were almost certainly something we could use.

Tracy followed my glance, and she understood what I was thinking, and she nodded, and then she slapped me on the bum again – she really, really liked to do that – and she said, with a smirk, "Oh, you are so intelligent, Misty Hoyt. How is it you get yourself in these terrible fixes, about to be offered up as a sacrifice to Baluchi of all people?!"

The young guard laughed. "I'll leave you now," he said, bowing slightly, to all three of us I noticed, and he saluted.

"No, why don't you come along – join the fun," said Sonia, giving him a big smile. "I'm sure Sergei would agree. We may need a man to help us if the situation gets out of hand. You never know what might happen."

"Well ..." He grinned and shrugged.

"Do you want to check with Sergei? I'm sure it will be alright. I'm sure he would approve."

"No, no, well, yes, if I can be of service to you ladies. I shall come with you then."

I wondered what Sonia was doing – but then I realized, or thought I did. The young man had a pistol and a submachine gun, a cluster of magazines of ammunition, and a knife and a walkie-talkie. We had no weapons. He was our walking arsenal.

"What is your name?" Sonia said. "I think you are new. I haven't seen you before."

"Anton. I worked for Sergei in Moscow until last week. I just got here three days ago."

"Ah. Well, I am Sonia. That is Tracy. And our charming manacled guest is Misty – Misty Hoyt."

Yes, I have seen you, all of you. You were ... ah ..." He seemed a bit embarrassed; he looked down.

"We were wrestling in the mud."

"Yes, yes, that is it. It was a real show, very, ah, exiting. It made the men very, very, well, very happy."

"We try to provide entertainment," said Sonia, and she gave him the most unbelievably beautiful smile.

Anton blushed, I swear – he blushed. My earrings and chains jangled, and he glanced at me, and he saw – and understood – that I had seen him blush. He half closed his eyes, looked down, and smiled a sheepish smile.

We went through the arching gothic entrance. There were guards outside, but inside, the big vestibule was empty. The fire was still burning in the fireplace. Betty was curled up in her Plexiglas cage.

"I think Betty can help us," said Sonia. "You don't mind snakes, do you?" she turned to Anton.

"No, not at all," he said. He was definitely flattered to be accompanying the three naked slaves on their mission, and particularly Sonia, who, though known to be a "slave" was, in fact, Sergei's lover and advisor and had survived in that role for almost three and a half years, which was, so the lore went, a record.

Sonia knelt next to the cage and opened the cage door. The flames of the fireplace reflected in oily ripples on the long, fine lines of Sonia's body, delineating the stipples of grease and sweat and mud. Degas would have loved to draw her, I thought, or Ingres would have painted her as a goddess, yawning, stretching her body out to its full voluptuous length, or Delacroix would have sketched her in quick strokes and splashes of color as a lounging, long-limbed, and tragic harem girl, enslaved to a muscular libidinous bearded sultan in billowing trousers, his flashing eyes and his scimitar lingering, shining and sinister, in the penumbra of draperies and tapestries. Feeling Sonia's presence, Betty uncurled herself and stuck her head out of the cage; she flicked her tongue inquisitively and pushed her snout against Sonia's offered hand; and then she came slithering out and wrapped herself around Sonia's arm and then around Sonia's body, hanging from Sonia's shoulder and looking around, her snake eyes taking us all in, her head turning this way and that, swaying back and forth, and her tongue flickering. Sonia closed the cage door, turned the dial to lower the temperature inside the cage, and stood up. "Do you mind looking after Betty, Misty?"

"How am I supposed to ...?" I was handcuffed, after all, with my arms pinioned behind my back; how could I handle a snake?"

"Don't worry. Betty likes you."

"Well, I like Betty too, but that doesn't mean ..."

"Here. You two are made for each other." Sonia looped Betty over my shoulders. Betty accepted me as her perch and slithered off Sonia and settled down on me; her head riding above my shoulders; she swung out in front of me and stared at me, only about three inches from my face, her tongue flashing and her serpent eyes considering me, calmly, then, seemingly reassured, she curled around me, part of her body going down between my legs, and wrapping itself around my thigh and my waist and my breasts, making the rings and chains of my breasts and ears tinkle. She tickled. It was not unpleasant. It occurred to me that Betty, perhaps combined with a fig leaf, would be quite a nice costume to wear for a philosophic evening at, say, the Café Flore in Paris. Maybe James and I should adopt Betty if we managed to survive all of this. But I was not sure I would approve of Betty slaughtering ten kilos of rabbits or whatever she needed a day, and I would have to get her the rabbits, poor things, or goats or whatever she ate. So, on second thought ... Betty was tickling my ear with her tongue and had decided to examine my scarlet topknot. Her head was lying flat on my skull, rattling some of the earrings, and, as we passed a full-length mirror, I saw that her tail was wagging out behind my bum, as if I had a pointed, mottled, café-latte Louis Vuitton patterned tail myself, and was wagging it.

Such frivolities aside, the relevant thing here – I suddenly realized – was a curious item in the briefing we had uploaded on Nassir. He was a very courageous and deadly fighter; he had survived six assassination attempts, by Mossad, by Shin Bet, by the Soviet Intelligence Service, by French Special Forces, and by the Iranians. He was tough. But a footnote held this interesting tidbit: Nassir was terrified of snakes. And it seemed this was a deep dark secret; none of his collaborators knew of this fear. I only hoped the intelligence was accurate.

"Betty does seem to like you," Anton said.

"I think she does," I looked at him. It was the first time he had spoken directly to me. "And I like her. She's a super accessory."

Anton shook his head as if bemused by so much perversity gathered in one small Grotesque Tattooed Punk-Goth package, and a shackled prisoner to boot.

We went up the grandiose marble staircase, the click-click of our high heels muffled, luckily, by the lush richly patterned Persian carpet, held down by goldplated metal rods, which covered the marble steps of the staircase. And, then, two floors up the spiral staircase, we came to the balcony-like platform outside Baluchi's suite of apartments. Everything was gilded and ornate, and hanging close above us was a monstrous golden and crystal chandelier, its myriad lights blazing, lighting us up as if we were on a stage. In one of the gilded mirrors hanging on the white marble walls, I caught a glimpse of myself – a naked girl cartoon kaleidoscope with a scarlet topknot and a creamy white eight-foot python curled around her. Behind the three-meter-high oak doors, inside his suite, Baluchi was being beaten and threatened by Nassir Khalid. At the door were two of Khalid's men, both armed with submachine guns.

"Stop! What are you doing here?"

"Sergei Platonov told us to bring our prisoner Misty Hoyt and Betty – Betty's the python – to help Nassir work with Baluchi. He thought these two might be useful." Sonia pushed me forward so my splendor – and that of Betty – could be fully appreciated and, before he could think of refusing it, she handed my leash to one of the guards – "Here, hold this!" He looked at the leash and then at me, and as he said, "But what do I do with this –?"

Sonia thwacked him on the side of the temple, and in one smooth movement as he fell, she grabbed his submachine gun – it had a silencer, I noted – and with a short, muffled burst, she felled the other guard before he could even turn around. Two down – one to go!

Anton said, "What the hell, what are you ...?"

"Shush, Anton." Tracy had her razor wire tight around his throat, poised for the kill. "One move and you are dead."

Betty hovered just off my right shoulder, out in front of me; she was lazily slapping my left buttock with her tail. Her head – with its narrow triangular snout and crafty serpent eyes – seemed interested in what was going on; she swayed back and forth, following the action. Slowly and carefully, I slipped out of the handcuffs, so as not to alarm the python. She turned her snout around again, quizzically, and stared at me with her sleepy snake eyes, as if to ask: What are you doing, what is going on? "Everything is cool, Betty," I said in my most soothing voice. She seemed reassured and went back to watching the little drama playing out between Sonia, Tracy, and Anton. I rubbed my wrist and reeled in my leash. I didn't want somebody grabbing it and dragging me around.

Sonia knelt down and relieved the unconscious guard of his sidearm, pulling it out of the leather holster and – after checking that it was equipped with a silencer – she shot him through the temple, just as he was opening his eyes and beginning to groan. He was a handsome young man, and his eyes remained open, just the hint of a startled expression frozen on his face.

"What is going on?" Anton was red in the face; the razor wire was pressed tight against his jugular.

"I'm sorry, Anton," Sonia said, lifting the pistol and turning it towards him, "We didn't have time to explain."

"Explain what?" Anton coughed. A ribbon of blood showed at his throat, where Tracy held the razor wire tight. Without razor wire to hold her ponytail in place, her hair had once again tumbled free, a luminous tangle glittering in the lights of the golden chandelier. Anton's eyes were wide in terror. He knew she could kill him in an instant.

"Nassir is torturing Kaleem Baluchi," said Sonia. "These are Nassir's men. We have come to capture Nassir, rescue Baluchi, and interrogate both of them."

"Agent 452," Anton said, over his shoulder, to Tracy.

"What?"

"You are agent 452, or Curly Sparkles the Third."

Sonia kept the pistol aimed straight at Anton.

Tracy stepped back, letting the wire fall away from Anton's neck. She blinked at him. "What's the black thumb?"

"Istanbul."

"What's the red thumb?"

"Soho."

"Which Soho?"

"London."

"What is the worst food in the Moscow canteen?"

"Chicken curry, particularly if Svetlana's mother makes it."

Tracy nodded.

"So?" Sonia was still pointing the gun; it was clear she was mistrustful of both Anton and Tracy.

"Everybody, please keep cool." I went to the staircase railing, still clothed in Betty, who did seem to like to cling to me. I looked down. There was no sign of life. Nobody, it seemed, had heard the shots. Nobody was coming up the grand marble stairway.

Anton was talking quickly. "Moscow central got the information, four days ago, from Paris, that James Hewitt Spencer had been kidnapped. We also got information that Sergei Platonov had acquired nukes from Baluchi. I had already infiltrated Sergei's gang in Moscow. I got myself sent here." Anton rubbed his neck and looked at the blood on his fingers. "Tracy, we thought you were dead. Agent 452 was dead."

"Yes, I thought Moscow thought so." Tracy was still holding the deadly wire.

I turned and came back toward them, with Betty, my guardian angel, hovering over my shoulders. The earpiece began to speak; it was James funneled through Paris. "Misty, Moscow says Anton is theirs, he's a colleague of Tracy's, though she has never met him; just now they matched his voice patterns with their audio files; Anton is authentic. Moscow insists he can help you, and they ask you to trust him. Anton is an expert on Khalid Nassir, and he speaks perfect Arabic."

"Okay," I said. I turned to Sonia. "Paris says that Moscow confirms that Anton is one of theirs. They've matched his voice patterns. They ask us to trust him. He speaks perfect Arabic, they say."

Sonia looked doubtful, but she said, "Okay, Anton."

"Good," he said, rubbing his throat.

"Sorry," Tracy looked contrite.

"No problem – I would have done exactly the same; in fact, I probably wouldn't have hesitated the way you did. Thank you."

Again, James spoke in my ear. Hearing his voice this way was so intimate and so comforting I almost shivered in delight. "Misty, I'm going to turn the lights off and on in Baluchi's apartment. I can do it from here. That way, he will be a bit distracted. And then Anton can shout, in Arabic, 'Nassir! There's a problem.' Nassir should open the door, and then you get in. Remember: Try not to kill him."

"Okay," I said. And I relayed the information.

Anton was looking at me rather oddly.

"Earpiece," I said, "I'm linked to Paris and Moscow and Washington and to James back in the bunker."

He nodded and looked me up and down, carefully examining me for the first time. Betty aimed her snout at him as if curious, or perhaps jealous of her perch, which was me, and ready to defend it.

We got into position, around the door.

"Now," James whispered in my ear.

"Now," I said.

Anton knocked on the door, and shouted, in Arabic. "Nassir, there's a problem!"

After what seemed a very long moment, Nassir opened the door. We slammed our way through it, and before Nassir could say anything, he was stomach down on the floor, arms behind his back, pinned under Anton. Tracy glanced at me, "Handcuffs!" I handed her the handcuffs, and she snapped them onto Nassir, pinning his arms against his back, and locking the cuffs.

Betty and I went over to Baluchi, who sat rigid on the chair, his arms tied tight behind his back.

"Hello, Master Baluchi," I said, and I bowed slightly; Betty swayed out in front of me, aiming her curious triangular head at Kaleem Baluchi. He was naked except for that old loincloth; he glowed with sweat; his belly seemed even more enormous than before. There were bruises on his face, he had one black eye, and a trickle of blood at the side of his mouth. "Ah, Goddess Misty Hoyt," he said, "Goddess, have you and your nymphs and warriors have come to save me?"

"In a sense, we have, Kaleem Baluchi." I bowed. His round eyes roved up and down my body, where the chains he had adorned me with were still attached to the rings; they jingled as I bowed; Kaleem had a strangely lascivious and worshipful glow in his large brown eyes; he licked his lips; he blinked at Betty who swayed towards him and then swayed back.

"You are truly a goddess from ancient times, Misty Hoyt," he said, gazing at me with an increasingly weird expression. "You are a kaleidoscope of sacred imagery, the ultimate principle of being in all its multifarious splendor bodied forth in polychromatic glory – like a living temple of the goddess Devi."

"Thank you, Master Baluchi. You are extremely gracious." I bowed again, thinking that Baluchi was becoming rather grandiloquent and theological; perhaps this weird form of piety, and perversion – for all the glories of paganism are now seen as perversions – if it was a genuine feeling, could be put to some use; Betty swayed with me, examining Baluchi, and then turning a quizzical snout towards me, her flickering tongue almost touching my lips, a gleam in her serpent eyes.

"We have to stop the nuclear bombs, Master Baluchi, the bombs you sold to Sergei Platonov and which he sold to Nassir, and which we think are now in place, and ticking away, and threatening to kill millions," I said. "We are counting on you. Your humble Goddess, Misty Hoyt, is counting on you."

"The problem is this, Goddess Misty. That man Nassir – who is an unprincipled terrorist – is going to kill my daughter. And he already knows too much. He has set several of the bombs going. I do not know how to stop them."

Sonia and Anton set handcuffed Nassir down on a chair. He said nothing; his fierce eyes glared, their dark brilliance focused on me.

Baluchi glanced at Nassir and swallowed, "As I said, that evil man has set several of the bombs ticking. He is going to kill my adopted daughter if I don't give him the codes for the other bombs, Goddess Misty. And he has an agent who will set another bomb ticking.

"Which bombs are ticking?"

"Paris and New York. The New York bomb is probably being set right now. The Tel Aviv bomb is not yet in place. It is on a yacht headed for the Tel Aviv yacht club. The Moscow and Tehran bombs are in place, but the timers have not yet been set in motion; on the spot, they cannot be set in motion unless someone has the code – and from a distance, they cannot be set in motion unless someone has the telephone number and the code. Each bomb has its own code and telephone number." Sweat gleamed on his forehead; his eyes were big and sad.

"Where is the Paris bomb?"

"I don't know. Nassir knows, I think he knows, but even he may not know."

"And how much time?"

"Oh, Goddess, you must save my daughter."

"I will. We will. We'll try, Baluchi. Where is she?"

"She was in Provence, in France, going to school in Cannes. She was kidnapped on her way home. It was not reported to the police."

"How long do we have – in Paris, in New York?"

Baluchi told me what he knew; or what he claimed he knew. It turned out the bomb was to go off in Paris in about three hours, but we didn't know where it was. Baluchi had his computer with him and a secure cellphone. His computer had a specific coding device, and it was the only one that could stop and reprogram the bombs.

"So, you are saying, if we don't use your computer, we can't stop the bombs."

"That's right." Baluchi cleared his throat. "You have to ring the numbers from my computer and enter the codes from my computer."

I looked at the computer. It was a top-end laptop, but a small package just the same. It had been sitting on his bed. Now it was sitting in front of me, on this table, innocent and innocuous-looking. It was the doomsday machine.

"I was able to block most of the bombs. Not all. That's why Nassir was ... so unpleasant to me."

"Unpleasant."

"Yes, a trifle. It is my daughter Sara that is important."

"May I?" I motioned towards the computer.

"Of course, Goddess Misty Hoyt. What's mine is yours."

Baluchi, I decided, was crazy, mad as a hatter. But we could use his craziness. He gave me his password, and I opened the computer and set to work tracing the calls he had made and the codes he had inserted. And I downloaded all of his computer's contents to Paris, which sent the results onward to Washington, London, Moscow, and Jerusalem. The Iranians had been linked into the network too. I sat there, working on the computer, while Baluchi, my respectful worshipper and one of the great murderers of the world, sat just behind me, still tied up on the chair, and sweated.

"But only Nassir knows how to stop the bombs that have already been set ticking, right?" I turned to Baluchi.

"That is correct, Misty Hoyt. He set them using his computer, which is there. And he changed the 'stop' code so I would not know how to stop the bombs, nor would anyone else." Baluchi nodded towards another computer; it was another laptop, sitting innocently on the other side of the bed.

I frowned and fingered my nose ring: This was a complicated jigsaw puzzle, with plots overlaying plots, codes overlaying codes.

Betty swayed out from my shoulder, turned her snout toward me, and tickled my ear, making the earrings rattle. She did it again and seemed pleased.

"So, Kaleem, to summarize: you sold the nukes to Sergei?"

"Yes."

"And Sergei sold them to Nassir?"

"Yes, Goddess, that is correct."

"Hmm." I stood up. Betty swayed and tightened her grip. I needed to get a clear image of this – oh, what a tangled web! I stretched. Betty swayed easily out from me, her head dancing in the air, up and down, just in front of my face. My chains and rattled, and my loop earrings jangled. Sonia and Tracy and Anton all turned to stare at me.

Tracy puckered her lips in a giant smooch and blew it off the palm of her hand towards me.

I looked down at myself. My body gleamed with sweat; sweat dripped from the nipple-rings, and drops of sweat like silver beads hung from the silver chains. Every inch of skin was varnished to highlights of dazzling color. I shimmied and stretched my arms straight up over my head and pirouetted around. Betty swayed and allowed herself to be carried with me. I was a one-girl circus.

I turned to Baluchi, who was staring up at me with his giant wet brown eyes. "And, dear Kaleem, when you realized that the nukes had gone to Nassir, you were not happy."

"No, Goddess, I was not delighted. I am an arms dealer. I do business with anyone and everyone. But I abhor fanatics."

"So, you tried to stop him – by blocking the bombs."

"Yes, my computer was still linked into their programs, and I have the telephone numbers to reach all of them, almost all of them so that I could stop the clocks, by remote, but ..."

"But?" I sat down and swiveled the chair around, so I was facing him.

His big brown eyes stared at me. He cleared his throat. "But, as I said, he re-coded some of the bombs. He knows the new codes; I don't."

"So, we have to discover his codes and use your computer to phone the bombs, insert the codes, and stop the timers and prevent the bombs from going off."

"Yes," Baluchi cleared his throat. "That is the situation, Goddess Misty Hoyt."

I loved the idea of being Goddess Misty Hoyt, but there was no time to celebrate. "You are a very naughty boy, Kaleem Baluchi, selling those nasty nukes to a bad man like Sergei Platonov!"

"Yes, Goddess, Misty Hoyt, I am very naughty. I must be punished." He looked down. The sweat on his forehead and belly glowed like a lacquer of silver and gold. There was a thin, sly, childlike smile on his lips; he undoubtedly was imagining me or somebody like me, naked and all in a lather, wielding a whip and giving him a good spanking, or a perfectly wonderful whipping.

"You will be punished later, Kaleem Baluchi. I promise it." I lifted Nassir's computer off the bed and placed it on the desk next to Baluchi's computer; one computer could turn off the bombs; the other computer might lead to the codes which would be needed to turn off the bombs; it might also tell us where the bombs were.

Okay – time to play!

CHAPTER 9 – APOCALYPSE

The next few hours were exciting.

I asked Paris to find and rescue Baluchi's daughter. French intelligence had been monitoring Khalid Nassir's European network; they knew about many of his safe houses and many of his contacts and accomplices.

Now they used street cameras, traffic cameras, and highway cameras on the toll road to locate the vehicle used for the kidnapping. It was last seen heading up the D4 road behind Antibes, towards the little town of Grasse, famous for its perfumes.

One of Khalid's known bases was a farmhouse in the mountainous foothills fifteen kilometers from Grasse. Secret cameras set up on the roadside and in the hills near the farmhouse had already been monitoring activity there. That was almost certainly where Sara was being held prisoner, if she was still alive.

Orders were given to surround the farmhouse. If the information proved correct, then French Special Forces would assault the farmhouse and try to free Kaleem's adopted daughter. Sara was twelve. She had been kidnapped by one of Khalid's sleeper cells and almost certainly transported to the farmhouse.

James, back in the bunker, was able to process more data faster than I was, as he had access to more computer power than I, and he kept feeding me a stream of information.

It was exciting and a strangely erotic feeling, being so close to James, and yet so far, with his voice whispering in my ear for only me and Paris and London and Washington and Jerusalem and Tehran and Moscow to hear.

Nassir was sitting rigidly in the chair while Sonia and Anton and Tracy grilled him about the whereabouts of the bombs, the codes, and the time left. He refused to answer any questions whatsoever. Even Betty seemed unable to convince him, though he cowered and recoiled each time her snout approached his face, and he shivered in what I suppose was a mixture of fear and disgust when she wrapped herself around him.

Baluchi whispered to me. "You like the chains, goddess?"

I glanced at him, I was busy typing, and trying to hack into Nassir's secret files. They were doing the same in Paris and Moscow and Washington, I was sure.

"I adore the chains, Master Baluchi," I said, out of the corner of my mouth. "You are a very fine and loyal worshipper, Baluchi. And soon, I shall arrange for exemplary punishment. Perhaps you should be tickled to death."

He grinned at me, a huge smile, as if I had given him the greatest of gifts. Reflections danced off his forehead and his enormous smooth round belly. The loincloth was barely visible underneath his vast sagging girth.

He was truly weird, this Kaleem Baluchi; underneath my banter with him, I seethed with anger and indignation; he had sold arms to some of the cruelest most bloodthirsty governments and tyrants in the world, and he had smuggled arms into some of the worst civil wars in the world, and now he had unleashed this nuclear nightmare. And here we were, he and I, chatting like old buddies in our little playland fantasy where he was the worshiper, and I was the fetish goddess. I wasn't sure whether he was really crazy, secretly a serial killer and sadist who would dismember me as part of some sort of private ecstatic ritual, or where he was totally rational and merely playing me along, buying time, or whether he really did in some weird fetishistic way worship me – James in my ear thought the last hypothesis was the right hypothesis, "After all, Misty," James said, "I worship you, and I also think this new name of yours, Misty Hoyt is an exquisitely ridiculous choice, yet another twist in your adorable complexity," James said, "Humor Baluchi. He's become half-crazy probably. If you do what he does, trading in mass death, you have to become so indifferent to human life, as to become crazy, in the end, unless you are a pure fanatic like Nassir."

Seeing that Nassir was resistant to interrogation, Baluchi, still tied in his chair, took it upon himself to lecture the fanatic. "Your god is a poor abstract and absent thing, Nassir, sublime, perhaps, but merely a figment of your imagination."

Sonia looked at Baluchi and grinned. Sonia decided Baluchi would be an effective interrogator. She untied the ropes and released him. Baluchi stood up and flexed his arms. Betty reached out to him, and decided he was perhaps more interesting than I. I let her go. She would be a very nice addition to Baluchi's nakedness.

"Your god is unreal, Nassir, and you are a fool, a cruel fool, but a fool!"

"Shut up," Nassir snapped back.

Baluchi was not to be shut up so easily. He ambled over, a giant Buddha dressed in a loincloth and wrapped in a python, and sidled up to Nassir. "Here, in Misty Hoyt, you see the true symbol of divinity, the goddess, in flesh and blood, an incarnation of the eternal principles of life and death, desire and fecundity, a multicolored gateway to the mysteries."

I thought, the gateway to the mysteries – me? That was pretty rich, but perhaps it is true, out of the womb, mysteriously, it must have seemed to our ancient forbearers, life. And life is a mystery. I stared at the screen: if only I could understand how Nassir had coded the timers? Hmm ...

"Obscene fool," Nassir hissed.

"Now, now," said Sonia, "Don't be tetchy."

"Obscene fool," Nassir repeated, and he spat.

Baluchi chortled. "Oh, I am perhaps not so foolish, nor even so obscene. In Goddess Misty Hoyt, we see the generous, the maternal, the female principle, far beyond the crabbed, and cruel, death-dealing, death-worshipping patriarchal macho vacuity you call your God, an evil parody of an obscene old man, a wicked tribal elder, the abomination before which you, my dear Nassir, prostrate yourself, a tangle of cruelty and prejudice and vengeful sadism that you wish all human beings to submit to. You wish to reduce everyone to your insignificant level. You are blasphemous in the disservice you do to God, even to your version of God. I am sure that your God would turn away from you in disgust."

"Silence, you fool." Nassir strained to escape his bonds.

Anton walked back and slapped him, hard. "Sit still, Nassir."

Baluchi blinked his eyes, and, with a strangely bland, almost benign expression, he gazed down at Nassir. "The only true virtue your God possesses, Nassir, is that He doesn't exist." Baluchi's belly glowed with sweat, and he towered over Nassir, who stared back at him with his coal-black fiery eyes.

Betty, draped over Baluchi's shoulders, swung herself out towards Nassir. He shuttered and drew back, and, foaming at the mouth, he spat out the words, "You will all die, all of you, and I will see you die. If I die, it is nothing; it means nothing. I die a martyr."

"But, my dear Nassir, you are a martyr to what and for what?"
"God."

"Ah, to God, for God. How wonderful, how sublime, how

senseless, how absolutely without meaning, my dear Nassir. You are a most accomplished nihilist, dear Nassir, dying for something which does not exist. In your heart of hearts, you most assuredly do not believe in Him. You believe, and I am sure of this, in nothing."

Nassir spat towards Baluchi, but the spit fell short; Baluchi had pirouetted out of range.

Betty noticed the spit, and spun her head towards it, and then she followed it to its origin, swinging her attention, aroused now, attentive now, back to Nassir, she drew back as if to strike at him: perhaps she sensed the spit had been an attack.

Nassir trembled. If he could have raised his arm to protect himself, he would have.

Betty waited, her head swaying slightly, then she relaxed, and stretching out from Baluchi's arm, she approached Nassir's face slowly, her head tilted to one side.

Baluchi continued his lecture. "But, what is unpardonable, dear Nassir, is that you will kill millions in your folly, and as you know millions more will die because of your ridiculous cult of martyrdom, since those you have attacked, will attack back and lay waste to all the cities and countrysides."

Betty's snout was now only an inch, maybe a centimeter, from Nassir's face. She hovered there, the end of her forked tongue flicking up and down.

Nassir trembled. He stared as if hypnotized at the snake. Betty continued to hover, not moving, her tongue flashing and flickering. I wondered what she was thinking. What does a python think? I suppose that is a mystery I shall never solve, and a question to which there is, probably, no answer that humans will ever know.

Baluchi nodded toward me. "Behold, Nassir, here, in the person of Misty Hoyt, is the true divinity. Not cold, not dead, not imaginary, but real, alive, a divinity of flesh and blood, passion and intelligence."

Oh, boy, Misty Hoyt, the goddess – a rival to Yahweh, God, and Allah! Flattering, I suppose but utterly ridiculous. I'm an old stock Yankee girl, English, and Scottish, with some Huguenot French and Native American blood way back, or at least so I have been told, and that's about the sum of it. I turned my attention back to the keyboard.

"You see, Nassir, the goddess is multiple and is multicolored and present in all things; her sensuality and forgiveness are infinite, and she embraces all experience, all forms of life and death, all of life is in her, and many goddess and goddesses inhabit her spirit, it is as if the memory and sensuality of all of the human race, from its very beginnings, were present here, here in this one place. Look, look at this, look at the dragon, look at the serpent, look at this blossoming emerald flower, look at the silver chains, the embodiment of beauty enslaved and contained, look at the fierce energy, the light of life, in her eyes, look at the delicacy of her movements, of her gestures, of her fingers as they dance over the keyboard, of her thoughts ..."

Anton came over, crouched down, and stared at the screen. "How's it going?"

"Not fast enough, but it is going."

Anton stared at the screen, flashing rows of code. "We could torture Nassir, but I don't think it would do any good. He's tough; he's a true believer; whatever we do, he won't crack; it would take too much time – time we don't have."

Tracy and Sonia joined us. "I agree," said Sonia, putting her hand on my shoulder. "Let's not waste time on Nassir. He can be interrogated later, if we get out of here."

"Yes," said Tracy.

"Yes," Anton nodded.

I was listening to their discussion and to Baluchi with half an ear and watching the little drama with half an eye – and busy typing and thinking about how to penetrate the codes. I agreed that torture would be messy and ineffective, and, as to Baluchi and his theology, I wasn't sure where all this praise and all these hosannas to the painted, particolored, pagan Goddess Misty Hoyt would lead. I certainly didn't think they would convince Nassir that I was lovable or to be worshipped and obeyed. Nassir had had five wives, dressed them in potato sacks, was known to hate women of any independence of mind or spirit, and to rape any woman – and, when the possibly presented itself, young boys – on the slightest pretext – which always involved evoking God's will, and other such wicked self-serving self-righteous pseudo-divine bullshit for which I, personally, had the utmost disdain and no patience whatsoever: it was criminal and ridiculous all at once. Nassir's education had involved, mostly, reciting verses from the holy book, over, and over, and over, and interpreting all the subtleties that such recitation involved, in tone of voice, emphasis, and rhythm; and in having his own voice, in recitation, amplified by loudspeakers, broadcast to the faithful. Easy to take oneself for God, or certainly for His voice on earth, in such circumstances. After all, yours is the voice of God. Nassir's mind, I presumed – and I knew it was a presumption – had almost certainly never been truly opened ever, not to anything – not to doubt, not to respect for life or for people just because they existed, not to any sense of true equality and humility, not to any sense of the fallibility and relativity of knowledge and belief. He had studied computer science at the University of Manchester and was extraordinarily clever, but that had not, it seemed, turned him into a democrat or secularist or even into a moderate. A wounded and vulnerable identity and high intelligence stiffened by inculcated dogma is a difficult sickness to cure.

Baluchi, walking up and down, was delivering his sermon. "You see, Nassir, a world filled with wonder – with nymphs and satyrs and wood-sprites, and chimeras and goddesses and gods, all randy and desirous, all in love, or consumed by hate, a world where every brook and stream and mountain is sacred, where every animal has its spirit, its inimitable being, where every pathway leads to adventure, where every conscious being is unique, such a world is a much richer, more delightful, more human world that the world abandoned by your sterile arrogant lonely and unreal god, a god who worships only death, not life, who has no sex life and no desires, who is nothing and nobody and nowhere."

Nassir flared, screaming. "You are a fool, an apostate, a pagan. You worship all that fades and dies and is pure filth and wickedness. You will go to hell."

"Yes, certainly, Nassir, you are right. I am a pagan," Baluchi said. "As for hell, and going there ..."

I glanced up. Baluchi's huge belly glowed even more than before; under it, his loincloth hung low, just a glimpse of white dangling cloth. He winked at me. I sketched a smile – a goddess must be gracious – sighed, and turned my attention back to the keyboard.

Baluchi grumbled. "Stupid ideas of honor robbed me of much that makes a man, and, yet, still, I have tasted to the full many of the pleasures of this life. I am not afraid of the next life because there is no next life. So it is that death means nothing."

"You will burn in hell."

"Ah," Baluchi shrugged, "That too, dear Nassir, is an illusion." Betty slid off Baluchi's shoulders, and Sonia picked her up, allowed her to swing off her arms, and she carried the snake over to Nassir; Betty hovered in front of Nassir's face, and then she slid off Sonia and onto Nassir and curled herself around his shoulders; her head hovered out in front of him, considering his expression.

Nassir was terrified of the python; he resisted her blandishments and caresses – he merely shivered and closed his eyes, a cold sweat breaking out on his forehead.

Sonia lifted Betty off Nassir's shoulders and came over to me.

"Sit on Nassir's lap, Misty," said Sonia, "Give him a taste of true pagan glory."

"Yes," said Baluchi. "Give him a taste of divinity, Misty Hoyt."

"I don't have time. I'm decrypting," I said, scowling at the screen. I was eager to beat Paris and the others to the answers; really, it didn't matter who "won," but one of us – in Paris, Washington, Moscow, Jerusalem, and Tehran – did have to win; otherwise the bombs would almost certainly go off – and millions would die. James was whispering suggestions in my ear regarding codes and deciphering strategies – he was, I think, almost as good at this stuff as I.

"Please," Sonia came over and knelt next to my chair, crouching low, staring up at me.

"Hmm." I frowned and looked down at Sonia. She looked delicious. I began to reconsider the idea of torturing Nassir: Why didn't they just tear out his fingernails, or poke out one of his eyes? I didn't want to get close to Nassir. He gave me the creeps. Fanatics are the worst and most dangerous kinds of human beings. Their faith in their stupid ideas makes them incapable of empathy and fellow-feeling and capable of any cruelty, and, mostly, it makes them ethically obtuse and incapable of honor. They have no respect for anything or anybody, except for the obscenity of their crazy dogmas. Nassir was, in my eyes, incurable and utterly despicable. And he was an insult to the glory of a great religion – Islam – which he claimed to represent.

"We need you," said Sonia.

"Yes, this nut refuses to crack." Anton favored me with a grin.

"Okay, okay." I stood up, stretched, jingling my divine and holy chains and earrings, and glanced at Nassir. He glared at me.

"I don't think anything will make him crack," I said. "He wants to be a martyr, so nothing we can do to him will make a difference. Might as well give him a nice coffee with sugar and make him comfortable."

"Ha, ha, he's afraid of you, Misty," said Baluchi. Sweat dripped down his forehead. He blinked. His eyelashes were rimmed with silver drops. A rivulet of sweat ran between his breasts.

Nassir spat.

I turned to the self-proclaimed prophet. "Really, Nassir? You are afraid of me? What are you afraid of?" I walked towards him, giving to my walk the most sensual undulating gait I could manage; in this, the stilettoes were a great help. My breasts swayed back and forth, the nipple-rings sparkled, and the silver chains jingled and rippled with lamplight; and, I am quite sure, the sweat and oil made my tattoos glow, extra vivid, extra colorful. I was a walking poster – a crazy circus of perversity.

Anton gagged Nassir so that he couldn't bite. The man squirmed and twisted, but Anton was strong.

I swayed up to Nassir, and then I lowered myself down onto his lap, slowly, carefully, adjusting my position. At first, he was stoic, he went rigid, tried not to move, not to budge.

I gave him my best, most flirtatious, smile, which I am sure was supremely grotesque, mouthing pouts and grins with my tattooed gargoyle mask: in fact, I'm sure it was terrifyingly horrible. I ran my tongue over my lips. I fluttered my eyelids and gazed into his eyes. I was tempted to gouge out his eyes. This man raped women without compunction; indeed, killing women and children was part of his mandate from God, or so he claimed. He really was blasphemous, and insult to Islam, to all religions, to all forms, secular or mystical, theological or mundane, of righteousness. He loved to cut off people's hands and stone them to death and bury them alive or cut off their heads while the cameras were running. He adored taking selfies with his victims. "What are you afraid of, Khalid? Do you want to rape me?"

He growled, and his fiery dark eyes blinked at me.

"Are you afraid I will rape you?" I got off his lap and knelt before him. I put my hand to his crotch and massaged it. He stirred and winced. He was beginning to have an erection.

"Oh, mighty prophet, I see you are awake." I looked up at him. He glared at me, and he tried to shift his position. He tried to kick me away, but his legs were tied to the chair. I continued my little act. The erection, under his trousers, became harder. That was enough. I let it be. Caressing it would truly be an obscene act. Giving him pleasure, even if it was pain, was not something I wanted to do. Erections, for me, were sacred, both comic and holy and vaguely terrifying – a form of homage and desire, and in the right context, an act of love, but whatever dark secrets any particular erection held, I didn't want to know or even try to fathom what lay behind Nassir's excitement.

I put my hand to his beard and began to caress it very softly. "What are you afraid of, Khalid?" He squirmed. His dark eyes glowed with true fire, brilliant embers. He was an extremely handsome man. But I was getting tired of this; I had better things to do.

I bent forward and reached out my hands both thumbs extended; he squeezed his eyes shut. I think he thought I was going press my fingers in, pop his eyeballs, and gouge out his eyes. I kissed him on the forehead and held his face between my hands. He opened his eyes. I kissed him again, on the forehead. "Do you think only cruelty is divine, Khalid?"

I stared at him. Our eyes were now locked in a staring contest.

"I know that for you, I am an obscene monster, Khalid." I tweaked his nose. "I know that in your eyes, my body has been desecrated and that I am an abomination. But I know too that you don't know anything about me, or about anybody else either; you are too closed in your certainties and dogmas to be open to anyone else. You have followers, of course, people who worship you, people who will die for you, but you are alone, utterly alone. You have no imagination for other people's thoughts or feelings, no empathy, no understanding. Oh, yes, you can manipulate people, just like any skilled sociopath, but that is not empathy, it's not understanding, it's not humanity. But – I forgot. You are not human; you are a prophet; you are the voice of God; you are God. In your own mind, you have replaced your God with your Self. I am sure that is so."

He growled and squirmed, straining against the bonds.

"I think, and I say this with all modesty, Khalid, that you are the real obscenity, not me. It is too bad – you are a handsome, strong, intelligent, brave man, wasting your life in fanaticism and hatred and murder, trying to hasten the end of the world. And this world, Khalid, is, I dare say, the only world we have or that we will ever have. So, your war of hatred, your crusade or jihad, is a useless distraction from the real business – living and helping other people to live. It's just too bad that in some other time and in some other world you and I could have been friends. But, of course, you worship death, Nassir. And I love life. You are death. In fact, you are already dead, soulless, and dead. You don't know what it is – to be alive."

He glared at me. I knew from the beginning that it was useless. Fanaticism is like the plague. There is rarely a cure.

I stood up. "I give up," I said. "He's not human."

Anton nodded. He handed me the knife. "You do it," he said, "You do it."

I took the knife. I sighed. I leaned over and kissed Khalid again on the forehead. He stiffened, unsure whether I was going to stab out his eyes or cut his throat. Then, careful not to scratch him, I cut away and opened his gag.

He drooled, and he glared at me. "Whore, bitch," he muttered, "Filthy abomination."

"Thanks for the compliments," I said. "So, will you tell us where the bombs are, the bombs that are designed to kill millions of people?"

He spat at me – a huge gob of spittle, catching me in the cheek. I felt it, looked at it, smeared it on my breast, and I said, "Do you really believe in your God, Khalid, or is your God just a projection of your own poisonous ego?"

He spat again. But this time he missed. There is no dealing with some people. I winked at him and said, "Okay, well, I guess we agree to disagree." I turned away and sashayed my way, jingling, back to the computers.

"The natives are getting restless," James said in my earpiece. "I've been watching them on the monitors. They are getting nervous since they haven't seen Sergei for at least two hours now. I'll try to set up a distraction."

"We could stage an air alert," I said.

Baluchi spoke up. "You were too kind, Goddess, to such an evil man. But, of course, in your eyes, I am evil too. Well, let me tell you, Goddess, I am evil in my own eyes."

"There are many forms of evil, Master Baluchi," I said, "And, yes, I am certain you are evil; but, then, who is not?"

"You should not call me Master, Goddess. You should reserve that for your lover."

"My lover?"

"James Hewitt Spencer."

"What do you know about James?" While Baluchi answered

me, James, through the earpiece, told me that he and Baluchi had done business in the past.

"Oh," I said, and then I remembered, "The armored cars for that African country."

"Yes, the armored cars."

"Right," I whispered. James had been involved in a lot of tricky stuff, and he had shared with me, sometimes in the midst of our games, sometimes over a good meal, sometimes on long walks in the country or swimming expeditions, many a hairy tale of intrigue and skullduggery, so I was not entirely innocent of the shadowy side of his business and of the arms trade.

While Baluchi was droning charmingly on about nymphs and goddesses – he seemed to know the names of virtually every goddess that had ever existed – James was whispering in my ear, giving me an update on another looming problem: the huge storm Paris had mentioned was coming in and the Estimated Time of Arrival of the storm was now predicted to coincide with the ETA of the American-Russian airborne force; James had more access than I did; his computer had access to radar and multiple channels; while I was narrowly focused, concentrating on delving deep into Nassir's files. Much of the material was in English since he had studied computer engineering in Manchester, and many of his minions didn't speak Arabic.

I suddenly realized that I had cracked through to something important: a series of maps, and they had markings on them. This, of course, could be old material, but, no, it had been used recently, in fact, the file had been sent only a few hours ago. "I think I have something," I said, to Sonia and Tracy and Anton, to Paris, to James, to the various listening networks.

Betty had not been able to break Khalid either, so she had been returned to me. It was distracting, but it was stimulating too. She curled over my shoulders like a large boa, which

I suppose was only appropriate, and then she peered down at the keyboard and at the computer screen, and then she slipped upwards as if she were going to try to climb to the ceiling, and then she settled down again and just watched my fingers do their dance.

Sometimes obliquity, coming at problems from the side, the indirect, distracted approach, is the best way to solve a difficult problem. "By indirections, find directions out," as the Bard said. Being conscious of Betty lolling around on my body, as if I were a convenient tree or coat hanger, somehow increased my concentration. "I have three addresses for Paris," I said. I gave them the addresses.

Sonia, who had been searching through Nassir's files, said, "I think we have to get back to the bunker – and the command center – if we are going to neutralize the anti-aircraft defenses."

"Yes," I said, "And the computers there are much more powerful than what we've got here. They'll be useful for searches and communications."

"Right," said Tracy, "But how are we going to get back to the bunker. We'd have to take Nassir and Master Baluchi with us."

"Misty, the natives are quite possibly coming to visit you," James said again. "I see them on the monitor. Nassir's men are leaving their SUVs, they are having some sort of argument, and they are clustered in front of the front entrance. I think they are deciding what to do – maybe they are going to come up and check with Nassir. I imagine they are used to hearing from him, or his guards, regularly, and the silence – perhaps has alarmed them."

"Okay, we have to distract them."

"An alarm of some kind – maybe an aerial alert. That would help us see how they activate the system, too," I said.

Baluchi had been listening. "Goddess ..."

"Yes, Master Kaleem," I said, glancing at him. This goddess game was fun – up to a certain point, but there seemed to be no irony in his voice, none at all. Maybe James was right; maybe Baluchi was totally nuts, and, in his own picturesque way, in love with, or obsessed with, me. After all, I was a painted totem, an icon.

"Yes, Master Kaleem," I repeated.

"I am going to be punished, I know."

"Well, yes, I suppose you will be punished, Master Baluchi. But if you help all these good people – and help save millions of lives – you will have some powerful friends in Russia, in the West, in Israel, and even in Iran."

"Yes, yes, I understand. Under the bed is my suitcase, well, more a trunk than a suitcase."

"Really?" How had we not thought of that? Nobody had looked under the bed.

"It is full of weapons – grenades, in particular. They are very powerful. It also has my personal communications system. And, no, it is not bobby-trapped."

"You swear on the honor of me your Goddess Misty Hoyt, re-incarnation of the Great Mother Goddess, and of Isis and Hera and Asherah and so on and all the goddesses that have ever been and ever will be, and on the honor of my faithful servant Betty the python so help you God and forevermore, that it is not booby-trapped, amen?"

"I swear." He looked at me with his big droopy eyes. He glowed with sweat. "I swear on the honor of the chained and tattooed supreme Goddess Misty Hoyt and on the honor of Betty the python and etc. and all the fine print."

"Okay, then," I said, "Thank you, worshiper Kaleem Baluchi." I returned his glance with my most uppity Misty Hoyt Goddess stare, and glanced at Tracy: should we take a chance?

Tracy and Sonia nodded. Tracy bent down and crawled and wiggled under the bed and began to haul out the Kaleem's giant suitcase.

"And I would like you to liberate my pet." Sweat poured down Baluchi's forehead.

"Your pet?"

"You met her."

"Ah." Now I remembered. She was the deaf-mute blonde, the musician Sergei had turned into a deaf-mute, destroying her vocal cords and her eardrums. "She's tied up in some bedroom. Where is she?"

"In the next room, through the invisible door, hidden, safe from Nassir, behind that tapestry."

"An invisible door? We are idiots," said Sonia.

"Yes, yes, we are." Anton had his hands on his hips and was staring around, looking for other hidden surprises.

Sonia took her submachine gun, moved the curtain aside, and she and Anton pushed a painting aside, the secret door opened, and they went through it, while Tracy was hauling the big case out from under the bed and I sat there with Nassir and Baluchi – and Betty.

The girl, as I had seen earlier on the security screen, was tied up spread-eagled, face-up, on a bed. She had been waiting, patiently I suppose, for something to happen and since she was blindfolded and gagged and totally deaf, she had no idea what was going on, and she hadn't been able to make a noise – not even growl or moan. Sonia freed her, and the girl then insisted on going to the bathroom and having a quick shower, which she did, and then, still toweling herself, she joined us, wearing only her collar. We made a fine pair, she and I: the chained collar-wearing goddess and the collar-wearing deaf-mute slave.

"Ah, my dear!" Baluchi grinned at her. The girl went straight to him and kissed him on the lips, held him by the shoulders for a moment, and then bowed in front of him, but it seemed to be a friendly kiss and a friendly bow; then, suddenly, I understood: Baluchi was her savior and her protector; since he had bought her from Sergei, he had probably rescued her from further mutilation and probably a quick death.

Betty had been curled around Baluchi, but she now decided she might like to return to me. She stretched herself out to the very limit. Sonia picked her up and brought her over, and I reached out an arm, and Betty slithered across until she was perched on me. She rested her head on my topknot and curled herself around my body, being careful – or so it seemed – not to interfere with my typing.

I plunged back into the computer. I was drilling down as deep as I could into Nassir's secret files. His encryption techniques were really quite primitive, which surprised me, I half expected a trick, and decoy set of files. "Okay, I've got a couple of addresses in New York. The last address Nassir accessed was this – it's probably where the bomb is, at least it's my best guess at this moment." I gave them the address.

"Yes, Misty, that checks with what we found – we got to that information at exactly the same time as you!"

Everybody on the network had decided I was Misty; maybe this new identity – and appearance – was going to stick. I might even have to keep Betty. She peered over my shoulder at the computer screen.

Tracy had pulled the giant suitcase – it really was more a trunk than a suitcase – out from under the bed; now, she dragged it over towards Baluchi. The "suitcase" had a combination lock. Was the man going to blow us up with himself? I stood up, and Betty and I knelt before him. "Master Kaleem Baluchi, we are trying to save your adopted daughter. And we are trying to save millions of lives. You are not going to play a nasty trick on your most humble goddess and her friends, are you?"

"No, I swear."

"Okay. Your goddess trusts you."

The girl was watching my lips closely; when she realized that I was calling myself "goddess," she laughed and then covered her mouth, shyly, with one hand. It was a very graceful gesture.

Baluchi, speaking in slow, measured tones, gave Tracy the combination.

She opened the "suitcase." Inside was a cornucopia: grenades, a mobile phone, a walkie-talkie kind of device, guns, and a very small fold-up rocket launcher. There were rolls of duct tape, and handcuffs, and blindfolds, and various pistols.

"These are live?" Tracy looked up at Baluchi. She wiped her brow. Her hair was plastered against her forehead. She blinked away some sweat. Her eyelashes were beaded with silver. It seemed to be getting hotter and more humid in the apartment, and Tracy, like all of us, was glowing, soaked in sweat, golden, muddy, her hair loose, in strands down her face and neck. Her dark eyes bright, almost turning to liquid. I blinked and licked my lips. Time seemed to have folded up like an accordion, collapsing all the hours together into one, packing all the moments into one; and then, suddenly, it opened up again with a swooping sound, and it seemed like what happened only a short time back, was eons away, another life, another me. Only a few hours ago, Tracy and I had been pole dancing, then waltzing, and then performing in a variety of live sex acts before the crowd in the SS Marquis. It seemed like a lifetime.

"Well, well," said Tracy; she wiped her forehead, shook her head as if to rid it of cobwebs, and began to examine the weapons; her back glowed, pure gold, with sweat. The temperature must have been at least 40 degrees Celsius, the humidity 85 percent. "These are live?" she repeated the question.

"Yes," Baluchi coughed, "they are not for display. They work."
He glanced up at his "slave." She was standing beside him, and
she had put one hand on his shoulder and was following what
we were doing with what looked like great interest; she was obviously a highly intelligent – but deeply traumatized – young
woman.

"Good." Tracy picked up a grenade and examined it.

"And what about this?" Tracy held up the fold-up rocket
launcher.

"Yes. It works. It's very effective."

"These are the ammunition for it?" She pointed at a box of
neat little ten-inch shells.

"Yes."

To prepare him for our trip back to the bunker, Sonia and Anton were gagging Nassir, blindfolding him, taping his arms to his
sides and putting a hood – consisting of two pillowcases – over
his head. He was for the moment useless; he was not going to
give us anything.

Tracy held up the rocket launcher and a shell. "And it uses
these shells, like this?"

"Yes," Baluchi said, "I can help you, show you how to do it
quickly."

Tracy looked up at him. "Why are you helping us?"

Kaleem Baluchi was dripping sweat. Big drops of sweat were
falling from the end of his nose. "Because you are in the right.
Because I am tired, because I do not care if I die, because I worship Misty, my pagan goddess who has sacrificed and risked all
for the man she loves, and because you have all promised to save
my adopted daughter, because you have freed my pet Sandra,
who is my friend and is an innocent. I have loved few things –
aside from myself – in the world, but I love my daughter, and,
in my own way, I love my pet, Sandra. And Misty knows and

understands what and who I am. So, I shall fight to defend you, and I shall not harm you – I swear on the life of my daughter and on the life of Sandra."

We all glanced at each other.

Tracy, still kneeling next to the cornucopia of armament, said. "Okay, Baluchi, show us how the rest of this stuff works – and be fast about it."

Kaleem knelt next to Tracy, his great belly bulging over his skimpy loincloth. He truly did seem like a Buddha, but, of course, he was no Buddha. He was probably as far from Buddha as you could get. In the next few minutes, he showed us how to set the grenades, how best they were to be thrown, and how the fold-up rocket launcher worked.

Sandra, his "pet," acted as his assistant, holding the various objects up, and demonstrating them, as if he were a magician – a magician of death – and she his assistant. She was calm and competent. She was not just a pet.

"Let's hope we don't have to use all that stuff," I said, still sitting at the computer, still typing, still feverishly trying to figure out how to stop the bombs. Meantime, James was briefing me on what was happening in Paris and in New York. Emergency crews were headed to the addresses we had found in Nassir's files. I was getting almost a blow by blow account. Meanwhile, Nassir's men were going back to their SUVs. They were getting extra weapons. They were onto something: they were coming to get us.

"I do have another idea," said Baluchi.

"Yes."

"I have ten men and women, all extraordinary fighters, downstairs, in three vehicles off to the right, by the first gate. One of the vehicles is an armored car, with a high-powered machine-gun and a light cannon. They are not far from Nassir's men and his vehicles."

"Ah." I swiveled around to look at him.

Kaleem continued, speaking now, through my earpiece and me, to James and to Paris and the rest. "You can inform my people, James, by speaker, and in Sergei's voice, that I was being held prisoner by Nassir, that Sonia and Anton and Tracy have liberated me. And that they are going to take me, and Nassir – now our prisoner – to Sergei."

"Ah."

"That will set off a gunfight down on the ground."

"Perhaps we can get to the control room and to James – and avoid being slaughtered. Otherwise, they will all come storming in here, and there will be a slaughter."

"James, can you do that?"

"Yes, I can." James paused. "I could put a lot of static on the line, and they might think I am Sergei. But perhaps – if we are going to trust Kaleem – It would be better if he could talk directly to his men. And not do it through me. Do Baluchi's men have earphones connected to his system direct?"

"Yes, they do," Baluchi said.

"And, Kaleem, do you have access to your coms system?" James asked, through me.

"My coms system is here," said Baluchi, holding up his personal com set that Tracy had just lifted out of the suitcase. "My men would hear it from me, in their earphones. That would create a surprise, since Nassir's men would hear nothing. I could instruct my men – and women – to attack immediately, to kill Nassir's men or take them prisoner. Killing, though, would be quicker, easier, and more certain. Nassir's men are fanatics."

"Yes," said Sonia, "Killing would be safer."

"Yes," said Tracy.

"Definitely," said Anton.

"Yes," said James in my ear.

"Okay," I said, "there's probably no other way. Kill them."

"There isn't any other way," said Tracy.

"Okay," said Sonia, "If this works, we'll take all our equipment from here, and we'll concentrate in the bunker, and we try to reach the control room inside the bunker to neutralize the air defenses."

"Do we all agree?"

"Yes, Kaleem Baluchi sets off a gunfight to neutralize or eliminate Nassir's men."

"And we head to the bunker."

"And James will get Sergei's men to cooperate, by using their earpieces – maybe by transmitting orders through Boris."

"Right."

"We can use my armored car to go to the bunker," said Baluchi.

"Hmm," I said, "This is getting very cozy, Master Baluchi."

"Yes, it is," Baluchi beamed at me.

"You heard all of that, Paris?" I asked.

"Yes, Misty. The consensus here is that you are right. Do what you have to do and Godspeed!"

≈

The next twenty minutes were total confusion. We broadcast through their earpieces, separately, to Baluchi's men, and to Sergei's men, that Nassir had broken the deal; that he had taken Baluchi prisoner, and was preparing to execute him, but that Baluchi had been freed by Sonia and Anton and Tracy; that Baluchi's and Sergei's teams should, when Baluchi gave the signal, immediately eliminate Khalid's men; that we – Baluchi and Sonia and company – would be leaving the castle and heading back to the bunker, back to Sergei, and we would be taking Nassir as a prisoner with us.

We came down the stairs, carrying Baluchi's weapons, and his com set, and our computers. When we reached the door, Baluchi gave the signal through his handset and, within 10 seconds, the firefight outside began in a thunder of fire, cannon blasts from the armored car, and rat-tat-tat.

Nassir wiggled and struggled, but he could do nothing; he was blindfolded and gagged and had two pillowcases tied tight over his head, and he was handcuffed, and his arms were pinned to his sides with duct tape.

When we came out of the baronial entry, bullets were flying every which way. I crouched down. We threw two grenades at Nassir's cars. One of the vehicles exploded. Nassir's men had been taken by surprise, but they had reacted quickly. One of their remaining armored cars was spraying the area with bullets. Many men were down. Two of Nassir's SUV's were already on their sides and burning.

Sonia gave Kaleem Baluchi a pistol.

"You know how to shoot?"

"Yes, my dear, I know how to shoot."

For such a heavy man, and a eunuch, Kaleem was amazingly agile. I had a pistol and was taking potshots at the enemy. Betty, who was swinging from my shoulders, seemed indifferent to all the action. Baluchi's men were now by our side, with five of Sergei's guards.

"Does your friend know how to shoot?" Sonia nodded at Sandra, who was helping me carry the computers, slung over our shoulders.

"Yes, Sandra knows how to shoot." Baluchi wiped his forehead. "In fact, she is an excellent shot. I trained her."

Sonia handed Sandra a pistol. Sandra looked at it, checked the magazine, and gave Sonia a thumbs-up.

Two of Baluchi's men, strangely, were women. One of the women, wearing a headscarf, gave me a startled glance and then wide-eyed looked at Sonia and Tracy – and at Sandra: The Naked Brigade.

We made it to Baluchi's armored car, got it going, and running beside it and using it as shelter, we fought our way up towards the bunker; halfway up, the car was hit and swerved and skidded to a stop, the driver – another of Baluchi's warrior women – bailed out and joined us, so we abandoned the armored car, and hunkered down behind a low wall, near the ditch where earlier we had had our mud tussle and where I had almost been executed. Once again, it began to rain. The clouds were low, and the humidity was high, and by this time, it must have been about 45 degrees Celsius.

Bullets and grenades exploded all around us.

We ducked and splashed down in the muddy hot slush. Sandra was right beside me; she seemed to have adopted me. As we crouched in the shelter of the stone wall, I asked her how she was. She squinted at me, reading my lips, used her finger to write in the mud: "Still got a headache. Hangover." She grinned.

"Me too," I said. I turned to Baluchi. He was covered in mud. "Are you going to behave yourself, Kaleem?" I wasn't sure arming him was such a good idea.

"Yes, Goddess, I will behave myself," Baluchi wiped his forehead. "I am your servant, Goddess, even if I pay for my loyalty by going to my death or to prison for the rest of my life."

More bullets whizzed over our heads. They ricocheted off the stone wall. They shattered trees. They hit the blockhouse. They slammed into the mud. Sonia and Tracy were firing with submachine guns. Anton tossed grenades. Boris, with two of his men, came running down to help us.

"I am worried about Sergei. It's not like him to be so silent." Boris crouched close to Sonia. I was next to them, sitting with my back against the wall, Betty draped over my shoulders, and in my lap, her head coiled up, looking at me as if waiting for instructions. She, too, had gotten rather muddy but didn't seem to mind. I heard distant thunder, lightning flashes in the mountains, lighting up the mountain valleys, steel-blue flashes, far, far away, but coming towards us.

"Sergei is dead," Sonia said, looking Boris straight in the eye.

"Dead?"

"Yes, dead. "You, Boris, are now in charge."

"But, how, how is Sergei dead. How could he be dead? What happened?"

"I killed him."

"What?"

"I killed him so you could become chief, Boris."

"What? I cannot believe this."

"Well, I will take you to him, if you like."

"Yes, yes, do that." Boris stared at Sonia, with an incredible mixture of emotions, fear, desire, shock in his expression, lit up by the burning SUVs and reflections from the security lights, and I realized from the worshipful look in his eyes that he was in love with her. "Then we will talk, Sonia. Not everybody will follow me, you know that. We will have trouble, bad trouble."

"I know," said Sonia.

"The missile crews, they will not follow me. I'm certain." He was rubbing his, chin, thinking it through. "They'll fight."

"I know that." Sonia changed the magazine in her pistol, "They belong to Sergei's tribe."

"Yes." Boris slapped the side of his trousers. "We have to get back to the bunker. It's the only safe place."

"Yes." Sonia nodded.

This interesting conversation was punctuated by shells flying all over the place and by rippling explosions. Bullets zipped just above our heads, bouncing off the wall parapet, shards of stone careened down, thudding into the mud, splashing like meteorites, spraying all of us in clayey slime. I glanced at Sandra. She looked like a mud baby. Her blue eyes blinked at me, a bright smile in a mask of mud. She gave me a thumbs-up: I'm okay! I bounced it back with the same sign and a mud-soaked grin.

Alliances in this part of the world change in the blink of an eye. Boris and Sonia crawled along, knelt close to a bend in the wall, and loaded the mobile rocket launcher. Boris leaped up and fired. The launcher sent off a shell – a trail of flame arching off towards the Nassir's men. There was a whoosh and then a rippling explosion. I peeked through a chink in the wall. The missile had smashed into Nassir's last SUV, blowing the vehicle up. Two silhouettes, engulfed in flames, bailed out, rolled on the ground; their screams were faint; the fight was ending.

Nassir, gagged and hooded in the two pillowcases, was sitting on the ground, handcuffed, his arms tapped to his sides, his back propped against the wall, sheltered from the fire. Suddenly he somehow jumped to his feet, obviously meaning to run – which was absurd since he couldn't see where he was going. Before anybody could pull him down, a bullet smashed into his shoulder, with a thud. Nassir spun around, twirled like a drunken dancer, and fell between Sonia and me, splashing face down into the muddy slush. He must have been hit by a bullet from one of his own men. He lay there without moving. If he stayed like that, face down in the mud, gagged and blindfolded, he would suffocate. I crawled over to flip him on his back, but I was pretty encumbered, already carrying his computer, an automatic rifle, and a pistol, and Betty. I felt like a pack animal. Sandra was staring at Nassir's body, wide-eyed; she crawled over, to help me, but Baluchi waved us back. "No, my dears," he said. Sandra stopped, on all fours, obedient, doglike, dripping mud, her vast eyes staring out of her mud-smeared face, as if waiting for instructions. It occurred to me that she and I were mirror images of each other, both on hands and knees, in the canine doggy pose, filthy with mud. If we had tails, we would wag them. This pleasant image burned itself into my brain.

"I will help him, my dears, I will help him." Baluchi crouched down, his vast muddy bulk reflecting the flickering flames; he turned the terrorist over, lifted him up, and propped him against the wall.

"Time to go, people," Sonia shouted.

"On my mark," Boris shouted, "Now!"

And so, crouching low, we scurried away, leaving the shelter of the wall, following the slope downhill, and skirting the ditch where I had almost ended my days, by being shot in the back of the neck by my lovely friend Sonia.

Baluchi half carried, half dragged Nassir, who was alive but seemed to be only half-conscious. We circled down below the roadway, still sheltered by the retaining wall, and by covering gunfire from Baluchi's men and women.

Up in the mountains, blue lightning flashed; the thunder rolled in slowly, like distant artillery. It looked like a huge storm, but it would take maybe an hour to get to us, maybe more.

The shots from Nassir's men became feeble and sporadic; then, one or two last shots, and they ceased; they were probably all dead, or too badly hurt to fight. Their vehicles were burning, projecting an eerie warm orange glow into the humid air; then, with a great roar, they exploded, seemingly all at once.

"It is over," said Baluchi. Nassir was by now on his feet. Baluchi held the man by the handcuffs. Blood spread down from Nassir's shoulder. He looked pathetic, the pillowcases over his head, his arms taped to his sides.

Baluchi glanced at Sonia and Boris. They nodded, and Boris said to the group, "Go and check – see if there are survivors."

As we watched, three of Baluchi's men, and one of the women – who seemed to be in charge – went up towards the chateau and the parking lot. We saw them, silhouetted against the burning vehicles. There were a few isolated shots; then they returned to us, the woman leading, holding a clutch of captured weapons.

"They are all dead. The wounded were going to die anyway," said the young woman warrior, handsome and dark, holding her pistol in her hand. "We finished them off."

Sandra, standing with a computer strap slung over her shoulder and a pistol in her other hand, wiped her mouth, looked at the tanned young woman with burning eyes, and nodded.

"Sandra believes in pity?" The woman grinned.

"Yes, she does," Baluchi nodded.

We headed towards the bunker. Sandra kept close to me; I realized that, though her musical career and hearing and voice had been destroyed, she was probably just like an ordinary university student; she had written her 'hangover' message in English. I wanted to know more about her.

"As I said, she's American," Baluchi said, as if reading my thoughts, "Her parents are dead. She has no one. Sergei kidnapped her in Indonesia, I think it was. She was a tourist; it was a terrorist attack; the other tourists were all killed. I want to send her to university. She's deciding what she wants to study."

"But you were cruel. You made her drink ... You whipped her with your belt. You made her display herself on the table in the club."

"It was all a show, or mostly. Sergei insisted. Some of it was an act. I put water in one of the vodka bottles. Still, she drank quite a lot since Sergei forced another bottle on her. And we had to perform. Sergei was always watching. My cruelty was a necessity."

Sandra, who had been watching this conversation, looked at me and nodded. She mouthed, in English, "Yes, it's the truth."

"You are obviously an angel, Baluchi," said Tracy, giving him a grin that was not entirely unfriendly.

"Angel," said Sonia, "Oh, angel!"

Baluchi's woman guard said, "Kaleem is a good man, whatever you think. Our tribe would not have survived without him. We had to make ourselves useful. Sometimes to survive, you have to do evil things."

"I understand," Sonia nodded. There was a faraway look in her eyes; I wondered if she was thinking of the people she had shot, the Italian girl, the so-called Israeli spy, the others, which would have included me if the greater interest of the cause had required it. Her people had been very close to extinction; she didn't want to take any chances. It was as if she read my thought, "That's true, Misty, that's what I would have done; if it had been necessary, I would have executed you."

"I understand." I shifted the weight of the computers and guns, trying to make sure that both Betty and I were comfortable. Betty hovered out in front of me, turning her snout towards me from time to time as if to check on my thoughts or intentions. It was like having a cross-examiner perched on my shoulders.

We were soaked and covered in mud when we got back to the bunker. A few of Boris' men were waiting by the big entrance, they were nervous, they had seen the fight by the chateau, and they had their guns drawn. Boris said, "Sergei is dead. I'm in charge now." He glanced at Sonia, as if for approval. The men looked uncertain. Some of them looked at the points of their boots.

"So, you're in charge," one of them said, looking up from under his thick black eyebrows.

"Yes."

The men shuffled, uneasily; then, they nodded.

"You are our leader, Boris, but the others," the man nodded

towards the castle and the anti-aircraft positions, where the crews were just visible, silhouetted against the glow of the burning vehicles. The anti-aircraft crews had not taken part in the fight, which was interesting. They had remained concentrated on their own duties, single-mindedly.

"The others will come around," Boris said, "Or we'll deal with them. For now, we say nothing. I think they suspect something. We will deal with them, one way, or another."

They all nodded agreement.

Baluchi's men and women watched this exchange. The leader, the dark woman, smiled a brilliant smile. "Together, then," she said, "My name, by the way, is Jamila."

"Together, then, Jamila" Boris said and reached out his hand. Jamila accepted his offered hand, and they shook on it.

"Misty isn't handcuffed, and she has a gun," one of the men pointed out.

"Misty is with us now." Sonia blinked at the questioner.

"Really?"

"I can marry her right away, then," said my old admirer, Kirill, giving me a big grin; I decided the rather liked the big oaf, though I wasn't considering matrimony. I smiled back, blinking; then, I looked down, with a coy fluttering of my eyelashes, licking my lips, pretending to be shy.

They all laughed – the tension melted away.

"I'm getting jealous," whispered Tracy as she came close to me.

"Don't be! You know I love you."

"And you love Sonia," Tracy said, "And James; and maybe Sandra too; and your high priest, Baluchi."

"Yes, and Sonia, and James, and Sandra too," I said, thinking that, under the mud and tattoos, I would have blushed, were I capable of blushing, which I think I'm not, "I love everybody, especially my high priests and worshippers."

We entered the bunker, leaving most of the men and women warriors behind to guard the gate to the immense structure.

Once inside, Boris looked around, his hands on his hips, and turned to Sonia. "As I said, not all the men will follow me. The anti-aircraft guys will certainly refuse to join us. We are going to be in for a fight. What do we do now?"

"Now, we take the control room and try to neutralize the bombs Sergei sold to Nassir, and that are going to destroy everything we love," said Sonia.

"Yes," said Tracy, "Moscow, Tel Aviv, New York, Paris, London, Tehran, and possibly everything else as well."

"I see. Yes. So, we are going to save the world!" He grinned and wiped his forehead. "And Mr. Hewitt-Spenser – is he alive?"

"Yes, he's with us."

"Good, then," Boris said, "He can help us. I like him. He knows a lot, and he's a very brave man."

"No time to waste," Baluchi said.

"Let us go, then," said the dark, handsome warrior woman.

We rushed up the stairs to the control room, Baluchi's Jamila, Boris and Tracy, and Sonia and Anton leading the way. The men in the control room, who had seen the fight outside, refused to open the door.

In a blaze of fire, we smashed the door open. The three guys inside – who had said they would never surrender – put up their hands – but there was something shifty about their eyes. One of them had rolled a grenade our way.

Anton kicked the grenade, it bounced against the ceiling. We backed out of the door, just in time. There was a flash, and when we entered through the smoke and falling plaster, the three guys were lying on the floor, dead.

One of the guys had been decapitated. His neck ended in an elongated smear of red, and the remains of his head were splashed against the far wall, next to the bank of computers and monitors. I just hoped the machinery was not damaged.

I went over to the consoles and checked all the computers and monitors. The electricity was still on, and all the computers seemed to be intact, the security monitors were still functioning; they gave an overview of the castle and the fortress.

Betty had survived the excitement of the assault on the bunker and control center. She coiled herself comfortably around my shoulders, dangling on either side like an extravagant fur boa.

"Well, Betty," I said. I put down Baluchi's computer on the control console.

Sandra slid Nassir's computer down next to it. And Baluchi lowered Nassir himself down onto a steel chair, where the terrorist slumped, almost falling off, then steadying himself.

James came up from his dungeon torture chamber and brought Igor's computer with him. We slid the extra laptops into place on the desk, and we plugged them into the more powerful communications system.

I sat down on a bench in front of the control panel desk. Tracy slid in beside me, with James leaning on my chair and Sonia standing behind Tracy. Sandra stood by the door, staring at all the blood. She found a metal chair, unfolded it, and set it down next to me, for Baluchi, apparently. He might help us as we narrowed in on the bombs.

Boris and Anton and Jamila, and their teams took command of our defenses.

Working together on the computers, James and I – with help from Tracy who knew how the Russian-made technology worked – managed to ground almost all the defense drones. But we discovered that the anti-aircraft missile batteries had been separated from the main circuits and that they operated, as we had suspected, with their own radars. They were controlled by their own crews. They also had their own individual generators, so cutting the power was not a solution.

"We have to get them down now," said Tracy, "otherwise the joint force helicopters can't land."

"We'll have to attack them later," said Sonia. "The first priority now is to stop the bombs."

"Right," said Tracy. She walked up and down, banging her fist in her hand. The lights of the banks of computers gleamed off her slender mud-streaked golden body, "Of course."

Boris came back into the room and stared at his dead comrades. "I don't know," he said. He turned to Sonia. "What are we doing?"

"We are trying to stop Baluchi's or Nassir's nukes from going off. And we probably have to do it from here. And Misty is going to do it. Misty is a sort of computer genius."

"Misty?" Boris looked at me, "A genius?"

"Yes."

I was typing like mad, but I waved at him.

"A genius in disguise," said Tracy.

Boris sighed. "So she's a genius, and you and Tracy and Anton are spies. What fools we were!" Boris laughed, but it was more a snort than a laugh. "My family is in Moscow," he said, "and my sister lives in Paris – and I have a cousin in Tel Aviv and one in London. You are right, Sonia, we have to stop this. Sergei had gone mad. His sadism had spiraled out of control. He hated everyone; I think he hated himself most of all. In others, he saw himself, so he became more and more sadistic, and so he handed the weaponry over to Nassir, who wants to destroy everybody – the whole world."

"Well, then. Like you said, Boris, we have to save the whole damned world." Sonia's hands were on her hips, her impatient I-don't-have-time-for-this pose, "You are right, the problem with Sergei is – was – he'd gone mad. I had no choice."

"No, she didn't have a choice," said Tracy.

"Yes, I know, he was less and less stable." Boris came over to look at what James and I were doing with the computers. "The hardliners, outside, will fight, though."

"Yes." Sonia came up beside him.

Boris put his hand on the back of my chair. "Well, Sonia, well, Tracy, we will defend the bunker and control room, and then we will neutralize the anti-aircraft defenses so your US and Russian Special Forces, Tracy, can land. I just hope they don't kill us all."

CHAPTER 10 – BABY NUKES

Kaleem Baluchi stood there, a pistol in his hand, a free man, for the moment, guarding Nassir, who was slumped down on the chair.

Sandra stared at the three bodies, at the pools of blood and pieces of flesh. She disappeared for a moment and came back; somewhere, she had found a mop and pail. She filled the pail with water.

Sonia said, "Please give me the pistol, Baluchi."

"Yes," he handed it over, "But someone has to look after Nassir. He may bleed to death."

"Tracy and I will look after Nassir," Sonia nodded. "Sit there, Baluchi, by your goddess, next to Misty. I am sure you can help Misty and James sort things out with the bombs."

"Yes. Yes, I can." Baluchi sat down next to us in the chair Sandra had placed there for him. He explained once again that only his computer, which was sitting on the console next to me, could be used to defuse the bombs. That was something that Nassir did not know. Kaleem said that he had maintained control, or so he thought. "You see, when I realized who was going to be getting the bombs, I decided I had better try to be able to stop him – to stop the bombs from going off."

While we set to work, Boris went down to rally his troops and Baluchi's troops and to make sure Sergei's men didn't attack the bunker; one of Baluchi's women had come up to act as liaison with her boss Jamila; this young woman, Aisara, seemed totally unfazed by the nakedness around her; amused, but not at all shocked. Sonia and Tracy staunched and cleaned Nassir's wounds. He groaned, his eyes fluttered open, then they fluttered shut; they bound him with duct tape and left him lying on a fold-up cot in a corner, half-conscious.

I was exhausted. It had been a long night, and a fairly acrobatic one, when you added it all together. But the adrenaline began to pump as I realized what was at stake. This was a real challenge for Misty Hoyt!

Once again, I went over the whole thing with Baluchi. The bombs were on timers; the timers were coded; and the codes and the timers were linked into a computer control so that, if the bombs were used, say, for blackmail, they could be neutralized at the very last minute – by Baluchi's computer – if the blackmailer decided to stop the bomb; that is the timer could be stopped, and it could be stopped by remote control; it could be stopped by a telephone call and by a code which consisted of coded orders – a simple letter-and-numbers sequence, that is, if all went well, but that code had to be sent from Baluchi's computer; this was protection and safeguard Baluchi had set for himself. He would be able to stop any of the bombs, as long as he knew the codes, and he had thought he knew the codes and numbers, but on several of the bombs, Nassir had changed them. The bombs could also be set off instantly, by a variant of the code, bypassing the timer, and this too could be done through a simple telephone call from anywhere in the world, and from any telephone. Somebody could pick up a phone in Caracas, dial a number, then the code – and Paris or New York or Moscow or Tel Aviv would be vaporized, many millions would be dead. To stop the bombs that were already ticking, only Baluchi's computer could be used.

This was pretty complicated.

Nassir had accidentally – through a security breach – discovered the code for two of the bombs, and he had typed in the initial instructions before the bombs had been sent on their way, putting those bombs on timers. So the bombs in Paris and New York were ticking. The others were waiting for the fatal telephone call that would set them off instantly, or set the timer ticking.

Nassir had changed and encrypted the telephone numbers that gave access to the codes. So I had to get through Nassir's codes and instructions – that is, get the right telephone numbers – before I could insert Baluchi's counter-order codes, from his computer, and stop the bombs.

It was enough to give a muddy, naked, tattooed Punk-Goth waif a monstrous headache.

I typed furiously. "This is not going to be easy," I mumbled. Nassir had put an extra level of code, protected by some fairly sophisticated encryptions. "Do you see the problems, Paris, Washington?" I asked.

"Yes, we see the problems," a voice said in my ear. "Keep working. We are working on our side. If we come up with answers, we'll tell you. If we understand correctly, we need to use Baluchi's laptop to feed in the codes; otherwise, nothing will work."

"Yes, that's what Baluchi is telling me."

"So everything depends on that computer you have, a laptop."

"Yes."

"And on you, Misty, on you putting the right telephone numbers and the right codes in the right sequence for each of the two bombs."

"Yes." Sweat trickled down my tattooed back; it tickled my coccyx; I wiggled my sweat-covered bum.

"Damnation." It was Séverine's voice; behind her, I could hear a babble of voices in French, English, Russian, and German. There was also, I think, some Hebrew and Arabic and Farsi.

"Yes, Damnation," I said, wiggling my coccyx.

Tracy discovered a coffee machine in the control center kitchen and some espresso capsules and a refrigerator with sandwiches that were fresh and edible.

We were all hungry.

Sandra stopped mopping and hauling the bodies out of the control room to gulp down a coffee. She was streaked in blood and gore, blood up to her elbows, blood dribbling from her collarbone, her breasts smeared in watery blood. Slurping down the coffee, she gave me a thumbs-up sign and mouthed, "Good for the hangover."

"Yep!" I grinned and nodded. I liked the kid; we would have to find a way to help her.

Baluchi was too nervous to sit. Like a giant Buddha, he walked up and down behind James and me, making suggestions and wiping his face and belly with a dirty old oil-soaked towel. He was still in the loincloth since, as he said, it was too hot to dress like a civilized man; James, who usually favored very fine suits or impeccable jeans and shirts, was still in his blood-soiled patch of cotton. I liked him in his Tarzan-like outfit. As for me, well, I was of course, in tattoos, oil, mud, sweat, rings, my puffball tuft topknot, and Baluchi's chains. After all, I was a totem, a fetish, an icon, a goddess, all of which was very satisfying. And I was wearing Betty as a boa, though she had developed a fondness for James too and would sometimes reach out and rest her head on his shoulder before swinging back to me.

James followed my work, giving suggestions – good ones – at each nodal point. "Yes, yes, that's good," I said. His hand was on my thigh. His presence was always intense, and now he radiated a special strength and confidence. He knew we could do it! I typed as fast as I could.

"Okay, I think I've got access." In one swallow, I gulped down a full cup of coffee. If we didn't solve these problems, well, we'd be doomed. I couldn't even think about it: millions would be dead. Two of the greatest cities in the world, New York and Paris, would be turned into radioactive wastelands, and some of the other greatest cities would be under threat of annihilation.

I stood up and walked back and forth. Betty slapped at my backside with her tail, exciting my sensitive coccyx: Back to work, she was saying. I was so concentrated I sometimes forgot she was using me as her castle.

I sat down and set to it. Betty, wrapped around my shoulders, hovered out in front of me, fascinated I think by the shifting patterns of the computer screen, or perhaps the by the heat the computer was radiating. Maybe it was something to eat – yummy!

Sonia and Tracy were glued to a radio set and following the progress of the airborne group and also the progress of the weather. Boris and Anton were using the intercom to try to convince the rest of Sergei's men to surrender or change sides; they were not having much success; loyalties depended on families and tribes, and you don't shift those overnight. Sandra brewed more coffee and discovered a big box of chocolate bars – pure 99% Swiss chocolate. Ideal energy food!

By this time, we were all running on nerves. We had narrowed down the possible site of the bomb in Paris to one very probable and two less probable addresses, and we had done the same for New York. Of course, where the bombs were, was secondary to discovering the telephone numbers and codes to stop the bombs.

With one ear, I followed events in Paris and New York. Martine was with the unit in Paris that was headed to the most probable bombsite. When they got there, they wouldn't be able to do anything – without risking an immediate explosion – because the bombs – I discovered as I raced through Nassir's files – had been booby-trapped against any direct outside physical effort to break the circuits. Damn it. So it depended on me, with Baluchi and James helping, to break the codes. He had, Baluchi told me, a solid memory, and he had memorized all the codes. But we had to get through Nassir's encryption to the level where the codes could be used. Meantime, to keep Kaleem happy and cooperative, we had to make sure that his adopted daughter Sara was safe. I was keeping one ear open for the results of the rescue operation in the south of France, hoping the little girl was not already dead and that she could be saved.

"We're almost there, to the first suspected bomb site," Martine said into my earpiece. And she added, "Good luck, Misty."

"Thanks, Martine, Good luck to everybody." I was sweating and balancing a million thoughts, but an image of Martine flitted through my mind, and I saw dozens of images of the two of us, things we had done together, laughing, running in the streets, dining with Philip and James; she and I, alone, sleeping entangled, embraced; and I also saw the two of us doing wonderful things in the future, on a sunny beach with sand dunes reaching up to cliffs, and little waves breaking against the shore, if we survived this, and we would do wonderful things with each other and with James and Philip too, yes, if we survived this.

The minutes passed. Outside, a fight broke out between different factions of Sergei's gang.

I could hear, through some of the security monitors, gunfire, and explosions outside the bunker. When the fight broke out, Sonia and Tracy and Anton – and Kaleem's men and women led by Jamila – plus Boris and his men had gone down to the entrance to the bunker, and they were now fighting to keep us from being overwhelmed by Sergei's loyalists. Not everybody had accepted Boris as their leader. The Sergei loyalists were trying to get at us.

I glanced at the bank of monitors that showed what was going on all around the fortress: yes, there they were, the glorious girls and boys, the Naked Brigade – Sonia and Tracy – and all the others, Boris, his team, and Kaleem Baluchi's mixed-sex brigade led by that handsome woman warrior Jamila, all fighting like mad to keep the enemy at bay. Flashes of fire filled the screen, and smoke. When it cleared, our guys were still standing. The dissidents – or loyalists – had been driven off. But they still controlled the anti-aircraft missile batteries.

Sandra – an Uzi slung over her shoulder – had stayed with us to watch over Nassir, and bring us coffee and look after security inside the bunker.

On one screen, the radar showed the storm approaching from the mountains; it was enormous.

"Look at that," I said.

"Yes, one more little challenge," said James. He was scribbling a little diagram on a piece of paper, the route we would have to take to solve our decrypting problems, a sort of tree diagram. James nodded towards Baluchi. "We do need our friend," he whispered.

"Dear Kaleem," I asked, "can we really stop the bombs from here?"

"I have the codes, Goddess, and I think they will work," he said. "But, I want my daughter Sara saved first."

"First. Kaleem, there is no time. Millions of people will die."

"Or one person will die," he said, "What, Goddess, is the difference? Do we not love the least of God's creatures?"

"Yes, we do," I said, thinking that this was not perhaps the best time for a discussion of theology. Each little sparrow or chickadee may be as loved by divinity – whether monotheistic or polytheistic – as much as divinity loves anybody else, including Mozart and Einstein and Mother Teresa and Doctor Salk, but for the moment ...

There was news: French special forces had just surrounded the house where Nassir's men were almost certainly holding Baluchi's adopted daughter Sara in the mountains outside Grasse, just above the Mediterranean, and now the men inside were threatening to kill the girl. I went to Nassir and knelt next to the cot where he was lying, bandaged, and tied down. "You can save a girl, Khalid Nassir, and if you don't save her, you don't gain anything but a wanton bit of cruelty."

I heard through my earpiece, in French: "Sharpshooters are in place. Mini-drones in place."

Nassir, lying bound down on the cot, glared at me. His bandages were bloody, but his color was better. It looked like he was going to live. He spoke, barely a whisper. "I want revenge on him; he is a traitor; he betrayed me; he betrayed our cause."

Sandra stood next to me; she had the Uzi cradled in her arms, pointed down at him; she followed his lips, and I think she understood – quite clearly – what Nassir was saying.

"Our cause?" Baluchi came up beside Sandra, put his hand on her shoulder; his enormous bulk towered over Nassir, "You are a presumptuous and deluded fool, Nassir. It was never our cause."

Nassir tried to spit at Baluchi, but the spittle barely left his lips, and dribbled on his chin. Sandra shifted the Uzi to her shoulder, knelt down, and wiped the spittle away. It was a delicate gesture, done with tenderness, almost with love. She put her hand on his forehead. He blinked at her but said nothing.

I had no time for this. "So, Nassir, you refuse to talk to your men? You refuse to give the order to let her go?"

"I refuse. Let her die!"

"That means your men will die."

"Ah, yes, so much the better: They will be martyrs. Life is of no importance. Your weakness is you Westerners love life. You are decadent cowards. We love death."

"Okay, so be it." Such evil nonsense – superstition, and presumption, all wrapped up in one malignant package – was tiresome. Death, being nothing but the cessation of life, means nothing. Believing in life doesn't make you a coward, on the contrary. If you realize what you are giving up, then it does take guts to die; if you are fool enough to believe in the paradise nonsense, then it does not require courage, only illusions. Well, that's the easiest spin on it. Even cruel suicidal fanatics can be brave; I'm not going to deny that.

Kneeling next to him, Sandra looked up at me and nodded. She put a damp cloth on Nassir's forehead, and his eyes flashed at her, and for a moment, I saw something like gratitude in his eyes, a brief suggestion, which quickly vanished. She continued to bath his face, the naked deaf-mute girl giving succor to the sacred warrior-terrorist who hated the flesh, hated women, hated the world, and hated almost everything. He closed his eyes. He whispered, softly. "They must die; they all must die."

I turned my back on Nassir, and I whispered to Paris. "Okay, you heard him. He refuses to save the girl, or his men. Go in – priority is to save the girl, absolute priority."

Sonia and Tracy came back into the control room. The battle – except for the anti-aircraft batteries – was over. Boris and Anton and Jamila were holding the line below, a sort of uneasy truce with the anti-aircraft batteries.

"What's happening?" Sonia came up to the screen, followed by Tracy.

"They're going to try to rescue Sara, Kaleem's daughter."

"Let's hope it works," Tracy breathed. She glanced at Baluchi.

Events were patched straight through. There were explosions

and the rattle of automatic weapons; then there were shouts, in French, Arabic, and English; then there were two or three more shots, and then silence, dead silence. I waited. The silence was unnerving. Baluchi stared at me. Nassir, lying on the stretcher, his eyes closed, had what looked a grin on his face. I was tempted to smash his beautiful teeth. Sandra, still crouched on the floor next to Nassir, saw the expression in my eyes. She shook her head – "No," she was saying with all the eloquence of her beautiful eyes, "No, he is horrible and a killer and a sadist, but no, he is weak now, and we will not hurt him, you or I, that is not what we are, that is not who we are." I bit my lip and nodded back. "Yes, Sandra, you are right – that is not what we are."

"They're taking too much time," James whispered.

Baluchi paced back and forth, wiping at his forehead, anguish on his face. "Oh, oh, oh," he groaned, like a mute creature in agony, "Oh, oh, oh, oh, Sara, oh, oh, oh ... It is all my fault; it is all my fault!"

Sandra stood up and went to him and put her arms around him – not an easy thing to do – and held him.

"Oh, oh, oh," he sobbed, his vast smooth dark body shaking like jelly, and the chalk-white naked girl comforting him, making cooing sounds, stroking his sides, kissing his forehead.

"Damnation, this is not going to end well," I whispered, glancing at James. He kissed me on the cheek and put his arm around me.

In the earpiece, I could hear more shouting, but it was in the distance; I couldn't make out who was speaking or what they were saying.

Baluchi sat down, heavily. He looked up at Sandra, his big dark eyes glossy. "You would have loved her," he said. Sandra stroked his forehead. "You would have loved her," he repeated. He began to cry, his huge body wracked by tears. "You would have loved her, and she would have loved you." Sandra crouched next to him and held his hand.

I felt tears in my own eyes.

James put his hand on my thigh.

And then, I heard, in the earpiece, a voice in French saying, "Package intact, package intact."

"Please confirm that," I said.

"Yes, package intact. The little girl – and it is her – she's fine. A bit shaken up, but she's fine."

"You're sure?"

"I'm sure. She's here. Just a second, hold on," the voice said; there was static on the line, and then the voice said, "She's next to me."

"Let us talk to her," I said. I was trembling; I was covered in sweat and sweat gleamed in little beads down the chains and on the rings and dripped from my nipples. I was submerged in a gluey shower, drip, drip, drip … "They say they have Sara, and she's safe."

Kaleem stood up and came to stand next to us. "Is it possible, is it true?"

"Yes," I said, "They say she is alive."

They opened another line, through the computers, not the earphone, a video connection, on the screen, potentially open for all to see.

"Papa Kaleem!" It was a girl's voice.

"Oh, thanks to all the gods and goddesses. Thanks to Misty Hoyt. All praise to Misty Hoyt!" Baluchi seemed to glow. Tears streamed down his face.

"Can we shift that to the computer system, James, with visuals on the big screen?"

"Shall do, Misty," James pushed a few buttons on the console.

"So I'm Misty now, am I?"

"Definitely, Misty," he grinned.

I swiveled my chair to be even closer to him, so our knees could touch, and he leaned forward, and again he put his hand on my thigh, "We have an image now too."

On the screen, a box appeared and in it was a beautiful young girl, dark-skinned, her jet-black hair cut short, her face streaked with tears, perhaps 11 or 12, but she was smiling and clearly very excited. Behind her were security personnel, people talking, smoke rising, a jumble of impressions. James enlarged the image so it would fill the screen, and he activated the cam camera on the computer, so the girl could see Baluchi.

"Papa Kaleem," she said, "You are not wearing any clothes."

"I have a sort of loincloth, such as holy men in some religions wear," he said. "I have been meditating and learning wisdom as they did in ancient times."

"And what is that beside you, a painted goddess?"

"Yes, that is a painted goddess. She is a friendly, painted goddess. She is helping me better myself." Baluchi said, glancing at me, as I slipped out of the frame; I hadn't realized I was visible to the camera and I'd forgotten I was not exactly presentable. The girl laughed and then Betty slid into the frame. "Papa, you have a snake – a big snake!"

"Yes, it is a holy snake, and it is the friend of the painted goddess. Now, you let the good people take care of you, and I shall see you soon. Right now, I have work I must do with the painted goddess."

"Bye, bye, papa!"

A French policewoman, blond with a smart little cap tilted at a rakish angle, and a ponytail, came into the frame. "Sara is fine. We'll take her for medical checks and to a safe house outside Nice and then – when this is over – to Paris. Don't worry!" She saluted smartly.

All of Nassir's men – and two of his women – were dead.

The image was gone.

"Alright," I said, "now the codes."

Baluchi said, "Now, goddess, I give you my full attention. Whatever I can do, I shall do."

Indeed – the clock was ticking

Khalid Nassir lay there on the cot, deathly pale, but smiling with his bright teeth rimmed in blood. His men had died as martyrs – for him and for his God. At least there was that. So what if the girl was saved. Who cared? The more people died, the better; his real religion, in my opinion, had nothing to do with Allah or God; it was pure nihilistic narcissism. Utter destruction was what Nassir wanted. It was truly a stupid and evil combination, his pride, his fanaticism, and his indifference to other lives and other people. It was a violation of all that was best in all religions.

"We have about twenty minutes," said James.

Tracy and Sonia crouched next to us. Tracy clasped her hands together in a prayer-like gesture, rolled her eyes heavenwards. "Everything depends on Goddess Misty Hoyt!"

"Amen," said Sonia, puckering a kiss and blowing it towards me.

This was surreal, but it was also more and more real. I typed and typed. Sweat streamed down my back, pure terror. Until now, I don't think I'd really absorbed the reality of what was happening.

Séverine's voice came into my earpiece, "We think we have located the bomb, just off the Quai de Conti in the 6th Arrondissement. We are approaching the site."

"Give me the code, Master Baluchi." I could picture in my mind Paris – the Quai de Conti, on the Left Bank, not far from where I lived, not far from the Louvre across the river, not far from the Gare d'Orsay Museum, not far from ... everything ...

"Stand up and dance for me."

"Are you crazy, Kaleem Baluchi?

"Just a tiny, modest pirouette," he grinned at me.

"Do it," James whispered through his teeth, "Fast."

"Master Baluchi, you are crazy." I stood up and turned around once or twice, the high heels making it interesting, as always, and Betty turning with me, swaying out in front of me. I kept forgetting she was using me as her nest. She seemed to be part of me now, it was so natural having her entangled with my body. I swayed, and danced, and the chains rattled, and the rings jingled, and I thought, yes, I guess I do belong in some ancient pagan temple with incense rising to the skies and humans and animals being prepared for sacrifice and with all my worshippers falling to their knees and breathing out sacred hosannas. That was my new profession – a sacred prostitute and goddess. Well, enough of that. I stopped. "Now, Kaleem Baluchi, let us get to work."

"Yes, yes, Goddess, now we get to work."

He stood over me while I looked at the schematics. "There is an automatic trigger device that will go off if you try to tamper with the wiring."

"Oh, shit," I heard someone say, in French, in my earpiece.

"We already knew that," said Séverine's voice.

"But Kaleem says we can override it from here," I said.

"Well, do it!" Séverine did sound just a bit edgy.

"Yes, sir, yes, ma'am," I was tempted to smile. Even Séverine was losing her impeccable cool.

But – In twenty minutes, a huge part of Paris and of New York could be obliterated, and hundreds of thousands or millions of lives.

In New York and Paris, the authorities were trying to decide whether or not – now they knew where the bombs were – to give any warning to the public. It was really too late – the only result of a warning would be mass panic.

So no warning would be given.

No last-minute embraces. No $500 bottles of wine. No making peace with one's Maker. No prayers, no hosannas, just instant death, and hideous mutilation, and endless suffering.

In a few minutes – about 20 minutes for both cities – there would be a mass flash and obliteration.

"We're approaching the address," said Martine's voice, police sirens and a babble of voices in the background – Séverine giving orders, Frederick shouting something. "We're almost there," Martine said, with what seemed admirable cool, exactly her normal voice.

I was drilling down, deeper and deeper, through the levels of code. The clock was ticking, faster and faster it seemed. I glanced at it. Damn! I glanced over at Nassir. He turned his head and smiled. He was sure we would lose the race, and millions would die. He was a smug, handsome, evil bastard! Sweat was getting in his eyes. Sandra knelt and wiped his forehead.

James was standing beside me, and Kaleem, both of them staring at the screen. James pointed to a figure – a little string of orphaned code – on the left side of the screen. "Try that," he said.

"What? Oh, yes, right. Hey, James, you are a genius."

He slid onto the chair beside me, his arm brushed my shoulder.

Kaleem Baluchi leaned over us. "Yes, that's it; I think that's the last gateway."

"Well," I said, "It is official: James Hewitt Spencer is a genius."

I went through the gateway, and there was a code, a jumble of figures and for some reason, I figured I would be able to crack it, it would respond to a simple algorithmic formula, I was certain of it.

Sandra and Tracy and Sonia walked up and down. They stopped and looked at the computer screens, and they just stood there.

Nassir began to giggle and laugh. Sandra looked at him, wide-eyed, and crouched down next to him. Kaleem's women warrior, Jamila, a fierce, beautiful, deeply tanned young woman who had her jet-black hair cropped short, had come into the room and was now standing over Nassir.

"What is so funny?" she glared down at him.

"You are."

"Oh, how so?"

"You are all going to die – infidels, whores, abominations, apostates!" He coughed up blood.

"I am tempted to smash you one, to shut you up," the warrior woman said, "but you are not worthy of my attention."

"Ha, ha, ha. You will be obliterated. All of you – all apostates and infidels."

Hmm, I thought.

Sandra knelt down and wiped the blood from Nassir's lips. He glanced at her again – a flash, something like gratitude. She was a ministering angel. There was a human person inside Nassir, somewhere, though that person was lost, of course, lost for all eternity. Sandra put her hand on his forehead.

"You are too good to him," said Jamila, in English, and crouching close so Sandra could see her lips.

Sandra shrugged and smiled. It was a saintly sort of smile.

"Kaleem told me you were a holy woman. Now I believe him."

James whispered, "I don't like that grin of Nassir's. Misty, maybe you'd better check the programs controlling the other bombs – the two bombs that are stored here, downstairs, in the trucks."

I rolled my eyes. "Yes," I said. "Damn it! Why didn't I think of that?"

Kaleem Baluchi was leaning over me again. He put his thick, soft hand on my shoulder. "This had not occurred to me. James is right. Nassir could have set them on countdown, intending to stop them later."

"You'd better check it out," said Sonia. "If we blow up, we won't be able to stop the other bombs."

"Yes," Tracy pushed back her hair. "Nassir would like us all to go up in a whoosh of flame. Perhaps that was his plan all along. Kill millions and then die in a flash of light – martyrdom writ large."

"A sort of collective suicide," I whispered.

"Precisely. It is the sort of trick the man would play," Baluchi wiped his forehead. "He hates life, and desires death – for himself, for everyone. For him, it's the cult of death that makes life worthwhile. It is like a vampire, sucking out life to rejoice in death. And besides, Sergei's castle is a nest of infidels, wickedness incarnate – as we can see all around us."

"Quite," I said, rather primly, "Absolute wickedness." Yes, I was a naked pagan fetish goddess, but in truth, I didn't feel particularly wicked. Actually, I thought I'd behaved rather well, given the circumstances, and all things considered.

I did a quick sashay to the other bomb codes. Indeed, the two bombs stored in the trucks downstairs were ticking away, their timers were on, and linked to the computer. We had 34 minutes. That was longer than for Paris and New York. I guess Nassir had wanted to be sure the apocalypse had truly occurred before he committed hara-kiri. "Well, well," I said. "We'll deal with them later."

"Thank you, James," said Baluchi. "That was very good thinking."

"Sometimes I surprise myself," said James.

I switched back to Paris and New York. We now had 18 minutes. I wanted to pee, but I didn't have time. I wiggled, hoping that would help. My coccyx itched. I felt my body encased in a gooey, greasy varnish. Sweat trickled down my spine, tickling my coccyx, and it flowed down my belly, gathering in my crotch, coating the labial rings, a stimulating but irritating sensation, arousing, when I really didn't need to be aroused. Betty slithered back and forth between James and me; she seemed to be enjoying herself. My silver chains and steel rings dripped sweat. Betty liked to jiggle them. The tattoos glowed sweat. I truly felt like an ancient idol, a goddess. And, in spite of myself, I was a goddess of life and death. What I had to manage to do in the next few minutes was ... was ... well, no, it didn't bear thinking about.

A soundtrack came through the computer from New York: sirens and the voices of the emergency responders, then from Paris, then all at once. I was getting several tracks – through the earpiece, from the computer; it was like a multi-audio-track hallucinatory drug trip, a prelude to the end of the world in real-time.

Séverine's voice chimed in from Paris. "Okay, we've found it. We are here. It's in a delivery van, parked on the side of the road, just off the Seine on Quai de Conti. I am looking at the trigger device and watching the countdown. Bomb disposal units are here, but now we will wait. Any interference with the bomb here will almost certainly trigger it, until the bomb has been disarmed by you – if we understand you correctly."

"Yes, that's what Baluchi says. I have to stop the clock before you can do anything."

"In any case, even if we could, we don't have time to do anything here."

"No, you don't," I said.

"Okay, we'll sit tight," said Séverine. I could hear Martine's voice in the background, and Frederick's. And there were those sirens, that particular Parisian sound, the pulsating siren sound. It made me wince with nostalgia for our flat on the Left Bank, for the Café Flore, for the Boulevard Saint Germain, for the plane trees that cast a sweet fluttering shade on the sidewalks, for the little books stands along the river, for the Seine itself, for Notre Dame, for the croissant shop at the corner, for the school kids going to the little school at the corner, for Zoe Parillaud and her father, for Martine and Philip, for all the places and people that held memories of what had become my life. And I thought of all the people I knew, just casually – the newspaper vendor at the corner, Mrs. Chang and her Chinese restaurant, the waiter at Café Flore, Madam Golikova, our baker on rue de Buci, the ...

Everybody might be vaporized or die in horrible agony – in only a few minutes.

"Okay, give me a few minutes, guys," I said. I puzzled. Okay, yes, the code was this, so the answer was this. What if he had coded it backward? I looked up at Kaleem. "What if he coded it backward so that by trying to stop the clock, I'd actually trigger the bomb?"

I saw doubt flicker in Baluchi's eyes. "No, I don't think he had the time."

"You don't think," I repeated the phrase slowly. For Paris, there were three minutes and fifteen seconds to go. I had the code. I could insert it, and push "execute."

"Okay, Séverine," I said, "I've got the code. I've got the telephone number. I'm going to try to stop the clock now. But, Séverine, there is a small chance that this will trigger the device immediately."

"I see," she said. I heard people talking around her, but it was muffled, and I couldn't hear what they were saying.

"I don't think I'll share that nugget with anybody, Misty. And, there's no time to hesitate, dear Misty," she said, "Do it."

"Okay. Here goes." I rang the number, and it answered with a suave female voice – which was a nice touch I thought – and the suave female voice said, "Please enter your code now," and I punched in the code on the reserve pad, double-checked that it was right. I noticed from the side of my eye that Betty had draped herself over James' shoulders. "Okay – now," I said.

I pushed the final button. There was an instant of hesitation, and the clock on my screen stopped. There was silence on the line. "Has it stopped?"

There was silence.

Just silence.

I shifted in my chair. James' arm tightened around my shoulder; Betty was now wrapped around both of us, hovering out, looking at the screen – it occurred to me that probably the heat, which had been building up, was attracting her more and more.

"Paris?" I said. "Paris?"

"Yes," Sévérine whispered, "It has stopped. We are checking for booby traps, pressure triggers, and so on, and if we have the all-clear, we are going to remove the weapon immediately – get it out of Paris to an isolated ship-borne laboratory. You probably can hear the helicopter now."

"Yes, I can," I said. I heard the whap-whap-whap sound, and I could picture it lowering itself onto the Parisian street. They had webcams with them, Martine had told me, but there was no time for that.

"Okay, we're heading to New York," I said.

I switched to the New York program.

"Hi, New York," I said.

"Greetings to you, Misty Hoyt!" said a very New York voice. "Have you any news for us?"

"I will in a few moments, I hope." Kaleem and James were pointing at the same spot on the screen – it was the entry point. James had been working on preparing our New York entry while I had been concentrating on Paris.

Betty hovered out from James' shoulder, aiming her snout at the screen, curious as to what was happening, what all those little blinking lights meant. Why were all her human perches focussing their attention on those points? The clock said two minutes and thirteen seconds.

I drilled down three layers – it was relatively easy – and I came to the final little bit of the puzzle. Yes, a similar algorithm, but applied backward. Some math junkie had designed this for Nassir. I would like to sit down with whoever it was and discuss their technique.

"Hmm," I glanced at the clock. Okay, it was now just two minutes and three seconds. The team in New York would be crouched around the weapon, watching the little red letters countdown: 01.59, 01.58 ...

"Okay, here goes," I said, "Oh, wait a minute; this is a little bit of tricky code." I ran a few possibilities through my head and then without really thinking it through, I chose one, inserted it. It was an intuition, a gamble, a risk. Then glancing at the clock, I saw how much time we had: 1 minute and 20 seconds. I said, "Okay, I'm doing it now!" The number rang. The suave female voice spoke. There was no time to warn New York that this might have been a double-double-cross, that Nassir had played a little joke on us, and that they were going to be consumed in a flash of heat and fire and that an estimated 1,650,000 people would be vaporized instantaneously without even knowing what had happened to them and that several million more would suffer untold agonies, and that works of art and architecture, and manuscripts gathered from over the centuries and millennia would be obliterated in a nano-second. Wonderful images of Manhattan and all that it meant to me and to everybody else raced through my mind in an instantaneous kaleidoscope. Little bookshops and art galleries in Soho, the wind tunneling down streets in winter, the ... And Claudia, my grandmother, and almost certainly grandfather, were probably in Manhattan.

I pushed the button. Silence.

The clock stopped.

I waited. "New York?" I said. I waited.

Nothing on the line, just static, just hissing silence, just nothing.

"New York?"

James put his arm around me. My shoulders felt very small, very fragile. I put my hand on his hand. Why don't they answer? Baluchi was leaning over us. I could feel and hear his breathing. Anton – who had just come back from the battlefield – and Sandra and Sonia and Tracy and Jamila were all staring at the screen, and at me. I had stopped breathing. I might have just killed millions of people!

"You're grinding your teeth," said James.

"I am?"

"Yes. You do it, sometimes, in your sleep."

"I do? You never told me."

"No, but ..."

"Right now, I want to grind my teeth. This is crazy, this is ..."

Then it came, a bit of static, and then ...

"Yes, Misty, this is New York. The clock stopped at zero minus one minute and 13 seconds. Like Paris, we will be testing the weapon to see if it can be moved and to make sure there are no physical or other booby traps."

"Great," I said. "We've got two live bombs here in Sergei Platonov's fortress, so we're going to be dealing with them now."

Somewhere, as if he were in another universe, I heard Nassir groan. His plots, up to this point at least, had been foiled. The apocalypse would have to wait. Now the question was whether we would all die in the next few minutes, or survive to live and love and fight another day.

The next five minutes were taken up with stopping the clocks on the two bombs, which were sitting in a truck five floors below us. I was not inclined to let myself be vaporized by the machinations of a terrorist religious fanatic. The trigger devices on these bombs were simpler – and so I stopped both of them, at least the computer said so. And no instantaneous flash and total obliteration indicated that the computer was wrong. Tracy went down with Anton to have a look at the physical bombs. They reported through the bunker intercom that the bombs had stopped ticking. So we were not going to die right away, not instantaneously at least.

Then we located the Moscow, London, Tel Aviv, and Tehran bombs – none of the clocks had been started. And the bombs were examined, the booby traps disarmed, the timers neutralized, and the bombs made secure. We receive messages of thanks from Moscow, London, Jerusalem, and Tehran, some of them on the screens at the same time; it was like a party.

Nassir raged and foamed at the mouth.

"Shut him up, he's bad for concentration," I said.

Sandra, under the watchful eye of the woman warrior, knelt and very gently, but firmly, gagged Nassir. He made a muffled sound of protest; then, he was silent. Sandra remained crouching. She wiped the sweat from Nassir's forehead. Nassir glared at her, almost as if he were terrified. I think her kindly and very womanly ministrations – and her nakedness and beauty – were even more painful for him than defeat and capture.

I stood up and stretched. I kissed James, and he embraced me, our sweaty naked bodies pressed to each other. "Oh, Goddess Misty Hoyt, you are truly a wonder," James whispered into my ear, ticking and jangling my loopy steel earrings, and caressing my naked skull. He, like Betty, seemed to like my scarlet topknot, and he fussed with it, and flicked it back and forth. Then he stood back a bit, gave me the once-over, and then gave me the deepest kiss I think I had ever had, my steel nose ring making it even more spectacular.

Under his loincloth, James had an erection. I reached down and took possession of it, and I whispered, "Later, later, Darling James. We still have another fight to win."

"I know that, Misty, but I can't resist." James kissed me and touched me, and I realized that I was fully aroused and totally ready, but then, grinning, we pulled back from each other. Betty, who had been part of this embrace, hissed gently, and then settled own, draping herself over my shoulders, her head hovering out just in front of my breasts.

"Love birds," Sonia rolled her eyes. "I am truly jealous."

"Me too," said Tracy.

"You people!" said Jamila.

"Naughty, naughty," Baluchi favored James and me with a heavy wink. He was very jovial for someone who was facing life in prison – or perhaps in witness protection. Perhaps he felt he had let drop a great weight of guilt and responsibility from his shoulders. He reached out and took Betty away from me and allowed her to drape herself over him. He was a comfortable mountain to explore. She slid up and down his body as if exploring a new universe.

"Now, there are the anti-air defenses," said Sonia. "Tracy's and Anton's airborne force is approaching. And so is that monster storm."

CHAPTER 11 – MUD & BLOOD

We were outside – a new battle was about to begin.

The Special Ops helicopters were thirty kilometers away, flying down the valley of the Beckistan River.

Lightning flashed.

The thunder was deafening.

We were out in the open now, fighting our way through mud and rain. I was wielded a computer – for communications – and James, I discovered – well, I already knew – was very good at wielding a submachine gun.

We'd left Nassir under guard with two of Kaleem Baluchi's people – a man and a woman. They were from the same tribe as Kaleem and utterly loyal to him. They hated Nassir, and we had to get them to swear that they would not hurt him. He was gagged, now, and blindfolded, and had two pillowcases over his head and was tied up and taped with five layers of duct tape to the metal cot. It must have been hot and sweaty and difficult to breath under the pillowcases.

Betty had stayed behind as part of the guard. She seemed to have developed a fondness for Nassir and liked to curl up, perched on him, as he shuddered and squirmed; it was almost comic; I think she sensed the fear and liked it; perhaps Betty the python was a sadist; she must have spent too much time with

Sergei. In any case, we didn't have time to provide Khalid Nassir with a luxury suite.

The guards later told me that they took pity on Khalid and took Betty away from her perch on Nassir's shoulders and let her wrap herself around one of them. Betty did not like to be alone, and we didn't want her wandering off by herself.

Jamila, Beluchi's glamorous commander, told me that she very much liked Betty. "Betty would be absolutely at home in my village," she said, "Lots of rabbits."

While slogging through the mud, I communicated with Paris and through Paris with the incoming US-Russian Assault Team. "The two outside missiles launchers have been taken off-line; the crews, who are hostile to us, are going to operate them manually; we'll try to capture the guns and disable them before you get close. We're going to be in contact throughout; at least, I hope we are." I took a deep breath. "Paris, are you still listening?"

"Yes, Misty, we are here."

"You heard what I said?" I asked as James helped me as I stepped over a slippery patch, up to my ankles in mud. Thunder roared, and lightning flashed, and the rain began again, powerful sheets and downdrafts of rain. "Paris, you heard what I said?"

"We heard, Misty – we've been patching you through in real-time to the assault helicopters."

The lights flickered as the power went on and off and then on again. This was serious.

One of the remaining mini-self-directed drones buzzed down out of the rain – I wondered how it had escaped – we'd turned off all their guidance systems. I thought we'd killed them all. This one was confused and not very bright, and, as it spiraled down, sputtering, and aimlessly sending out a spray mini-bullets, James shot it out of the air. It lit up like a miniature Roman candle, careened downward, and splashed into the mud about two yards from us.

We sheltered under the old stone wall that had protected us before. Tracy and Sonia were next to me, with Anton and James and Sandra and Jamila and some of Baluchi's men and women on the other side.

The missile launcher was up on the cliff face, and we could see it from the bunker, and James and Anton went out onto one of the support structures and threw grenades. The missile launcher exploded. Several of the crew leaped to their death from the platform, landing with a splat far below. I sighed. That seemed pretty simple. Boris and his men headed up to the burning missile site and to the chateau for a cleaning-up operation.

The other missile launcher was on a platform sticking out of the wall, and it was protected by another wall and the only way to get close was to go through the muddy low ground. It was raining steadily. A wall of thick fog was moving down the valley. The moon disappeared. Then it came out, all raggedy and misty, from behind ripples of steel-dark clouds – with flashes of lightning high in the blue mountains and down on the plain. Then the moon was gone again. We hunkered down in the mud.

Bullets whizzed over our heads, one shattered a bit of stone just next to my head.

I looked up and realized that, from the top part of the gun platform, I was exposed, out in the open. So I splashed belly down in the mud and lay there clutching handfuls of liquid clay; I looked up, sniffled, blew my nose – my nostrils were full of mud; the nose ring was caked in mud which made it difficult to breathe. I wiped the slop of clay from my eyes. I shimmied and crawled forward. The chains weighed down by mud, felt very noticeable, tugging on all the rings, once again making me acutely conscious of my body and its over-decorated state. I crawled until I got to the low stone wall. Then, carefully, I sat up with my back against it, blinking. Sonia and Tracy and Anton had been caught in the blast of fire and had dropped into the mud. They were just as slimy as I was.

I sneezed and wiped at my nose – the big steel nose ring always meant wiping my nose was a weirdly uncomfortable, sensual, and not always simple operation.

Sonia blinked at me, her eyes bright in a mask of mud. "You okay?" she asked.

"I'm hunky-dory," I said, "And you?"

"Perfect," she smiled, her teeth a sudden flash of moonlit brightness in her absolutely muddy face. Like me, she and Tracy and Sandra were still naked. Clothes didn't seem important. Besides, it was stinking hot. Like a sauna. The rain was a fine, soft drizzle, just enough to give us an extra slimy sheen, not enough to wash off the clay.

The missile launcher crew knew we were coming to get them; shots pinged down, splashing in the mud, exploding against the wall, ricocheting off the cliff across the road. There were only a few of them left, so they were not going to attack us. They were diehards; they just wanted to fend us off – and, I suppose, die with "honor."

"Misty," James crawled up beside me; he was carrying Kaleem Baluchi's miniature rocket launcher, "I've used this weapon before. So I'm pretty familiar with it. Anton and Sonia agree. I'm going to try to take out the rocket launcher with it. I want Sonia and Anton to cover me, as well as Baluchi's people. You and Tracy and Sandra stay down, under the cover of the wall, as backup and for communications. Tracy can hand me the shells."

"Right," I put my hand on his chest. Somehow James had avoided getting covered in mud, but his loincloth had been reduced to a torn muddy rag; he might as well have been naked, and he glowed with sweat. "You look very pretty," I said, "In fact, you look absolutely yummy."

304

"So do you, darling Misty Hoyt," he mimed a kiss.

It pleased me that we should be naked together like this, lost in a stormy world of violence and struggle. In the brief interludes of moonlight, the scars and the burn marks stood out on his chest and legs, and the places where Igor had thrown acid on his chest were smooth ragged splotches and glowed like silver.

"You look particularly beautiful in the rain and mud and moonlight," he grinned and touched his finger to my muddy chin and pinched the end of my muddy nose.

"You too," I whispered. I rubbed my muddy ringed muzzle against his shoulder. Then, I left him. Keeping low and slithering zigzagging on my belly through the slime, I crawled over to Sonia and Anton. "James is going to fire missiles at the rocket launcher. He wants you and Baluchi's people to cover him, on my count."

"Right," they said. Anton crawled down the wall to pass the word to the four warriors from Baluchi's group. Jamila was crouching on her haunches, conferring with Anton. She gave me a big grin, very bright, beautiful teeth, in her dark, handsome face. She also gave me a thumbs-up. Anton, who by this time was totally covered in clay, came crawling back.

He and Sonia and Jamila would leap up at the last minute, and fire off a volley of semiautomatic fire, just as James stood up and fired a miniature missile. Tracy was next to James, on the other side, crouched next to the wall, on her knees, unpacking the case of small missiles for the launcher, and ready to hand James a second missile the moment he had fired the first. She looked so slender and petite, like a child; her hair was plastered down, and strands of hair and mud crisscrossed her face, and hung down, framing her eyes and lips. She glanced at me. Her eyes were gigantic and bright in her muddy mask. She stuck out her tongue, a bright flash of teeth, and a smile.

I wasn't sure at first what precisely she meant – but I knew she was flirting, saying something like, look at us, two filthy naked girls, lovers and sex performers, and you are even more filthy than I am, so do not make fun of me. Sandra put her hand on my shoulder and pulled me down. I'd been distracted and I'd put my head up too high. I might have gotten my brains splattered all over the place. And, in fact, just as she pushed me down, bullets whizzed right over us. "Thanks," I mouthed. "You saved my life!" She grinned and made a gesture which clearly meant that I had done the same for her. I figured she and I were definitely going to be pals.

Baluchi's people were exchanging sporadic fire with the men up on the platform, two or three shots, then silence, then two or more shots. A couple of shots pinged over my head. Sandra crawled over next to Baluchi, and crouched in the mud. She held her Uzi at the ready; she looked eager for action.

"Okay," James said, "Let's do it: On the count of three."

So I counted, and held up my fingers, giving the signal, and on "zero," Sonia and Anton and Jamila and Baluchi's people sprang up and started firing like mad, a ripple, and blast of shots. James stood up slowly, steady, calm, taking his time, with Tracy and me crouching at his feet. And he fired the missile.

It went with a whoosh, leaving a trail of fire. There was a huge explosion. James dropped down. Tracy handed him another missile. James loaded the weapon, deliberately, carefully. Reflections of the flames flicked on his shoulders, on his tousled muddy hair and classic profile, and on Tracy as she knelt and helped him, and on the streel-gray of the tube-like weapon. The enemy was still firing, a blaze of fire, hitting the wall, shattering the stone, sending of shards flying in every direction.

Sonia stood up to fire, there was a thud, and she spun around and dropped face down into the mud. She started to get up, fell back, and was still, her face under inches of slime. Anton glanced at her, ducked, and then got up and started firing.

James again stood up. Shells and lightning flashed around him. The rain bounced off his shoulders, lit up like electric sparks. It seemed to me that James was doing everything in slow-motion – he was being very deliberate, taking aim carefully, slowly – and then firing. It occurred to me then that James was a very brave man, which I already knew, but it also occurred to me that he was a passionate man – and that, after the torture, he had suffered and after the threats to me, and after leaning what Sergei and Nassir planned to do with the bombs, he was furious, and that, with admirable self-control, the cool, understated self-control of a true warrior, he was focussing and channeling his anger so that it would be useful. Each gesture was measured, precise, and machine-like. And, yet, with me and Tracy and Sonia, and even with Baluchi, he was gentle, considerate, always thinking of what we might be thinking, feeling, needing. In that instant, my love for him surged to new heights.

James dropped down, crouched against the wall. Tracy handed him another shell. Her hair was plastered tight against her skull. Her eyes seemed even larger than usual. Thunder and lightning were rattling everything. The rain came down sideways in great hot gusts, and the clouds seemed so low they were touching the ground, and in the midst of this, the fighting was raging as shells and lights seemed to be showering all over the place. I felt we were caught in a tsunami of rain and an exploding series of Roman candles. I crawled, on all fours, towards Sonia.

James glanced at me; he wiped the rain from his eyes; his body glistened in the flames and streaming flashing lights; a shell of some sort ricocheted off the wall just next to him, sparks showered in all directions; James didn't even duck. Tracy, like a Degas miniature molded in clay, was kneeling next to him, calmly helping him reload and adjust the launcher. I could see from the way her head was bent how she was concentrating on the task, oblivious to the danger, oblivious to everything around her.

Keeping as low as I could, I crawled and wiggled my way to Sonia, fearing she was dead. But then I saw that she was slowly pushing herself out of the mud.

"Keep down," I shouted, putting my hand on her arm. I helped her turn over, so her face was out of the slime. Her eyes were wide open, a ribbon of blood, darkened by the mud, was at her temple. "I can't see anything," she blinked, her eyes bright blue pools, "everything's gone black. Is everything dark, or is it just me?"

"It must be a shock or concussion," I said, "Your eyes look perfectly okay." I guided her, so together we could crawl and slither back into the shelter of the wall.

James stood up, silhouetted by the silver curtains of water and the orange glow of the fire, and launched another missile. Again, he was slow, deliberate, seemingly relaxed. There was another huge rippling explosion. In the echoing silence, interrupted by more thunder, the firing from the other side ceased.

"There may be some of them left," said Anton, crouching down next to me. "We'll have to go in and check."

James crawled over, and sat next to me, his back against the wall, his body glistening with rain and oil, the silver scars like pools and rivers of satin. "Misty, darling, can you patch through to the copters? Tell them both missile launchers have almost certainly been eliminated. We're going to check now. They should try to come down on the helipad, just up there, beyond the road. It's clear, no electric wires or buildings nearby."

"Yes. I will, if all the mud hasn't clogged this thing up." I propped myself against the wall, with Sonia sitting beside me. She was shaking her head and muttering to herself: "I can't see a damned thing! This is stupid, so stupid, so fucking stupid, so fucking stupid!"

I spoke so my earphone could pick it up. "We think we've brought down their last missile launcher. We're going in to check on it now." There was a pause, and I heard their reply, a nice American accent, I figured somewhere down south.

"Right, roger that, honey. We're approaching. If we don't have confirmation that the gun is down in three minutes we will launch missiles, and take you all out. Do you understand? Three minutes."

I swallowed. "Yes, we understand. I'll be back to you."

"Another thing, honey; if we get any radar locking onto us, we're going to fire right away. That will mean we'll be firing at you. We and our Russian friends agree on that. Understood?"

"Understood."

I turned to James and the others. "They are going to fire in three minutes if we don't confirm all systems are down. And if any radar locks onto them and they will fire that instant."

"Okay, we've got to do this." James and Anton and the others, including Tracy, went over the top, and headed up towards the burning missile launch site.

Sonia held out her wrist. "Here's my watch, Misty. I can't see it, so it's no use to me. And you are so naked you don't even have a fucking watch."

"Stick with me, Sonia, you'll be my watch."

"How dark is it?"

"Not so dark, the moon's come out, just now, and a couple of fires are burning from where we destroyed the missile launchers and part of the fuel depot. It'll be dawn soon."

"Fuck," she grinned. "Now, I will definitely have to be your slave, Misty Hoyt; if I can't see a fucking thing, you'll have to keep me as your fucking pet and lead me around on a fucking leash."

"You've never sworn so much since I met you, Sonia. If you're my slave, it will definitely be a role-reversal," I put my hand on her shoulder. "Or I could be your seeing-eye dog, and you lead me around on a leash. That would still make you the boss."

"That's better. I like that, I like that idea," she said, and she grinned, "We have had some fun, though, haven't we!"

I heard a burst of shots.

"Oh, oh," I said. "Maybe they are not all dead. Keep down." I peeked up over the wall. I could see James, in silhouette, outlined against the flames, the rocket launcher slung over his shoulder, and Tracy and Anton standing next to him, with Jamila and Baluchi's people a bit further along. Tracy was holding a pistol, and pointing it at something and that something was getting up – a human silhouette, hands in the air. It was one of the survivors.

James turned and waved at me – I must have been quite visible lit up by the flames. I waved back. "All clear," he shouted. "Tell them it is all clear."

"Okay!" I shouted. I slid down so I'd be protected – you never know what might still be lurking in the darkness. I spoke into the earphone. "Okay, it's all clear; the last of the missile launchers has been eliminated. Okay?"

"Roger that. All clear. We are holding our fire. We're coming in."

More clouds spilled over the mountains; the moon disappeared; the night was even darker than before – except for the fires burning here and there. The rain returned, a deluge, with flashes of lightning, a wild unceasing drumbeat of thunder, and a flood of warm rain, a Niagara. Visibility dropped to near zero.

I held Sonia's hand. She was sitting against the wall, her blue eyes staring straight ahead, bright blue diamonds; blood trickled down one side of her face. James lowered himself from over the wall and sat down in the mud beside us. Rolling thunder echoed down the valley, and flashes of lightning lit up everything. I caught a brilliantly etched image of Tracy climbing over the wall to us, with Anton and Sandra and Jamila and the others, all in vivid silhouette, coming just behind her. One was a prisoner, his hands tied behind his back. Then it was all darkness, just the moon, which suddenly appeared, and a ragged trail of clouds, and the rain slashed down, and James held my hand and I held Sonia's hand. I was thinking that we needed a doctor.

Boris and his men had assaulted and finished off the other missile site and flushed out the few hostile snipers who were left. Boris had been nicked in the head and was bleeding from one arm. He crouched down and stared at her. "Sonia?"

"Hi, Boris," she said, turning her muddy face and bright unseeing eyes towards him.

He glanced towards me as lightning flashed and we were lit up in a ghostly bluish brilliance.

"Sonia was hit; she's ... she can't see."

"Misty is being gentle; I'm blind."

"It's shock; it won't last," I said.

"I hope you're right, darling," Sonia turned her face and grinned at me.

"She is right," Boris said. "You said Misty's a genius, right? Well, she must be right."

"Oh, Boris Konstantinov, you are a dear." She reached out her hand, and he took it.

We heard the whap-whap-whap of the helicopters before we saw them, and lightning flashed as they landed – like giant dark, blinking, hovering birds – on the helipad, which was lit up by the burning fires.

We climbed up onto the platform, and we were there to greet the troops, as they poured out of the copters, ready to give battle, arms pointing every which way, leaping down, crouching, taking defensive positions, it was like they were going to slaughter us. After all, they were coming into dangerous enemy territory;

they didn't really know if we had managed to take over the whole place. I half expected them to open fire and kill us all.

But, when they saw us, standing there, lined up, and lit up in the rotating flashing lights, they froze, taking it in: a lineup of men and women – one almost naked man, James, and a cluster of naked women, including a tattooed wonder, and then guerrilla warriors, men and women, and one giant Buddha-like man in a loincloth.

"Shit," said one of the Americans, staring at us, "Shit. What the hell are you folks?"

"It's a long story," James said. I looked at us. Well, we were a fairly motley lot. Baluchi had remained as he was, clothed in only a loincloth, so there he was, huge, bald, glowing with sweat, his belly hanging gloriously out, and wiping his forehead with a small handkerchief. "I'm going to become a naked mystic," he said, "in honor of you, Misty Hoyt." Sandra, naked as always, and wearing her collar, and holding an AK slung over her shoulder, was beside him, holding his hand. Then there was James, handsome, scarred, covered in mud, and wearing only a tattered loincloth, with a miniature missile launcher slung over his shoulder. And there was Tracy, also covered in mud and sweat, and just as naked as she had been when she and I had cavorted in the mud. Next to me was Sonia. I was still holding her hand. She leaned close, her arm and shoulder rubbing against mine.

I had asked her if she wanted clothes, now that the Russians and Americans were arriving. "No, not really, we don't have time," she'd said, "Besides, do you see any clothes?"

"No, I don't, just dead bodies and burned bodies and a few rags."

"Well, then, Mistress Misty Hoyt, you keep me as I am, your very own pet, au naturel. Later we can get cleaned up and get some clothes and become human again."

I took her face between my hands, and I kissed her. "You'll see again. I'm sure of it." In fact, aside from a ribbon of blood at the hairline, there was no sign that Sonia had been wounded at all, just the extra – empty – unfocused brightness of her eyes.

Then, as the star attraction of our motley crew, there was me, James' girlfriend and Baluchi's painted goddess, naked, tattooed from head to foot, with a scarlet – but mud-soaked top-knot, metal and chains, and with an ancient AK-47 slung over one shoulder, and a computer over the other.

Jamila, Baluchi's woman warrior, the chief – came over and touched my topnotch. "Ever since I saw you, I've been wondering: are you really real?" she grinned. "May I?" she touched my breast and tugged, gently, on the nipple ring and chain. "Kaleem says he worships you," she said, grinning and looking back at Baluchi.

"He has a tiny bit of a fixation, I believe," I said.

"He is the most perverse and complicated man in the universe." She laughed, leaned forward, and brushed my cheek with her lips, put her hand on my shoulder, grinned, patted my cheek, and turned and walked away.

An American officer came walking up to us, with a Russian beside him. "Shit," the American said, "shit." He had a cheroot in his mouth, and he took it out, and he spat and then he put it back in his mouth and he lit it up and he grinned, "What sort of folks are you?"

"We're the Naked Brigade," I said. And I explained who the members were: James, Tracy, Sonia, Anton, Boris, Sandra, Jamila, Baluchi, and his people. When I told him how we'd all come together, he professed not to believe me, "Shit, darling, I've heard some tall tales, but this one takes the cake!" The Russian officer had been listening to this little exchange; now, very seriously, but with a twinkle in his eyes, he saluted Tracy and Anton. "You are both safe, then."

"Yes, sir," Tracy and Anton replied, saluting.

It was funny to see the reaction of the troops to our motley and naked band. None of us thought it worthwhile to dress in any particular way. Our nakedness and our loincloths were our badges of honor. We had formed our own little Naked Foreign Legion.

But we soon turned to serious business. After all, Anton and Tracy were Russian agents (with Tracy on loan from the Americans), Sonia was an Israeli agent (one of their best it turned out), and James was well-known in international espionage circles. Kaleem Baluchi was, of course, a big prize, and, even more so, Nassir. Nassir was wanted by virtually every nation on earth. And, as it had turned out, we in the Naked Brigade, with help from Jamila and Baluchi and his people and Boris and his men, had foiled a huge act of terror, one of the deadliest plots ever hatched.

Kaleem surrendered to the Americans and the Russians. He was one of the greatest arms dealers of the age; his bodyguards, who were essentially tribal warriors, were freed; they had helped save New York and Paris from certain destruction. Sonia said we had to find a home for Betty. One of Jamila's women warriors – her name, I discovered, was Tamika – had been looking after Betty. She said she had discussed with Jamila and they would take Betty to their village, in a prosperous, warm mountain valley, there was plenty to eat. She was sure Betty would have a fine time – lots of rabbits.

James and I managed to shower – in the same shower where Tracy and Sonia and I had had fun amusing ourselves a few hours before. Under the steaming hot water and in the mist, my tattoos and chains and rings seemed brighter than ever. James kissed me. And then, covered in perfumed soapsuds, we made love. We were just calming down, and James was on his knees and kissing my belly and my breasts when Sonia and Tracy arrived.

"Oh, you are worshipping the goddess, I see, James," said Tracy.

"Indeed I am," said James, and he didn't stop. "You are welcome to join me."

"Well, she deserves all the worship we can offer her," said Tracy, leading Sonia by the hand.

"I wish I could see clearly. I'm beginning to see," Sonia said, "The American medic said it was a shock to the optic nerve, and that I'll probably be okay in a day or two. Misty Hoyt, the genius, was right, just as Boris predicted."

"That is wonderful," I said. James stood up and kissed me. And so we stood there, kissing, our hands exploring, while our two friends, stood, showering, a few feet away, Tracy soaping and shampooing Sonia whose bright blue eyes stared straight ahead, blinking, but her mouth was smiling. And she did allow Tracy to kiss and caress her, and she did return those favors until the two beautiful women were entwined in a passionate and sublime embrace. This, I thought, was a true expression of the Naked Brigade's esprit de corps.

CHAPTER 12 – RETURN

Two days later, James and I were in a safe house in Germany for the debriefing. James and I were in separate rooms, but we did have a door which allowed us to communicate.

"Soon this will be over, Misty." He gazed at me. "You are a goddess, Princess."

Then he coughed. As the tension of the fight drained off, the strain he had been under, and the effects of torture, began to tell.

I said, "For a few days, you're going to need a nurse, Master, not a goddess."

Baluchi was to go to a luxurious prison where he would be debriefed on all his arms deals in the last twenty years; Nassir was to be interrogated in a joint operation by the Russians, the Americans, the French, the British and the Israelis. I found this degree of international cooperation quite amazing; but so much the better. The Iranians – the Secular Republic of Iran had recently become a friend to Israel – were going to receive some of the transcripts and were being consulted on some of the questions Nassir might be asked.

Without Baluchi to look after her, Sandra – it turned out, her name was Sandra Salvatore – was alone. She had no family. James and I decided – and we did consult Baluchi – that she should be given a scholarship and a generous stipend so she could study whatever she wished to study.

It turned out she was interested in mathematics, and very good at it, and though she couldn't speak, her vocal cords having been cut, she was fluent in French, since she had studied music in Paris and her parents had been stationed in France before they were killed; and so, in a way, she and I became colleagues. Baluchi had set up a very substantial trust fund in her name. She decided she would study in Paris. Martine and Philip arranged for a flat on the Left Bank, not far from Saint Germain des Prés, so we would all be neighbors. Sara, Baluchi's daughter, would go back to school in Nice; there were to be no money problems for Sara, since quite a bit of money had, long ago, been transferred to a trust fund for her and the authorities decided they would not try to expropriate that money, which had come, mostly, from some of Baluchi's legitimate businesses; Baluchi would be able to talk to Sara – and to Sandra – via WhatsApp.

James and I decided Rome was a good place for recovery.

It was already night when our special executive jet – courtesy of the Italian air force – got in, landing at Leonardo Da Vinci International Airport. We didn't have to go through customs, and we were driven in a special diplomatic car into Rome, along the E80 and then along the road past the EUR – the new city Mussolini had planned in the 1930s with its surreal-looking buildings – and along via della Magliana and then along the Tiber, and finally into the little streets of the center.

It was a dark night, low clouds, no moon, and fog filling the streets. The air was clammy, so damp it almost felt like continual drizzle. Everything felt sticky, my clothes, and the seat of the car. "Oh, James, oh, Master," I leaned my head against his shoulder. His arm was tight around me, holding me close. He kissed my shaved skull. "Oh, Princess," he whispered. I was still in full Punk-Goth freak mode; now dressed in heavy black hobnailed boots, short elastic black hot pants and the little skimpy open black vest I'd worn when the oil rig guy, alias Harry Redford Cornwall, had beaten me up, on that little rainy street in Typhilis, the capital of the New Democratic Republic of Old Transbeckistan.

By the time we arrived in our little street, I'd forgotten what I looked like; I was so eager and happy to be back. While the car waited, with its engine running, and the mist thickening in the street, and while James was getting some of the things we had picked up out of the trunk, I opened the little door in the big gate, and I knocked on the porter's door, Maria's door. It opened a crack. Maria looked at me as if she had seen a monster. Her eyes went wide, she stifled a cry of horror, and she recoiled in fear. She was going to slam the door.

"Maria," I said, "It's me – Gwendoline."

Maria hesitated, looked doubtful.

"I know I look like a monster, Maria, but it is me."

"Oh, Signorina Gwendoline – is this you? Oh, what happened? Oh, dear, Giuseppe, come and look at Gwendoline! Oh, oh, oh," Maria's face was comic to see: pure horror mingled with confusion and with joy.

Giuseppe appeared on the doorstep, in his undershirt. "Oh, Mother of God," he said, "what has happened? What is this?"

"It's Gwendoline. It's Signorina Gwendoline."

"Mother of God," Giuseppe repeated, staring at me.

"Don't worry, Maria, don't worry, Giuseppe, it will all go away," I said, though I was beginning to have my doubts. Part of me thought that perhaps the tattoo artist Lou-Lou Jade had played a trick. She did say she was experimenting with new techniques; and that I was to be her masterpiece, and she clearly was a fetishist and – in her own endearing, cute way – a sadist, and …

Giuseppe, standing right behind Maria and with his hand on

her shoulder, was struggling to regain his composure. "Well, Signorina Gwendoline, it is certainly very interesting. Perhaps you will set a new trend in fashion." He patted Maria on the shoulder and then turned her around and pulled her to him and kissed her on the forehead and then on the lips, which I found very touching and then he turned back to me and said, serious now, "But it will go away, won't it, Signorina?"

"Absolutely, Giuseppe," I said, but, yes, secretly, I was beginning to have more and more doubts; just how sadistic was Lou-Lou? She positively drooled at the idea of doing me over as a Punk Gothic freak. Perhaps she would really have liked to lock me forever in the "look" she had invented, and make me forever a creature of her art, an object in her personal museum and portfolio. One day I might get to be displayed in a glass cage in the Museum of Modern Art as a post-Pop fetish artifact.

James was outside, leaning over, thanking the officer who had driven us into the city. As the limousine drove away, James turned around. His face was still marked; there were deep shadows under his eyes. Maria put her hand to her mouth. "Oh, Professor, what happened to you?"

"I was in a bit of a tight spot, Maria. Some evil devils had me in their clutches; they had been doing some quite unpleasant things to me and were about to top it all off by killing me, which would have been even more unpleasant. Gwendoline jumped in and saved my life. To do it, she had to put on a disguise, and this is the result." He nodded towards me and put his hand on my shoulder and kissed my shorn skull.

"Oh, she sacrificed herself! She sacrificed her beauty for you!"

"Yes, Maria," James put his free arm around me. "Gwen sacrificed everything for me." He again kissed my naked tattooed skull, rattling my big jangly loop earrings, and making my bold scarlet topknot sway.

"Oh, Signora Gwendoline," Maria put her hands together in the praying supplication position, as if offering her soul to the Virgin Mary. Her eyes filled with tears, "Oh, Signorina!" She put her arms around me and pulled me to her, "Oh, Signorina!"

Giuseppe and Maria both helped us with our bags, and stowed us away in the overcrowded creaking little elevator; then, we were on our way up to our flat. In the small, cramped little space, James kissed me. "Well, Misty Hoyt – How do you feel?

"Perky, Master," I said, "And I am going to make you soup and hot chamomile and I'm going to put you to bed."

"That sounds just about right," he said.

$\approx$

James had lost a few pounds. They had starved him and given him strong laxatives – as the Italian Fascists used to do with their prisoners – so he would shit himself, lose strength, and feel humiliated. It really hadn't worked. James had an almost mystical ability to detach himself from his own body, and his own humiliation and pain. He had defied them, and he had the badges to prove it: scars on his back and on his chest from where they had whipped him and branded him, and splashed acid on his skin.

"I'm going to fatten you up," I declared. I was exhausted too, but he was much more exhausted than I was. He'd kept going during the fighting with pure nervous energy.

The first few days, he slept, and mostly he didn't sleep alone.

"James?"

He yawned. "I'm an old man, Gwen, I'm broken. You'd better give up on me."

"Oh," I stood with my hands on my hips, in my most annoyed and preachy pose, "So, Master is a coward, Master is a shirker." I pouted, then I relented and crawled into bed next to him and lay next to him and stroked his chest. "Does it hurt?"

"Not really, no, not at all, but it's as if I have been burnt out. I am angry with myself for my sheer stupidity in allowing myself to be kidnapped like that, and, worse, I put you – and many other people – at risk. I can't forgive myself."

"Oh, I'm sure you are not burnt out. And there is nothing to forgive," I said, "For me, this has been a wonderful adventure." I ran my fingers lightly down his belly, I touched the scars, I touched the penis, limp in my hands – and I was afraid.

James was breathing regularly. He was already asleep. For two days, I tiptoed around the flat. I slept next to him during the day and during the night. Sometimes I lay in bed next to him and read a book and made notes. He didn't mind the bedside light. He just turned on his side and slept. Sometimes he turned toward me, and slept with his arm across my body. I worked as silently as I could. "Oh, Princess," sometimes he would whisper, and favor me with a caress, even as he slept.

One thing was strange. We were, as adventurers and spies, totally anonymous, which was, of course, as it should be. Nobody knew that the world had come within a few seconds of a nuclear meltdown, and that Paris and New York, in particular, had been saved only seconds away from a huge flash, obliteration, and the creation, in the heart of Manhattan and Paris of long-term no-go zones, uninhabitable for centuries.

I didn't leave the flat. I would have been a sensation – looking the way I did – if I had left the flat and questions would have been asked. So, Giuseppe and Maria, who had been sworn to secrecy and who did, it seemed, obey that particular order, did the shopping and brought the old-fashioned hardcopy newspapers and all the other necessities of life, and our favorite restaurant sent us a few marvelous meals, with Giuseppe doing the deliveries.

I looked at myself in the mirror. The tattoos were not fading.

"It will take time, lots of time," Lou-Lou said, giving me a wicked smile over WhatsApp from Paris. "Stand up, and turn around, Misty, and take off your clothes, so I can look at all of you," she commanded.

"Yes, Mistress," I replied. I slipped out of my vest, and my hot pants, and I stood up and I turned around, giving her a full view, so she could look at all of me.

"These will take months to wear off," she said, "turn around again. I particularly like that one on the back, there."

Secretly, I liked Lou-Lou's sadistic masterful gaze, which defined me as her very own creation and creature, and I was rather pleased with being a custom-designed, tailor-made freak. It has been one of my fantasies since my earliest memories of having fantasies as a girl, a fantasy of being transformed by a monster, an evil witch or sorcerer, into a fellow monster, something out of a wicked fairy-tale told to you late at night with the wind blowing against the windows; in these fantasies, my monster lover and I would merge into one monstrous love affair; we would become one. I did harbor a small fear that my freakish state might not be reversible. "You can keep the tattoos brighter if you put on this special oil," Lou-Lou said, and she gave me the name of the oil. "Some people get addicted," she said. "Addicted?" I looked down at myself, and I again turned around so she could see the full effect.

"Addicted to the look, addicted to the feel," she said, "You, Misty, are a marginal or borderline case, tempted, but not fully tempted." And then she added, looking off-screen, "Hey, Yo, come and look at Misty Hoyt."

Yo appeared beside Lou-Lou; she was wearing a thin T-shirt and no bra, her nipples showed, her skin glowed gold, and she looked like a beauty queen. I was jealous. "Oh, you are fantastic, Misty Hoyt. You are truly our masterpiece."

"Well, I am delighted you are pleased," I said, feeling both miffed and proud; what, after all, is a collector's item really supposed to feel?

"Where did the chains come from? They are a nice touch," Yo said, giving me a sweet smile.

"Oh, that was one of my admirers. He's convinced I'm a reincarnation of some over-decorated pagan goddess from olden times. I like the effect, so I put them on if I'm around the house, and I'm mostly around the house. Actually, I don't dare go out."

"That sounds charming. You are a prisoner. We must come and visit you in your dungeon. Is James happy with the new you, Misty?"

"James is delighted. I'm no longer his urbane, sophisticated innocent boring chalk-white Gwendoline; now, I'm hard-living, hard-swearing, hard-drinking, tattooed and pierced, backwoods, tell-it-as-it-is Misty Hoyt, a waif from the Appalachians."

"That's great! We are delighted!" Yo and Lou-Lou said in chorus, grinning. They kissed, right there on the screen, maybe wanting to make me feel jealous, or aroused, or amused. It was a nice long slow smooch, a delicate flirtatious little dance of lips, and a nice contrast too between pure golden Yo, with her sharp, perfect features, and Lou-Lou's tattooed and pierced and partially shaved head. Then Lou-Lou turned to the screen and grinned. "Remember, just apply the oil I told you about, nice deep massage, and you will remain bright and shiny – a goddess forever," said Lou-Lou before they hung up and the screen went dark, and I returned to a page of mathematical calculations I'd been working on, and, as I worked, I thought about myself in my new guise as Misty Hoyt. If the tattoos took months to wear off, then for the moment at least, I would remain a world-class freak. Part of me rather liked it, and if I was going to be a freak I should shine, so I had Maria buy me a bottle of the magic oil, and I had James give me an in-depth massage, and thus I had everything refreshed so I would look spanking brand-new; in fact, I would make sure the tattoos were so bright I positively glowed. I shaved the sides and the back of my head so they would be ultra-smooth, and I shaved my eyebrows, so I had no eyebrows, and this way only the glorious scarlet puffball tuft remained. I dyed it, so it kept its glowing pristine comic splendor. I was Misty Hoyt! Gwendoline Clermont was packed away in a cupboard.

Three days later, in the afternoon, I tiptoed into the bedroom. It was in shadow. James was on his back, asleep, and he looked like Andrea Mantegna's dead Christ lying face up almost naked on the stone of unction, the stone bier, and about to be anointed with the sacred ointment by Mary Magdalen. Like Mantegna's Christ, my Master was scantily clad; he was wearing just torn faded jean short shorts, and he was lying on top of the covers, and the ceiling fan was turning lazily above him, making a whispering sound. The tuft of Kleenex in the box on the bedside table fluttered gently. His iPad and yesterday's Financial Times and International New York Times and Le Monde and Corriere della sera lay on the bed next to him, the pages stirring, making a soft crisp rattling sound. I went out to the kitchen and made a vitamin-laced banana smoothie in the blender. And I carried it back into the bedroom, put it on the bedside table, and I crept onto the bed and lay down next to him; I kissed him lightly on the lips. His eyes fluttered open and I saw recognition dawn. "I was dreaming," he said.

"A nice dream, I hope."

"We were on a beach, just you and I, alone in the world, and you were walking into the water. You were naked, and as white as ivory and your hair had grown back, and you glanced over your shoulder and said, 'Come on in, you coward, the water's lovely' and I splashed into the water, and I took you in my arms, and we sank into a sea of bubbles."

"Ah," I said, "it sounds like paradise. Here, drink this."

He sat up and groaned slightly. He drank the banana smoothie, looking at me as if I were a schoolmarm, and he a naughty schoolboy.

"I want to lie next to you," I said, "Is that okay?"

"That is a delightful idea, Misty Hoyt."

I pulled off my T-shirt and my shorts, and I lay down next to him, and I kissed him on the shoulder and then on the lips. His lips were cool and welcoming and tasted of banana smoothie. Then, as he slept, I lay next to him, listening to his breathing, thinking how easy it is to lose someone you love.

I turned on my side, and laid my arm across his chest. He put his hand on my arm. I drank in the warmth of his body, the smooth curve of his muscles, and the rippled roughness of his scars.

Soon his sleep deepened. I let my hand lie there, dormant, but on the alert, sensitive to his breathing, to each nuanced spasm of his muscles, to every little sigh and groan. The body is a temple, it's true, and like a ruined temple, many ghosts live inside it – past selves, past loves, past lives, and lives to come.

He put his arm around me. So – he was not entirely asleep. My hand snuck down his belly. I touched his penis. It stirred. So, his cock was alive, his libido was returning, desire was not dead.

"Wicked, dangerous Misty," he whispered.

"Indeed, Master, I am wicked dangerous, Misty Hoyt."

"Yes, you are."

His cock was now definitely showing signs of life. "May I kiss it, Master?"

"I hereby grant you permission to land, Misty Hoyt," he whispered, moving his hand over my smooth, freshly shaven skull, playing with the tuft-ball on the crown of my head – a sadistic parody and reminder of the thick jet-black locks that once were my pride and joy.

I got up and then knelt beside him on the bed, I took the hem of the loose shorts he was wearing between my teeth, and I slowly pulled the shorts down. I pulled them from his ankles. His eyes were closed. It seemed almost as if he was asleep. I leaned over him and bent down and I began to lick and I almost held my breath waiting to see if the magic of desire would return. The ceiling fan turned languidly. I felt its breeze gently tickle my shoulders and caress my shaved skull. I worked away, thirsty, hungry, desiring, acutely aware of my body bending over his, crouched in adoration – for, truly, I did adore him: he was mine, he was my man, he was my destiny; he was my life. His cock returned to life. He opened his eyes and he sat up and he said, "I will sit on the edge of the bed, Misty, and you will kneel on the floor."

"Yes, Master." I slid off the bed. He sat, like a god now, and I knelt, tattooed, collared, shaved, pierced, chained, and naked before him; I gazed up at him for an instant; then I bowed my head and licked his cock; I toyed with it and teased it, and it rose up before me like a proud little fellow, then a proud big fellow, the original totem, lingam and pillar of ancient cults and religions; James was stroking my head, playing with the little perky round tuft. I licked and licked some more, and then cock was fully erect, oh, we were going back to the good old days; and then it was huge, its old proud self. I opened my mouth and I welcomed it. I licked and caressed it and sucked it, and for a long time, this continued, with James stroking my head, and whispering, "Easy, Misty, easy, Misty."

And still with my mouth full, still sucking and licking, I looked up with a question in my eyes – wondering how strange and monstrous I looked, totally tattooed and with no eyebrows and only a tuft, and the oversized ring in my nose, and he nodded, "Yes," to my unspoken question.

I let him go with a last, parting, sumptuous lick and slurp. He lay back on the bed, and I climbed up and crouched over him, and I licked again, a final little liquid polish, a sparkling lacquer of saliva. Then I sat back and slowly, carefully, guiding him, I lowered myself onto him.

"Easy, easy, dear, dear Misty," he whispered, and he kissed my breasts, his tongue flicking the nipple rings, as I leaned down to him, and then he kissed me on the mouth; the nose ring, as always, made it feel strange, and weirdly even more intimate, a branding as well as a kiss. I slid up and down. I rode him. I kissed him. He kissed me again, and again, and again. And he touched my breasts and the two nipple rings, and the chains, and I felt that, yes, truly, I was his, I was his slave, I was his forever! I arched my back, up and away from him. He was thrusting deeper and deeper into me, gently at first, slowly at first, then faster and faster, and there was a crescendo, and I was on the edge of orgasm, and then he slowed, "Oh, evil Master," I whispered, and he whispered, "Oh, beautiful Misty, I want you to suffer the maximum taste of ecstasy, I want to balance you right there, forever, on the knife-edge, teetering, tottering."

"Oh, cruel, cruel, cruel!" And so there I was, tattooed, bejeweled, naked Misty Hoyt, suspended on the knife-edge, groaning, drooling. He tightened his grip on my waist, and thrusting still deeper into the heart of me, and still deeper, and deeper, and I rode him, and he moved, faster and faster, and deeper and deeper, and the pressure of the rings in my labia, and the nipple rings on my breasts, and Kaleem's silver chains, all pressed upon me, moving, touching the flesh, tugging, making my nipples strain in an agony of desire, and then, in the same moment, in a rippling rising uncontrollable rush, we both came. I screamed, and then

328

I screamed again, and then I sobbed, and then I screamed, and then I laughed, and then I screamed, and tears flooded my eyes and ran down my cheeks.

"Oh, oh, oh ... Oh, Master," I whispered, "finally, oh, finally."

"Yes, Princess, yes, Misty, yes, my love," he said.

He began to move in me again – his force was not spent.

"Oh, boy, oh boy," I whispered, "You are cruel, my Master."

"Yes, my adorable slave, Misty."

And we were once again a single being, male and female, master and servant, worshipped and worshiper, mingled and all in one, riding each other in a rhythm that didn't want to stop, that seemed it would go on forever. And we came, once again, we came, overwhelmed by the quick tempest, the tension, and release. We cried out in the very same moment, and then he turned me over so I was under him, and he kissed me, a deep fiery kiss, and I opened my legs and welcomed him into me again and for a long lazy time we made half-love, just a thrust and parry, a thrust deeper, and then shallow, and then deeper, and then shallow, with me tightening and loosening, squeezing and releasing, and I kissed him, and licked him and touched him everywhere.

I was now covered in sweat. The ceiling fan turned and turned in its lazy, indolent way, projecting rotating shadowy patterns onto our gleaming bodies. Rays of sunlight from the French doors reflected on the ceiling, painting flickering gray-and-cream-and-gold designs; the white muslin curtains wafted gently inwards, bringing with them the sounds and smells of a warm damp afternoon; it was as if summer had suddenly returned to Rome. Finally, James let me go, releasing me slowly, oh, so slowly, withdrawing from me, gently, in stages, like the long-drawn-out slow withdrawal of moonlit ebb tide on a smoothly sloping sandy beach.

I lay on his chest, and his arms enclosed me and held me tight.

Later, I carefully untangled myself from his embrace and stood up. For a long time, I gazed on his sleeping body, the pure beauty of it and all the marks of suffering and torture which remained like shadows from the past, then, while he slept splayed out on top of the sheets in the rising simmering heat of the Roman afternoon, I went to my office and sat down at my computer and began to prepare my next paper – on the analysis of terrorist networks and how they recruit their personnel and how they chose their targets. I was given access to Kaleem Baluchi, via a highly secure video feed, so that I could help in his interrogation – they called it "debriefing" since he was cooperating – and so I could use my math to build predictive models of the future evolution of the illegal arms trade and the methods used by illegal arms merchants to evade the law and to recycle and launder their profits. Baluchi called me "his goddess" and insisted that I appear on the screen, which was another reason for keeping, for a while, my image as "Tattooed Punk-Goth freak" and "Pagan Goddess" intact and bright and shiny. Even better, during these sessions, if I was covered in oil – then I had an extra sparkle, and Baluchi was even more cooperative, eager to please his "Goddess Misty Hoyt" and, on those occasions, he talked on and on, revealing all he knew. Baluchi was also cooperative because James and I had helped Sandra, and we were in constant touch with her. Before coming back to Paris to start her studies, Sandra was in New York, staying with my grandmother Claudia, who had adopted her, just as she had adopted Kate and Martine, as another new, sparkling granddaughter. James and I, and Martine and Philip, were also going to keep a special lookout for Baluchi's daughter Sara, and when she came to Paris, she had a place to stay with James and me or with Martine and Philip.

I was sitting at my computer clicking away on the keys when James came wandering out, yawning and rubbing his eyes, and dressed in shorts and wearing plastic flip-flops. He stood behind me and kissed me on the top of what he called "your adorable tattooed naked noggin," and then he fiddled with my topknot.

"Ouch, that tickles," I wiggled and giggled – and my earrings rattled and clanged, and my rings sparkled and Kaleem's chains – yes, he too had left his mark on me – swayed as my breasts swayed, and, looking down, I noticed that my nipples, poor indefatigable and easily swayed little creatures, were erect, engorged, and that I was, once again, all liquid in desire, excitement, and anticipation.

I swung my chair around so I could face my Master. I kissed him on his beautiful flat muscular belly, and then I stood up, very slowly, kissing my way up his chest, pausing at each whip mark and at each burn, I worked my way, a kiss at each station, to his shoulder and to his neck, and while I explored his body with my lips and my hands, his hands too were, it seemed, all over my body, everywhere, on every part of my anatomy, all at once, his fingers electric on my buttocks, breasts, belly, groin, thighs, back. I sighed and kissed him deeply, on the mouth, and James smiled, kissed me back, and then he said, "I will cook tonight, and you will be my assistant, Misty, that is, if you agree."

"Certainly, Master, Misty Hoyt does agree."

"I do like this new tattooed look," he smiled, and he kissed me and then tugged gently at the nose ring and at the two breast rings and, smiling, he played with the chains Kaleem had adorned me with. "Turn around, Misty. Let me see you."

I stepped away and turned around. The stilettoes gave an extra lift to this little pirouette. The light from outside, coming through the closed shutters and the drifting white muslin curtains, made matching patterns on our bodies. He gazed at me. This was truly the possessive patriarchal masculine defining gaze, ancient and imperious – and I hungered for it. I was consumed by it. I felt worshipped by it, desired by it. I felt a thrill ripple through my belly. I wanted to kneel before him and begin again our lovemaking and a little passion play of mutual desire. I licked my lips and gave him a desperate look, which I am sure expressed my pure absolute shameless unbridled needy lust, and need for him to take me right away there on the floor of the studio. I got down on all fours.

James slipped out of his shorts, and even abandoned his flip-flops, and with the afternoon light rippling over us in waves of pure voluptuous rhythm, he pleasured me as rarely a woman has ever been pleasured before, except, of course, it was exactly as women have been pleasured since the beginning of time, and exactly as women have pleasured men from time out of mind, but, then, enacting and re-enacting an ancient ritual – as our ancestors have done for millennia and millennia – is always satisfying, is it not?

≈

"Dinner," James decreed, "will consist of lemon spaghetti, with an arugula salad, ripe Bosco pears, wedges of parmigiana, and a bottle of chilled Chablis and a large jug of water."

James cooked, standing there in his ragged shorts and flip-flops, slaving over the skillet and over the big pot of boiling water, testing the spaghetti to see if it was al dente. I stood beside him, and click-clacked around the kitchen's tile floor, in stilettoes, freshly showered and perfumed and oiled, my tattoos glowing, my topknot freshly dyed scarlet, with all my chains dangling and glittering, and my collar on, its leash dangling, and I handed him the utensils he needed. I felt totally fulfilled being his maidservant, as he, my love, in his skimpy shorts, slaved over the hot stove.

I peeled and chopped the fresh garlic, took the capers out of their bottle and drained them; I peeled the salty anchovies free from their little clusters where they were clinging desperately to each other; I sliced up some luscious tiny cherry tomatoes, rinsed and drained the arugula, and squeezed the lemons and grated the lemon peels to make a fine shower of lemon zest, I also did the same to three limes, for a bit of variety. I combined balsamic vinegar, and extra virgin olive oil, salt, and pepper, to make a very simple salad dressing. I whisked the cream for the lemon spaghetti into a frothy bubbly smooth concoction, and handed it to James. Each order he gave me caused me to shiver in pleasure. It was fun, playing house like this, particularly after our deadly adventures facing down Sergei Platonov and Khalid and even my friend Kaleem Baluchi.

"Hand me the garlic, Misty." He kissed me lightly, one hand on my shoulder.

"Hand me the tomatoes, Misty." He laid his hand on my bum and slapped my rump gently.

"Hand me the little jug of lemon juice, Misty." He caressed my breast, letting his hand run under the undercurve, toying with the rings and the chains. "Ah, Master," I sighed, "Here you are, here, Master, here is the lemon juice."

It was a warm evening, so we decided to eat on the terrace. I carried the plates and settings out, and to keep my hands free – what with the glasses and bottles and knives and forks and serviettes and table cloth I had to carry – I held the thick tress of the black leather handle of my silver chain leash clenched between my teeth, which made me drool, and gave me too, a tiny suggestion of what it might be like to be a pony with a bit in my mouth, and that gave me an idea of what I might possibly do to Martine the next time she and I found a moment to play some of our Mistress-Servant games. She would be my little pony, and I would outfit her – "tack her up" – with an impressively cruel bit-and-bridle and trot her up and down the beach or perhaps lead her down a lamp-lit cobblestoned street some moody, sultry summer night. I lit candles and I set the table.

The awing was up, exuding a slight canvas smell, a smell of hemp, from the long hours it had spent baking in the hot sun.

The moon was a polished coin, silver in a misty, humid sky, the mid-summer heat building up, early in the season.

We sat down, and I served, while James sat very erect, like a king on his throne. I kissed him on the shoulder as I served him and then we sat very close so we could touch each other. "I shall feed you, Goddess Misty," James said. And he spooned the spaghetti into my mouth and he ate while I chewed and he poured the wine and he lifted the glass to my lips and I swallowed, allowing from time to time, a little bit of wine to drip from my lips and this allowed James, now my servant and worshiper, to lick and kiss the wine from my lips, from my chin and from my breasts.

While we played, and kept ourselves in a softly excited state of continuous titillation and smouldering desire, with lots of kissing and touching, we talked of many things – of the implications of the Platonov affair for James' work, and for my work; of the balmy clinging weather and the sensations it aroused in us; of museums and art galleries we planned to visit – the Musée d'Orsay in Paris, and of course the Louvre where we liked to pass an hour or two, every few weeks, when in Paris; and the various art foundations and collections in Venice we were eager to see; and of the world economy and what was happening to it; I was always amazed at the range of things James knew and at the range of his curiosity and interests and how his thought was organized in such a way that he always seemed to pluck precisely the most pertinent and relevant information or anecdote and made it fit smoothly into what we were discussing, using it to make precisely the point he wanted to make; it was truly an art, and he did it very lightly, not at all, unlike me, in a heavy pedantic way, and with lots of wit and humor; it made him a formidable debater, whenever we disagreed on anything, I had to maneuver like crazy, and pull out all the stops, otherwise he would simply – with a gracious smile and a kiss – obliterate me. We decided we would visit Florence and Venice and that when we were back in Paris, we would increase our regular visits to the Louvre, so that we could "learn to see as the great artists saw," as James put it, "and learn to appreciate all the techniques and creative strategies by which they created their masterpieces," and he kissed me on the lips.

We washed the dishes together, splashing the water, and generally making a gentle little mess, which I cleaned up with a little mop, getting down on my hands and knees to do it so James could admire me as I crawled around at his feet. For some reason, I found this position, with his gaze posed upon me, deliciously titillating, and it reminded me of our little tryst on the floor of my studio in the afternoon. My breasts, with their rings and chains, particularly enjoyed the gravity of the situation, and they swayed gently as I crawled around and made the tiles glow with pristine clarity.

I stood up, conscious of every detail of my own body, and of his. "So, what shall we do tomorrow, Master? Martine and Philip are coming to Rome tomorrow afternoon, and we should do something special." I was dying to see Martine – just the idea of her aroused me – and I was itching for a bit of adventure; I – that is, Misty Hoyt, the person I had become – had not been out of the flat since we had come back to Rome. Maria and Giuseppe and James did the shopping. I remained a prisoner in the castle, a marked creature, a freak and sport of nature that could not be displayed in public, lest we cause a riot – or a horrified stampede of frightened and disgusted citizens.

"What shall we do tomorrow?" He laughed, took me in his arms, kissed me, and slapped me on the bum. "Let's see, tomorrow night, perhaps, we will go out, you and I and Philip and Martine. But it is difficult to see how to dress you, Misty, as you are entirely dressed already – tattoos and rings and chains make a splendid costume."

"Yes, Master," I said, "but perhaps the authorities will not appreciate the fact that I am splendidly dressed, if in fact, and in the eyes of the law, I am stark naked, albeit pierced and painted and chained and adorned with a searchlight topknot."

"Oh, well, the authorities." James waved the authorities away. Such dismissive and almost aristocratic insouciance was, I thought, a tiny bit shocking. After all, I was the one who would be arrested, handcuffed, carried off in chains, and put in a cell with other ladies of the night, which might, in itself, be an adventure, but not necessarily comfortable or amusing. "Oh, the authorities," he repeated.

"You have returned to your old wicked imperious patriarchal self, Master, I see."

"Indeed I have, Misty. You, Misty, have brought me back to life." He took my face between his hands and kissed the end of my nose. "Tomorrow night, Misty, two movies are playing in an open-air theater, outside, like an old-fashioned drive-in, but without the cars, a sort of old Greek or Roman amphitheater, on the edge of the Tiber. Fellini's La Dolce Vita is in a double bill with Ridley Scott's Blade Runner. About a twenty-five-minute walk along the river. I think we should do that. Do you agree?"

"Yes, certainly, Master, your slightest wish is my command, but how shall Misty dress, if you think she should not be dressed at all."

"Have no fear, Misty, your master has a solution."

I licked my lips and bowed my purple plumed scarlet-and-black noggin in obeisance: Master knew best.

Having agreed that we would go out the next evening to the movies with Martine and Philip, we went to bed, but not before James suggested I give him a massage, which I did, out on the terrace, perched on his back, and spreading oil over his shoulders, and he sighed and groaned with pleasure and then he insisted on returning the favor, so he massaged my back, my buttocks, my belly, my breasts, and so it turned out we were covered in oil, and made love in this oily naked state, out on the terrace while somewhere not too far away – perhaps in the trees along the Tiber embankment – an owl spoke owl speak – to-wit, too-woo – reminding me of when I too had been an owl and could only speak owl – to-wit, too-woo – and while the Roman traffic, along the Tiber embankment boulevard under the plane trees, sounded far away and muted, the moon drifted in the heavy warm mist, and then finally, exhausted, we lay on our backs and stared up at the sky, and let our thoughts wander, speaking whatever came into our minds, making a little duet or tapestry of words, mingled thoughts, mingled breath, and his hand strayed over to my breasts and my belly, and with his fingers only, like a genius concert pianist, he made love to me again, and I arched up, bending my legs, tense with pleasure, and then, again, with his tongue he teased me, made love to me, held me, brought me to the very edge of obliteration, "Oh, oh, oh, Master, oh!" And I lay and stared at the moon, whimpering with pleasure, and totally passive, as his fingers played with the nipple rings and my nipples were so erect that they were positively painful and my breasts felt so full that I felt I must be swollen up, fertile, and heavy with milk, and ready to suckle and be suckled, a primitive creature, pure animal, no longer me, no longer Gwendoline, no longer Misty Hoyt, no longer human, just a nexus of pure pleasure, pure sensation. I cried out, "Oh, oh, oh! Oh, my love, my love, my love, oh, oh, oh!"

Finally, we showered together, which was nice and long and lazy, and then, exhausted and walking around, dazed, almost as if in a dream, we fell into bed, and entangled in an endless undifferentiated embrace, we slept.

CHAPTER 13 – MOVIE NIGHT

The next morning it was raining, a gentle gray rain, and, feeling absolutely refreshed, I worked at my computer. I had an interview, via a secure video connection, with Kaleem Baluchi. For my dear friend Kaleem, and he was the only one allowed to see me, I displayed the goddess in all her splendor, so he was very forthcoming, and afterward I got an extremely complimentary note from the US State Department and the CIA and MI-6: the information acquired was invaluable.

I was feeling pleased with myself, as I sat there, fingering the chain that dangled from my right nipple, and pondering how best to extend my analysis of the arms trade based on the additional tidbits Kaleem had provided – particularly the ones regarding the role of important banks in London and New York in secretly covering and facilitating and financing illicit transfers of arms and arms technology. Those banks are all-powerful and do not like to be tampered with; I would proceed with caution.

Evening approached. I wondered what thrills James had in store, how I could possibly go to the cinema and appear in public in my new guise, without being covered up and wrapped in a chador or perhaps a head-to-toe niqab reinforced with big wraparound black glasses or maybe bound up in bandages like a walking mummy, which sounded like fun. And I was wet with anticipation – with an acute nervous fluttering in my tummy – thinking of seeing Philip, freshly back from India, and above all Martine again. What would Martine think, how would she feel, seeing me still as Misty Hoyt, no longer as Gwendoline?

It turned out James had a rather ingenious and bold idea regarding how I was to be costumed. I was to be dressed in ultra-high heels, black patent leather stilettoes of course, and – here was the bright idea – in a flimsy, thin, black plastic raincoat that James had picked up at a roadside stand in a flea market just outside Rome and kept in reserve, as he did so many such weird trinkets collected from hardware stores, dollar emporia, and sex shops, which he felt would add to our fun, and which he stored away until he could find the right and ideal scenario for whatever trinket it was. And that was all, as far as clothes went, so this was to be my official unveiling or vernissage: Misty Hoyt made manifest and visible. I was to be adorned, too, with my thick leather collar, with its ring, and I was to be led on a leash, to supplement my wonderfully abased and abominable state as a submissive tattooed Goth-Punk work of art. James added to the fun by cutting deep vertical slits on both sides of the raincoat, a glimpse and a tease, as it were, flashing hints of the glowing tattooed and pierced wonders that lay beneath the cheap glossy fluttery black plastic. Any combination more perfectly meretricious would be hard to conceive.

James and I were going to meet Philip and Martine at the outdoor amphitheater cinema, on the edge of the Tiber, about two and a half kilometers downstream.

It was already dark when we set off – sneaking out without Maria or Giuseppe noticing, and slinking down two little cobble-stoned side streets to the river, luckily encountering nobody on the way, for I did feel a residual sense of shame, of violating a taboo, which in itself, provided a titillating thrill and sense of danger; we climbed down the stone embankment stairs to the river and headed along the Tiber, walking on the lonely and sheltered stone quays, down below the high 19th century stone embankments, and close to the dark, turbulent muddy water; it is a place where few people walk, particularly after sunset. The night was sultry, humid and close, and even clammy, which made the fluttering crackly black plastic stick, here and there, to my skin and made me conscious of every millimeter of the surface of my body, of every millimeter of skin, of every muscle and every tendon, of every piercing and every ring, of every dangling and taut length of chain I licked and lapped at my nose ring. It felt nice and warm, and yet cool and smooth; by now, it was part of me.

At one point, we stopped to examine a waterfall, rapids of foaming water, and James asked me, Gwendoline, aka Misty Hoyt, the two-legged walking encyclopedia, about the history of the Tiber, and about the rapids and the bridge. I cleared my throat. I was so plunged into my role as Misty Hoyt the backwoods tattoo fetish icon that I'd almost forgotten that I was also Gwendoline, a world-class pedant, and erudite show-off pain-in-the ass. I gave him a kiss, pressing my nose ring against his cheek, and I began, "Well, Master, you asked for it. Misty will now speak." I cleared my throat. "The Tiber River begins with two springs, called the "veins" that gush out of a rock face in a beech forest on the south face of Mount Fumaiolo, which is part of the Apennine mountain range; the two springs, now reduced to one, are located more than a kilometer about sea level, and over 400 kilometers north of Rome. The Tiber, in fact, is just over 400 kilometers long, and enters the Tyrrhenian Sea just west of Rome. Rome was probably created here because there is an island in the middle of the Tiber at this point, which makes it easy to cross the river, and ..."

While I spieled my spiel, James fiddled with the light flimsy plastic raincoat that was my only raiment and protection from the elements; it had two big round plastic buttons to hold it shut, and his deft fingers quickly unbuttoned both. The plastic swung open, and, clinging only to my shoulders and my arms, it drifted around me like a flimsy, feathery cape. As we walked, I felt the air move freely against my skin, a gentle breeze, coming upstream, meandering its way up the Tiber valley from the beaches and the Tyrrhenian Sea. The breeze is then, as it approaches Rome, trapped between the high, sloping embankment walls, so it must tunnel itself gently into the heart of the city, wafting over the muddy turbulence of the river, picking up all the delicate and primal smells from the clay and the volcanic tuff, from the fields of pine and cedar, and from the sunburnt earth and sand. And now this sacred breeze touched my skin, tickled my epidermis. It was delicious, subtle, cool, and revealing, stripping me bare, touching and exploring me like a curious lover. James smiled, realizing the effect the moving air and the open, rustling plastic was having on my aroused senses. He stopped walking, held me, and kissed my breasts, as I continued my learnèd lecture, expatiating now, with a certain perverse pedantic insistence, on the history of the river, and of its bridges, and on the story of the Isola Tiberina, or Tiber Island, while James ran his hand down my belly, playing with the chains, and with the ring in my bellybutton, and then his hand was between my legs, exploring the rings, and gently opening my labia, already wet in anticipation, and I gulped and sighed and tried to keep a steady keel on my stream of thought – and on my stilettoes – babbling on, in great detail, about how one of the Popes had a little boat to cross the Tiber and visit his lover, and so they named the street where she lived the Street of the Little Boat, and James finally shut me up by kissing me, and

I unbuckled his belt, plunged my hands under his jeans, and seized his erection.

"You were saying?" he said, as he sighed, and his erection became even harder and larger.

"Master is cruel to Misty, making her speak of geology and ancient history, of the Apennines and Tuscan volcanoes, of popes and concubines, when she should be concentrating on other things." I kissed him and cleared my throat, and continued my tale. "Tiber Island, which provided a convenient spot to cross the river, became a center of healing and health, and the site of a hospital because it was easy to isolate people there, quarantine them, on the island, and prevent contagion, and ... " And on, and on, and on!

James tensed. His erection was grandiose. He took a deep breath. "Well, that was very interesting, Misty, about the Temple of Aesculapius, and about why they sculpted the island to make it look like a boat, and why a hospital is located on the island, and I liked the part about the ancient Roman sewer system," James continued, keeping his cool, though his erection was as hard as steel – I barely exaggerate – and his voice had become a bit foggy, perhaps indicating a high state of readiness and arousal. My man was all primed, eager to spring into action.

We stood there for perhaps five minutes, teasing each other, kissing and touching, with me prattling on, giving a veritable history of the city of Rome and its relation to the Tiber and to the geology – mountains and plains and rivers and harbors – of Italy itself, with James caressing me, exciting me, teasing me, and asking me increasingly erudite, complex questions.

Then, suddenly, he said, "Oh! Dear, Misty, if we don't hurry, we are going to be late!" He gave me one last deep kiss, and he buttoned me up – well, just one button this time – and we continued, James striding ahead with my leash clutched in his fist, me tottering along on my stilettoes making a damp, muffled, click-clack. "Ships used to come up the Tiber, right to the Port of Rome, which was … in Testaccio, and close to where that river port was, there is a mountain, or hill, Monte Testaccio, made of millions of broken amphorae, or jugs, brought in by ships …" And so I went, blah, blah, blah, teetering along, click-clack, aroused, all tumescent, the damp fecund breeze wafting in under the thin floating plastic …

The outdoor amphitheater movie palace was only a few steps from the Tiber, but we did have to climb up a steep, narrow stone staircase to the top of the embankment, and walk along a short length of narrow cobblestoned street. It was dark on the street, with no cars, but, in the darkness, the streetlamps formed misty little circles of bright light, like spotlights, through which we walked, and the few pedestrians – mostly romantic couples and lonely film lovers heading to the movie theater – opened their eyes wide when they saw me all lit up, and I heard a current of remarks and whispers wash behind us and around us as if I were a grotesque ocean liner of sin and depravity leaving spreading waves and a wake of scandal and rippling shock behind me.

We entered the theater through a little stone archway. People turned and glanced our way; some stared; some turned away. It was interesting, being a freak, and, of course, for me, perversely exciting. I was like a wild tiger who had been let loose in the center of an ancient civilization, or an outcast marked with dangerously unsettling stigmata. People could turn away and ignore me; they could run, or they could stare.

Martine, who was in a skintight, micro-thin, single-piece black latex dress, the exact echo of the dress I had been wearing the day – which seemed so long ago – I was transformed into Misty Hoyt, took one look at me, opened her arms, grabbed me, kissed me on the lips, then on the forehead, then on the cheeks and

344

then stood back, with her finger hooked through my collar ring, and whispered, "Oh, Misty, we really do have to exploit this look while it lasts."

Philip cleared his throat, and gazed at me, saying, "I hear you have been a true hero, Gwen, though I don't know in what way you were a hero – Martine says she can't tell me – and I believe it is top secret and I am not to mention it." He kissed me on two cheeks. He stood back, and blinked, taking in the new apparition that was me. He did look shocked. Martine had warned him, but the effect in person, I had been told, packed a real wallop, a punch in the visual gut.

The fact that James and I were with two famous people, the actress Martine Aubin and the director Philip d'Este, added to the spicy curiosity of my freakish, multicolored appearance. While we sat down, Martine and I, in the bleachers, James and Philip went to get popcorn and beer. Martine, who was a model of sexy elegance, her blond hair cut short and absolutely perfect, her lips a bright scarlet, her skin lightly tanned and without a blemish, her blue eyes bright, and her black latex dress – which was as I said the exact twin of the one I had been wearing the night I had climbed over the rooftops with Zoe Parillaud to escape from the kidnappers in Paris – revealed just about everything about her body and how perfect it was.

It was already dark in the amphitheater – a sort of smoky twilight with only dim floor lights guiding people to their seats. Ignoring the spectators sitting around us, Martine leaned close, tickled my ear, and jangled my earrings, first with her lips, then with her tongue, and whispered, "We are going to have fun, I think." I whispered back, putting my hand on her thigh – damp from the dampness of the night – that I was indeed ready for fun.

Even in the obscurity of the smoky dim twilight, people did glance at us, and then they glanced away. James and Philip returned, their hands full, with big buckets of popcorn, and a bottle of very cool white wine. "They didn't have any beer left," James explained, "So we decided a dry, tangy white from the Roman hills would do be even better."

The dim floor lights went down, and everybody concentrated on the movie. As far as tattoos went, I was not alone, of course; there are multitudes of beautiful girls and guys with elaborate tattoos, but very few people – particularly women – had the sort of elaborate face tattooing I was decorated with, or the elaborate piercing and bald scarlet topknot look.

At the intermission, I, of course, was sent – with Martine – to get another bottle of wine and two buckets of fresh popcorn, while our two gentlemen lolled back and discussed the deeper meaning of the first film – Federico Fellini's 174-minute-long La Dolce Vita.

Martine led me out to the food and drinks stand on my leash. She and I ended up standing in line. Lots of film folk were there, and Martine knew most of them, so simultaneous conversations ensued in every direction. Lots of "Oh, darling!" "Oh, love!" And lots of embracing and cheek-kissing. It was very showbiz. Martine introduced me, "You know Gwendoline Clermont, of course." And they all said they knew me, or had heard of me, or had seen photoshoots of me, or TV and video shorts of me – almost always with Martine. But they had never seen me like this.

Eyebrows were raised, and people complimented me on the "bold statement" I was making.

In spite of what Misty Hoyt had declared to Sonia, way back, I was not really sure I was "making a statement," but it was better than nothing. Having an ideology or a philosophy or a manifesto behind you can always help you get away with the most imprudently excessive behavior. Big words and a theory will excuse almost any form of tomfoolery. The real story behind the tattoos

346

could not, of course, be told – at least not yet. As for "Misty Hoyt," she was an underground agent, and could not be named or even spoken of, except among the cognoscenti, James, Martine, Philip, and me.

Then other people, particularly the young women, began to show us their tattoos, which led to Martine insisting I show, for the girls alone, the totality of my tattoos and my piercings. So we women all went off into a little garden which was at the side of the amphitheater, and I opened the raincoat and then – Martine said, "Don't be shy, my slave, take it all off."

I gave her a look, stuck out my tongue, and I slipped out of the raincoat. Martine reached out her hand, gave me an imperious, commanding glance, and took the raincoat, and folded it over her arm.

And so I stood there in the humid Roman night, naked, in the circle of young women. There were a few who said, oh, oh, oh, and a few too who wanted to touch the rings.

"Go ahead," I said, bowing my head submissively, "if my mistress allows it, of course."

Martine, looking every inch the sleek dominatrix in her black latex and high heels, said, "Go ahead but don't pull on them, don't hurt her, she belongs to Mr. James Hewitt Spencer and to me."

I glanced at Martine and licked my lips and stuck out my tongue, but I was pleased thus to be branded – their possession. I belonged to both of them.

We still had five minutes before the second film – Blade Runner. So some of the women touched the rings, and ran their fingers and hands over my belly and my breasts and my ass and the small of my back. I was public property and branded as such.

Two of the girls took off their T-shirts and displayed their piercings and their tattoos. And one, briefly, stripped entirely. She had labial rings and a dragon rising out of the scarlet and orange tattoo of flames on her pubis and belly, plus a bellybutton ring. I touched the dragon, whose fiery open mouth consumed her left breast, and gave the ring a little circular caress. The girl put her hands on my shoulders, and then gave my nose ring a cute, gentle little tug. She had freckles on her face, and, aside from the tattoos, a creamy white body, with super generous breasts, and two front teeth which stuck out giving her an eager startled air, like a beautiful chipmunk. She looked very interesting, I thought, and I saw Martine give me a warming smile of complicity; she had seen the flicker of interest and arousal in my eyes, and she felt it too and she both approved of it, and warned me she would be extraordinarily jealous – her revenge would be terrible and wonderful – if I were to succumb to this slight momentary tempting fantasy, which of course I wouldn't.

The bell rang. The women all said, "Oh, that's too soon!" and "Oh, this was fun!"

I slipped back into the raincoat – which was truly the thinnest and flimsiest of things, James being impeccably precise in his erotic calculus – and we returned to our seats, bearing the drinks and the popcorn. We found James and Philip deep in a discussion of the more arcane aspects of existentialist philosophy as manifest in Marcello Mastroianni's masterful performance as a dissolute corrupt journalist who loses his innocence in his pursuit of meaning in a world which, with post-war capitalist prosperity and the decline of the family and of religion, is losing all meaning, all reference points, all anchors. Or something like that.

"Ah, there you are, Misty," said James in his most genial tone. As the lights went down, he slid his hand through the slit in the raincoat and rested it on my thigh, and his fingers crept up, and my excitement rose, slowly, as we watched Blade Runner, and his fingers cleverly massaged me, played a little melody on my mons veneris, and indirectly teased my clitoris, until I was ready to scream.

"I see my Master has fully recovered from his trials and tribulations and from the extreme exercises and acrobatics of yesterday and early this morning," I whispered from the corner of my mouth, trying to keep my voice from turning into a primal animal screech.

"Indeed he has," he touched my ear with his mouth, and he kissed me full on the mouth and then he opened the raincoat, slipped it off my shoulders, and put his arm around me so that, enclosed by his love, I sat there, naked, in the midst of the public, in the darkness, and lost myself in the world of Blade Runner, a future image of Los Angeles where "replicants," specialized humanoids created for special purposes, in particular, to amuse humans, or provide sex, have escaped from their prisons in space, and are hunted down by bounty hunters. It poses the question, over and over: What makes us human, and where do the frontiers lie, truly, between the human and the non-human, between "them" and "us"? I thought the question applied as much to me as it did to the replicants. Misty Hoyt was not human; she was a fiction; and so was I. I had invented Gwendoline Clermont, bit by bit, piece by piece, every time I learned to do something new, every time I overcame a fear, every time I dared to love, every time I allowed myself to feel something new; but maybe that's what we all do, being the authors of our own destinies, the inventors of our own fictions.

≈

"Blade Runner is a fantastic film," I said, as the credits stopped rolling, and the dim lights went up, revealing a full house, still at this late hour, shadowy figures rising from their seats. James pulled the raincoat up, so that it covered my shoulders, but when

I tried to stand up the raincoat almost stuck to the seat and almost slipped off me. James, who was still sitting, winked up at me as I stood, carefully pulling the flimsy covering back into place and buttoning one of the two buttons. James stood up, put his arm around me, and took my leash in his other hand.

"There are several versions of Blade Runner," I said, becoming automatically my encyclopedic self. James looked at me with the indulgence of a parent for a precocious child.

Martine smiled and licked her lips. I could see she thought I was being very cute reverting thus to my pedantic and encyclopedic self and she wanted to kiss me. But Philip, a true movie buff, took my point seriously, and said, "Yes, of course, Gwen, oh, sorry, Misty – yes, of course, Misty is right. And sometimes, in my opinion, producers – I hate to say this – can protect directors from themselves. And different markets, of course, offer different possibilities of interpretation. Now, in this example ..."

And we had a little discussion, until we were the only people left in the amphitheater. James and I said we were going to walk home. So we said goodbye. Martine gave me a kiss, wrapped her arms around me, slid her hands down, lifted the raincoat, and patted my bum and said we had been apart too long. And she adored my new look, "We will definitely do something with it." She was going to be in Rome for at least a few days and she would phone me, tomorrow, she said, about a little project we might do before I ceased being fabulous Misty Hoyt and returned to being boring old Gwendoline. We kissed and hugged and waved and then Philip and Martine sauntered away, turning to look back a couple of times, and waving. Martine blew me a last kiss. Then they turned a corner and were gone.

As James and I left the theater and stepped into the street, a group of young women went by – including the creamy freckled girl who had stripped to reveal her dragon. They all waved and cried out, "Good night, Gwendoline! It was great, Gwendoline! Goodnight!"

"You already have a new fan club, I see," said James.

"Yes, there was a little striptease and tattoo competition during the interval while Martine and I were getting that popcorn you and Philip had set your hearts on. Some of the other women had really interesting tattoos and piercings."

"We suspected as much," James laughed. "Philip said, 'What's taking the girls so long?' and I explained that you and Martine were undoubtedly putting on a show of some kind, and Philip nodded sagely and said, 'Yes, yes, of course.'"

James kissed me. "People do love you, you know, Gwendoline – my delicious little Misty."

I kissed him back and leaned against him and stroked his hair.

It was almost three a.m. and there we were, James and I, outside, alone, in the sultry Roman night, and we had a thirty-minute walk to get home.

We sauntered lazily down the narrow little cobblestoned street, which was closely confined between two towering crooked ancient brick walls, my heels clicking, and the plastic sticking to my skin, with tendrils of mist curling up from the river; and then we climbed down the steep embankment steps to the quayside walkway. The Tiber embankments had been built in the 19th Century to channel the Tiber and stop the flooding which had plagued Rome for centuries; the quays below these big walls are stone, and are rarely visited, particularly late at night. They are romantic and spooky and grandiose places, and, with the smells of the river and mudflats, they are a sensual and sensuous refuge from the city which is invisible and hidden above.

We were alone. Fog curled under the arched bridges and drifted over the water in long, lingering, thick, serpent-like tentacles. I thought of Betty the python, and I wondered how she was doing in her new home, and if she missed me. She had, during our adventures, seemed quite fond of using me as a perch, and dangled from my shoulders or curled around my body every opportunity she got.

"You're thinking of Betty," James said, and ruffled my topknot.

"Yes, the ribbons of mist ..."

"Remind you of her."

"Yes."

The lamps were shrouded in moving mist; it moved against our skin, almost as thick as a drizzle. "Oh, Misty," James said. He looked up and down the quay. There was not a single person to be seen.

"Yes, Master, I am yours, Master. Misty Hoyt is yours." I lifted off the raincoat, and put it over my shoulders. It fluttered in the damp, gently moving air; it was so light.

"Here, I'll carry it," James said. And he took the raincoat and put his arm around me, and we walked that way, me naked and my high heels going clop, clop, clop, on the paving stones of the quay. The air was so moist it condensed on my skin, sparkling beads of water, brightening the tattoos, glistening on the rings and chains, making me doubly conscious of my nakedness, my vulnerability.

I turned and kissed James, full on the lips.

"Ah, Misty Hoyt," he said, "you are unique, a true pagan goddess."

We walked under one of the bridges. Some people were sleeping under the arches of the bridge on the far side of the river, little heaps of cloth, burlap and plastic and canvas, and sleeping bags laid out on the quay; they were sheltering in the shadow of the bridge; they had lit a fire that was burning low; the smell of burning wood, cedar and pine, mingled with the rushing, tumbling, roaring smell of the river, a fresh smell of ozone, and with a fecund earthy smell too, since the Tiber carried silt downstream from the north, from the lands of the Etruscans, and from the mountains.

Up above the high gray walls – that sparkled with humidity – we could hear the muted murmur of sparse late-night traffic. We came to a stone bench.

"Let us sit down," said James.

"Are you tired, Master?"

"No, but I have been neglectful of you of late, my dear Misty."

I sat down on the bench, as instructed, and James knelt on the stone pavement and looked up at me. He put his hands on my thighs and looked into my eyes and then caressed my breasts and kissed my belly; his tongue played with the two nipple rings; my nipples were excited, erect, aching for him; he touched them with his lips, lightly, and then he kissed and sucked and licked them and kissed them again, and blew upon them gently. And then he kissed my belly, and the navel ring, and then, as I leaned back and opened myself to him, he kissed my brightly tattooed mons veneris. Then, with slow liquid motions of his tongue, he opened me, slowly, gently. I was melting with excitement, all fluid, leaning back, dazed, staring at the branches of trees above me on the roadside above the embankment, hearing the roaring water rushing past the island and tumbling, crowded into a Niagara by the piers of the bridge, foaming and racing under the stone pillars and arches, and seeing too, out of the corner of my eye, the yellow fire of the encampment of the vagabonds and homeless men and women who were sleeping across the river sheltered by the bridge, and all the while feeling James, deeper and deeper within me, his tongue, which was lighting me up like liquid fire, touching my very soul, and I cried out "Oh, oh, oh, James! Oh, oh, oh," and then, after resisting and resisting and resisting, I realized all resistance was vain, and I came – with an echoing soaring sensation of excitement, there, naked, me, Misty Hoyt, vagabond, orphaned, false-Appalachian white trash, there, splayed open, on that wet stone bench beside the roaring muddy gray water of the Tiber. I lay back, and sighed, barely conscious. James continued to caress me, his tongue and his fingers, masterful and subtle and strong. My fingernails scratched at the wet stone of the bench. I cried out again, and then again.

I lay there for a long time; finally, I stood up, and looked down at James, who was on his knees. James looked up at me, and he kissed his way up my body to my mouth and then he kissed me on the mouth, the mingling of him and of me, and then he said, "Do you mind if I take you and possess you here, my dear Misty?"

"No, Master, I do not mind at all. Indeed –"

I was not able to finish my thought. He shut my mouth with a violent, long, deep kiss.

"Undress me, Misty," he said. He stepped out of his sandals, and I unbuttoned and lifted off his shirt, and his jeans and his underpants, and folded everything neatly on the bench, and I looked upon my work, his nakedness, his muscles, the scars and acid marks left by the torture sessions, and I sighed and said, "Oh, man, oh, my man, you are so beautiful!"

He slid his arms around me, and he held me and then he kissed me. We walked, arm in arm, to the very edge of the water, and watched it for a long time, the primal water, rushing past, rich with the fertile smells of earth and mountain, volcano and limestone, sulfur and soil. We kissed and walked back to the embankment wall, where I stood with my back against the soaring barrier of stone, while he, my man, my naked man, knelt before me, and again his tongue opened me.

"Wait, Master," I said, and I knelt before him, and I licked and sucked so that he was well lubricated and shiny, and I stood up and leaned back against the damp stone, and he entered me, and held me, and he pulled me away from the wall, and spun me around, and it was almost like a dance step, waltzing, until he again pressed me against the stone of the wall, and I wrapped my legs around him, and he was deep in me, thrusting, thrusting, thrusting, and "Oh, oh, oh ..." I bit him, I scratched him, I howled and screamed and ululated, and licked and kissed and sucked and I cried out, and I came ...

He had transformed me. I was no longer human; I was a wild screaming inarticulate thing, a wailing banshee, freed of all humanity, of all civilization, casting off all limits; I wanted to dive into the swirling muddy river, I wanted to growl and crawl on all fours, I wanted to lie on my back, open my legs, and bay at the moon. I licked my lips, and I growled, and I stretched, and I got down on all fours and I looked up at him. And I kissed him, and, rising up on my knees, I kissed his belly. I growled, "Let us run naked through the streets! Let us dive into the river and swim to the sea! Let us go naked to Saint Peter's Square and ask the Pope to join us in singing a hymn to the moon and the tides and the nymphs and satyrs and gods of the ancients!"

"No, Misty, no, Goddess, no," James said, smiling gently, and he put his arm around me.

I licked my lips, growled and snarled, baring my teeth, a werewolf woman, snarling, gnashing, slobbering, eager to fight, eager to tear up the earth with her claws, eager to bound through the grasses of the vast savannah, to snarl with her fangs, to lick her long spiny whiskers and eat the bloodied heart of an antelope, and to flee and howl under the ragged clouds and stars; and then I looked down, contrite, returning, briefly, to my neatly contained old human self, Misty Hoyt, font of all wisdom. "Yes, Master, you are wise; you save me from myself and my infinite folly."

And then I dressed him, most reverentially.

"Well, Misty Hoyt, how do you feel now?"

"I feel fulfilled, Master, I am happy to be of service to my master."

"And I am happy to be of service to you." He kissed me, and we walked farther on, until we came stairs that led up to the bridge closest to our home, and I slipped back into the raincoat, and we climbed up the steep damp mossy stone steps that glistened like tarnished copper under the amber-tinted lamplight, and we crossed the bridge, where the fog had become thicker, and the air was rich with all the early-morning smells of the city: damp sun-baked stone, bread baking, espressos being served, coffee being brewed in the few coffee shops that were already open and invisible to us but only a few streets away, in the markets, in the squares and small streets, and we went up several narrow little cobblestoned alleyways and streets, feeling very wicked and daring, particularly when a garbage truck went by and the garbage men glanced at us, and one whistled a perfect, admirable, admiring wolf-whistle, and we entered our own street, all the cobblestones glowing, and we came to the giant closed wooden horse-carriage doors of our palazzo. And we entered through the tiny Lilliputian human door, and went up the stairs, and halfway up, James asked me to take off the raincoat, which I did, and he kissed me and held me and then, finally, we were in front of our own door, and James turned the key, and we went into the flat.

"Whew," I sighed. "Now, it is time to sleep."

"Perhaps," said James, "perhaps."

"You have certainly recovered your spark, Master," I said.

"Yes, I think perhaps I have, my dear Misty, my dear Gwendoline, and it is all thanks to you. In fact, without you, dear Misty Hoyt, I would be dead and my remains – whatever was left of them – would be rotting in an unmarked grave somewhere in the New Democratic Republic of Old Transbeckistan."

CHAPTER 14 – ICON

The next morning James and I were having breakfast on the terrace under the awning when Martine phoned and said that she had a great idea: we should do a photoshoot while I was still truly a spectacularly tattooed freak. A cutting-edge fashion magazine would love it, and we could accompany it with an essay of our choice.

James, who was buttering my toast, nodded his approval.

"Okay," I said to Martine. "Okay, in principle, though we'll have to check the security issue. After all," I said, rather pompously, I must admit, "I was on a top-secret underground mission."

"Well, you check, my darling tattooed Mata Hari, and if our friends the spooks give permission, this will be a new mission and add to your luster and notorious shamelessness – and it will, quite possibly, stir controversy and get us into deep hot water and that can be useful. Any news is good news, right?"

"Hmm, I guess so. I'm putting you on speaker," I said, and I took a big bite out of the toast and plunged my fork into the bright yellow yolk of a luscious-looking, very runny egg, one of four that James had prepared. I was dressed in hot pants and the flimsy little vest, so I was feeling proper and civilized, unlike my usual early-morning naked self.

"Good morning, James," Martine said.

"Greetings, Martine. We are just having breakfast."

"Well, Bon Appetit to both of you," said Martine, "I think our friend Misty should jump at this chance. She is unique, and this is a unique opportunity."

"We have to double-check," I said. "Of course, Lou-Lou has the rights. And then there's security."

It turned out that the security problem was a non-problem. Frederick said it was a one-shot deal, so I could expose myself. In any case, no one would know why I was tarted up the way I was. "It might even be a good diversion from your ... ah, from your other work. We can suggest that Martine and Lou-Lou put you up to this, or that you felt inspired for some reason of your own, that it is some sort of artistic Punk-Goth-Retro experiment and you are their work of art," Frederick laughed. "It will divert attention from the cloak-and-dagger stuff," he added, alluding to my math and decryption and hacking efforts that should not really be put into the spotlight; he said he'd like me and Martine to come in, but later, in a few weeks perhaps, for a detailed, very informal, debriefing. Martine, he added, had been very helpful, briefing me on my new identity as Misty Hoyt, providing diversions with my double, and generally facilitating communications with Misty Hoyt. Martine and I, of course, agreed. A joint debriefing sounded like fun!

Lou-Lou's skill was public knowledge. So we decided we would put on a show – it was essentially a photoshoot for one of the edgy glossy fashion and art magazines that hover right on the frontiers of a dozen kinds of cultures and subcultures, feeding the products of those subcultures – graffiti, SM and bondage, fetishisms, political slogans, and logos, local and ethnic and street culture creations – into a sophisticated sort of mainstream, and doing erudite, subtle essays on rap artists, on street art, on tattoos, on the traditional avant-garde and even on the art of the

Renaissance, or of Persia, or Africa, mixing old and new, classical and revolutionary, and generally being hip and street-savvy, catching trends as they are born, surfing the Zeitgeist on the perilous frothy cutting-edge of the wave.

It was a great idea, of course, but it was going to create some huge problems which none of us foresaw.

≈

It was early morning when Martine picked me up so we could go to the photoshoot together. Our narrow cobblestoned street – mostly restricted to pedestrians – was filled with the warm gray-silver morning light so typical of Rome. A few people were hurrying by on foot on their way to work. I was waiting, hiding, just inside the gate to our building, a cowering invisible freak. Maria was standing lookout. "Here she is, Signorina Gwendoline! Here is Signorina Martine!"

Stopped in the little cobblestoned street was a sleek, long, highly polished black Mercedes limousine. Martine got of the car, saluted gallantly, and opened the door for me. She waved and flashed her biggest smile at Maria, "Hello, Maria!"

"Signorina Martine, hello, hello. You look beautiful."

"Thank you, Maria. So do you! Giuseppe is a very lucky man!"

Maria was utterly charmed, as was everybody, by Martine and, of course, this morning, Martine didn't disappoint. She was in her simplest minimalist style, black jeans, black T-shirt, black sandals, chic, and understated, just perfect.

"By-by, Maria," I said, "wish us luck!"

"Good luck, Signorina, Good luck!" Maria stood there, wringing her hands; in a way, she had become a surrogate mother and older sister for me, and she was just as anxious as a real mother would have been, watching out for her wayward undisciplined and perverse daughter. At the same time she was thrilled that I was so notorious and so present in the tabloid press and Internet and that I was the pal – and more than the pal, the lover – of Martine Aubin, who was a real star now, and known just about everywhere in the world where people go to movies or watch TV or go online.

I was an absolute contrast with Martine. I was the invisible freak, the dark side of my tanned, buff, sunny, blond lover. And, for the moment at least, I was under semi-wraps, to be revealed publicly in full glory only when the magazine came out. Our midnight movie outing – and my for-girls-only striptease – had been an aberration and an exception. A few surreptitious selfies and snaps had appeared from that night, but nobody had revealed or seemed to know what they represented. Since then, I had stayed strictly hidden creeping around the inside flat like a dark shadow – which was in itself thrilling. Only James was allowed to see me, and Maria if she came to the flat, or Giuseppe if he came up to check on the plumbing or electricity.

For this occasion, I had put on big wraparound dark glasses so I wouldn't have to stare back at people who were staring at me – if anybody did spot me – and a loose-fitting black sweatsuit and pull-on black wool beanie, and thick socks and running shoes, and thick, flesh-colored makeup, so that my tattooed features were as invisible as possible.

The windows of the Mercedes were tinted. I felt like a star or a VIP, or maybe a prisoner being spirited off to anonymity in some frozen wasteland or desert Gulag.

"You look adorable. It's like you were wearing a burka," said Martine, lifting off my glasses and giving me a very sweet kiss.

The car maneuvered its way through the little streets, and then out onto the boulevard along the Tiber, and it began to go faster, zipping through the traffic with ease. The plane trees and palatial four- and five-story residences sped past us, like sepia-tinted friezes on an unspooled ribbon, only dimly visible through the dark glass.

Martine explained how it would all happen and what the strategy was: We already had a whole lot of photographs from the archives, taken of me before the tattooing, close-ups and full body shots, and then there were shots of me with the tattoos, already taken before the adventures in the New Democratic Republic of Old Transbeckistan; these were details of the tattoos – the themes, the flames, the dragon, and the skulls, the emerald serpent, the extremely dense abstract Maori-type face black-and-scarlet tattooing.

A well-known Italian-German fashion photographer, Irene von Plato, had been chosen for the job, and Lou-Lou and Yo had flown in from Paris with an assistant. This, I discovered, was a big production. In fact, it would go on for several days, almost a week. I was glad I'd brought an iPad, and a keyboard, and a couple of ballpoint pens and a notebook; I might be able to squeeze in some work in between shots.

We were to do the shoot in a big converted warehouse outside Rome, with huge high ceilings and one wall of windows and various screens that controlled the light and separated the space into separate working spaces. Irene von Plato and her assistants had set up lights and screens and various props and also a green-screen type of background. Dim, chalky light came through the vast industrial windows, but we were largely shielded from it by semi-transparent screens, and, in any case, the outdoor light was overwhelmed by the photographer's lights.

Within half an hour of arriving on the site, I was sitting on a very high wooden stool, naked, and being photographed. It was a pretty drafty exposed position. Yo and several of Lou-Lou's makeup assistants were continually fussing around me. My skin had been polished, matt powder to minimize reflections had been sprayed and brushed everywhere, and I mean everywhere, and the tattoos touched up and renewed – though they hardly needed it, so I was as bright and perky as a neon sign. There were a few journalists and writers present. This was a "performance" – a piece of "performance art" – and an "event" as well as a photo-shoot. Luckily I was allowed, from time to time, to take sips from a big mug of strong coffee.

"Are you appropriating Maori art?" a journalist asked Lou-Lou, "I mean, look at her face tattoos ..."

"All art is appropriation," Lou-Lou said, rather curtly, I thought, as she strode up and down, and circled around me. "In fact, virtu-ally every thought we think, even when we are thinking alone, all by ourselves, is a form of appropriation."

"What do you mean by that?" the journalist, who was sitting on a fold-out metal chair, and swiveling around to follow Lou-Lou, had her pen poised, and her recorder on.

"Well, we are speaking English, Italian, and French, right?" Lou-Lou came up and adjusted the chain hanging from the ring in my right nipple. She exploited the moment to pinch the point of the nipple and gave me a beautiful smile. I muttered "Ouch" and stuck out my tongue. Lou-Lou was enjoying this – displaying her very own little totem and creation, her exercise in total objecti-fication and reification: me. She turned to the journalist and re-peated. "We are speaking English, and at least half a dozen other languages here, right? Let's see, English, French, German, Italian, Mandarin, Vietnamese ..."

"Yes."

"Well, we didn't invent the bloody words – somebody else did. And it's the same with Russian or Swahili or Spanish or any lan-guage" Lou-Lou was now ruffling my topknot, my scarlet tuft, to make sure it was in exactly the right ridiculous comic poodle-tail puffball shape – perversity as parody, or vice-versa, I guess – and while she did so she was looking straight into my eyes and continuing to talk to the journalist, and she was saying, "I come from a Dutch-German and French background, with – I have been told – some Native American far back on my father's side. So I've appropriated the English language, which my ancestors, who were French and Dutch, had appropriated before me, and then, when we returned to live in France, and I was still a kid, I appropriated – I learned – the French language." Lou-Lou stepped back to examine how I looked. "Hmm, Gwen, could you touch your right breast, the ring, and the nipple? Thanks, that's it, that's it exactly. Hold that pose. Does that work, Irene?"

"Perfect," said Irene von Plato, who was angling one of the big lights, "Wunderbar! Fantastisch!"

Lou-Lou turned to the journalist. "Look at Picasso, he robbed and ransacked the whole tradition – Renaissance Art, African Art, Christian art, secular and classical art, ceramic art, iconography from bull-fighting. And all those earlier art forms borrowed from what went before them. We live and learn by appropriation. So, I appropriated some Maori patterns, maybe, I wasn't even aware of it, but if I did 'appropriate' them, I have changed them a whole lot. I don't think any Maori would recognize them as Maori."

"Isn't this exploitation?"

"The Maori are sophisticated people – they can look after themselves. Maori artists use ideas and themes that come from other cultures. They wear business suits and use computers from Korea or Japan and ideas and images from everywhere. If you oppose 'appropriation,' you create mind ghettos – and economic ghettos too. Actually, I think it would be impossible to be human without appropriating things. Culture is appropriation. Humans learn to be human by imitation. Monkey see, monkey do."

Irene von Plato peeked out from behind the camera a couple of times, blinked at me, did a thumbs-up, and shot two or three photographs, with me pinching my right nipple, with the ring and silver chains dangling, and the labia rings, touched with oil, glittering.

Lou-Lou had stood out of the frame while the photographer was shooting. Now she went to check on the images – electronic and instantaneous. She and Irene discussed, and pointed, and laughed, and Lou-Lou gave her approval. While she was with the photographer, and the two of them were consulting on the next shots, Yo circled close around me, touched up the makeup and spray-on powder here and there. "How are you doing, Misty?" she whispered, handing me the coffee mug.

"Hunky-dory," I whispered. I took a sip, and handed the mug back to her. "Thank you," I whispered. It was a bit like we were in a cathedral and had to be very quiet and reverential.

Yo winked and moved back to stand beside the photographer.

Lou-Lou returned and again began to circle around me, talking to the journalist as she went. "Anyway, as I said, it's impossible to live in a culture without appropriating images, ideas, words, themes from other cultures or subcultures – that's the way our minds work, that's the way creativity works, that's even the way we construct our identities, we are all a hodgepodge of influences. We're mimics and copycats, that's what makes us human. If postmodernism taught us anything, it should be that." She turned towards Martine, who was standing to one side, barefoot, naked, and wrapped in a towel. "Could you drop the towel, please, Martine? No, don't drop it, please, hand it to Alfred."

Martine handed the towel to Alfred, a very dark bearded and beautiful young man, wearing short shorts and a skintight T-shirt, who had the sweet high-pitched melodically plaintive voice of a young woman. I wondered whether he was a guy, or a transsexual,

364

or transitioning from male to female, or female to male, or something else. He seemed to be a special assistant to Yo.

Martine was naked, which pleased me. Lou-Lou glanced at her. "Martine, sit on that stool; we want to place it next to Gwen's stool. Alfred, help her, please."

Alfred placed the stool right next to mine, got it just right; his legs, I noticed, were entirely hairless, very smooth, and shapely. He or she or they was very intriguing. Frontiers are increasingly porous.

Martine sat down, perching on the stool. It was a nice contrast – naked, unmarked Martine and Multicolored Chained Gargoyle Gwen. "You look fabulous, Misty," Martine whispered, "I can see why Baluchi has made you his goddess and totem."

"And you, Madam Martine Aubin, are my goddess," I whispered.

"You are so sweet, my goddess, my totem, my taboo," Martine whispered. She narrowed her eyes and licked her lips: a cat contemplating milk.

"What do you think, Yo?" said Lou-Lou. "What do you think, Irene?"

"Just a bit to the left," said Irene, glancing at Yo, who nodded. A lot of eyes, I was discovering, were needed to make these things work.

Lou-Lou was now circling Martine and me, like a possessive and protective herd dog, while continuing to lecture. "Culture is made of bric-a-brac, piecemeal do-it-yourself improvisation, it's 'bricolage' as the French anthropologist Claude Levi-Strauss said; it's the cobbling together of the stuff we find lying around – mental stuff, real stuff – it's tinkering with concepts, ideas, fragments of a story, scientific models, mental pictures of the atom – bits of wire, a screw or two, a piece of wood – a squiggle or smear on a piece of paper – and making new patterns from them. If culture is made of bric-a-brac, so are our minds and personalities."

Lou-Lou closed in on Martine, and signaled to Yo who stepped forward and started to work on Martine, finishing and touching up some matt makeup on her face, darkening the mascara, and the eyelashes, and adding a touch of gloss to the bright scarlet of Martine's lips. "There, that looks good!"

The shoot went on for hours, with Lou-Lou improvising lectures on the history of tattoos, and on the magpie bricolage cobble-it-together make-do-with-what-you-find-to-hand nature of creativity and art. William Shakespeare, she said, was like a kid in a garage working with lots of bits and pieces, screws, nuts, bolts, masking tape, wire, a light bulb or two, words, phrases, myths, old wives' tales, fragments of syntax, rhythmic patterns, and rhyme, old historical and literary characters, clichés from popular theater and religious processions, classical Roman comedy and tragedy, cookie-cutter patterns from old drama and popular entertainment, bits of wisdom from the Bible, formal structures, like the sonnet, a sort of mold into which he poured words, and deep archetypes that were floating around or welling up, and who came up with Hamlet. "That's the way Thomas Edison worked," she said, "bricolage."

The next day and evening, we worked out in the streets, usually in out-of-the-way places.

At one point, we had Martine, in stilettos and dressed in a G-string, and a black-and-red topless vaudeville corset, and wearing a cone-shaped party hat with tassels, leading me on a leash – our usual relationship – down a Rome boulevard, out near the film studios of Cine Città, and then near the restaurants and bars of Testaccio. Some of the locals got a chance to clap – which added to the spectacle and the frisson.

Then Martine and I – both of us naked and on all fours, were being led attached to leashes, on the Appia Antica, by a very muscular young man dressed, skimpily, in the skirts of a Roman

Legionary. Irene von Plato, the photographer was brilliant, precise, and very demanding, everything had to be done over, and over, and over.

Then Martine was chained to a dungeon wall, while I, the tattooed underground girl, pretended to whip her. And then Martine on her knees, begging, while I stood over her with a whip.

And then the both of us, naked, in an empty, chalk-white flat, with me, the tattooed freak, dominating her, the impeccable golden blonde, and then we had a series, with Lou-Lou transforming Martine into a clown, via makeup. Here the whole process was laid bare, with photos of Martine in all the different moments of her transformation. This was an echo of our charity performance out at the Loire chateau where I was the Owl and Martine was the Fool brightly painted in motley.

And then we were on a windswept beach – James came to join us – with Martine in dominatrix gear, with the leash, of course, and with a whip for good measure.

"I'm not sure I'm as fond of whips as I once was," said James.

"No," I said, "Brute reality can intrude on fantasy, can't it." I was hugging myself, since the wind – even if it was warm – had risen and I was naked except for a loose bathrobe. Irene von Plato was busy doing shots of Martine in her dominatrix gear, facing the waves, and standing, looking very domineering, up on a ruined and rotten wooden wharf, as if she were King Canute commanding the seas and tides to turn back and retreat from the land.

For two of the shots, Jo, the black choreographer and dancer with whom I'd done my Paris Performance, joined us, to add a bit of racial or racist variety and piquant to the mix. Her partner Marlene – an artist herself, and German, and very articulate and opinionated – came and added to Lou-Lou's and the art director's and Irene von Plato's woes by giving her own imperious opinion on almost everything, though often, I thought, her ideas seemed quite interesting.

Jo, wearing a semi-transparent white catsuit, led me on the leash into a fashionable beachside restaurant. The reactions of the clients became part of the show. This little event was videoed as well as photographed.

Jo and Martine paraded me out onto the beach, and into an old abandoned barn, where the light, full of dust motes, streamed down through gaps between the weathered and warped boards. Jo, Martine, and I posed with a bull, and with a herd of cows.

And also, we were in an empty silo, covered in oil, Jo, Martine, and I, our bodies, glittering with the stuff, making a nice contrast with the gritty cement wall. I was on my knees, holding a very large white toy bone in my mouth, as if I were Fido enjoying a good chew. Jo also attached bells to my nose ring and breast rings for the occasion.

We played the whole fetish gambit, in so far as Irene and Yo and Lou-Lou could imagine it. Marlene had a few extra ideas which we put to the test. I poured a bucket of molasses over Martine, and then we had to wash her off. It was sticky. "My eyes are stinging something dreadful," she said. "Lucky you are not filming next week," I said.

For the last shoot, my topnotch was dyed coal-black, to go with the rest of my face mask. And the 'tattoos' were temporarily refreshed since they were just beginning to fade. It did make a pretty frightening look.

We took a break for lunch and ate in a closed-off section of the terrace of the beachside restaurant. We were fenced in by bamboo stakes. The weather had turned warm. We were a sweaty crew. I had a loose silk nightgown which I left open. We didn't drink and we didn't eat too much to avoid swollen bellies which might be not exactly photogenic. I had coffee and a tiny sandwich.

"I look like a cannibal," I said.

"I'm not sure that is politically correct," said Lou-Lou, "One should not criticize or insult cannibals. I hear they are getting organized and have their own union and have hired lobbyists."

Jo grinned. "You are absolutely right, you shouldn't insult cannibals. That is an absolute No-no. The cannibals have formed a union. Their slogan is Eating People is Hunky-Dory, and no one is allowed to object." Jo had her own strict sense of moral rectitude, a touch of the 18th Century Enlightenment and libertine attitude and was not fond of the currently fashionable "politically correct" and so-called "cultural relativism" trends, and if you think of it, the practitioners of politically correct thought, which is self-righteously moralistic, and cultural relativism, which denies the reality of any legitimate values and therefore denies the legitimacy of any platform from which one can be self-righteous, should destroy each other since logically they shouldn't be able to stand for anything, their relativistic beliefs and their moralizing shrillness are contradictory and incompatible, but then, logic too, patriarchal and phallic and binary as it is, is suspect in the brave new world, so ... so we can't get anywhere discussing anything; simpler just to scream at each other. But, on the other hand, racism is real, as Jo pointed out, and it can impact you every minute of everyday. "We are all blind to what doesn't wham into us and affect us personally, I think," I said.

"Ain't that the truth, now," said Jo and gave me a very sweet kiss.

Martine growled and curled her claws.

Lou-Lou then demonstrated her art on a beautiful young model, Oriana Ricci, who had been prepared to look just like me. This was so the whole process could be demonstrated for the article, and for the website, which would be dynamic and interactive. The girl's head and pubis had been shaved, except for the topknot, and her eyebrows had been shaved, and then she was to be tattooed with precisely the same patterns that covered me.

We did side-by-side shots of her being done, but incomplete, and me, as the completed result. When she was finished, there were lots of mirror images of the two of us – and in fact, Oriana and I did look like exact and freakish, twins.

"This is fun, but sort of scary," Oriana said. "You're telling me!" I said. I did like looking at this twin, but it was sort of eerie too as if I had been dispossessed of my uniqueness; I was no longer me, not even as Misty Hoyt, now I was a mirror image, multiplied, potentially, to infinity, a sort of Andy Warhol silk-screen knock-off.

Quite a few of the photographs made a play with this, using mirrors, reflecting mirrors, like in a Midway Hall of Mirrors: Me kneeling before Oriana; her kneeling before me, and all sorts of visual role-reversals.

It was mystical in a way, this interchange of identities, "I am you," and "You are me." I said to Oriana, "I love it," she said. "Me melting into you, and you melting into me."

During the breaks in the shooting, when I was either sitting on a stool or walking around, I explored my own thinking on the subject: My own feeling was that mysticism and fetishism and perversion and the sublime forms of love and abandonment of self and loss of all sense of self, in ecstasies which can be secular and sexual, or religious and sexual or, ostensibly at least, non-sexual, all overlap in the most intimate and extraordinarily unpredictable ways, mixing the sublime and the ridiculous. We are all mysteries, everybody is a universe, or a circus, or a chamber of horrors, a clown or a saint or a sinner, depending on how you want to look at it, and depending on the mood of the day. Most prophets, who can also be seen, if you consider them with a certain detachment, as clowns, or, at best, as jesters, or, at worst, as fools, take themselves much too seriously, at least that is my opinion on this weighty matter. Shamans and jesters are never far apart, and being "two-sprited" leads one to wonderful heights, and, sometimes, to impossible depths. Rumi, the 13th-century Persian poet captures so much of the mystical side of self-abandonment: "Stop acting so small. You are the universe in ecstatic motion," and, "The wound is the place where the Light enters you."

It was a long exhausting week. At the end of it, I just wanted to fall into bed with James and whimper, but on that last day, after taking just enough time for a quick shower, we all went out to dinner in a country restaurant just outside Rome and right on the beach. My double Oriana and I were in a state of minimal dress, skimpy vest, tiny hot pants, stilettoes, collars, and leashes, so that we could show off the artwork, Jo in her ballerina's catsuit white body stocking – the creamy white contrasting perfectly with her silken black skin – and Martine was in her single-piece, skintight, black latex number. Philip, who had been working in Paris, managed to fly in for the occasion, and he put on a tuxedo, as did James. Irene von Plato, a beautiful woman and ex-model, was dressed in a glittering sequined catsuit. She offered a toast to all of us. A full moon was up. Beyond the golden lamps of the terrace, it turned the sea to sliver.

James looked pale under his tan, and I was worried about him.

It was late when we drove home, a warm night, and we had all the windows open. I was sitting in the front seat, next to James. I watched his face, as he concentrated on driving. Yes, he was paler than usual. He was blinking a lot, as if he were trying to stay awake. We drove along the edge of an old canal, used to drain some of the swamps near Rome, and the air was full of the smells of the night; Martine and Philip were talking and giggling in the back seat, and I think they were enjoying themselves. We got to the city, left Martine and Philip at their hotel and drove to the garage where we parked the car. Then we caught a cab home.

"You're tired, James," I said.

"Just a tiny bit. You're the one who should be tired, Misty."

We undressed, showered together. I soaped him all over, and he soaped me all over, and we toweled ourselves down, walking around on the terrace, letting the breeze caress us, touching each other, hardly talking at all. And then we slid into bed, and when I woke up, it was morning, and James was in the kitchen, and I could already smell the rich aroma of coffee.

≈

There were huge close-ups of me that went on billboards and images of course all over the Internet. Once again, I was infamous, now it was as an icon of Goth-Punk-Retro perversity.

Lots of articles spoke about self-mutilation and how I must hate myself, and I was elected to lots of Internet lists as the "most disastrous this" and the "most catastrophic that" – worst tattoos, most horrendous make-over, grotesque plastic surgery, and so on. There was no mention of course that the whole charade had been orchestrated for the purpose of an undercover operation. That was top secret. Nobody knew that I was Misty Hoyt. Nobody knew that Martine had acted as a decoy and intelligence agent. Nobody knew that two arms dealers – Sergei Platonov and Baluchi and one terrorist had been "neutralized." Nobody knew Paris and New York had barely missed obliteration and other cities had been saved from destruction. Frederick and Séverine said that the fetish-fashion caper was an excellent distraction and cover for what had really happened.

≈

A few weeks after the photo shoot, I was scheduled to give several seminars for the University of Cambridge. I should have traveled to Cambridge to do the seminars, but traveling on a commercial airline – as exhibit number one of the most awful of everything – might be distracting, so I got Professor Higgins' agreement to do the seminars on a video hookup. I planned not to show my face, but just a sort of blackboard with diagrams and equations.

There was a bit of a discussion about this – since for some reason they wanted to see me – so I told them they could see me at the end of the seminar and that would be their reward, seeing me in my Goth-Punk Transformation. Before they could catch this magic glimpse, however, they would have to listen to me natter on about inferential and deductive logic, and the role of mathematics in the scientific revolution, and so on.

It was fun doing the seminar with just the blackboard. I dressed for the occasion in my full Misty Hoyt outfit, skimpy vest, hot pants, and stilettoes, and I was wearing Baluchi's chains as an extra attraction. Baluchi, in his way, was a subtle psychologist, a master of the nuances of perversity. The chains always made me ultra-conscious of my body as subject and as object; they touched my skin and marked me as a prisoner and a fetish, the stigmata of sexuality all linked and marked, a fetish for myself and for Baluchi, and possibly for others; James had insisted on helping transform me into Misty; he attached the chains, in which act, he said, he took great pleasure; he slipped me into the hot pants and the stilettoes; and he slid me into the vest, and adjusted it, with just one button holding it closed. He stood back and contemplated the result and said, "Perfect!" While I gave the seminar, James lay on a deckchair on the terrace, dozing off. He still slept a lot; and more and more, I worried about him. I began to think he was having a delayed reaction to the torture sessions and the shock of having been taken prisoner.

Once the seminar was over – and it seemed to be a success since they asked for two supplementary seminars on related topics – this meant more homework for me – I exposed myself and showed them a few of the tattoos, making sure that I did not expose anything too indecent; I was a mathematician after all.

They asked a few questions, mostly about why I did it – I said it was a fashion statement that I had proposed and that Martine Aubin and I had agreed upon with body artist Lou-Lou Jade and her assistant Yo and the photographer Irene von Plato, and the choreographer Jo Delyle, and it was "a way of exploring the alienated and alienating concepts of female beauty and how they had evolved over the ages and in different societies," and it was part of a campaign for the "awareness of the body being simultaneously object and subject" – and "an exploration in the transformations of identity" – were some of the answers that I came up with – prompted by Lou-Lou, Martine, and the intelligence people. The students and professors were very complimentary and kind to me, and they didn't need to see any more of me than my head and shoulders and back and breasts, since I was, they told me, already displayed naked on a giant billboard in the market square in Cambridge and the image there left nothing to the imagination. "Oh," I said, "Perhaps I shall never dare show my face again."

"Oh, don't worry, Gwen," said Professor Higgins, "everybody here loves you. And we all follow your adventures with great interest." As a consultant to MI-6, Professor Higgins suspected the real reason for my body art escapade, and so he was particularly courteous, but I think he truly liked me and he proposed, in a follow-up email, that we write an article together on one of the questions I had raised. I agreed right away and told him I was thrilled. It would be great to work with him as he was one of the most fertile and inventive minds in the field.

When the seminar and follow up notes were all over, I flipped off the computer, stood up, stretched and yawned, and went out onto the terrace.

374

It was a beautifully warm day – about 27 degrees Celsius – just over 80 degrees Fahrenheit – but with a wintry Roman sun, paler and yellower, than the rich orange ochre sun of Roman summers. I stood under the awning and looked at James. He was lying in a deckchair on the terrace, wearing ragged faded jean shorts and no shirt, and he'd tossed off his sandals, and he was sleeping. His skin was tanned again – he tanned very quickly, and the acid burns made interesting whirls and patterns on his shoulder and above his left nipple. The welts and scars were there still, on his chest, but paler now, and I felt they were marks of beauty, badges of courage. He had suffered, and he had not given an inch. His eyes were closed, and he was breathing regularly.

I stood looking at him for a long time. I was awe-struck with the privilege of knowing such a person, loving such a person, and being loved by such a man – a man who understood me and accepted me and laughed with me and played with me and who protected me, just as I was determined to protect him. We are all islands, of course, but then we meet another island – and when we combine, the beauty is too great for words.

I went into the kitchen and made coffee, and I tiptoed back out onto the terrace and sat down, not far from James, so I could watch over him. I opened up my iPad and went to the file I was studying, and I read over the notes, and on a paper pad I scribbled down a few equations, and I laid out some questions I thought Professor Higgins and I should ask when we were defining our approach to the problem we wanted to study – how networks generate their own nodal points which are sources of both strength – or resiliency – and weakness – or vulnerability. This analysis would be relevant for defending legitimate networks and for attacking illegitimate criminal and terrorist networks, and also for studying the spread of diseases. If you could quickly identify and even predict strategic "chokepoints," you could perhaps cut off an epidemic – of disease, of crime, of terrorism.

I was soon deep into the question, scribbling notes as fast as I could, but I glanced up from time to time and just gazed at James, and my heart ached for what had happened to him. His eyes opened, and he smiled a sleepy smile and yawned, and he said, "Hello, Princess. Hello, Misty. Ah, Misty Hoyt, what an untamed beauteous wild Appalachian girl!"

I got up, knelt next to him, and kissed him.

"I love the nose ring," he said, "And I like the kiss and I the taste of that coffee you have been drinking."

"Master, I shall bring you a brimming mug of strong coffee, right now."

"Thank you, Misty," he stroked my side. "But take off the vest and pants, if you don't mind. I want to look at all of you. I want to see you, here in this brilliant light."

"Yes, Master." Still kneeling next to him, I slipped out of the vest and stood up and wiggled out of the hot pants and stepped out of the panties. "Well, here it is, Master, once again, the living art gallery."

He reached up and touched my breasts. His finger lingered on the nipple-rings, which he touched lightly, and tugged it gently. "You are truly a work of art," he said, he smiled, and I leaned down and kissed him again.

"I will be right back, Master." I blew him a kiss over my shoulder and headed for the kitchen to make a fresh cup of coffee. While the espresso machine worked away, I went into the bathroom and looked at myself in the full-length mirror. My face was a pattern of bright black and scarlet lines, the thick bold ring hanging from my nose, my eyes were surrounded by kohl-like darkness, and my lips were black, and my eyebrows had only now begun to grow back; the scarlet puffball just above my forehead was still there, and still shone brightly, but my hair was beginning to grow in, jet-black as before, and both sides of my skull were now covered with jet-black stubble that almost covered the elaborate tattoo designs that covered my skull. Three bold earrings in each ear, and, the rest of my body, well, it was a colorful, total, design, which covered everything and went down to my ankles. It seemed as bright as the day Lou-Lou had applied it. That girl didn't fool around.

I turned to leave the bathroom, and paused, just for a second, to look over my shoulder at the weird creature in the glass. All her back was brightly colored too. The Chinese dragon flared up like a flame, from the buttocks to the nape of the neck. Truly, I was a masterpiece of the tattooist's art.

I carried the coffee out to James. He was sitting up now, and he had placed the mattress – our very favorite mattress – on the terrace floor, in the delicate, vibrant blue shadow cast by the terrace awning, on the wonderful bright ceramic tiles. "Thank you, Misty," he said as he took the coffee.

I knelt in front of him. "What does my master wish of me?"

"I wish a kiss, dear Misty."

I leaned forward and kissed him.

"I think, Misty, we should make love."

"Do you really, Master?"

"Yes, I do."

"Can you accept a circus freak as your lover, Master?"

"Oh, Misty, Misty Hoyt!" He sighed, smiled, and kissed me, and took a long swig of the coffee, and then he slid out of his shorts and knelt by me and kissed me. I kissed him back.

He lay down and said, "You must be a gentle princess, oh, my wonderful Misty Hoyt."

I crouched next to him and kissed him. I kissed his cock, and I caressed it, and licked it. I glanced up at him. "I will kiss it and make it better."

It was instantly erect, my own servant and prince, and I softly caressed it, and I softly held his testicles, cupping them, stroking them, and I said, "Master, are you content?"

"Very," he said, and his hands were moving over my shoulders and collarbone, and he caressed my breasts and played with the rings, and he kissed them, and then he caressed my waxed and tattooed mons veneris, and then he opened the ringed labia and he knelt over me, and his tongue licked me, and opened me, and his tongue captured my clitoris, and seemed to hold it prisoner, to enthrall it, and I sighed and my hands were in his hair, and I cried out, "Oh, Master," and I came in a convulsion of love and desire and thankfulness.

He lifted me up, and I straddled him, and he was in me, his fingers exploring me, each inch of me, my shoulder blades, my breasts, my belly, my spine, the two dimples low on my back, my buttocks, my waist, and I leaned down, the nipple rings dangling, and I kissed him, and I was liquid, entirely liquid, and it was strange to feel the rings pressing against me, and his presence in me, and I felt that truly I was his slave, and marked by him and for him and that the rings and the tattoos were marks indicating that my body was no longer my own, that my soul was no longer my own, that I belonged to him, all of me, body and soul. I kissed him, and I felt him deep in me, and he seemed to know me, all of me, as if he knew precisely what nerve ending to touch, what subtlety of feeling to evoke, what ghost of vanity and fear to caress and console, what ultra-sensitive button to push. I kissed him again, and I bent over him, and I whispered, "You are truly my master, and I am truly your slave."

"No, Princess, I am your slave," he whispered, and his breath was sweet, and his lips were sweet and his tongue and my tongue mingled just as our thoughts and our breath mingled and he was deeper and deeper inside me as if he would cleave me in two, and it was delicious, exquisitely delicious, and my particolored thighs gripped him, and as I realized, what a sight I was, seeing myself through his eyes, and seeing myself from outside, through the eyes of an invisible but curious and lascivious observer perched on the terrace balustrade, seeing me as an object, a tattooed and pierced slave, re-enacting the ancient ritual, and realizing that I was his, forever his, irrevocably his, and, suddenly seeing myself in this shimmering vision, I thrilled with fear and exaltation at the weirdness of it all, and I came, and in that moment the shudder overwhelmed my loins, he came too, in the same instant, and both of us cried out together.

We lay for a long time, and I held his cock in my hand, and then I slid up onto him, and I kissed him. "Does it hurt?" I asked. "Nothing hurts when you are with me, Misty," he said, his hands caressing the erect scarlet puffball at the top of my skull, and his fingers working their way down the stubble on the sides of my skull and tinkling the rings that hung from my ears. "On, Misty, Misty, Misty," he sighed, and he kissed me, and he gently moved, so that I could kiss his cock again, and I knelt over him, and I licked and I sucked and I caressed and I licked and it swelled up to a new degree of pride and fervor and so once again I climbed onto him, and I rode him, and the light was shifting as the awning rippled and there was a warm breeze crossing terrace, light and shadow playing on his wounded chest and the awning above us gently rippling, slapping sweetly, a sound like a sail on a sailboat at sea in a gentle breeze, almost becalmed, and I felt we were embarking on yet another of our adventures, two lonely sailors on the vast, unpredictable sea of life.

He turned me over, so I was under him, and he held me, his prisoner now, crucified now, and he went deeper and deeper into me, and my excitement rose until the world went black, and I blinked, and it was all luminous silken blackness, and I cried out in abandonment and wonder and I cried out too in hope and love.

≈

The shower was steamy. It made the tattoos even brighter, as if I were coated in oil. James held the bottle of special soap. "It seems a shame," he said. "Well, we can do it again, or we can leave it as is," I said. The special soap would begin to remove the tattoos, or so Lou-Lou had said.

"How long will it take?" I had asked, and she told me about a month – maybe two. Then I would be like new, except for the piercings.

James kissed me. I pressed my body against his. The water poured down on us.

"Do you want me like this forever?" I spoke into his mouth, my mouth and his lingering together in a kiss, as the water poured down and as the steam rose around us.

"I love you, whatever way you are." James poured some of the liquid soap into his hand, and then, carefully, he began to soap my breasts, and then my shoulders, and then my face, and I adored his touch, it was like a consecration. He was so slow and thoughtful, yet strong, each touch was its own little drama, with its rising tensions, its complications and complexities, its ironies and teases, then its resolution. And with each caress came a new kiss, and he explored everywhere and touched me inside and outside, and I was covered in drooling lines of foam, and I felt like a steamy golden girl.

"I must be washed each day, twice a day," I said, "that's what she said."

"It will be a pleasure, each day, every day, twice a day," he said.

"Hmm." I nibbled at his lips, and bit his right nipple, but tenderly, gently, for it had been tortured.

Finally, still steaming and dripping water, we stepped out of the shower.

"It looks brighter," James said, "not paler."

"Hmm," I said. I turned around in front of the mirror. Yes, I looked like a neon sign. I could be hanging glowing from a building in Tokyo or Hong Kong or Times Square. The turquoise and gold and crimson dragon twirling up my back shone in all its pagan glory. 'Maybe I will be like this forever," I pouted, "will you still love me?"

"Oh, my very own monster, oh, Misty Hoyt, I shall love you to the end of time." He lifted me up, and I caught a glimpse of the two of us, the naked deeply tanned man, covered in scars, and the naked multicolored masked harlequin, dangling loop earrings sparkling, and with circles of steel glistening at her breasts and between her legs.

That night it turned cooler, but still crisp. James decided we should drive to the beach and eat in a beachside restaurant. So, dressed in a thick black turtleneck sweater and in tight black jeans, and high black boots, I looked at myself in the mirror.

"That looks excellent," James said.

James had decided in the afternoon that the scarlet puffball should change identity, so I had dyed it black, as it had been for the photoshoot with Martine and Jo and Lou-Lou. That and the face patterns, which so far had not seemed to fade at all, made me look quite sinister. Over the black turtleneck, I put an open leather jacket.

"You look like a crazy biker," James said.

"Crazy, certainly." I pulled up the collar and pulled the jacket closer, zipping it up partway.

The drive took a sensual, relaxed forty minutes, out of Rome, and then down some winding country roads. And then, we were in the little fishing village, stars overhead and the street full of the rich smell of wood fires, and soon we were seated in an inside terrace, drinking wine and eating marvelous seafood as the cool winter night drew in.

I recognized one of the men – he was a friend of Nicole's, the man she had waved to while she and I were having lunch at the Babington's Tea House on the Piazza di Spagna. He nodded, and when on his way to the appetizers buffet table, he stopped at our table, reminded me he was a friend of Nicole's and said he was an admirer of mine, and also of James, and so we had an interesting chat. It turned out he and James were aware of each other, and had quite a few mutual interests – so you never know what sort of connections will be revealed in the oddest of contexts.

CHAPTER 15 – OUTRAGE

The magazine "Daring Chic" sold out, and its website was overwhelmed. Comments rained down from every direction and pundits pronounced on every possible aspect of our misbehavior. Lots of people liked it and thought it liberating, we were knocking down taboos and clichés, and we were having fun with them, and we were making fun of ourselves doing it, and liberating a few fantasies at the same time.

But the photoshoot also created a backlash.

"Everybody" was outraged. Well, they said they were "everybody," and they said they were "outraged." Essentially they were some archaic hard-line paleo-feminists who had somehow morphed into believing that women are sexless, helpless, hapless, virginal wallflowers who need to be protected from men, from advertising, from society, from passion, from sex, and even from their own imaginations and perversities or quirks if they dared have any, which some of these weirdly passionate ideologues denied was possible since women were devoid of any quirkiness or evil or strength of character and incapable of doing anything interesting anywhere anytime whatsoever whether evil or good. On the other side, there were religious and social conservatives, who worshipped different gods or different versions of God, and who basically despised everybody who disagreed with them. These zealots loved judging everybody who didn't think or feel like they did; they felt that sex should not be experienced unless it aimed exclusively and only at pro-creation; it had to be exclusive heterosexual love consecrated by the All-Seeing State or the All-Seeing Church; they preached that passion had to be severely disciplined and channeled and, basically, despised sex as something "dirty" and "filthy" and "sinful" and that sex of whatever kind was inherently polluted and a result of Eve eating the bloody fictional apple and the fictional phallic serpent seducing her – giving her knowledge – which, as we know, is a very dangerous thing – and the conse-quence was the Fall of Man and our expulsion from Paradise. Everybody among these true believers, it seems, has a monopoly on truth, but in each case, it is a different truth. On the other hand, one very prominent Islamic scholar, who did very inter-esting mathematical work, wrote me a very nice letter, alluded delicately to my "show business side" as he called it, and then went on to pick up – just where we had left off – an intriguing and stimulating discussion with me of some tricky points of math we had already been analyzing together, though we had never met nor even talked to each other; and two Jesuit math-ematicians wrote me, joking about how "naughty" I was, and then picked up with an ongoing debate we had been having about Artificial Intelligent as if nothing had happened. I love such open-minded, forgiving people!

Being "outraged" seems to me to be one of the silliest, self-in-dulgent, and presumptuous of emotions or claims. It's a form of mob justice, a bit like a lynch gang, even if the violence of the mob is confined to the inside of one's own head. My blood began to boil. I stormed around the room in a froth of outrage and self-righteousness. "Grrh, grrh, grrh!" I was acting just like the people I criticized!

James looked up from his paper, "Calm down, Misty, calm down! Getting excited won't help."

"Grrhh," I said, "Grrhh!"

"Now, now, Misty." He smiled.

"Grrhh," I stopped and stared at him, hands on my hips. "Grrhh!"

"You're very attractive when you foam at the mouth."

"Grrhh, Grrhh, Grrhh!"

Some people started a movement to ban me from the university and from teaching because I was a "disgrace." It was a cabal of two different hysterical and politically correct ideologies. Fundamentalists of various religions – patriarchal monotheists all of them – shouted that my lack of modesty, my exhibitionism, and my – evident – fetishism, masochism, and bisexuality – were a challenge to female modesty, a shameless travesty of what it meant to be human and a woman, and a profanation and act of defiance towards God, and certainly towards the authority of those who claimed to speak for God. I had violated the sacred temple of the body, they said, which was a gift of God and not to be trifled with or doodled upon.

One preacher thundered from his TV pulpit, syndicated in many countries, that I was damned and would shortly be in hell, and he encouraged his followers to send me there as quickly as possible. This seemed to be the equivalent of those fatwas by which certain Christian or Islamist preachers suggest it would be doing God's Work to shoot a doctor who provides abortions or a writer or blogger who criticizes religious leaders and their – multiple – absurdities, or a young woman who says it would be a good idea if women learned to read and write and perhaps drive a car or even become a doctor.

I sent the reverend – he was a bit of a firebrand with his red hair combed over his forehead and glaring blue eyes and a command of words which had few equals in the preaching and rabble-rousing department – in any case, I sent him an email saying I would be delighted to come and preach in his church, and explain myself, if he wished me to. Some of his followers tried to hack my site; they failed. I didn't bother to hack theirs – well, actually, I did, in a minor way. I sent them a sweet little letter with a smiley face which popped up – with a photograph of me – whenever anyone opened their site. They asked me to take it down since I had made it almost invulnerable to interference. I said, "Okay." And I removed it. They didn't thank me.

Then some radical feminists, or people who claim to be feminists, saw all representations of "degradation" and sex – playful or ironic or not, consensual or non-consensual – as part of a campaign to degrade women and to encourage violence and rape. I was deeply into "objectifying" women, they said, and was therefore profoundly evil. I had betrayed my own sex, I had betrayed all women everywhere, and in particular, I had betrayed those brave women who had sacrificed to make our present freedoms possible. I was, in fact, a despicable traitor, an instrument of internalized patriarchal oppression – a bearded old patriarch, or a modern advertising executive, was sitting in my head, in the driving seat, telling me what to do, what to feel, how to dress, and who to be. In any case, I was playing all my pathetic tricks for the patriarchal male gaze, and I had obviously, so the argument went, internalized the most retrograde patriarchal values, which explained why I was such a freakish idiot, and why I had so mutilated and degraded my body.

Petitions were signed, and I was pelted with eggs and flour and mud at one point, when coming out of a seminar on "Statistical analysis and the Prevention of Rape."

People marched up and down outside a seminar I was trying to give on "Crime Networks and Human Trafficking." They were chanting that I was an abomination and an obscenity and that I should be driven out of academe and out of the country.

Luckily, my academic supporters were a stout-hearted bunch, and did not cave easily before threats and ideological hysteria.

And, some people, those obsessed by pop culture, blamed my transformation into grotesque freak on Martine Aubin. Her sadism, they said, had driven me to mutilate myself. I had flirted with somebody, they suggested, and Martine, in her rage to take revenge, had forced me into turning myself into a creature no one could possibly desire. "Now evil Martine Aubin has turned our adorable Gwendoline whom we once loved into a circus freak no one could possibly love."

Well, there were lots of things to say about that. For one thing ...

Oh, well, why bother!

The anti-Martine movement became a huge movement, and a potentially dangerous movement. Philip talked of providing a bodyguard for Martine. She refused. He insisted and put somebody on the job anyway. Martine spotted the person – a female – and let her trail along, but only at a certain distance.

A pie was thrown at Martine during a gala opening of her latest film. The bodyguard threw herself in front of the protester, so only part of the pie hit Martine – the rest hit the courageous, quick-witted, young bodyguard. Martine said the pie tasted good and did her interviews, smiling, with half her face covered in cream, with dribbles of cream streaming down into her plunging latex cleavage, and with her heroic bodyguard, also covered in cream, standing beside her. Martine had lots of fun with the whole episode, and so did the interviewers. Of course, the pie-in-the-face made all the front pages, all the websites, and all the gossip-and-show-business Internet columns and lots of talk shows. Philip was glum, and but he had to admit, "We couldn't have bought so much publicity."

Martine and I decided that, perhaps, it was time for a counter-attack.

"You know Antoine Parillaud and his daughter, Zoe, right?" said Martine, on the phone from Paris. I was out on the terrace, in Rome, cutting my toenails.

"Yes, absolutely," I said, "They are our neighbors, and Zoe was key in my getaway from the killers."

"Well, Antoine's talk show is the biggest talk show in France."

"Right," I said. And I phoned Zoe.

"My God, Gwendoline, I've seen all the pictures. What have you done to yourself?" Zoe sounded utterly horrified; I explained what I wanted.

≈

I flew to Paris to go on Antoine Parillaud's talk show – to talk about desire and the idea of fetishism. I dressed in the skimpiest of semi-transparent hot pants and my flimsy, false leather vest, attached by a single button, and of course, stilettoes.

Antoine knew the background – after all, Zoe had almost died in a hail of bullets when she and I were escaping from their flat. So he knew that my tattooed and pierced self, mysteriously, had something to do with an intelligence operation. But, as he said when we were negotiating my appearance on the show, "We will definitely not go there. That is anti-terrorism stuff, and I've been told quite clearly by the Ministry of the Interior and the Quai d'Orsay to stay away from it, and that many lives are at stake. You agree, Gwendoline?"

"Absolutely," I said.

The other guests included a famous call girl, dressed in a short leather skirt, net stockings, and a white blouse, a handsome philosopher with very long wavy hair, and a rather severe-looking but extremely – I say, extremely – handsome feminist, who turned out to be very intelligent and quite reasonable and who smiled at all the jokes anybody made and whose skirt, quite tight, was slit very far up the side. On many – most – issues, I would count myself as a feminist. And one part of feminism, in my books, is liberating female desire, whatever shape it takes, as well of course as equal pay, and maternity and paternity leave, elimination of glass ceilings, credit to women's work even when unpaid or in the "informal" economy – that is at home and so on – and on and on; it is an endless battle, not only with men and stereotypes, but also with ourselves, and with the plurality and contradictory nature of our desires: in spite of the slogan, "you can have it all," you definitely cannot always have it all. Nobody can, not even men. I am ultra-privileged; I have almost everything I could desire, and even I don't have it all. As for men, they often simplify themselves into reified and petrified idiocy – becoming their job or totally defining themselves by their social roles – much more easily, I think than women. Our complexity, and the complexity of our priorities, is a problem for us women, but also a delight. Oh, well ...

The big question was: "Why did Martine Aubin do this to you?" Antoine kicked the ball right off. I noticed that Zoe was in the audience, looking at me wide-eyed.

"Well, Martine had nothing to do with this," I said. "It was my idea. I wanted to experiment."

"I don't believe you," said the philosopher. "You are putty in her hands."

"I don't believe you either," said the feminist. "You have succumbed to passionate erotic love and allowed yourself to be defined by Martine Aubin's possessive imperial gaze, the patriarchal gaze of the iconic phallic female, an icon, a macho in travesti, a star well-known for her passionate intensity and steely determination, the Napoleon of actresses. She has forced you to destroy your beauty, your power. She has forced you to castrate yourself."

"Yes, it is terrible, what you've done to yourself," Antoine raised his eyebrows, allowing himself a theatrical frown.

"Let us see. Let us see the full horror." So, I opened the vest and bared as much skin as was possible – painted-on pasties helped – and showed it to the world. I had also put Baluchi's tinkling silver chains on for the occasion.

"The chains were somebody else's idea," I said, "Not mine."

"Well," the feminist said, "I feel it is a nice touch, like the poodle top – a sort of parody, as it were. The stigmata of sex and desire and femininity are marked by rings and chains. Martine wanted to castrate you, symbolically, of course. And she has effectively done so. Your beauty, which was your power, is gone, totally transformed."

"Well, as to the symbolism, I think you are right," I said. "That's exactly the point. Symbolic castration is an allusion to absence – something that is not there, the phallic power that has been removed, excised, the symbol is a reminder of something that has been lost, that is gone, so the ridiculous topknot is a negation, a reminder, and a memorial." I couldn't help myself; I could see, in my mind, James, who was in the control room, grinning at my pedantry. I had to remind myself to reign in my blabbermouth bluestocking side.

The philosopher ran his fingers through his long hair, looked very serious, glanced at me over the top of his glasses, like a Grand Inquisitor, and declared, "So you have become a work of art – an objectification of the body as a symbol of capitalism in its late stage which objectifies and reifies everything and turns everything into a commodity, even our most intimate fears and desires – say, our fear of mutilation – say, of loss of desirability – say, of exile and being ostracized – it turns everything, even the most sacred things, even the most obscene things, into merchandize and into show business, pure glitz, making of everything a mere ephemeral cog, as it were, in the eternal cash nexus machine, by which surplus value is extracted from the worker bees, and our various conditions of alienation, psychic, physical, bodily, and monetary alienation, are continually reproduced in continually new forms, and thus the parodic topknot as you call it is a monument to so-called 'creative destruction' typical of capitalism as described by Joseph Schumpeter and also as sketched out by Karl Marx and Friedrich Engels in 1848 in the Communist Manifesto, in their famous phrase 'all that is solid melts into air'."

"You got it!" I gave him my most grotesque naïve Appalachian mountain girl Misty Hoyt smile. "My body is a Marxist tapestry, a gloss on alienation, if you like, and my body is a commentary, too, as I am sure you are aware, on the works of Antonio Gramsci, on his concept of hegemony. I am the embodiment of the internalization of the hegemonic ideology of the ruling patriarchal, capitalistic class, all their fetishism and desire inscribed, on her own body, by a helpless and self-loathing member of the alienated subservient class and, what is more, of the alienated, self-loathing female class. I am a pathetic, but iconic individual, whose body and desires are not her own but have been kidnapped mentally and ideologically and now consist merely of memes turned out by the consent-manufacturing capitalist rightwing media. Capitalist alienation has been literally inscribed in my flesh."

Antoine gave me an indulgent smile. The French adore this kind of rigmarole, and he knew I was making an idiot of the philosopher by butting heads with him on his own turf, though, frankly, there was something in what he said.

The handsome philosopher – he was so very French – looked at me for a bit over his glasses, trying to figure out if I was serious, an ironist, or merely a bubblehead exhibitionist American goof-ball with an unusual command of syntax and Marxist allusions.

"That was very interesting, Gwendoline," said Antoine, who seemed to be enjoying himself. One of his specialties was baiting the fashionably pompous.

"I'd like to hire you, Gwendoline," said the call girl. "You are unique. I mean, you've taken it all the way. We are always looking for something new, and you've carried the tattoo gimmick to its logical philosophic all-encompassing conclusion. I'm sure that with your gift of the gab, you could talk even the most unruly of our clients into whimpering impotence, instantly, tout de suite, presto! After listening to you going on about Marx, Engels, and Gramsci, he – or she – probably wouldn't even want any sex anymore – ever. I'm definitely a fan."

"Thank you." I blinked at her and looked demurely down into my lap.

"Well, there are, in the sex industry, a great many special interests, and I'm sure Gwendoline, who is already a famous mathematician, could add a few skills, a few arrows to her quiver," said Antoine. "Now, let us turn to –"

"I have an extra guest for you, if you like," I said.

"What – this was not scheduled." Antoine looked around with a silly grin and pretended to be confused. The audience cheered and whistled because a little light lit up telling them to do so, and because they were familiar with the game and how Antoine telegraphed his reactions with this comic mimicry and clowning.

"I have the artist who did this. You all know from the photoshoot who she is."

"Really?" Antoine's eyebrows shot up. "Well, Gwendoline, you are really full of surprises."

"Her name, as you all know," I said, "is Lou-Lou Jade."

So Lou-Lou came on – to loud cheers, clapping, and cat-whistles.

She was fairly elaborately tattooed, or made-up, one half of her face looking like a clownish mask, her head half-shaved and the swath of hair that remained dyed phosphorescent pink, wearing too, her scholarly looking pince-nez metal-rimmed glasses, and a vest and hot pants that matched mine, plus military boots, which contrasted with my flirtatious stilettos.

"If Gwendoline will stand up," Lou-Lou said, "I can analyze the various aspects and symbolisms and styles of the tattoos, and the implications of the piercings too, if you wish."

"Absolutely!" Antoine glanced at the audience, and they cheered.

So Lou-Lou explained about the symbolism. I stood there, the painting, her work of art, as she provided the exegesis, and I learned a great deal about where all the art on my skin had come from. In all the rush to get to the Republic of Transbeckistan, and then to save the world, I had not really had time to learn much about the whys of how I had been redesigned.

"Then, there's one extra thing perhaps we should explain," I said.

"Yes," Lou-Lou said, and turning to Antoine, she added, "This looks very real, doesn't it?"

"Absolutely. It is real, isn't it?"

"No, it will be all gone in about a month – maybe two."

"What?"

At this point, there was a bit of confusion.

"You mean it's not real?"

"Nope," said Lou-Lou.

I grinned, "No, it isn't."

"It's made to look real, ultra-real," said Lou-Lou, "You see, we even have ripples here representing the ink-injections along the edges. Not real, it's a special glue. And the fading effect, here, where the skin is flexed, near the joints in Gwen's arms."

The audience was confused, and then they cheered.

I turned around so they could see the whole – false – me. Then I said, "I have another surprise guest, if that's okay."

"Yes, okay, Gwendoline." Antoine grinned at the audience. "This has been an evening of surprises.

"I'm going to introduce the guilty person – the person who you say turned me into a freak, my torturer, who makes me suffer so much!" I paused. "Martine Aubin."

Martine was just off stage, invisible except to me and Lou-Lou and Antoine. I could see her taking a deep breath – I could see her steeling herself. She was dressed in that superb one-piece black latex, almost a trademark uniform. She took another deep breath. Martine's secret is that, actually, she is shy, and each performance involves taking a deep breath, squaring her shoulders, and screwing up her courage. Her exhibitionism – the daring outfits and nakedness – are, for her, like a test, and not an easy one. She took another breath, straightened her shoulders, and came walking quickly out from the wings with a radiant smile, and confident long-legged stride – the audience reacted by a mixture of clapping and cheers, for the famous actress whom everyone loved, and cat-calls and boos for the perverse sadist who had forced poor innocent pristine Gwendoline to become the freakish creature she was – both personae wrapped up in the same radiant blonde. Martine made a great show of giving me a kiss, and I kissed her back, and, even surprising ourselves, we made it a very long kiss, and a full embrace, and then Martine stepped back, gazed on me for a long, drawn-out instant, and then turned to Lou-Lou and kissed her on both cheeks.

"So, here I am, the guilty party," said Martine, kissing Antoine on both cheeks and then perching on the stool beside him.

"So Gwendoline, as we see her, is your creation? Your creation and Lou-Lou's?"

"Well ..." Martine hesitated, pretending she was reluctant to confess.

I stepped forward. "Now, I'd like to say, again, that Martine had nothing to do with this. In fact, she was against it."

"Is that true?" Antoine glancing at Martine and then at the audience, and his startled, comic expression meant that he should perhaps be ashamed of himself; that the public, that vast amorphous being, should perhaps also be ashamed of itself; that we should all be ashamed of ourselves, because we had blamed poor innocent radiant Martine for something that was not her fault. There was suspense in the air. A murmur rippled through the audience that was sitting close to us, in serried ranks, and a very good-looking bunch they were too. But like all publics, like all crowds, they were emotional, and easily swayed. I thought of the saying, "Your rabble, sir, is a great monster!"

"Yes, I was," said Martine, "I was absolutely against it."

"But I prevailed," I said, putting my hand on her shoulder, and she lowered her head, as if she belonged to me and I was the mistress and master.

"And you had your reasons, Gwen," said Martine, looking up, blinking at me with that worshipful look she had, and then glancing at Antoine and the audience. "But I quickly realized that Lou-Lou and Gwendoline were really onto something and that it would be great to be part of it."

"So, Martine, after fighting us like a tiger, you surrendered and joined in with us," said Lou-Lou.

"And so I joined in, and we did a photoshoot – and some videos – to document the experiment with Lou-Lou, and a brilliant young Italian model, Oriana Ricci, and Gwen, and Yo, who is Lou's assistant, and Jo, the fabulous dancer-choreographer, who is a friend of ours, and the photographer, Irene von Plato."

The feminist looked over her glasses and said that this

exercise demonstrated that women were masters of their own bodies, or should be, and that our bodies could be our canvases, our works of art; they could be, they had to be, the place where we could redefine our relationship with ourselves and with our past, and with our future, what else was fashion after all, but a continual effort at definition and self-definition. "Female desire can take many forms. Men have no right to a monopoly of perversity and quirkiness and fetishism! And if we want to truly liberate ourselves, then we must be able to display all our quirks, all our perversions, all the various forms desire can take."

The audience cheered. How quick the tide can change, I thought. Martine glanced at me, blinking from under her eyebrows, as the same thought flashed, simultaneously, in our minds. Love truly unites two souls, making them one.

The philosopher said that the rage for tattooing and piercing reflected a need in an excessively tame and unadventurous society for a sense of adventure, for a connection to roots, for a means of self-definition that transcended the mere fashion of changing wardrobes. Permanency amid flux he said, continuity in the continual disruption created by Late Capitalism in its mania for "creative destruction," everything being ceaselessly transformed into something else, all social relations and identities continually being revealed as fragile, ephemeral, ultimately unreal, flimsy social constructs, to be swept away in the next instant by the transformation of production and property relations. The tattoo was both a sign of generational conformity, a style, and also a residual bit of revolt, with a hangover odor of rebellion from the gangster, underground, and mercenary-military background, a desire for the permanency of a monument, a rejection of Jean-Paul Sartre's concept of contingency ... So he went on, and on.

Then the philosopher and Lou-Lou got into a heated argument about some of the particular work that had been done on my anatomy, and while I stood there, like a living statue, though I did clown about a bit, they discussed what was under my left breast, on my right buttock, or snaking up my back, or on the back of my skull; and Martine, to complete the show, demonstrated the concept of "Gwendoline's Body as Object," by using a stick – that Antoine handed her – as a pointer, like an old-fashioned schoolmarm, to indicate the features Lou-Lou and the philosopher were fighting about, the serpent on my shoulder, the dragon rising from my bum, the criss-cross mask of my face, the ring in my nose.

The call girl, who was very sweet and very sharp, came up and gave some pointers about which tattoos were erotic – why they had their particular appeal and to whom they appealed – and which features weren't erotic and about the meaning of various piercings, and talked about some of her clients – and some of her fellow sex workers – who had tattoos, what tattoos meant in underground culture, and how the cult of tattoos had evolved over the last 100 years.

They all got into quite an argument – everybody talking at once – which Antoine tried – in vain – to calm down. The fuss boiled over, with everbody shouting and the audience whooping.

While this was going on, Martine – who in the last few minutes had not said a word – moved in close to me and gave me a long kiss and slid her hand in under my vest, tinkling the chains and rings, caressing my breasts, and I returned the kiss. This last little performance – the audience roared its approval – shut the debaters up and shot ratings through the roof and was immortalized in an infinite number of loops on the Net where, whenever I want, I can look at that kiss repeated over and over.

"Thank you, Martine, thank you, Gwen," said Antoine, who was very pleased that we were able – with our long kiss and lascivious embrace – to quieten things down.

After the show, Lou-Lou, her partner Yo, Martine, and I, and Philip and James, all went for dinner to La Coupole. Antoine came, with his daughter Zoe – who looked at me and grinned like the schoolgirl – well, university student – she was. Jo and Marlene joined us, adding to the quirky glitz. Zoe whispered to Martine that she wanted to kiss me; Martine whispered back, "Watch out, kid, she belongs to James and to me. But, if you send us a very polite formal hand-written letter with a big postage stamp and ask permission ..."

Talk buzzed around us, which was quite pleasant. A few people – journalists and writers and actors mostly – came over to chat at our table, particularly since Antoine, Martine, and Philip and Jo were famous and very public people, and I, of course, was increasingly an icon of perversity and a supposed math prodigy. I thought, looking around, Boy, this is a long way from the upstairs bedroom in the house outside Boston, Mass, only three years ago. James, who, like Martine, seemed automatically to capture my slightest mood or quickest most ephemeral thought, leaned over and kissed me. "Remember the night we met, you out running, and you were sick, and ...?"

Professor Harris and a number of the people in my Cambridge seminar sent texts saying it was all great, and I got especially nice notes from Kate, my old roommate and buddy, who was in Hong Kong but had followed the event on the Net, and from my grandmother, Claudia in New York who said I was a phenomenon. Claudia, who had been showing Sandra, Baluchi's wonderful "pet," Manhattan, and who had been briefly under police protection, had been briefed, by the Americans, on the Sergei caper, and so she knew – in vague terms – the real reasons for my temporary metamorphosis. It was not just show business.

The whole show put an end to attacks on Martine and the whole kerfuffle of "outrage" faded quickly away as most examples of mass hysteria and mob justice do, though of course the questions of style and objectification, and the alienation of the body, and the quirks and difficulties we all have with our body image and self-consciousness as women, and the exploitation of these images and feelings, and the real nature and range of female desire, and the force and nature of the "male gaze" – all those questions remained on the agenda, as well they should, because they are legitimate burning topics. The fanatical imams and preachers quickly forgot about me and moved on to their next bit of mischief and their next target where they could arrange for a stoning or an execution or a book burning or whatever struck their presumptuous and fevered fancies.

≈

The weeks passed, and I remained in Rome, staying mostly indoors, just working away, and giving my seminars via video or on the Internet and writing. Maria and Giuseppe kept me supplied with food and the restaurant sometimes sent up elaborate meals, and once or twice when James was away, Martine came to Rome alone to keep me company and stayed overnight. James traveled quite a bit, since his business was becoming even more complex. He consulted me, and, when he was away, we usually spent at least an hour on a video linkup each night. Some of those sessions were memorable.

James acquired the Czech biotech company, and as partners, he had some friendly intelligence agencies or their proxies. It was important to keep the technology away from hostile powers and, even more, from terrorists. What remained of Sergei's operation was rolled up. The Russians had been very unhappy with him because, as a Russian officer explained, aside from planning to nuke Moscow, the guy had been in bed with some other Islamist terrorists – not only Khalid Nassir – and was going to sell them access to dangerous biotechnology via the Czech Company. In Sergei's castle and fortress, enough information had been found to "roll up" the rest of the organization. But, of course, when you destroy one of these networks, another one will spring up to take its place. But at least that particular group was out of the way.

Sonia, our Mossad Agent friend, passed through Rome; her eyesight was back to 20/20. We had a quiet dinner at home, just James and Sonia and Martine and Philip and me with a nice little fire in the fireplace.

"You guys were not bad for amateurs," said Sonia. She was flying to Berlin the next day and then onward to Israel. She was wearing a black leather jacket, black T-shirt, and black jeans, with black boots. I was still a freak, a fading freak, but still a freak, so I just wore myself – all my etiolated tattooed glamor – plus a T-shirt and jeans. Martine was demure in a one-piece black latex dress that was semi-transparent. Our two men were in jeans and open shirts.

"They are so lovely," I nodded at Philip and James, who were out on the terrace talking.

"Yes, let us drink to men," said Martine.

"To men," repeated Sonia, "in spite of everything, what would we do without them?"

Sonia told me that, just as Jamila and Aisara had promised, Betty had found a very happy home in a beautiful village, had become the village mascot, and was supplied with a continual diet of rabbits.

Tracy was back in the States working as an intelligence analyst, and she also was teaching at Georgetown University. Boris had been recruited by Russia to help train some Special Operations troops and was happy in his new – extremely challenging – job. Anton was doing something top-secret for the US and Russia in East Asia.

CHAPTER 16 – POPCORN

By early summer, I was without any marks, except for more or less invisible scars where the piercings had been. I asked James if he wanted me to keep the breast rings. And he kissed my nipples and caressed the rings and toyed with them and said that it would entirely depend on me. I said I thought I'd keep them for the time being, as a reminder of the adventures we had been through. "Yes," he said, "that is right, darling."

Love is strange – it is an accumulation of so many things, big and small, it is a moving totality of memories we shared, and feelings we shared, and it is a natural unspoken animal comfort we felt in each other's presence. It is the exchange of glances where we instantly understand each other – our thoughts, our feelings, our doubts, our desires.

I would not be really me if I didn't feel his gaze upon me – even when he wasn't there – and I would not be me if I didn't feel his thoughts within me – even when he was far away.

Summer began, and we went for long walks along the Appia Antica – the ancient Roman road that headed south towards Naples – and on the beaches, and we often lingered, working and holding hands, at cafes on the terraces of Campo de' Fiori. Martine and Philip came by often, and we all flirted with each other.

When both James and Philip were away, and Martine was in Rome, she and I slept together or went out to little restaurants together and acted like the lovers we truly were. She dressed as I ordered her to dress and it was always very sexy, and I adored the feeling that she would obey me and I adored her courage too, when she was nervous about making a display of herself – but doing it for me, or, on alternate occasions, for Philip.

"You are a cruel mistress, Misty Hoyt," she whispered.

"I know," I whispered back.

James was away, and Martine and I were in the Rome apartment sitting on the big flurry rug in front of the television watching a really spooky horror film. It was almost midnight, and outside it was raining, and flashes of lightning lit up the windows. I had made popcorn. I was in shorts and a T-shirt. Martine was naked and handcuffed and gagged. She was sitting on the rug, her knees up, her arms manacled behind her, with her back propped against the divan; we watched the film get scarier and scarier.

Outside, the thunder roared, and the lightning flashed. Inside the room, the only light was the light from the screen. Martine squirmed a bit and made gurgling sounds, her eyes wide, miming fear and terror. A slick of saliva made her chin and lips glow silver; she was drooling. A long glittery drip of saliva drooled down from her chin. She squirmed. "You are drooling, darling," I said. "Gurrmph," she squirmed and blinked at me with her wide blue eyes. The collar, attached by a taut chain to the back of the divan's steel frame, held her in place. Her body in the reflections of the light from the TV screen looked ghostly as if sculpted in bluish-white marble.

I stopped the video. The screen went blue.

"Gurrmph!" She squirmed.

I took off my T-shirt and shorts and panties, and I got down on all fours in front of her and growled. She squirmed. "Gurr-mph," she gurgled and blinked at me, her mouth forced open by the ball-gag, saliva leaking on both sides. I kissed her nipples and bit them gently, feeling the rings on my own nipples brush her skin when I leaned in close. "Gurrmph!" She growled and closed her legs around me to try to trap me. I let myself be trapped. I kissed my way down her belly, and she opened her legs and let me lick and suck and kiss her and play with her with the tip of my tongue. "Gurrmph!" She stirred; she wiggled; she groaned, "Gurrmph!"

"Gurrmph, Gurrmph, Gurrmph!" She came, a truly neat orgasm, a rippling series of inarticulate spasms that went on and on, even more intense because she couldn't scream. Beads of sweat stood out, silver, on her forehead and breasts. I could feel her heart beating, feel her blood throbbing.

I looked up, and kissed her belly, and worked my way back up to her breasts. I liked the sweet, sweet sweat and beautiful saliva of my love, and my lover, and my mistress and my slave.

"Gurrmph!" She stared at me with her cool blue beautiful eyes, blinking, helpless. I nibbled at her nipples, carefully pinching and teasing and twisting them with my teeth.

"Gurrmph! Gurrmph!"

"Okay, my darling." I knelt next to her and undid the gag and lifted the rubber ball out of her mouth. She took a deep gasping breath and tried to lick back the saliva. Her blond hair, dark with sweat, was plastered to her forehead. "Oh, Misty," she sighed, "You are so cruel, Misty!"

"Now you eat popcorn," I said.

"Oh, no, no, Misty, you are too cruel – not that! Not popcorn!" She squirmed and twisted, turning her face away.

"Yes, popcorn!"

"With butter?"

"Yes," I grinned a wicked villain's grin, "With butter, real, greasy, dripping, sticky butter."

"Oh, no, no, no, Misty! Not that! Not butter!!"

I set the movie going again. The monster was just outside the room where the heroine was crouching in pure fear, her beautiful ball gown torn to shreds from her earlier encounter with the werewolf whose clutches she had narrowly escaped under the cliff and under the waterfall just beyond the enchanted woods during the most awful thunderstorm you could imagine.

"This is scary, but popcorn with butter is scarier," said Martine, shifting a bit, to make herself more comfortable; her arms and shoulders pinned back by the manacles, making it look like she had no arms, but had been amputated at the shoulders.

"Eat now," I said.

"Ugh," she made a face.

"Open up!"

"No!"

"Open up!" I began to tickle her.

"No! No! No!" She resisted, turning her head to one side, but then she started to laugh and laugh and laugh.

"Open up!"

"I give up! I surrender! I am yours, Misty. Do with me what you will!"

"Open up!"

The opened her mouth wide, and I fed her popcorn with lots of gooey dribbling salty butter, which I licked from her lips.

"This is messy, and I'll get pimples," she pouted.

"I'll love you with pimples." I forced more popcorn into her mouth.

"Gurrmph!" She chewed and swallowed and licked her lips. Now her breath was buttery and salty. "No, you won't," she said, "And Philip won't, and the camera won't."

"Too bad, then," I kissed her on her salty, buttery lips.

"Sadist," she whispered.

Using my mouth, I fed her kernels of popcorn, one butter-dripping kernel at a time.

"Oh, oh, each popcorn is a kiss," she whispered. I kissed her again, this time without popcorn, and I kissed her collarbone, and I kissed her breasts, and her belly and then I kissed her deep, and she opened her legs again, and I kissed her deeper, and deeper, and teased her and caressed her breasts, and I brought her slowly, slowly, up to orgasm, and I teased her, feeling I knew precisely what to do, what cord to strike, what nerve to touch and tease and tantalize and, on all fours, I felt I was her servant and her slave, and I felt myself coming too, just like that, and so, as I licked and kissed and teased her, I touched myself, and, then, the tension rising, she and I came in one explosion of excitement, and ripple of after tide and ebb and almost blackness of unconsciousness and then I lay next to her and looked up at her.

"Cruel, cruel, Misty," she said.

I released her chain from the divan, and then I sat on the divan while she knelt in front of me and, still shackled, with her arms pinned behind her back, she pleasured me.

"Oh, cruel, Misty."

Later, we showered, and then we got a bottle of wine and some cheese and a fresh baguette, and we sat curled on the divan, and set the movie going again. And we watched it to the end. The girl in the tattered ball gown made it to the end; she was the only survivor, but there was a hint, just at the end, that having been scratched by one of the monster's fangs, she was perhaps infected, and she perhaps was going to become a monster too, and that, as she entered the house where her lover was anxiously waiting for her, she would sprout fangs, be suddenly covered in fur, extend her long, curled, yellowish claws, and eat him up, yum, yum, yum.

Towards dawn, we went out on the balcony, and we stood in the rain and we held each other and then we went to bed and fell into a deep sleep and the next thing I knew I woke up and Martine was still sprawled on her tummy half under the covers and I was curled against her and I smelled fresh coffee. Someone was in the kitchen. I got up, slipped into the black silk robe that James had just bought me, and tiptoed into the kitchen. James was standing there, splendid in jeans and shirt and sandals, making bacon and eggs and making coffee in the espresso machine. He turned and grinned. "Good morning, Misty."

"Good morning, Master." I kissed him and pressed myself to him.

"It looks like you two ladies had quite a night." He put his arm around me and kissed me again.

"We did."

"Hello, James." Martine was standing, in white silk pajamas, in the doorway looking rather sheepish.

"Greetings, Lady Martine," said James. "Philip and I were on the same flight from Paris. He's just getting some fresh croissants from Camp de' Fiori."

"Oh, boy." Martine sat down at the kitchen table. "What a night! We watched a really spooky movie." She poured herself some of the coffee, "And Misty tied me up, and gagged me, and kept me as her prisoner, and forced buttered popcorn down my throat, and she had her way with me in ways you positively cannot imagine."

"That's just like Misty," said James, "But perhaps I can imagine." He winked and handed me a mug off coffee.

We ate on the terrace, and James and Philip told us about the news from Paris and the latest news from everywhere because, for the last 14 hours, Martine and I had somehow been living on our own little island, isolated from the world of mere mortals.

≈

Later the day we went to the beach early and ate in a seaside restaurant, breathing in the wood smoke and eating fresh fish and watching the breakers and the seagulls, and then we drove back to the city.

When we returned to the city, Philip and James both had business to attend to – Philip in the Cine Città Film Studios – and James with some bankers who were staying at the Hilton Hotel which sits on top of a hill overlooking Rome – and told us they would not be back until late. Martine and I went for a walk in the center of Rome; it was a glorious, warm, dry day.

"I am a tiger," I said to Martine.

"That's a very good idea, Misty," she said, "If you are a tiger, I am a tiger too."

"Really? We're both tigers?"

Martine said if we were going to be tigers, we should look like tigers. So we made a phone call, and Nicole said she'd be delighted, and we spent four hours Nicole's makeup studio, getting painted in non-smear paint, both of us striped like tigers, with tiger faces. The paint would need a special body shampoo to be removed. Nicole and her daughter Justine had fun turning the two of us into tigers. And we went back home dressed in what looked like total burqas.

When James and Philip came home, two tigers, naked tigers, were waiting for them. We two tigers growled a lot and didn't seem to speak or understand any human language at all.

But we were very affectionate and tender tigers. We were so well trained, we even prepared perfectly acceptable drinks and snacks.

And after watching a movie and nibbling on the snacks, each wild tiger retired, with her man, to a separate and very cozy bedroom.

And so it was that the tigers and the humans did battle until, exhausted, tigers and humans declared a truce and fell into a long and dreamless sleep.

CHAPTER 17 – TENDER LOVING CARE

"James, you need a full checkup and you some tender loving care," I said. I was sitting at my desk, and just happened to look up at him. He was standing in the doorway, gazing at me, wearing shorts and a T-shirt, a coffee mug in his hands. He had come back the night before from a week in New York – we were in Rome – and I again noticed the pallor under the tan.

"Tender loving care?" He raised an eyebrow.

"Yes, darling, tender loving care," I got up and kissed him and held him, and leaned my head against his chest. He ran his fingers through my hair – now fully returned to normal, as were my eyebrows, and as was my Bermuda Triangle. No visible trace of Misty Hoyt remained, except the nipple rings. Once again, for the world, I was Gwendoline Clermont.

"Let's go to the waters," he said.

"The waters?"

"Yes, the waters. Let's go to the hot springs, north of Rome, hot sulfurous springs, they are at a waterfall, with mud baths, out in the open, just pools of mud – no attendants, no walls, no admission fees, just open fields – and a cascade of hot sulfurous water; they are about two hours away, in Tuscany. Let's stay there for a couple of days."

"That, Master, is a brilliant idea."

So we drove north in the Porsche convertible, and at one point, on a country road, James suggested that I might like to undress, and strip down to a sort of G-string he had provided me with.

"Yes, Master, I shall do so, if it is your pleasure."

"Yes, Misty," he winked at me, "It is indeed your master's pleasure that you should be naked or almost naked."

"Well, then, Master, your wish is Misty's command." I wiggled out of my T-shirt, and I levered myself out of my shorts and my panties, and I fished the G-string out of my purse and shimmied my way into it as we drove under a grove of trees, the shadows flickering across us, bright alternating shadow and light, and the perfumed breeze.

James checked us into the hotel. I waited in the car, parked down the road. We were in our own little cabin on the edge of a steep hill that looked down over rolling fields, a small river, and in the distance, other hills and perched on top of one of the hills a small village.

James hitched a backpack onto my back.

"I am your pack horse, then, am I, Master?"

"Yes, Misty."

We walked down the edge of the winding hillside road, me essentially naked, a skimpily clad pack horse, with high-heeled mules stirring small circles of dust.

Several cars passed by; one tooted its horn, and I saw a woman staring at me as she whizzed past.

"Turn left, Misty, if you please."

"Yes, Master, your little packhorse Misty will follow your every desire and order to the letter."

We went down a muddy and dusty little path that went through a farmer's field, with wheat that reached up to my shoulders, and then the path wound through a meadow with very green grass, and we came into a grove of trees, shadowy and perfumed, and then we were walking along the bank of a tiny river or canal, only about five feet across, and we met a women, who was naked, who smiled at us, and walked past us. Hmm, I thought; I was not alone. We came to the ruins of an old mill, a two-story pile of ancient stone. The air smelled of hay, or flowers, and, vaguely, sweetly, of sulfur.

We came to an open space. People were sitting on rough wooden chairs at a rough wooden table drinking wine and eating – spaghetti, cheese, bread, salad, and sliced meats.

The sun was blazing down and the fields smelt of hay and rich sun burnt earth, and, vaguely, of sulfur.

James lifted the backpack off my back, and we sat down, introducing ourselves to all of the people. The men were in jeans and T-shirts and bathing suits, and two of the women were, like me, topless, with just bikini bottoms though my costume was the skimpiest of them all.

The wine was delicious and cold, and the food was scrumptious, and the conversation lively. I forgot I was next to naked. It seemed the most natural thing in the world.

We walked across the field, down a narrow path between bushes, and James said, "I think we should make love here, but first ... First ... the mud baths.

"Oh, the mud baths."

"Yes ..." He held me, and he kissed me, and he slowly slipped a blindfold over my eyes and snapped it shut, then he kissed me again, holding my arms locked behind my back.

"You are a wild animal," he breathed into my ear, "and I have to control you." He kissed me again.

"Yes, I am," I breathed, dizzy in the darkness, feeling the soft breeze against my skin, hearing the rustling of the wheat and of the leaves and the gurgling and rush of the water in the little channel of smoky sulfurous water.

And he slid the G-string down, to my thighs, and he touched me, and pressed into me, and suddenly I was totally liquid, totally ready, and eager.

"Oh, Master," I breathed. I kissed him and bit his lips, pressing myself into him.

"Yes, Oh, Misty." He held me by the shoulders; he kissed me on the forehead, and then he knelt and slipped the G-string down further, to my ankles.

"Step out of it."

"Yes, Master." I stepped out of the G-string. I felt the hot sulfurous breeze against my skin. His hand went down my back, pressing me to him. He had, under his jeans, a steel-hard erection. "Oh, my, what shall we do with that? What, Master, shall we do with that?"

"Wait, darling, wait," he whispered.

We kissed. My tongue and his tongue seemed to be one. It is amazing how a kiss can make you merge into another being, become one with another person.

"Step out of the mules."

"Yes, Master." I did so, and now I felt the soft wet earth of the muddy path squishing under the soles of my feet. I breathed a small sigh of sensuality, the feeling was strange.

I reached up and kissed him again, and, blindfolded, in the sweltering sulfurous darkness, all I felt was him, his kiss, his mouth, hungrily exploring, conquering mine, and his chest against me, his erection, prisoner of the denim, hard against my belly, not yet possessed, but waiting, waiting for me to liberate him, enclose him, to consume him, and I felt the hot breeze, moving through the hay, and perfumed, and I thought might just swoon, it was so sublime.

I began to unbuckle his belt, and his hand stopped me, and his hand softly opened me, making me even wetter than before, and he whispered into my ear, "No, later, Misty, later. First, we'll visit the sacred grove."

"Sacred grove?" Saliva was rising. I was hungry for him. I wanted him inside me. I wanted to be down on my hands and knees, blind and naked, and his ... I yearned to lick and kiss and caress.

His hand gently massaged my naked pubis, pressing the mons veneris, all naked and smooth, and putting just the right pressure on the clitoris, back and forth, back and forth, up and down, round-and-round.

"Oh, oh, oh," I whispered, "oh, oh, oh!"

I shuddered and came, I couldn't stop it. I came, shameless, standing there, naked and barefoot, on the dusty footpath between the hayfields ...

"Oh, boy, oh boy, oh, darling, darling, darling ..." I cried out as he held me as the shuddering rose and fell, and I wanted to scream, but he sealed my mouth with a hard kiss, and the kiss lasted, and lasted, and his erection was hard against me, the cloth of his jeans pressing into me.

I went limp, and finally, the tail-end of the scream became a whimper. I was covered in beads of sweat.

"You are cruel, Master." Cloaked in silky darkness, I beat my fists feebly against his chest.

"Cruel," he repeated, and though I couldn't see it, I could feel his smile. I kissed him. "Thank you for being so cruel," I said, "but I want you to come too. You sometimes make me travel to heaven all alone."

"I'll come, later." He slid his hands down my backside, and slapped me gently on both buttocks, then caressed me, so that now I again wanted to be down on all fours, on the dusty path of fine white clay, and I wanted him to take me, there and then, under the sun.

Now, what happened next was interesting ... He took a leather collar out of the backpack and snapped it around my neck.

"Ouch," I said, though it didn't hurt. To the collar was attached a leash; I felt it dangle between my breasts.

"You belong to me," he said.

"Yes, Master, I belong to you."

"And I belong to you," he said.

"And you belong to me. So why aren't you wearing a collar?"

"Do you want me to wear a collar?"

"No," I said, "No, I'll wear the collar. It is a badge of honor, Master."

He lifted off the blindfold. I blinked against the light, shimmering in the hot hair. The gleaming of the golden wheat was blinding, rustling, and moving, close around us. I felt, now, suddenly, how my body was beaded in sweat. He hooked the backpack over my shoulders.

"Okay, let's go," he said. "You lead the way."

The path narrowed, became more and more like a tunnel. The hay and long grass brushed my hips and thighs and breasts and the fine hot dust was silken under my feet. I was still dizzy and dazed by the orgasm and dazzled by the brightness of the sun and the hay. I shifted the weight of the backpack. The weight of the leather straps and canvas against my shoulders and back made me feel even more naked.

A woman and a man came along the path. The woman was naked. The man was in a speedo bathing suit. Both were heavily streaked with mud.

The woman glanced at me, looked me up and down, her gaze lingered on the leather collar, and the straps of the backpack, and staring at me from under her very black eyelashes she blinked, her tongue ran along her lips, then she smiled.

"Is she for sale?" she asked.

"Display only," said James.

"Too bad," said the woman. She caressed my arm and the side of my breast as she squeezed past. The man gave me the once-over, in a nice way, and smiled. "Very nice," he said.

"Hmm," I nodded. I glanced backward as they disappeared down the path.

"You have admirers," James said and slapped me gently – an echoing liquid little slap – on the left buttock.

"For display only," I murmured, and I turned and kissed James on the lips and pressed myself against him.

"You inspire desire in all who see you," he said, "I have to mark my territory." He smiled.

"Ah, incorrigible," I sighed. I kissed him again and pushed my hand down under his belt, and squeezed him. He was still fully aroused. And I was flattered by his aroused, though I knew it was not just me, it was the situation too.

Suddenly, the path opened up. I could hear a waterfall. Four kids, young boys, maybe about ten or eleven, were standing there, some of them streaked in mud, and one of them was naked, they turned and looked at me, their dark eyes focussing on me for what seemed a long instant, and then they turned away. One of them was crouched next to a pool of water, and he was digging out dripping handfuls of dark gray mud.

Beyond them was a woman in topless covered in mud and so I was given my instructions.

"Well, I think you should enjoy the mud bath." James lifted off the backpack, and he unlocked and opened the collar and freed me.

"Go!" he said.

"And you?"

"I'll see you later," and he kissed me, again on the mouth, twisting me back as if he were going to ravish me and lift me into the sky and wing me away to some celestial blue paradise.

Then he was gone. I was alone.

One of the boys came and offered me a handful of dripping mud.

"Thank you," I said, I took it, smoothed in on my arm. It was very sticky.

The boys giggled. "There's more down there," said one of the boys, and pointed down the path.

"Thank you," I said, and headed down the path, smearing some on my shoulders. It was very smooth, a voluptuous sensation, like sliding into a sea of warm butter. I climbed down beside an old mossy wall. Then there was a waterfall, and on the side, more pools of mud.

I waded into one of the pools. I crouched and scooped up some mud, and a woman asked me to put mud on her back. She was wearing a bikini. I had forgotten I was naked.

"Can you undo that?" She asked. I helped her slip out of the bikini. She tossed it to the shore. I smeared mud on her back; it was thick, as if I were covering her in dark gray paint.

She turned and looked at me and began to do the same to me, so that instead of smearing the mud on myself, I was smearing it on her, and she on me.

"Everywhere?" I asked.

"Everywhere." She nodded, looking at me with her very dark eyes and holding my gaze.

Other people were watching or just doing their own thing. I covered her in mud, everywhere. Then she smeared it over my hair and my face and my breasts and between my legs.

"You are beautiful," she said.

"That's very kind. You are too," I said, swallowing. And it was true. She was exceptionally attractive. We were by now two statues of clay.

We stepped out of the pool.

"The sun will dry us," she said. "It's excellent for the skin."

We sat on a ledge of rock and watched the others in the pool. The young boys had come, and they looked at us shyly and waved. I waved back. It was a strange sensation. They seemed to be very casual with all these naked women around. There didn't seem to be any naked men that I could see. I wondered if this should be the subject of a learnèd article in some academic review of gender studies.

Then James was beside us. In his bathing suit.

"All over again," he said.

"All over again," I said

I said goodbye to my new friend and I followed James down the path and then down another little path to a small side waterfall. We were alone. He slipped out of this bathing suit, and he helped me wash off all the mud. It was quite intimate and a strange sensation, the steaming smoky water pouring down over us, in the middle of the woods, with the sunlight streaming down between the trees. Then we walked out into the field and found an isolated spot where we made love under the shifting shadows of a tree, and we heard, in the distance, a combine and a tractor moving through the field and coming closer and closer. Finally, we headed back down the little path until we reached the roadside, where, about 200 meters farther on, the car was waiting. James pulled on his bathing suit, and he handed me the G-string, I pulled it on and wiggled and snapped it into place. I hitched the backpack onto my shoulders, settled it in place, and then slipped my feet into the high-heeled mules. Once again, I was James' little packhorse. He fitted me with the collar and leash and led me along the side of the road to the car. I unhooked the backpack and put it in the back of the car, and I slid into my seat. The leather was hot from the sunlight. We drove back to our little lodging. That night, wearing shorts and a T-shirt, I dined with James in the hotel dining room. The air had turned chilly. A bright fire was burning next to our table. We ate and ate and ate – and drank a very nice bottle of red wine.

That night, in bed, I kissed James over and over, sliding up and down his body like a friendly, hungry little serpent.

"I think Martine is head over heels," he said, running his fingers through my hair, "head over heels in love with you."

"It's reciprocal," I said, "do you mind?" I caressed his forehead.

He kissed me. "No, I don't, not at all, as long as I don't risk losing you."

"Never fear," I said, "I think you are trapped. I am needy and addicted, and you are my drug," I said. "I'm not going away unless you send me away."

"I will never do that, Gwen," he said, "never again, never, never, never."

For the next seven days, we lounged, we took the waters, we toured the region, we ate big meals, and we slept and slept, our bodies pressed against each other; we took long walks. One day we went to visit the tombs of the Etruscans, and while we were eating lunch in a very pleasant little rustic restaurant out on a shadowy terrace we decided on a little game – James had remarked that we were perhaps too articulate, too addicted to talking – and so I proposed that we remain silent.

"What? How?"

"We shall not say a word, Master, total silence will be our rule."

"I'll bet you can't keep to that, Misty." He grinned.

"That, Master, is a challenge. It is unwise, Master, to challenge Misty Hoyt when she has set her mind on something. So, from this instant – shush!"

His lips twitched, as if he were going to say something. I put my finger vertical, against my lips, and gave him my most ferocious imperious Gwendoline Clermont gaze.

The waitress wondered at the silent couple. We motioned and gestured, and we smiled, and we gave her a very substantial tip, but we said not a word.

And then we were out in the hot sunlight, on baked earth, and in fields where the grass was long and burnt dry by the summer sun, and we both bent low as we crawled into the Etruscan tombs and we looked and appreciated and walked for hours in the blazing heat. And then at night when we came back to the hotel we said not a word, but went to our room. I took off his clothes and he took off mine, and then we stepped into the shower – quite big enough for the two of us – and we washed and shampooed each other and then I toweled him down and he toweled me down and neither of us spoke a word and he took me in his arms and held me for a long time and wrapped in towels, we went out on the balcony, and we watched the light fade over the mountains, and then he began to trace with his fingers every detail of my body. I dropped the towel and lay back on the deck chair. For a long time he knelt next to me and kissed what he had once upon a time– in the days when we still spoke – called the special parts, under my chin, the nape of my neck, the crook of my arm, the little hollow behind my knee, the arch of my foot, and two dimples in the small of my back, and he kissed his way up my spine to the nape of my neck, and then he turned me around and kissed my forehead, my eyelids, and then he kissed me on the mouth.

I pushed him down onto the balcony rug, and I positioned myself astraddle him, and I slithered down onto his body, until I was lying on top of him and I slipped lower and lower and I took his sex in my hand – he was already erect, hard as steel – and I licked him, and kissed him, and I wanted to say all sorts of soft ridiculous things, but since silence was the order of the day, I said nothing, but I licked and kissed and glanced at him from under my eyebrows, and I could see he was making a great effort to control himself – he was truly a Phallic Narcissist – he wanted to maintain control at all costs – and I kept at it, as if I were exploring something very interesting, an archeological relic of enormous importance for reconstructing some ancient and lost civilization – and my mouth was full, absolutely full, of him, and this was strangely satisfying, orgasmic-like, and quite overwhelming, taking me right to the edge of ecstasy and abandon, and beyond, but I controlled myself, I realized how excited I could be just from exciting him, and then finally, I gave a final sloppy lick and released him, and I got up on my knees, opened my thighs, and lowered myself slowly down, taking him into me, a bit at a time, teasing him, over and over, knowing, now, that two could play the teasing game, and then, finally, relenting, and soaked and quivering with desire, lowing myself down, all the way, liquid, riding astride him, and bending down to kiss him and the kiss became fierce and he was slippery and immense inside me ... and I thought I would die ...

La petite mort, the French call it.

The little death.

Orgasm.

≈

Really, it is quite mysterious.

I wanted to cry out. But our rule was monastic silence. Not a peep, not a word.

I whimpered, and stifled the whimper.

I cried out, deep in my throat, but I smothered the cry.

I kissed him and curled my fingers, making fists in his hair.

His eyes were wide open. He was watching me. I kissed his eyelids, shutting his eyes. I shuddered. I was riding up and down, up and down, and I leaned back, maximizing the leverage as my professor of physics would have put it.

I came!

He came!

We came!

"Oh, darling," I wanted to cry out, "Oh, darling, I love you, I love you, I love you!"

But I didn't say anything; words were against the rules. Neither Misty nor Gwendoline will allow themselves to be undone by pure passion! I gritted my teeth; I sealed my lips; I held my breath; I swallowed my soul. My love was so strong I almost choked on it. And so I left unsaid all those things that lovers say, and perhaps – no, almost certainly – it was best that way. Or maybe not.

≈

When we got back to Rome, I insisted that James undergo a complete checkup. He fought me, but then he agreed.

And it turned out that he had a low-grade infection that only needed a short treatment with antibiotics, and then, within a week, it was gone, the pallor disappeared, and James was as vigorous as he always had been.

Hallelujah!

I took him out to Alfredo's to celebrate, and we had a long meal which was relaxing and totally normal, and then we wandered home, hand in hand, talking softly as true lovers have always done.

≈

And we did get to play some games. Indeed, the games never stopped. For this particular game, we were, after a brief interlude in Paris, back in Rome, with James entirely reinvigorated and deeply tanned.

He was wearing an eyepatch, an open canvas vest, bouffant

striped trousers, high floppy-topped boots, and looking every inch a pirate; I was dressed as a cabin boy on a British man of war circa 1743; we were fitted out to battle pirates or to be pirates.

I had a kerchief over my head and a canvas vest and canvas trousers, and nothing much else except leather sandals with silver buckles.

We were going to a costume ball at the French Embassy in Palazzo Farnese, just a short walk from our palazzo, and I found I was rather popular, as a cabin boy, among the diplomats and military men – and I even cut a swath, so I could see, among some of the more sophisticated ladies, for whom, it seems, the ambivalent androgynous impertinent, rakish boyish look held some sort of mysterious fascination. Shakespeare, writing Twelfth Night, knew what he was doing.

I thought I might have to walk the plank to escape from some of my admirers, but my master rescued me, and seized me around the waist and swept me off onto the dance floor.

"You have pluck, boy."

"I do? Well, sir, thank you very much, sir. And thank you for rescuing me!"

"It is a pleasure, boy, rescuing you. I shall rescue you anytime, under any circumstances."

That night, on our terrace, under a crescent moon, on hands and knees, next to the terracotta vases, and with the breeze from the distant sea rustling in the palm tree and rippling the striped blue and white awning, I, the intrepid cabin boy, was fully rewarded for my pluck. And it was a most satisfactory experience indeed.

EPILOGUE

Two weeks later I was sitting on a stool at the bar in the kitchen thinking some deep mathematical thoughts – though I now forget what they were – and slowly sipping a glass of cool water as it was a warm summery day, and I was wearing panties and nothing else since I had long ago decided that when the weather was hot, I thought deep mathematical thoughts best if I was wearing next to nothing, not quite nothing, but almost nothing, since the little difference between nothing and not nothing was, for some reason I have not yet elucidated to my own satisfaction, particularly inspiring, to the mathematical mind and way of thinking. James appeared in the doorway, barefoot, wearing jeans and a T-shirt, and he stood there without moving.

"Hello, Master. Shall I make you coffee?"

"I ..."

"Would you like a biscuit, a croissant?"

"I ..."

"Would you like a snack – a salmon and avocado sandwich?"

"I ..."

"I'll make coffee, Master. You look like you need a coffee." I stood up and turned on the espresso machine, flipping in the little container of pre-ground beans. I turned back to James. He looked extra nervous. He was still standing there, handsome, tanned, and virile, but utterly still, as if frozen, in the doorframe.

"I think, Princess ..." He was looking at me with a sort of quiz-zical tenderness as if he were frightened to say what he was going to say, "I think, Misty, I mean, I think, Princess ..."

"Yes." I looked at him from under my eyebrows. "Yes, Master, what is it you want to say? Tongue-tied is not your usual style, Master."

"I think, Princess, I think, ah, Misty, we might, ah, want, I mean, Gwen, only if you want to, Misty, of course, Gwen, then we might want ..."

"Of course ..." I crossed my arms across my chest and gave him the intense look from under the jet-black eyebrows, the dark-eyed gaze that it was said could subdue anybody. I had no idea what he was talking about. It was totally unlike James to be tongue-tied and fumbling like this. "Of course," I said, "Of course, Master, only if I want what I want will we do what we want and what I want and what you want ... Is that what you are trying to say?" I paused. "Is this about getting the new refrigerator?"

I hoped it was about that; I hoped – I prayed – that it was not about splitting up, about him leaving me, about ... the end of the world.

A cold sweat broke out on my back.

My tongue went dry.

He swallowed. He looked so handsome, so cute, and so help-less. I was mortally afraid. I wanted to rush into his arms, kiss him, and eat him up. Yum, Yum, Yum! He swallowed again, and then, finally, after a long, excruciating silence, he swallowed again, and he said, "I think, Gwendoline, ah, that we might want to have a, ah, a baby."

I let my fiery dark look rest on him for a torturous minute. I lifted the glass of water, I took a long, slow, thoughtful slip. I licked my lips. My heart leaped. It turned somersaults. I kept myself, somehow, from grinning. "Well, Master, now that you raise the subject, I have a bit of news." I somehow organized my mouth into a severe schoolmarm pout. "You see, Master, last month, I forgot to ..."

Then, of course, we all lived happily ever after, and, let me tell you, that's when our real adventures began.

To receive a free book or novella
And to get notes on writing and other topics:

Sign up at

https://gilbertreid.com

Please write a short review!
Just two or three lines.
Post it to Goodreads or Amazon
or any other book group you may belong to.

And send it to Gwendoline:
gwendolineclermont305@gmail.com
or to: **gilbert@gilbertreid.com**

GILBERT REID is the author of two short story collections: *So This is Love: Lollipop and Other Stories* (2004, 2019) and *Lava and Other Stories* (2019). He also co-authored, with Jacqueline Park, the historical novel *Son of Two Fathers* (2019). He has written extensively for television and radio. Most notably he researched, wrote, and narrated two five-hour radio series: *Gilbert Reid's Italy* and *Gilbert Reid's France* for CBC's flagship radio program IDEAS. His many television series include *Paths of the Gods*, *For King and Empire*, *For King and Country*, and *Sir Peter Ustinov in Burma: Road to Mandalay*. After thirty years in Europe working as an economist, university lecturer, diplomat, script doctor, journalist, and adventure travel guide, Gilbert now lives in Toronto.

https://gilbertreid.com/